MOONSINGER

Baen Books by Andre Norton:

Time Traders
Time Traders II
Star Soldiers
Warlock
Janus
Darkness & Dawn
Gods & Androids
Dark Companion
Masks of the Outcasts
Moonsinger

MOONSINGER

ANDRE NORTON

MOONSINGER

This is a work of fiction. All the characters and events portrayed in this book are
fictional, and any resemblance to real people or incidents is purely coincidental.

A Baen Book

Baen Publishing Enterprises
P.O. Box 1403
Riverdale, NY 10471
www.baen.com

ISBN 10: 1-4165-2061-9
ISBN 13: 978-1-4165-2061-0

Cover art by Bob Eggleton

First Baen printing, May 2006

Distributed by Simon & Schuster
1230 Avenue of the Americas
New York, NY 10020

Library of Congress Cataloging-in-Publication Data:

10 9 8 7 6 5 4 3 2 1

Printed in the United States of America

CONTENTS

To Sylvia Cochran,
who guided so many "infant" pens

Moon of Three Rings

Chapter 1

What is space? Is it a wilderness beyond any man's exploring, even if he had a hundred, a thousand life spans in which to prowl the lanes between solar systems and planets, to go questing, to seek ever new and newer knowledge of what may lie beyond the next sun, the next system? Yet to such seekers comes also the knowledge that there must be no boundaries to man's belief, but rather an acceptance of wonders which would leave the planet-bound, those who follow familiar trails, incredulous and refusing to accept the evidence of their own senses.

Those who do venture ever into the unknown—the First-in Scouts of Survey, the explorers, and not the least, the Free Traders who pluck a living from the fringes of the galaxy—to these it is a commonplace thing to discover that the legends and fantasies of one planet may be lightsome or grim truth on another world. For each new planet-fall brings its own mysteries and discoveries.

Which is perhaps too much of a pseudo-philosophic beginning for this account—save I know of no better, not being used to making more than trade reports for that repository of some very strange facts—the League of Free Traders. When a man tries to deal with the unbelievable, he finds it a fumbling business, in need of some introduction.

First-in Scouts, from their unending quest for new worlds and systems, turn in many weird and strange reports to Survey. But even

1

the planets opened to human contact by their efforts can yield
hidden secrets, after they have been pronounced favorable ports for
wandering ships, or even for pioneer settlements.

The Free Traders who exist upon cross trade, having no fat plums
to sustain them as do the Combines of the inner planets with their
monopolies, face now and again things that even Survey does not
know. Thus it was on Yiktor—in the time of the Moon of Three
Rings. And who better can make this report than I, to whom this
happened, though I was only assistant cargomaster of the *Lydis*, the
last-signed member of her crew into the bargain.

Over the years the Free Traders, because of their way of life, have
become almost a separate race in the galaxy. They own no one world
home, nor do some ships possess a home port, but wander always.
So it is that among us the ship itself is our only planet, and we look
upon all without its shell as alien. Although not in this sense are we
xenophobic, for it is part of our nature that we have a strong bent
toward exploration and acceptance of the outer.

Now we are born to the trade, for families live within the larger
ships, it being decided long since that such was better for us than
casual and transitory connections in ports which might lead to a
man's losing his ship. The big space-borne ports are small cities in
themselves, each operating as a central mart for a sector where large
deals are carried out, where those who have a mate and children may
enjoy a kind of home life between voyages.

But the *Lydis* was a bachelor ship of the D class, intended for risky
rim trading where only men without ties would venture. And I, Krip
Vorlund, was well content to so set my feet on the ladder of trade.
For my father had not returned from his last voyage years back. And
my mother, after the custom of the Traders, had married again
within two years and followed her new mate elsewhere. So I had no
one to speak up for me at the time of assignment.

Our captain was Urban Foss, well regarded as a coming man,
though young and sometimes thought to be a shade reckless. But
that suited his crew, who were willing to have a leader who might by
some gamble advance them well into the ranks of those who had
solid credit at the trade center. Juhel Lidj was the cargomaster, and
my only quarrel with him, though he was no light taskmaster, was
that he guarded some of his trade secrets jealously, leaving me to
ferret hints for myself. But perhaps that was the best way of training,

putting me ever on the alert when I was on duty, and giving me opportunity to think much when I was not being official.

We had made two good voyages before we landed on Yiktor, and undoubtedly we felt that we were perhaps better than we were. However, caution is never forgotten on a Free Trader. After we planeted, before we opened hatches, Foss had us all in to listen to the guide tape carrying all the warnings for this world.

The only port, such as it was—for this was truly a frontier world—lay outside Yrjar, a city as far as Yiktor knew cities, in the middle of a large northern land mass. We had timed our arrival carefully for the great trade fair, a meeting of merchants and populace from all over the entire planet, held at two-planet-years intervals at the end of the fall harvest season.

Like fairs on many other worlds, this gathering had once had, and still possessed as a pallid shadow, religious significance, being the supposed date when an ancient folk hero had met and vanquished some demoniacal enemy to save his people, died as a result of his exertions, and thereafter been entombed with pomp. The people still enacted a kind of play of this feat, followed by games in which the lords vied with one another, each backing his personal champions. The winners of each contest carried off enough awards and prestige—not for himself alone but also for his patron—to last until the next fair.

Chapter 2

The government of Yiktor was at the feudal stage. Several times in its history kings and conquerors had risen to unite whole continents under their sway for perhaps their lifetimes. This unification sometimes extended into the following generation, or maybe two, but eventually fell apart through quarrels of the nobles. The pattern had held constant with no advancement. The priests, though, had vague traditions that there had been an earlier civilization which had risen to a position of greater stability and technical knowledge.

No one knew the reason for the stagnation at this step of civilization, and no native appeared to care, or to believe there could be another way of life. We had arrived during one of the periods of chaos wherein half a dozen lords snapped and snarled at one another. But none had the backing, audacity, luck, or whatever was demanded of a leader, to take over. Thus the existing balance of power was a delicate thing.

This meant for us Traders brain lock, weapon lock, nuisances though they were and much as we disliked them.

Far back in Free Trading, for their own protection against the power of the Patrol and the wrath of Control, the Traders themselves had realized the necessity of these two safeguards on primitive planets. Certain technical information was not an item to be traded, no matter how high the inducement. Arms from off-world, or the knowledge of their manufacture, were set behind a barrier of No

5

Sale. When we planeted on such a world, all weapons other than belt stunners were put into a lock stass which would not be released until the ship rose from that earth. We also passed a brain lock inhibiting any such information being won from us.

This might seem to make us unarmed prey for any ambitious lord who might wish to wring us hard for such facts. But the law of the fair gave us complete immunity from danger—as long as we stayed within the limits set by the priests on the first day.

For following almost universal galactic custom, one which appeared to be spontaneous and native to every world where such gatherings had existed for ages, the fair ground was both neutral territory and sanctuary. Deadly enemies could meet there and neither dared put hand to weapon. A crime could be committed elsewhere and, if the criminal reached the fair and was law-abiding therein, he was safe from pursuit or punishment as long as the fair continued. The gathering had its own laws and police, and any crime committed within was given speedy punishment. So that this meeting place was also a site for the cautious sounding out between lords for the settlement of feuds, and perhaps the making of new alliances. The penalty for any man breaking the peace of the fair was outlawry—the same as a sentence of death, but perhaps, in its way, more torturous and lingering for the criminal.

This much we all knew, though we sat in patience as the guide tape told it over again. For on a Trader one does not ever push aside any briefing as unnecessary or time-wasting. Then Foss launched once more into the apportioning of planetside duties. These varied in rotation among us from world to world. There was always a guard for the ship—but the rest of us could explore in pairs in our free time. From the morning gong until midafternoon we would man our own booth for meeting with native merchants. Foss had visited Yiktor once before, as second in command of the *Coal Sack*, before he had his own ship, and now drew upon his notes to refresh his memory.

As is true on all Free Traders, though the cargomaster handles the main cargo and the business of the ship at large, each member of the crew is expected to develop some special interest or speciality, to keep his eyes open, and to suggest new products which might add to the general prosperity of the voyage. Thus we were encouraged to explore all such marts in pairs and to take an interest in local produce, sniffing out a need of the natives which we might in the future supply, or picking up some hitherto overlooked export.

The main cargo from Yrjar was Lidj's concern; it was sprode, a thick juice pressed from certain leaves, then hardened into blocks which could be easily stored in our lowest hold after we had emptied it of bales of murano, a shimmering, thick silk which the Yiktor native weavers seized upon avidly. They patiently unraveled its threads to combine with their finest material, thus making a length go twice as far. Sometimes a lord would pay a full season's land tribute for a cloak length of unadulterated fabric. The sprode blocks, transferred at section base to another ship, would end up halfway across the galaxy, where they were made into a wine which the Zacathans declared heightened their mental powers and cured several diseases of that ancient lizard race. Though I can't imagine why a Zacathan needed his mental powers heightened—they already had quite a start on mankind in that direction!

But the sprode would not provide a full cargo, and it was up to us to discover odds and ends to fill in. Guesses did not always pay off. There were times when what seemed a treasure turned out to be a worthless burden, eventually to be space-dumped. But gambles had done so well in the past that we were certain they would pay off again for all of us.

Any Trader with a lucky choice behind him had a better chance for advancement, with hopes for not too long a time before he could ask for an owner's contract and a higher share in a venture. It meant keeping your eyes open, having a good memory for things recorded on past voyage tapes, and probably having something which our elders called flair and which was a natural gift and nothing learned by study, no matter how doggedly pursued.

Of course, there were always the easy, spectacular things—a new fabric, a gem stone—eye catchers. But these were usually right out in the open. And the fair steerer made very sure that the cargomaster saw them at the first sighting when the big merchants met. On such sales as these depended perhaps all a planet's lure for off-world Traders, and they were publicly hawked.

The others were "hiders," things you nosed out on spec, almost always an obscure product some native merchant had brought to the booths on spec himself—small items which could be made into luxury trade for off-world, light, easy to transport, to sell for perhaps a thousand times cost price to the dilettanti of the crowded inner planets, who were always in search of something new with which to impress their neighbors.

Foss had had a storied success on his second voyage with the Ispan carpets, masterpieces of weaving and color which could be folded into a package no longer than a man's arm, yet shaken out in silken splendor to cover a great-room floor, wearing well, with a flow of shade into shade which delighted and soothed the eyes. My immediate superior, Lidj, was responsible for the Crantax dalho discovery. So it was that a very insignificant-appearing, shriveled black fruit had now become an industry which made the League a goodly number of credits, put Lidj on secondary contract, and benefited a quarter of a struggling pioneer planet. One could not hope for such breaks at the start of course—though I think that deep down inside all of us apprentices did—but there were smaller triumphs to bring a commendation for one's E record.

I went with Lidj and the captain to the in-meeting on first day. It was held in the Great Booth, which was really a hall of no mean dimensions on a field beyond the walls of Yrjar, now the center of the fair. While most Yiktorian architecture tended toward the gloom and dark of buildings which must always be ready to serve as fortifications in time of siege, the Great Booth, being free of such danger, was somewhat less grim. Its walls were of stone but only part way. Inside there was an open space almost the entire width, broken only by pillars which supported a sharply peaked roof, the eaves of which extended far out from the walls to afford good weather protection—though it was the dry season in which the fair was held and usually fine weather. The light thus given to the interior was far more than you could find in any building elsewhere on Yiktor.

We were the only Free Trader in port, though there was a licensed ship under Combine registry, carrying, by contract only, specified cargo which we did not dispute. This was one time when there was truce between off-worlders and no need for sharp maneuvering, our captains and cargomasters sharing the high seats of the senior merchants in amicability. The rest of us lesser fry were not so comfortably housed. We rated on a level with their second guildsmen and by rights would have had to stand in the outer aisles, save that we each bore, with a great deal of show, counting boards. These served the double duty of getting us inside with our officers, and impressing the native population that off-worlders were rather stupid and needed such aids for reckoning—always a beginning move in shrewd bargaining. We therefore squatted at the foot of the high-seat platform and took ostentatious notes of all the exhibits displayed and praised in the offering.

There were some furs from the north, a deep, rich red with a ripple of golden light crossing them as they were turned in the hands of the merchant showing them. Fabrics were brought out by the bolt and draped over small racks put up by subordinates. There was a great deal of metalwork, mostly in the form of weapons. Swords and spears appear to be a universal primitive armament in the galaxy, and these were undoubtedly forged by masters who knew their art. There was chain-link armor for the body, helmets, some of them crested with miniature beasts or feathered birds, and shields. And then a last merchant came up with the air of one about to top the show of war materials. Two of his guildsmen exhibited shooting at a mark with a new type of crossbow which, from the stir his demonstration provoked, must have been a vast improvement over the usual.

The arms display, which was a very large item in the local market, was more or less of a bore for us. Of course now and then one picked up a sword or dagger to sell to some collector. But that was the smallest of private ventures.

It was a long session. The Yiktorians broke it once for refreshments, passing around tankards of their bitter, and to us undrinkable, ale and a "hasty meal" made of a fruit-and-meat paste between flat grain cakes. But it was near to sunset before we were dismissed. By custom Captain Foss and Lidj were to go on to the official banquet given by the fair authorities, but we second men would return to our ships. The junior representative of the Combine Duffoldan who had been sharing the same uncomfortable board seat with me at the platform foot, stretched and grinned after he slammed his note board between his middle and his belt for safekeeping.

"Well, that's safely over," he said, stating the obvious. "You free to port crawl?"

Usually Free Traders and Combine men do not mix. There was too much trouble in the past history we share, though nowadays things are better policed than they used to be. The League has a weighty hand and the Combine leaders no longer try to elbow out a Trader who can call upon such support. In the old days a one-ship Trader had no hope of fighting back. But the feelings and memories stemming from those times still kept us apart, so I was no more cordial than mere civility when I answered.

"Not yet. Not until after report."

"Same here." If my coolness meant anything he did not show it. Instead he waited for me to stow away my own board, which I did slowly to give him a chance to go, though he did not take it. "I am Gauk Slafid."

"Krip Vorlund." Reluctantly I matched step with him. The exit was crowded by native merchants and guildsmen. And, as is wise for off-worlders, we did not push in among them. I saw him glance at my collar badge, and I returned that check. He was in cargo, but his disk was modified by two bars while mine bore only one. But then promotion in the Combine, while leading perhaps to greater wealth in the end, came more slowly.

One can never judge the planet age of those who spend most of their lives in space. Some of us cannot even tell the number of our years by that method. But I thought this Gauk Slafid might be somewhat older than I.

"Done your spec-looking yet?" That was a question I would have thought too brash for even a Combine man, arrogant as they were inclined to be. Yet when I stared at him, I believed he did not honestly realize that that was one of the questions one did *not* ask, save of a kinsman or blood comrade. Perhaps he had heard of Free Trader customs and was drawing on faulty knowledge to make conversation.

"We are not yet port free." No use taking offense if his question was an innocent one, though in bad form. One learns to put aside offense when dealing with aliens, and the Combine in the past had been more alien to those of my calling than many nonhuman contacts.

Perhaps he read something of my feeling, for he did not pursue that line; but as we came to a thronged side street he motioned at its gaudy flags and banners, each bearing the squiggles of local sign writing, and proclaiming a number of amusements, both innocent and bordering on the vicious. For, as the fair gathered sellers and buyers, priests and respectable people, so was it the focus for those who earn their livelihood by offering excitement for the mind and senses.

"There is plenty to see here—or are you shipbound at night?" Was there or was there not a faint trace of patronage in that? I decided it was best not to explore beyond surface emotions. We were not engaged in any sale, and I was cautious.

"So I have heard. But I have not yet drawn my watch button."

He grinned again, raising his hand to his forehead in a gesture approximating a salute. "Fortune attend you then, Vorlund. We have already drawn and I have my night free. If you make it, look me up." Again he gestured, this time indicating a banner near the end of the line. It was not bright in color like those the wind tugged at around it, being an odd shade of gray, yet also shot with rose. Still, once you looked at it, your eyes kept returning, undeterred by the more garish lures surrounding it.

"That is something special," Slafid continued. "If you like beast shows."

A beast show? For the second time I was disconcerted. My mental picture of a Combine man suggested a far different taste in amusement—something closer to the sophisticated, almost decadent pleasures of the inner planets.

Then suspicion moved in me. I wondered if this Gauk Slafid was esper. For he had unerringly picked out the one entertainment which would draw me first, did I know of it. I allowed one of my mind-seek tendrils to uncurl, not actually to invade, naturally—that was the last thing I must do—but to seek delicately for any esper aura. There was none, and I was left a little chagrined at my suspicion.

"If I am fortunate," I answered him, "I will indeed follow your advice."

He was hailed then by a crewman wearing the insignia of his ship, and gave me that half salute once more before he joined his friend. But I stood for a moment or two watching that almost demurely colored banner, trying to figure out why it drew the eye so steadily. Things such as that are important for Traders to learn. Was it only me that it could so influence, or was it the same for others? Somehow to know the answer became so important that I was determined to bring someone, the most cool-headed crew mate I could find, to test it.

I was lucky to come away from the drawing with port leave for that night. The *Lydis* had so small a crew that only four of us were free, and it can be difficult for four pledged to go in pairs if they have very diversified ideas of amusement. Because of our junior status I went out with Griss Sharvan, the second engineer. Well, I had wanted a hardheaded companion to try my banner on, and in Griss fate had given me one. He is a born Trader, generations bred as all of us. But his first love is the ship and I do not believe that he ever, except when it was expected of him, searched for any trade. Luckily I remembered that the deep crimson banner of a sword-smith's display fencer flapped not too far from the beast show, and used that as a lure for Griss. Among our own kind Griss is a gambler, but that is another activity against which we are inhibited in an alien port. It can lead, as drinking, drugging, and eyeing the daughters of strangers, to trouble which would endanger the ship. Thus the desires for such amusements are blocked for us temporarily, and in our sober moments we agree that is wisdom.

At the end of the show street, now brilliant with lanterns, each as brightly colored as the banners above, each patterned with pictures through which light shone to advertise the fares within, I pointed out that of the fencer. The pink-gray flag was still there, but the lantern below it was a silver globe with no pattern breaking its pearl luster.

Griss pointed to it. "What's that?"

"I was told a beast show," I replied.

Living as we do mostly in space, Free Traders might be expected to have little contact or interest in animals. Long ago all ships carried felines for the protection of the cargo, since they hunted to rout out any pests stowing away. For centuries they were inseparable crew members. But their numbers grew less and less; they did not have as large or as many litters any more. We had forgotten where that animal had originated, so fresh stock could not be obtained to renew the breed. There were still a few at headquarters, highly prized, protected, tended, in hope that the breed might be reinstated. And we had all tried from time to time to replace them with various hunters from many worlds. One or two breeds had promise, but the majority could not adapt to ship life.

Perhaps this desire for companion animals gives us a strong pull toward alien beasts. I did not know about Griss, but I knew that I *must* visit the booth behind the moon globe. And it seemed that I would have no argument, for he came willingly with me.

From somewhere there was a dull, heavy gong note. The chatter, the laughter, the singing died down a little, the crowd paying tribute to a temple call. But the hush did not last, for while the fair had its religious side, that had faded with the passing of centuries.

We came under the shadow of the pink-gray banner into the halo
of the moon lamp. I had expected some pictures of the animals to be
strung up to entice an audience. But instead there was only a fabric
screen bearing tangles of native scripts, and over the door flap a
strange mask emblem, neither beast nor bird but combining the two.
Griss gave a small exclamation as he looked up at that.

"What is it?"

His eager expression surprised me a little. I had seen such a look
before only when he fronted a new and intricate machine.

"This is a real find."

"Find?" I thought of some piece of trade luck.

"A real sight," he corrected himself as if he knew my thought.
"This is a Thassa show."

Like Captain Foss he had visited Yiktor before. But I could only
repeat, "Thassa?" I believed I had studied the Yiktor tapes with close
attention, but the meaning of this eluded me.

"Come!" Griss pulled me along to where a slender native in a
silvery tunic and high red boots was accepting scale pieces for
admittance. The native looked up and I was startled.

Around us was the crowd of Yiktorians born and bred—human as
to form, with only slight differences between them and my own
species. But this youth in his pale clothing seemed more alien to the
world than we.

He had an appearance of fragility, almost as if the wind tugging at
the sign banner over us could lap around him and carry him off. His
skin was very smooth, with no sign that any beard had ever pricked
through its surface, and very fair—little or no color in it. His features
were human enough, except for the huge eyes, so dark one could not
be certain of their color. His brows slanted so far up on the temples
they actually joined with his hair, and the shade of that growth was
silver-white.

I tried not to stare as Griss offered a token and the native lifted
the tent flap for our entrance.

Chapter 3

There were no seats, but several wide platforms raised in a series of steps at one end of the tent, such as might be easily dismantled when the show moved. These faced a larger stage which was now empty, but backed by draperies of the same pink-gray as the banner. A series of moon lanterns hung from the center pole overhead. The whole effect was somehow simple yet almost elegant, and to me not in keeping with any beast show.

We had come just in time, for a fold of the back drapery was lifted and the master trainer came to face the audience. Even though the hour was early, there were a goodly number of people, many of them children.

Master? No, the newcomer, though she wore tunic, breeches, and high boots similar to those of the doorkeeper, was clearly a woman. Her tunic was not collared tight to the throat, but fanned out behind her head in an arc of stiffened fabric that glinted along the edge with small sparks of ruby light, the color of which matched her boots and wide belt. She wore also a short, form-fitting, sleeveless jacket of the same red-gold fur I had seen displayed in the Great Booth that morning.

She did not carry any whip such as most beast tamers flick about to enforce their commands, but a slender silver wand which could be no defense. It gleamed to match her hair, which was twisted into a high cone and made fast with pins headed by the sparkling ruby lights. In the triangular space between her long slanting eyebrows and the center of her hairline was an elaborate arabesque of silver and ruby which appeared fastened to her skin, for it did not shift with any turn or lift of her head. There was about her a sureness, a confidence that is a part of those who are master of themselves and of some great art.

I heard a quick-drawn breath from Griss. "Moon Singer!" His exclamation held a tinge of awe, an emotion rare among the Traders. I would have demanded an explanation from him, save that she who stood on the platform made a gesture now with her wand and at once all hum of speech ended. The audience paid her far more respect than the crowd without had paid the temple gong.

"Freesha and Freesh"—her voice was low, a kind of croon, leaving one from the first word wanting to hear more—"give kindness now to my little people, who wish only to amuse you." She stepped to the end of the platform and made another wave of her wand. The drapery at the back rose just high enough to allow entrance to six small furred creatures. Their pelts were short-haired, but very thick and plushy, of a dazzling white. They scurried on hind feet, holding small ruby-colored drums to their rounded stomachs with forepaws which had a distinct resemblance to our human palms and fingers, save that their fingers were very long and thin. Their heads were round, and from them projected furless, slightly pointed ears. As with their mistress, their eyes appeared too large in proportion to the rest of their faces, which were wide-nosed and rounded of muzzle. Each carried in a loop over its back a bushy, silky-looking tail.

They trooped, one behind the other, to the opposite side of the stage from their trainer, and squatted on their haunches behind the drums on which they now rested their long-fingered paws. She must have given them some signal I missed, for they began to thump out, not ill-assorted bangs, but a definite rhythm.

Again the draperies arose and another set of actors came forth. These were larger than the drummers, and perhaps less quick in their movements. They were heavy of body for their size, but they tramped in time to the drumming, their coarsely furred bodies dark brown in shade, their huge, long ears and narrow, protruding snouts making them seem grotesque and truly alien. Now they swung their heads in time to the rhythm, their snouts flicking at the tips.

But they only served as mounts for yet another troop. Small heads of light cream, with big rings of darker fur about the eyes giving the faces an eternally inquiring look, were held high. Like the drummers these riders appeared to use their forepaws as we might our hands; they also carried cream-and-dark-ringed tails pointing straight up.

The tapir-nosed mounts and their ring-featured riders paraded solemnly to the fore of the stage. And thereafter I witnessed sheer magic. I have seen many beast shows on many worlds, but nothing like unto this. There was no cracking of whip, no voiced orders from their mistress. They performed not as if they were doing learned tricks, but rather as though they were carrying out some ceremonies of their own, unwatched by those not of their species. And there was no sound from the audience, nothing save the different rhythms beat out by the furred musicians and the complicated series of cries the actors voiced now and again. The snouted beasts and their riders were only the first. I was too entranced to count all the acts. But when at last they paraded off stage to a roar of applause, which they apparently did not hear, I thought we had seen at least ten different species.

She who was mistress came once more to the center of the platform and saluted us with her wand.

"My people are tired. If they have pleased you, Freesh, Freesha, they have had their reward. They will appear again tomorrow."

I looked to Griss. "Never have I—" I began when there was a touch on my shoulder and I turned my head to see the youth who had collected admissions.

"Gentle Homos," he spoke in Basic and not in the speech of Yrjar, "would you care to see the little ones more closely?"

Why such an invitation had been given us, I had no idea. But it was one which I was eager to accept. Then that caution ingrained in us asserted a warning, and I hesitated, looking to Griss. Since he appeared to know something of these Thassa (who or whatever they might be), I left the decision to him. But he seemed to have no doubts.

We drew apart from those who were reluctantly leaving and followed our guide to the stage and behind the draperies. There were strange scents here, those of animals, but clean and well-cared-for beasts, of bedding of vegetable matter, of food alien to our noses. The space fronting us was perhaps three times the size of the theater.

Lengths of wooden screen had been erected to enclose the area. Stationed alongside them were vans such as we had seen elsewhere for the transportation of wares. There was a line of picketed heavy draft animals, kasi, many of them now lying at ease chewing their cuds. Set in rows, almost in the form of a town with narrow streets, were a series of cages. At the end of the nearest of such rows was the woman. Woman—no—though I could not set age to her, she looked at this distance far more like a girl of few years. It was the elaborate coiling of her hair, the forehead decoration, and her vast assurance which gave the patina of years closer looks denied.

She still held the silver wand, slipping it back and forth between her pale fingers as if it were an anchor of sorts. Though why that thought crossed my mind I could not have said, for nothing else in her expression or manner would lead one to believe that she had ever known uneasiness of any kind.

"Welcome, Gentle Homos." Her Basic was low-toned as the native speech she had used on stage. "I am Maelen."

"Krip Vorlund."

"Griss Sharvan."

"You are from the *Lydis*." No question, but a statement. We nodded in confirmation. "Malec," she spoke to the youth, "perhaps the Gentle Homos will take verfor with us."

He made no answer but walked rapidly down one of the cage streets to a lattice wall structure at the right of the picketed beasts. Maelen continued to study us and then she pointed with her wand to Griss.

"You have heard something of us." She swung that pointer to me. "But you have not. Griss Sharvan, what have you heard of us? And be no more silent about the ill than the good, if good there has been."

He was tanned darkly, as are all of us who live in space. Beside the fairness of this people he was almost black. And I was the same, but under that dark overlay he flushed now and I read self-consciousness.

"The Thassa are Moon Singers," he said.

She smiled. "Incorrect, Gentle Homo. Only some of us sing the Moon Power into use."

"But you are such a one."

She was silent and her smile was gone as if it had never been. Then she answered him. "That is the truth—as far as you know it, man of the Traders."

"All the Thassa are of another blood and kind. None of Yiktor, save perhaps themselves, know from whence and when they came. They are older than the lordships or temple-recorded time."

Maelen nodded. "That is the truth. What else?"

"The rest is all rumor—of powers for good and ill which mankind does not have. You can ill-luck a man into nothingness, and all his clan with him." He hesitated.

"Superstition?" she asked. "But there are so many ways of shadowing a man's life, Gentle Homo. Rumor always wears two faces, true and false, both at the same time. She must be harkened to and ignored. But I do not think that we can be accused of any overt ill-wishing by any now living on this world. It is true that we are an old people and one content to live in our own fashion, troubling no one. What do you think of our little people?" Abruptly she swung from Griss to me.

"That I have never seen their equal on any world."

"Do you think other worlds would welcome them?"

"You mean—take the show into space? But that would be chancy, Gentle Fem. The transportation of animals needing diverse foods, special care—some cannot adapt to space flight at all. There is a way of putting them into freeze between landings. But that has a high risk and some might die. I think, Gentle Fem, it would take much planning and perhaps a specially built and equipped ship which would—"

"Cost a fortune," she finished for me. "Yes, so many dreams shatter on that rock, do they not? But if not the whole show, perhaps some of the main attractions might travel. Come, see my people— you will find this an experience to remember."

She was very right. We discovered as she led us up one of the cage streets and down another that these were not places of confinement but rather, as she pointed out, places of safety to protect her people from the harm which might come from human curiosity. The inhabitants were at the front of their dwellings as she stopped before each one and formally introduced us to them. And the feeling grew in me that these were indeed "people" with minds and feelings, strange to but approaching my own. There rose in me a great longing to have one for a ship comrade, though prudence argued against such recklessness.

We were near to the end of the last street when someone came running. He was one of the ragged "odd boys" who haunted the fair, picking up tokens by message running, and perhaps by less legal means. Now he danced from one bare foot to the other as if he had a message of import yet feared to disturb the Thassa girl. But she cut short her speech and looked to him.

"Freesha, the beast seller. It is as you asked me to discover—he has a furred one in torment."

Her face seemed to narrow, her lips drew taut against her teeth. She was even more alien for an instant, and it seemed to me that she expelled her breath in a feline hiss of anger. Then her calm mask was once more in place and she spoke to us.

"It would seem that one has need of me, Gentle Homos. Malec will entertain you. I shall not be gone long."

What impulse then moved me I did not understand, but I said quickly, "Gentle Fem, may I go with you?"

There was no reason to believe that this was not her business alone. And I think she might have said so. Again her expression altered and she nodded.

"As you wish, Gentle Homo."

Griss looked from one to the other, but he did not offer to accompany us. He made his way to the living quarters with Malec as we followed the messenger. The late hour had filled the street here, though it was the rule that selling and buying, for the protection of the customer, must be done only in the bright light of day when all defects in the merchandise would be plain to see. It was the night hours that drew men and women to the amusements, and through that part of the fair we now made our way. I noted that when the natives saw the identity of my companion they made way for her, some watching her pass with a kind of apprehension or awe, such as might be given to a priestess. But she paid no heed to them.

Nor did she break the silence between us. It was as if, having agreed to my coming, she had then pushed me from her mind, to concentrate on a matter of greater importance.

We reached the end of the straggling collection of amusement places and found a rather pretentious tent of raw scarlet splashed with eye-torturing green, from which came the calls of gambling games. The clamor sounded as if such games depended less upon mental skill than upon uproar, though I caught a glimpse of one table near the open door where they were playing the galaxy-wide Star and Comet. And seated there was my acquaintance of the afternoon, Gauk Slafid. Apparently his ship did not keep the strict discipline of the Free Traders, for he had a pile of counters before him that towered higher than those of his neighbors who, by their dress, were at least the close kinsmen of lords, though they appeared too young to be feudal rulers in their own right.

He raised his head as we passed and there was surprise in his glance, a glance which became a stare. He half raised his hand as if he would either wave or beckon to me, then his eyes dropped to the action on the table. One of the lordlings was also staring, and continued to watch us, with so intent and measuring a gaze that I fell a step or two behind Maelen and returned that scrutiny steadily. Nor did he then drop his eyes, but met mine, whether in challenge or mere curiosity, I could not read. And I dared not loose esper in that time and place to find out.

Beyond the gambling tent there was a place of small shelters—the living quarters, I presumed, for those working in the various amusement places. An odor of strange cooking, of sickly scents, and lesser and worse smells hung here. We turned again, picking our way around the huddle of huts to a quieter area where there were parked the wains, or carts, of the small merchants.

And thus we came to another tent from which the smell was vile and nose-twisting. I thought I again heard that hiss of anger from Maelen as she thrust forth her silver wand, using its tip to raise the entrance flap as if she refused to touch the fabric with her fingers. Within evil stenches warred mightily with one another, to raise a choking cloud, and there was also a clamor of barks, growls, raucous snarls, and sputterings. We stood in a small open space in the midst of cages which were not cherished living quarters, but rather places of imprisonment for their occupants, and wretched they were.

A beast dealer who cared for naught save quick profit and many sales owned them. The man himself came out of the shadows, his lips stretched in a smile which never reached his eyes in the way of greeting. But when he saw Maelen that smile was wiped away as if it had never been, and the coldness in his eyes was lighted by a spark which I read for hate—tempered by a wariness of the powers of the one he hated.

"Where is the barsk?" Maelen wasted no greeting on him, her tone was one of outright command.

"Barsk, Freesha? Who in possession of his full bag of wits would do aught with a barsk save slay it? It is a devil, a demon of the moonless dark as all know."

There was a listening look about her as if among all that clamor of unhappiness she could detect a single note and was now engaged in tracing it to its source. She paid no more attention to him but walked forward. I saw hate burn away his fear, so that he prepared to take a stand. His hand went to his belt and my seeking thought was a beam of light, showing me the weapon there, a curious, secret, and very deadly thing, unlike honest steel. This was small enough to be near swallowed up in a closed palm, fashioned not as a blade but a hooked claw, and it was green-smeared with what would be more deadly than its bite.

Whether he would have used it, even eaten as he was by rage and hate for the moment, I do not know. But he had no chance. The stunner in my hold, set to low ray, froze his fingers as they grasped the hidden fang. He stumbled back against one of his smelly cages and then cried out as the creature within, only a dark shadow, flung itself in a frenzy against the bars, striving to reach him. Maelen glanced around and then pointed her wand. The man reeled back and down, crouched on the floor with his useless hand doubled against him, now slobbering with a rage that choked him so he could not speak.

Maelen surveyed him coldly. "Fool, twice fool! Would you have me accuse you of peace breaking?"

She might well have dashed a bucket of icy water into his face, so quickly were the flames of anger gone. Fear replaced hate in his eyes. The thing she threatened meant outlawry. And on Yiktor that is the ultimate in punishment.

He scrambled on hands and knees back into the shadows. But I thought it prudent to stand guard, and told her so.

She shook her head. "There is no need to fear this one. The Thassa are not to be befooled—as you will know—nather!" She did not speak scornfully as she addressed him with the name for worthless-hanger-on, but rather as one who states a fact.

So we went beyond a dividing curtain into a place of more cages and even worse smells. She hurried to one prison set apart by itself.

What was housed there lay inert and, I thought, dead, until I saw the bone-creased hide rise and fall in long-spaced breaths.

"The cart there—" She was on her knees before the cage, staring intently at its occupant, but her wand indicated a board balanced on four wheels, and I pushed that forward.

Together we lifted the cage onto the cart and then pushed it to the outer portion of the tent. Maelen paused and took from her belt purse two tokens, tossing them to the top of one of the other cages.

"For one barsk, five scales and two fourthers," she said to the man still crouching in the shadows. "Agreed?"

Mind-seek told me he wanted us out. But a spark of greed had awakened behind his fear.

"A barsk is rare," he half whined.

"This barsk is near dead and worth nothing, not even the hide, you have so starved it. If you agree not, petition the price judge in open hearing."

"Enough!"

I caught her amusement. We pushed our burden into the open. The lad who had guided us hither came out of the dark and with him one of his fellows. Between them they took over management of the cart and cage. We took another route in return, one which brought us through a swinging panel in the lattice wall. As the cage was trundled by the line of the burden beasts, they snorted, and several rose to their feet, their nostrils wide, their heads tossing.

Maelen stood before them, her wand weaving from side to side, her voice raised in a low, comforting croon which restored their peace. The boys pushed the cage to the far end of the line and stood by it, waiting. Malec and Griss came out of the booth and the Thassa youth stooped to peer into the cage. Shaking his head, he paid the boys.

"It is hopeless for this one," he told Maelen as she came from the now quiet kasi. "Not even you can reach it, Singer."

She stood looking at the cage with a brooding stare, her wand in one hand while, with the other, she stroked the fur of her short jacket as if it was a beloved pet animal, alive and breathing.

"Perhaps you are right," she agreed. "Yet perhaps its fate is not yet written in the Second Book of Molaster. If it must go on the White Road, then it shall begin that journey in peace and without pain. For now it is too worn out to fight us. Let the cage for the sick hold it."

Together they loosed the fastening of the cage and lifted the creature within to wider, freer quarters in one of their own places, a soft litter spread to support the bone rack of body. It was larger, I saw, than any of the animals that had been on the stage this night; standing, I would judge, if it could rise upon its feet, about as high as my lower ribs. The coat was dusty, befouled, dull, and ragged, but in color it was the red of Maelen's jacket.

In form it was an oddly proportioned animal, for the body was small and the legs very long and thin, as if the limbs meant for one beast had been fitted wrongly to another. The tail ended in a fan tuft, while from between the pointed ears, down the neck, and across the shoulders was a growth of longer hair of a much lighter shade, forming a brush of mane. The nose was long and sharp, showing strong teeth beneath black lips. All in all, had the thing not been so outworn, I would have said it was dangerous.

It aroused enough to snap feebly as they lowered it onto the bedding in the new cage. Then Maelen used her wand with a light touch, drawing it caressingly down between its eyes to the point of its nose, and its head ceased to move. Malec returned from the living quarters with a bowl from which he dipped liquid, dribbling it from his fingers onto the creature's head, and then down the belly, finishing by getting a small measure of it between the jaws and into the encrusted mouth from which a blackened tongue lolled.

Maelen stood up. "For the present that is all we can do. The rest—" Her wand drew a symbol in the air. Then she turned to us. "Gentle Homos, the hour grows late and this poor one will need me."

"Thank you for your graciousness, Gentle Fem." I found her open dismissal abrupt. It was as if she had once had some reason to seek us out, but it was no longer of importance. And somehow I disliked that thought, which might or might not be rooted in fact.

"And you for your aid, Gentle Homo. You will return." And that was no question, and not quite an order, but a statement of fact in which we both agreed.

On the way back to the *Lydis*, Griss and I did not talk together much, though I told him of what had happened in the tent of the beast seller and received his advice that I note it in my report, lest there be some future trouble.

"What is a barsk?" I asked.

"You saw. They provide the fur displayed this morning, that which Maelen wears as a jacket. They have the reputation for being cunning, intelligent, and dangerous. And they are sometimes killed, but I do not believe very often trapped alive. More than that—" He shrugged.

We were passing the port guards when all of a sudden I caught it—not the hatred of the beast seller alone, but that coupled with a strong and driving purpose. So joined were the emotions they struck the mind as keenly as one of the spears we had seen displayed by the armorers would tear into the body. I halted and swung around to face that mind-stroke only to see nothing but shadows and darkness. And then Griss was beside me, a drawn stunner in his hand. I knew that he, too, had felt it.

"What—?"

"The beast dealer, but also another—" Not for the first time in my life did I wish for the full inner power to read esper. As it was, sometimes a warning could cripple instead of armor a man.

Griss stared at me. "Take care, Krip. He may not dare to go against a Thassa, but he may deem that you are in his reach. This must go to the captain."

He was right, of course, though I hated to admit it. Urban Foss might restrict me to the *Lydis* until lift-off. Caution was a Trader's shield in strange places, but if a man always clung too tightly to his shield he might well miss the sword stroke which would free him from all danger. And I was young enough to wish to fight my own battles, not sit under cover waiting for the storm to sweep me by. Also, that thrust had been born of two wills and not one. I could understand the beast seller's enmity, but who had coupled that with another assault and for what reason? What other enemy had I made on Yiktor, and by what means?

Chapter 4

Talla, talla, by the will and heart of Molaster and the power of the Third Ring, do I begin my part of this tale thus as would any Deed Singer of some upcountry lordling?

I am, or was, Maelen of the Kontra, Moon Singer, leader of little ones. I have been other things in the past, and am also now under bonds for a time.

What did we care for lord or Trader in that meeting in a tent at the fair of Yrjar? Neither were more to us than the dust of the cities that stifle us with their dirt and greed and clamor, and the drab thoughts of those who will themselves into such confines. But it is not necessary now to speak of the Thassa and their beliefs and customs, only of how my own life came to be pushed from one future to another, because I took no care for the acts of men, overlooked them—something I would not do with the little ones I respect.

Osokun came to me at the mid-point of day, sending to me firstly his shieldbearer. I think that he held me so much in awe that he would not treat me as one less than his own rank, though the plainsmen profess to believe the Thassa wanderers and vagabonds, not saying so to our faces however. He craved speech with me, said this young cub of the forts. And I was curious, for Osokun I knew by repute—and that repute clouded.

It is of the nature of the lords that power among them shifts often. This one or that rises to draw under him or remove all rivals, to become for a space the High King. So it has been many times in the past, an endless parade of mountains and plains in their history. Under one man a kind of uneasy peace holds, then straightway does it fall again. And for a space of many twelves of years now there has been no paramount lord, only many quarreling among themselves.

Osokun, son of Oskold, had in him the fire for great things, that will to power which, when blended with luck and skill, can bring a man successfully to the high seat. But when it is not so companied it torments the one who contains it, consuming him utterly. And I did not believe that Osokun had more than ambition to arm him. Such men are a danger not only to themselves but to their kind.

Perhaps it is not well to be aloof as are the Thassa, looking upon others' quarrels with amusement or indifference. For this disarms wisdom and foreknowledge.

I did not refuse Osokun's coming, though I knew that Malec did not agree that in this I moved with any wisdom. I confess that I had a certain curiosity as to why he sought contact with the Thassa, since he professed to consider us beneath his notice.

Though he had sent his sword-sworn to arrange the meeting, he came himself with no escort, but rather with an off-worlder, a young man with an easy smile and fair words on his tongue, but darker things unsaid in the mind behind his searching eyes, whom Osokun named Gauk Slafid.

They gave formal greetings and we gave them a just due at our table. But that impatience which would bring Osokun and all his plans to naught plunged him quickly into a business which was indeed perilous—though more for him, should it be detected, than for me, as the laws which bound him were not the Standing Words of my people.

It was more or less this: Osokun wanted special knowledge of the superior weapons of other planets. With this and such arms in the hands of his sword-sworns, he could straightway set up as the war lord of all the land and be such a high king here as generations had not known.

Malec and I smiled inwardly. I schooled my voice not to betray my laughter at what seemed to me to be his childish simplicity as I made him an answer which was courteous enough:

"Freesh Osokun, is it not well known that by their arts all off-worlders hide such knowledge before they set boot sole upon Yiktor soil? And that they put also such safeguards upon their ships as locks not to be broken?"

He scowled, but then his face smoothed again. "There is an answer for both bars to what I must have. With your aid—"

"Our aid? Oh, we have ancient learning, Freesh Osokun, but none to avail you in this circumstance." And I thought then that sometimes our reputation among the plainsmen could be a disadvantage. Perhaps Thassa power *could* break off-world barrier, but it would never be so turned.

But that was not what he wanted from us. Instead he hurried on, his thoughts and desires so urgent that his words tumbled from his lips in a race like unto the current of a mountain stream.

"It is the Free Trader we must pillage," he said. "This Freesh"—he indicated the off-worlder who was with him—" has furnished us with information." He then took from his belt pouch well-scribbled parchment from which he read and then expounded. And all the while the off-worlder smiled, nodded, and strove to mind-search us and what lay about us. But I held to the second level of thought and he gained naught that would do him any good.

Osokun's plan was simple enough, but there are times when simplicity backed by audacity works, and this might be such a time. Men from Free Traders are encouraged to seek out new products. Thus Osokun need only entice some crewman of a Trader outside the boundary of fair law and take him captive. If he could not wring the information he needed from his prisoner, he could bargain with the ship's captain for his return.

To this Slafid agreed. "It is a point of honor among these Free Traders that they care for their own. Let one be taken and they will buy his release."

"And how do we fit into your plan—if we choose?" Malec asked.

"Why, you provide the bait." Slafid told us. "The beast show will draw some of them, for they are forbidden to drink, gamble, or seek out women on strange worlds. In fact they could not if they would, being conditioned to such a state. Therefore we cannot tempt them by ordinary means. But let them come to one of your shows, invite them farther into your life, interest them as much as you can. Then, make a pretext that for some reason you must move for a space outside the fair. Draw one of them to visit you again—and your part shall be over."

"And just why should we do so?" Malec allowed some hostility to creep into his voice.

Osokun looked at us both directly. "There are threats I could make—"

I laughed then. "To the Thassa? Freesh, you are a brave, brave man! I see no reason why we should play your game. Get you other bait, and such fortune as you deserve attend you." And I reached out my hand to reverse the guest goblet standing on the table between us.

He went very red and his hand was on his sword hilt. But the off-worlder lay his fingers on his arm. Though Osokun shot a look of anger at him also, yet he got to his feet and went with the other, saying no farewell. Slafid, smiling again, gave due courtesy, having about him the air of one not defeated but merely willing to try another path to his goal.

When they were well away, Malec laughed. "Why do they deem us fools?"

But I turned the guest goblet around and around on the smooth green board of the table and my question was:

"What made them think we would be their tools?"

Malec nodded slowly. "Yes, why that? What gain or threat did they believe so powerful as to in a manner wand-bind us from our powers?"

"Which makes me believe that perhaps I was not wise to dismiss them so quickly." I was irritated that I had done so with such lack of subtlety. "Also—why is one off-worlder ready to entrap another? Osokun would deal very unhappily with any prisoner he took."

"That much I can guess," Malec replied. "There is an ancient feud, though not much returned to in these days, between the men of the sealed cargo ships and the Free Traders. Perhaps that is now revived for some reason. But that is their affair, not ours. However"—he rose from his stool, his hands hooked in his belt—"we should let the Old Ones know of this."

I neither agreed nor disagreed. In those days I had some ill feeling toward certain ones in authority among us, but that was a matter private to me, not affecting any but my own house clan.

Our little people performed their own magic in the afternoon and the pleasure they gave was great. My pride in them flowered as the lallang blossoms under the moon. Also I did as I had in other fair years, set out scale pieces for these odd boys who trace down animals for me. For I have this private service to Molaster, that I bring out of bondage where and when I can such of the furred ones as suffer from the ill treatment of those who dare to call themselves men.

That evening, when the moon globes were lit and we set things ready for the evening performance, I said to Malec:

"Perhaps there is a way we can learn more of this matter. Should any of these Traders arrive to watch the show, and should they appear to you to be harmless men, do you offer to bring them here thereafter and let me talk with them. All we can learn will be food for the Old Ones for their understanding."

"Best not to meddle farther—" he began and then hesitated.

"It will go no farther," I promised, not knowing then how quickly such a promise can become a dawn web, vanquished by sun rays.

In this much was Slafid right. There were Traders, two of them, at the performance. I cannot read off-worlders' ages aright, but I believed them young, and neither wore many service bands on his tunic. Their skin was very dark, as comes from space, and their hair, clipped close to the skull for the better wearing of their helmets, was dark also. They did not smile ever as had Slafid, nor did they speak much with each other. But when my little people showed their talents, they were as enrapt as children, and I thought we might be half friends, were they of Yiktor.

As I had suggested, Malec brought them behind when the show was over. And when I looked at them closely I knew they were not as Gauk Slafid. Perhaps they were simple men as we Thassa judge most other races to be, but it was a good simplicity, not that of ignorance which can be made crooked by malice or ambition. And I was moved to speak to the one calling himself Krip Vorlund concerning my old dream of seeking other worlds with my little people.

In him I read a kindred interest, though he was quick to point out to me the many dangers which would hedge about my desire, and the fact that it could be accomplished only if one had vast treasure to draw upon. Deep in me sparked the thought that perhaps I, too, had a price. But that quickly vanished.

As his kind is judged, this off-worlder was good to look upon, not as tall as Osokun, but rather slender and wiry. And I think that, were he matched weaponless to Oskold's son, the latter would have a surprise in the struggle. My little people enchanted him, and they liked him also—which warmed me to him. For animals such as ours can read the spirit. Fafan, who is very timid in strange company, laid her hand paw in his at first advance and called after him when he went from her, so that he returned and spoke softly as one does in soothing a child.

I would have explored farther this man and his comrade, only Otjan, one of the run boys, came then with his tale of a barsk in harsh imprisonment and I had to go. This Vorlund asked to go with me and to that I agreed, I know not why, save that I wanted to know more of him.

And in the end it was his quickness which saved me trouble, for that torturer of fur people, Othelm of Ylt, would have used a snik-claw knife. But Vorlund used his off-world weapon, which cannot kill nor greatly harm, merely deter a would-be attacker, giving me time to wand-wish that nather. With his aid we brought back the barsk and saw to its housing. But then I knew that I could not be two-minded while I nursed that hopeless one, and I dismissed the Traders with what courtesy my impatience would allow.

When they were gone I wrought with the barsk as best I could, using all the skill of Molaster's servant. I thought that the body might be healed, but so dampened with pain and terror was the mind that never might I establish contact. Yet neither could I find it in me to send it along the White Road now. I left it in a sleep without dreams, to heal its limbs and body, to take away the pain of its thoughts.

"There is no use," Malec told me near dawn. "You will have to keep it in dream or make the sleep complete."

"Perhaps, but let us wait awhile. There is something—" I sat by the table, drooping with that fatigue which makes one's muscles and bones leaden and slow to answer to an equally slow mind. "There is something—" But the burden of my weariness kept me from probing then. Instead I stumbled to my couch and truly slept.

The Thassa can dream true, but only under controlled conditions. What I pictured then in the depths of sleep was a return of memory which flowed on to be mingled grotesquely with the present, to give birth to a possible future. For first I held in my arms one who cried herself into a bleak despair for which there was no comfort. And I looked upon another who, in the fair and unblemished body of youth, was empty of all reason, to whom no power could return.

Then I walked with the young Trader, not as I had through the fair this night, but rather in a mountain place, which I knew with sorrow and dread.

But man shrank into animal, and beside me paced the barsk who turned now and again and looked upon me with cold eyes full of menace, which became entreaty, then hatred. But I walked without fear, not because of a wand—which I no longer held—but because I had that which tied the animal to me in a bondage it could not break.

And in that dream all was clear and had much meaning. Only when I awoke, with a dull pain behind my eyes and no refreshment of body, the meaning was gone, I held only scraps of haunting memory.

But now I know that dreaming planted in the depths of my mind, or awoke there, purpose that grew within me until it influenced clear thought. Nor did I shrink from that purpose when the moment came to put it into action, because it had grown to fill my being.

The barsk still lived, and inner seeing told me that its body mended. But we left it in deep sleep, which was the best we could now do for it. As I dropped the curtain across its cage, I heard that metallic ring which had come to mean space boots to my ears, and I turned somewhat eagerly, thinking that mayhap the Trader— Only it was Slafid who walked there alone.

"Dawn light fair to you, Freesha." He gave greeting in the town tongue as one who was entirely sure of his welcome here. And, needing to learn the reason for his persistence, I gave greeting in return.

"I see," he said, looking about him, "that all is well."

"Why should it be otherwise?" Malec came from the kasi lines to ask.

"There was no disturbance here, but elsewhere last night—" Slafid looked from one to the other. And when we stood blank-faced to his gaze, he continued, "One Othelm of Ylt has made formal complaint against you, Freesha, and one he terms an off-worlder."

"So?"

"Use of an off-world weapon, theft of valuable property. Both are black crimes in fair law. At best you may be embroiled with the court, at worst expelled and fined."

"True," I agreed. I had no fears of Othelm's complaint myself, but the Trader's case was another matter. Osokun—was there any way he could turn this to his advantage? By port law the Traders had a right to wear body weapons, since the effects of those were relatively harmless. In fact they were less dangerous than the swords and daggers no lord or sword-sworn would move without. And Vorlund had used his in my defense, against a weapon that was outlawed and the very possession of which could condemn Othelm to greater penalties than I believed he would care to think upon. Only, any embroilment with fair law could set the Trader's superiors against him. We all knew of the strictness of their code on alien planets.

"Osokun's kinsman-by-the-third, Ocorr, is chief guard today."

"What would you say?" Malec fronted this Slafid, his impatience sharp in his tone.

"That perhaps you have done Osokun's will in this matter after all, Freesh." Slafid smiled his slow smile. "I think you might be wise to claim credit for it, even if you did not intend to have this result."

Now I could not bite back the question, "Why?"

Still he smiled as he leaned against a cage. "The Thassa are above and beyond plains law. But what if there be new laws, Freesha? And what if the Thassa legend be mostly that, legend only, with little in the way of deeds to back it should it be challenged? Are you now a great people? Rumor says not—if you ever were. So far you have kept aloof from the affairs of the plainsmen, you who are not men as they are men, nor women as they are women. How do you run under the Three Rings, Freesha, on two feet or four—or do you sail on wings?"

I took that as a warrior might take a sword in his vitals. For such words and what lay behind them were a sword, a weapon which, if used rightly, could cut down all of my clan and blood. So—this was the threat Osokun could bring to force us, or try to do so, under his hand! But I was proud that neither of us, Malec nor I, showed the effects of the blow he dealt us.

"You speak in riddles, Gentle Homo," I answered him in the off-world speech.

"Riddles others will begin to ask and solve," he replied. "If you have your safe places, Freesha, it would be best to gather there in days to come. You may have let war pass you by, as the occupation of lesser species. Now it seeks you out, unless you make alliances."

"No one speaks for many, unless he is sent under the talk-shield," Malec observed. "Do you speak for Osokun, Gentle Homo? If not, for whom? What has an off-worlder to do with Yiktor? What war threatens?"

"What is Yiktor?" Slafid laughed. "One small world of backward peoples who cannot begin to conceive of the wealth, the power, the weapons of others. It can be chewed and swallowed as one bites and swallows a thack berry. And with no more interest to the swallower than an instant of tart juice taste on the tongue, too small an incident for memory."

"So now we represent a thack berry to be swallowed?" I allowed myself laughter in return. "Ah, Gentle Homo, mayhap you are right. But a thack berry taken before the day of ripeness, or only slightly past that hour, can cause a vast tumult and discomfort in one's middle. We are a small and backward world to be sure, and now I begin to wonder what treasure lies here that great ones from beyond the stars are seriously mindful of us."

I did not expect to trap him so easily, and I did not. But neither did he, I think, learn aught from us—at least no great fact such as he had revealed when he had aimed that blow meant to rock us so we would be easy prey for his questions.

"We thank you for your warning." Malec's thoughts marched with mine. "For the court we shall have our answer. And now—"

"And now you have tasks which can better be performed in my absence," the off-worlder assented cheerfully. "I shall be off and leave you to them. You need not reverse the cup this time, Gentle Fem."

When he was gone I looked to Malec. "Does it seem to you, kinsman, that he went pleased with himself?"

"Yes. What he spoke of—" But even between ourselves, within the hearing of only our little people who might neither tattle nor betray aught their ears caught, he did not put more into words.

"The Old Ones—"

"Yes," Malec agreed to my thought. "Tonight the moon waxes."

My wand slipped through my fingers, not cool to the touch, but warm with the life my thoughts relayed to it. To do so, in the very heart of what might now be enemy territory was an act of possible danger. Only Malec was right, the need was greater than the risk. He read my assent in my eyes and we went to our routine of setting up the show.

Twice during the day did I visit the barsk, each time mind-probing. Its hurts continued to heal, but not yet would I lift the rest-slumber and try to touch its mind. There was no time for such experimentation with this other thing pressing us.

We drew good crowds as always, having to turn some away. And my little people were happy and content in their acts, both of us being careful to shield our minds so that our apprehension would not distress them. I looked to see the Traders, if not the two who had visited us before, then others. For, if Vorlund had reported what had happened in Othelm's tent, then surely some one of them would come to us about the matter. But none did.

At nooning Malec sent Otjan to see who dealt with customers in the booth that belonged to the *Lydis*. He reported that he saw neither Vorlund nor Sharvan there. But they were doing a brisk trade and there was evidence they might be sold out and gone before the end of the fair.

"Which would be wise for them," Malec observed. "And the less we now see of them the better. What quarrel these off-worlders have among themselves, or what Osokun would do with them is none of our concern. If possible we should also be packed and away this day."

But that we could not do. One could sense it in the air, the feeling of being spied upon. And by afternoon that uneasiness reached the little people, in spite of my efforts at maintaining a mind-guard to protect them. Twice I had to use the wand to wipe fears from their minds and I put out the high-power globes that night to blank-out the show tent. Yet on the surface there was naught. The fair guard had not summoned me to answer to Othelm's charge. I began to believe it might have been wiser had I made a countercharge first.

We caged the little people and I put the moon lamps at the four corners of their homes, setting up the middle power to protect them during the hours of dark. Together Malec and I inspected the barsk, and then went to take our messenger from its place.

The large winged form stirred uneasily as Malec set it gently on the table of our living quarters, half mantling its strong wings, blinking as if awaking from sleep.

I burned the powder and let it drink in the fumes, its beak half open, its thread of tongue flicking back and forth in increasing rapidity. Then Malec held its head steady between his palms so that I might fix my eyes upon the red ones set in its narrow skull. I sang, not aloud as was the usual custom, but with the hidden voice that no others might hear.

To that singing I put much effort, holding the wand between my two palms until it burnt fire-hot, yet still I held it steady that the power might be channeled through me into our messenger. And when I had done, my head fell back and I had strength only to sit upon the stool and not tumble to the floor. But Malec looked now into the messenger's eyes and he spoke in short, sharp whispers, laying in its mind the words it would repeat precisely as he said them in the far place to which it would fly.

Having done this he took up his cloak and drew it about him and the bird he held to his breast. He went out into the dark of very early morning, to seek the open field where our beasts sometimes foraged, well outside the place of tents and booths.

I did not have the energy to rise and leave that seat now hard to my flesh and bones. Rather did I fall forward, my arms stretched across the table, my head resting on the board. I was wearied to the edge of faintness but I did not sleep. My thoughts were too alert, running hither and thither beyond my control. And memory pricked through the present need for sane and careful planning.

Once more mind-pictures came to me, and in these the face of a dark Trader fitted over one I knew much better, and both were erased in turn by the snarling mask of an aroused animal. It seemed to me that all this had a meaning, but one beyond my reading.

There rose then in me the desire to beam-read—though I knew the concentration needed for it was now far beyond my power. But I promised myself that this I would do. Do we beam-read the future, or only its possible path? Once having beam-read, do we then unconsciously turn our feet into the way that sight has opened? I have heard this debated learnedly many times. And the half belief that it does influence the choice of one's future leads it to be looked upon with distaste by many of us. We can be called to account for its use by the Old Ones. But now this I must do, when my strength returned. So having made my decision, I slept, my body cramped and stiffening, my thoughts at last leaving me in a fleeting peace.

Chapter 5

The law of cause and effect is not one which our species, or any other I have ever heard of, has been able to repeal. One can hope for the best, but must be prepared to face the worst, so accepting ship restrict was now my portion and logically I had no quarrel with it. I was lucky, I supposed, that Captain Foss did not add to this relatively minor punishment a black check on my E record. Some commanders would have. I had the persona tape we all carried in our belts to give the true account of the fracas in the beast dealer's tent. And, to my credit, my hostile move there had been made in defense of a native of Yiktor, not merely to save my own skin. Also Foss knew more of the Thassa and their standing than I did.

Much as he would have liked to make my restrict entire, our limited crew prevented total imprisonment. I had to attend the ship's booth during some selling hours. But I was left with no doubt that the slightest infringement of orders on my part would end in complete disaster for one Krip Vorlund. And he told me that he awaited now some complaint on the part of the fair authorities. He would be my defender in any such trial and the tape would be my best argument.

Most of the morning in the booth was routine. I would have no further chance to go hunting on my own; I had forfeited that privilege on Yiktor. But I kept thinking in my free moments of Maelen's dream of a traveling beast show in space. As far as I knew, such had never been seen before. All the difficulties I had listed for her were only too true. Animals were not always adaptable, our tough species being one of the exceptions. Some cannot thrive away from their native worlds and can eat only highly specialized foods which cannot be transported, or they cannot stand the strains of shipboard life. But supposing a species that could overcome all such difficulties could be located, trained, taken out to roam the stars— would such a venture be profitable? A Trader's mind always turns first to that question, just as he is willing to leap beyond the next sun if the answer may be yes.

There I could judge only by my own reaction to the performance of the night before—and personal judgments were chancy. We had been long trained to use our own enthusiasm only to spark initial interest, beyond that to test and retest before committing a fortune to any venture.

I wondered about the barsk, why Maelen had been so determined to rescue it. There had been other ill-housed and presumably ill-treated beasts in that selling tent. But only the barsk had interested her. It was a rare animal, yes, and one seldom seen in confinement. But why?

"Freesh—"

A pluck at my sleeve brought me around. I had been standing at the open front of the booth and now I looked down at the ragged boy, shifting from one bare, grimy foot to the other, his hands clasped together over his middle as he bobbed his head up and down in a "salute-to-superior." I recognized him as the one who had guided us last night.

"What wish you?"

"Freesh, the Freesha asks that you come to her. There is that which she has to say with her own lips."

It says much for discipline that I hesitated in my refusal for less than a second. "Give to the Freesha," I dropped into the speech of formal Yiktorian politeness, "that I bide under the word of my liege lord and so cannot do as she desires. It is with sorrow that I must say this, by the Rings of the True Moon and the Flowering of the Hress."

He did not go. Then I drew a small scale token from my pocket and held it out.

"Drink sweet water on me, runner."

He took the token, but still he did not go.

"Freesh, the Freesha wishes this very much."

"Does the sword-sworn go about his own desire when he is under orders from his lord?" I countered. "Say to her as I have said, I have no choice in this matter."

He did go then, but with a kind of reluctance which puzzled me. For the excuse I had given him was sound and acceptable anywhere on Yiktor. A follower was bound to his lord, and his commander's whim must be set above, far above, any personal desires, even above his own life. Why had Maelen sent for me, an out-worlder who had no connection with her save that we had shared a small adventure last night? Prudence dictated that it was better to keep well away from the tent of the Thassa, from the little people, from all that had to do with them.

Still, I kept remembering her silver-and-ruby trappings, herself as she had stood, not outwardly directing her animals but as if she, too, watched them. I thought of her concern over the barsk, her remote contempt which had frozen the beast dealer as her wand had bound him. Strange powers were allotted to the Thassa by rumor, and there seemed to be some truth at the roots of rumor, at least Maelen gave one the suspicion it was so.

But there was little time for dreaming over puzzles, for two of the high merchants from the north swept into the booth as the boy departed. They were not dealers in sprode, but offered other wares to make up our light cargo, small luxury items which could be packed in the ship's treasure room and so realize good return for small bulk. Captain Foss greeted them, they being his own customers, enticed here not by our regular cargo but our own light wares. These were the true aristocrats of the merchant class, men who had founded their fortunes securely and now speculated in things to pull wealth from the belt purses of the high nobility.

I produced the talk cups, plasta-crystal of Farn, reflecting light with diamond brilliance, yet so light in the hand that they appeared to be water bubbles. A man could stamp a magnetic-plated space boot on their rounded bowls and slender stems, and they would emerge unshattered.

Foss poured the wine of Arcturus into them, that deep crimson liquid which made them shine as the rubies on Maelen's collar. Maelen—I put her sternly out of mind and stood respectfully, waiting to show whatever Foss or Lidj would signal for, needfully alert to unvoiced orders.

The four bearers the merchants had brought with them, all senior servers, took their places across the booth, the small chests they had carried hither before them. In spite of the peace of the fair they demonstrated the worth of their burdens by the fact they were all wearing, not the daggers of custom, but swords of defense.

But I was never to see what they guarded so closely. For there came a shrill whistle at the open front of the booth, and all the surge of noise to which we had become accustomed during the hours died away to a silence so complete one could hear the faint jangle of armor, the scrape of sword which heralded the arrival of a squad of fair justiciars. There were four of them, armed as if about to go against a fortified tower. Leading them was a man in a long robe that was half white (though marked with dust), half black, to signify the two sides of justice. He went unhelmed, a wilted wreath of Hress leaves sitting slightly crooked on his head, so that we knew him for a priest who had temporary duty thus, to remind, if only faintly, that there had once been a sacred meaning for this assembly.

"Hark and give heed." His voice was high-pitched, specially trained in the sacerdotal style of delivery. "This be the justice of the Moon of Rings, by the favor of Domtatoper, by whose will we run and walk, live and breathe, think and do! Let he stand forth who Domtatoper calls—even the off-worlder who drew weapon within the bonds of the Fair of the Moon of Rings!"

Captain Foss fronted the priest in one quick movement.

"Upon whose complaint does Domtatoper's sword-sworn summon my liegeman?" He made the conventional reply to the summons.

"Upon the complaint of Othelm, sworn on the altar and before witnesses. There must be answer made."

"There shall be," Foss returned. I caught the slight movement of his eyes and went to join him. He had my persona tape in his tunic pocket. It would be enough to justify my use of the stunner. But how soon we could get a hearing before the mixed tribunal of priests and merchants was another matter, and I knew that this present conference between the captain and the northern men was an important one.

"Let me go," I said in Basic. "If they propose to try me at once, I can send a message—"

Foss did not answer but called into the booth. "Lalfarns!"

Alfec Lalfarns, tube man, had no regular booth duties save to lend a hand in unpacking and stowing goods.

"This man," Foss said to the priest, "goes as my eyes and ears. If my sword-sworn comes to trial, he will inform me. This is permitted?"

The priest looked to Lalfarns and after a moment nodded. "It is permitted. Let this one," he turned to me, "lay aside his weapon."

He held out his hand for the stunner in my holster. But Foss's fingers had already closed about its butt and the captain drew it.

"His weapon is no longer his. It remains here—as is custom."

I thought for a moment that the priest was going to protest, but by custom the captain was right. For, by Yiktor reckoning, all weapons worn by an underling were legally the property of the lord and could be reclaimed at any time, especially if the lord considered that his sword-sworn had transgressed some ruling.

So without any means of defense I stepped forward and took my place between the guards, Lalfarns following a few short paces behind. While a stunner was no blaster, I had worn one for most of my life, hardly knowing that it hung at my belt. Now I had an odd naked feeling and a sudden wariness of all around me. I tried to believe that this was merely reaction to my disarming, to the fact that I was, for the moment at least, at the mercy of alien law on a world strange to me. Only my uneasiness grew, until I knew it for one of the forewarnings that come with even the slightest gift of esper most of us in the space-borne communities have. I glanced back at Lalfarns just in time to see that he, too, was looking over his shoulder, his hand going to the grip of his stunner and then falling away again, as he realized that gesture might be misinterpreted.

It was then that I took better notice of the way in which my guards were going. By right we should have been heading for the Great Booth wherein the court sat during the ten days of the fair. I could see the wide-eaved roof above the tents and booths ahead, but well to the left. We were edging toward the fringe of the fair, to the space which held the ornamented tents of the nobles who could not be housed in Yrjar.

"Follower of All Light." I raised my voice to catch the ear of the white-and-black-clad priest, who had quickened step so we must lengthen stride to keep the proper distance in his wake. "Where do we go? The court lies—"

He did not turn his head, or give any evidence that he heard me. And I saw now that we were turning from the last line of merchant booths in among the tents of the lords. There were no crowds here, only a servant or two in sight.

"Hallie, Hallie, Hal!"

They came out of hiding, that swirl of men, stampeding into our small party with their mounts trained to rear and smash at footmen with their heavy hoofs. I heard Lalfarns shout angrily. Then the guard to my right gave me a shove which sent me skidding, trying to keep my balance, between two tents.

There was a sharp pain in my head and that was an end to it for a time.

Pain sent me into darkness, and the throb of pain brought me out of it, or accompanied me on a reluctant journey into consciousness once again. For some moments I could not understand the sensations that racked my body. Finally I came to guess, and then to know for a certainty that I lay face-down across the back of a burden kas, bound there, and jolted painfully by every heavy-footed step the beast took. Around me I heard a jangle, the murmur of men, so that I knew I was carried in the company of more than one rider. But their speech was not of Yrjar and the few words I caught I could not understand.

I do not know how long the nightmare continued, for I slipped in and out of consciousness more times than my painful head noted. And after a while I prayed that I would not return from the welcoming dark the next time it engulfed me.

A body made tough by a whole life of space voyaging, a body inured to all the stress and strain and dangers, does not easily yield to ill treatment, as I was painfully to discover in days to come. I was forcibly dismounted from the kas by the easy method of cutting my bonds and allowing me to fall to a very hard pavement.

About was the flicker of torch and lamplight, but my vision was so fogged I distinguished my captors only as vague figures moving about. Then I was lifted by my shoulders, dragged along, and with a last push sent tumbling down a steep incline into a wanly lighted place.

More of the speech I could not understand and a figure clumped down after me. There was the full force of some liquid dashed into my face and I lay gasping. Water was good on my parched lips, though, and I put forth a feverish tongue to lick off the small moisture. A grip in my hair, which tore at the roots, jerked my head up, and more water was poured into my mouth, half strangling me until I made some shift to swallow.

It was not enough, but it was some small alleviation. The hand in my hair released me before I had more than a swallow or two, and my head thumped back on the floor, with force enough to send me off again.

When I blinked out of that swoon or sleep, or both, there was a darkness which was frightening. I blinked and blinked, trying to clear my vision—until I realized that not my sight, but the area in which I lay was at fault. With infinite effort I managed at last to brace myself up on one elbow so that I could better see the place of my confinement.

There was no furnishing save a bench, and that rude work. The floor was littered with ill-smelling straw. In fact there was an evil odor about the place which grew stronger the longer I sniffed it. A window slit, tall as my body, made a vertical cut in one wall. It was no wider than a couple of hand spans, but through it came a grayish light which did not master the corner shadows. On the bench, as my bleary eyes focused there, I saw an earthen jug, and suddenly that became the sole interest in my world.

It was impossible to get to my feet. Even sitting up left me so giddy that I had to close my eyes and remain so for a space. In the end I reached that promise of water by a worm's progress, mostly on my belly, across the cold pavement of the floor.

There was liquid in the jug, my hope and fear concerning which had warred all during my crawl. It was not water alone, for it had a sharp, sour taste which drew mouth tissues. But I drank, for I would have lapped up far worse and thought it wine at the moment.

Though I tried to limit myself sanely once the water was on my tongue, easing the dry torment of my mouth and throat, it took all my will power to put the jug aside while liquid still sloshed in it.

My head was clearing and, after a short time, I was able to move without bringing on a giddy attack. Perhaps the odd taste in the water had been that of a drug or stimulant. Finally I lurched along the wall to the slit of window, to see what lay without.

There was sun there, though its rays reached me only as a kind of twilight. And my field of vision was exceedingly narrow. Some distance away was a gray reach of solid wall that resembled any fortress of Yiktor. There was nothing else, save pavement which must run from the base of the building in which I was imprisoned to that wall.

Then a man passed across my slip of outer world. He did not linger, but I glimpsed enough to know that he was a sword-sworn of some lord, for he went in mail and helm and had a surcoat of yellow bearing a black device. I could not see the manner of that device, nor would I have been able to read it, the intricate heraldry of Yiktor not being one of the matters of Trader concern.

Yet—yellow and black—I had seen that combination of colors before. I leaned against the wall and tried to remember where and when. Color . . . the last time I had thought about color—silver and ruby—Maelen's costume—the pink-gray of her banner which had exerted such an odd influence—the banners of the other amusement places—Amusement places—the searing red and green of the gambling tent that had done more than beckon—it had screamed!

The gambling tent! Half memory sharpened into a mental picture . . . Gauk Slafid at the table, the piles of counters heaped into small towers of luck, and to his left the young noble who had watched me so intently as I passed with Maelen. He had worn a surcoat, too, glistening half silk of a forceful yellow—and the breast of it had borne a house badge outlined and stitched in black. But the bits and pieces I now held could not be fitted into any recognizable pattern.

Any quarrel with a native of Yiktor was with Othelm, not with the young man in black and yellow. I could not see a logical alliance between two such widely separated people. The beast seller would have no call upon a lord's protection. My knowledge of Yiktorian customs was as complete as Trader tapes could make it, but no one could absorb the fine nuances of social life and custom on an alien world without years of intensive study. It might well be that the brush with Othelm *had* led to my present predicament.

Wherever I now was, it was not within the boundaries of the fair. That was astonishing. I could remember part of a journey by kas back which meant, I was sure, that I had not been taken into Yrjar. But I had been forcibly removed from the jurisdiction of the fair court, which was so bald a refutation of all we knew of custom that it was hard to believe it had happened. Those who had so snatched me, as well as he who gave the order for it and any who conspired with him to bring it about, were to be outlawed without question as soon as the fact of my disappearance was known.

What made me worth such a desperate price? Only time and my captors could supply the answer. But it would seem that they were in no hurry, for the hours crept by and no one came near me. I was hungry, very hungry, and though I tried to ration what remained of the water I finished it and then knew thirst again. The dim light went with the day, and the night washed in, to drown me in waves of shadow.

I sat with my back against the wall, facing the ramp down which I had been pushed, trying to make my ears supply information. Now and again some sound, distorted and muffled, reached from beyond the slit window. Then came the call of a horn, perhaps announcing some arrival. I got to my feet again and felt my way back to the window. There was the beam of a lantern flashing across the outer wall, and I heard voices. Then a body of men crossed my line of vision, one wearing the cloak of a noble a step or two in advance of the other three.

Not too long afterward there was the sound of metal striking metal at the top of the ramp. Hearing it, some ill-defined need sent me back along the wall to my old position facing the upper door. Light thrust down, powerful enough to blind me, to hide those behind it. Only when they came down into my cell could I see a little through the glare.

It was the same party that had passed by the window. Now I was also able to identify the noble as the young man from the gambling tent.

There is a trick, so old as to be threadbare, but I held to it now. Remain silent, let your opponent speak first. So I did not burst out with any demand for an explanation, only studied them carefully as well as I could see them, determined to outwait their patience.

Two of the men hurried to draw the bench away from the wall, and the lord sat down as one to whom ease of body was his just due. The third follower hung the lantern on a wall hook to my left, and from that position it gave equal light to us all.

"You!" I do not know whether my silence had surprised the lord or not, but I thought I read irritation in his tone. "Know you who I am?"

This was the classic opening between Yiktorian rivals, a chanting of names and titles intended to impress a possible enemy with the weight of one's own reputation.

When I did not answer he scowled, leaning forward, his fists planted on his knees, his elbows angled out.

"This is the Lord Osokun, first son to the Lord Oskold, Shield of Yenlade and Yuxisome." The man who still stood beneath the lantern chanted in the voice of a professional battle herald.

The names, son or father, meant nothing to me, even the lands they represented were unknown. I remained silent. And I did not see any gesture from Osokun, nor did he give any order. But one of his bully boys leaped at me and slapped my face with his open hand, sending my head thumping back against the wall with a pain so intense that I almost fainted. Only will kept me swaying on my feet, and by will I tried to hold to a halfway clear mind. So it was going to be that way? Whatever they wanted of me they were prepared to gain by force.

And what they wanted Osokun made clear in a rush of words.

"You have weapons, knowledge, off-world skulker. Both you will give to me, if not one way, then another."

For the first time I made answer, my lips swelling from the blow.

"Did you find such arms on me?" I gave him no title of courtesy.

He laughed. "No, your captain was too clever. But you have the knowledge. And if he would see you again, we shall have the weapons also, within a short time."

"If you know anything about the Traders, you also know that we are mind-locked against such disclosures planetside."

His smile grew wider. "So I have heard. But each world has its own secrets, as you must also be aware. We have a few keys to open such locks. If they do not work, a pity. But your captain has a bargain to consider, which he shall be doing shortly. As for the rest— Get to it!" His last order had the snap of a riding whip.

I do not want to remember what happened thereafter in that stone-walled room. Those who took part in the questioning were indeed experts in their line. I do not know whether Osokun really believed that I could, if I would, reveal what he wanted to know, or if some monstrous compulsion drove him to enjoy such an occupation for its own sake. Much of it was afterward gone from me, past recalling. An esper, even to the smaller degree, can shut off parts of consciousness to save the balance of one's mind.

They could not have learned anything to their value. And they were expert enough in their dirty employment not to maim me permanently. But I was not aware of their going, nor of anything else for a period of time. And when pain again roused me, there was once more wan day beyond the window. The bench was back against the wall, and on it sat once again the jug, and this time with it a plate bearing a mass of something congealed in cold fat.

I crawled to that sustenance. I drank and felt the restorative of the bitter water, but I sat for a long space before I could make myself try the food. Only the knowledge that I must have strength of body for the future made me choke it down, nauseous as it was.

This much I knew: I had been kidnapped by Osokun, who hoped to exchange me for weapons and information—doubtless that he might use both in a bid for a kingdom. The boldness of this act meant that he either had backing so powerful as to set aside the laws of the fair, or else that he hoped to make his bid with such rapidity that the authorities would not have time to move against him. The recklessness of his act was so near the borderline of utter folly that I could not believe he meant it. Yet I had only the past hours here to realize that he had already far overstepped all bounds and could only keep on the same dangerous way. There was no turning back.

That Captain Foss would buy me with the price Osokun asked was impossible. Though the Traders were close knit, and one of their main rules was loyalty to one another, the *Lydis*, her crew, and the whole good fame of the Free Traders could not and would not be risked for the life of a single man. All Foss could do would be to turn to the machinery of the Yiktorian law.

Did he know where I was? What had the raiders done with Lalfarns? If our tube man had escaped, Foss must have already learned that I had been taken, and could have set in action all countermoves.

But I must depend not on vain hope but on my own efforts now. I had to think and think clearly.

Chapter 6

Now was I driven to loose a mind-search, exhausting as that could be. For this was the place and time in which only desperate methods were left. Since thought-seek operates differently between races and species, I could not hope for any open message, perhaps nothing at all. It was as if I tried to monitor a band of communication so high or so low that my pickup caught only an indistinct pattern. No words, no clear thoughts, but what did come was fear. So sharp at times was that emotion that I believed those who broadcast it did so in peril.

Prick here, prick there, perhaps each prick signaled the emotions of a different defender of this fort. I raised my head to look at the pale window slit, then I crept to it to listen. But there were no sounds without. I pulled myself up to peer through. Day, yes, even a small strip of sunlight on the other wall. All was very quiet.

Again I closed my eyes to the light, strove to thought-seek, to fasten on one of those fear-pricks enough to read the source of that unease. Most of them still swam in and out beyond my catching. I found one near to the very door which guarded my prison, however, or so I thought. And into that I probed with all the effort I could summon.

It was as if I tried to read a fogged tape which was not only overexposed but also composed of alien symbols. Emotion, yes, one could feel that, for basic emotions remain the same from species to

51

species. All living creatures know fear, hate, happiness—though the sources or reasons for these feelings may be very different. And of the common emotions fear and hate are the strongest, the easiest to pick up.

The fear that rode minds here was growing, and intermingled with it was anger. But the anger was weak, much overborne by the fear. Why? What?

My teeth closed upon my underlip, I gave all my remaining strength to the need for discovery. Fear ... of something ... someone ... not present ... coming? Need ... need to get rid ... rid of me! That breakthrough came so sharply that I straightened as if to meet a physical blow. Yet there was no one there to deliver it. But I knew as well as if it had been shouted aloud that my presence here was the cause of fear. Osokun? No, I did not believe that the lord who had tried to impress his will in this cell had had such a forceful change of attitude.

Prick, prick ... I readied my mind, pushed aside amazement, went back to the patient mining of those incomprehensible thoughts. Prisoner—danger— Not my present danger, no—but as a prisoner here I was a danger to the thinker. Perhaps Osokun had so overstepped the laws of Yiktor that those who aided him, or obeyed his orders, had every reason to fear future consequences.

Dared I try a countersuggestion? Fear pushed too far erupts in violence in many men. If I added to that fear in the mind I had tapped and concentrated upon, I might well bring a sword to my own end. I weighed one thing against another while holding the link between us.

What I decided upon was perhaps so thin a chance that it already lay under the shadow of failure. For I attempted to set in that wavery mind-pattern the thought that with the prisoner gone there would be no fear, and that the prisoner must fare forth alive not dead. In the simplest pattern I could devise, and the most emphatic, I sent that thought-beam along the linkage.

At the same time I edged along the wall to the ramp which gave entrance to this place. I stopped only to pick up the jug, drank the remainder of its contents, and then grasped it tightly in my hand. I tried to remember how the door above opened, though my eyes had been dazzled when Osokun had come that way. Outward—surely outward!

Now I was halfway up the ramp, braced, waiting ...

Free the prisoner . . . no more fear . . . free the prisoner . . .

Stronger—he must be moving toward me! Now—the rest would depend upon fortune alone. And when one sets his life on such scales it is a fearsome thing.

I heard the click of metal against metal—the door—I raised the jug— Now!

The door swung back and I threw outward not only the water container but also a blast of fear, directed down the link between mind and mind. I heard a cry from the figure silhouetted against the light. The jug struck against his head and he staggered back.

I scrambled up, putting all my weakening force into that dash, reaching and passing the door. The light was dazzling even in this inner corridor, but the man who had unlocked the door was slumped against the opposite wall, his hands to his face, and between his fingers trickled blood. He was moaning.

My first thought was for his sword. I staggered to him, making his weapon mine. Even to have an unfamiliar weapon in hand bolstered my confidence. He did not fight me. I thought afterward that the blast of fear had struck his mind a far greater and incapacitating blow than the shattered jug had inflicted on his body.

With a roll of shoulder, a thrust of arm, I sent him down into the pit from which I had climbed. He had most thoughtfully left the lock rod still in the door and that I turned swiftly and withdrew to take along.

So much I did before I looked around. The light here, while stinging my dark-orientated eyes, was, I thought, after a moment or two of blinking adjustment, perhaps that of late afternoon. How long I had lain below I did not know, the passing of days and nights had escaped me.

But for the moment, at least, the hall in which I stood was empty. I had made no plans beyond this instant. All I could do was try to reach the open, though I might not have such good fortune in another meeting with any member of the garrison. Mind-seek was too thin to use for scouting. I had tried my esper talent to the full when I had drawn upon it to unlock my cell. What I did now must be accomplished largely by physical means alone, and the weapon I carried was strange to me.

I staggered along the corridor, ever listening for any sound which might herald the coming of another. There was a sharp bend where another narrow window slit gave light. I paused there to look out.

Again I saw a small piece of courtyard bounded by a wall. And this showed me a portion of gate, now shut—such a portal as would serve a large party. If that was the only way out of this place, I tasted defeat indeed.

At the jog in the corridor the way turned left. Doors opened along it and for the first time I heard voices. However, there was no other way out save this. With my shoulder against the wall, a bared untried sword in my hand, I began my journey.

The first two doors, recessed in the thickness of the wall, were closed, for which I would have given devout thanks had I been able to spare any relaxation of concentration. Though I knew my esper was at a very low ebb, I tried to use its remnants to feel out any life ahead.

So faint a flickering. I already knew from the sound of voices that there were at least two in one of those rooms, and mind-seek confirmed this. But there could be a dozen more and I would not pick them up now. I shuffled along. The voices grew louder, I could make out separate words, but in another tongue. By the sharpness of the tone I thought they were quarreling.

Brighter light, cutting from a half-open door across the corridor. I halted to study the door. Like that of the cell, it opened outward and it was more than half closed. The lock looked the same as that of the prison, some inner system which was made secure by a rod inserted in a hole and turned. My left hand went to the one I carried. Could it be that the same one might be used successfully here?

First, could the door be entirely closed without arousing those within? I dared not show myself in the open space to see what or who were there. But the voices had reached close to the shouting point, and I hoped they were so engrossed that my next move would go unnoticed.

I put the sword in my belt, took the rod in my right hand. The left I placed palm-flat against the surface of the door and gave it a gentle push. But no such easy touch would work with this ponderous slab, I discovered. It needed shoulder muscles to move it. I waited tensely for some betraying creak, some lull in the conversation, to tell me that I had made the wrong choice.

Move it did at last, inch by inch, until finally it fitted into its frame. Within the voices continued as I fumbled, my fingers slick with sweat, to push the rod into the hole. It resisted a little and I was ready to leave it. Then it clicked into place and I thrust it up and down as I had seen such rods used before. My faint hope paid off—the rod locked.

From the continued noise within, they had not yet discovered they were prisoners. Twice now I had succeeded, but I must not take too much confidence from that, for such luck was too good to last.

There was another turn in the corridor with a window where once more I paused to look out. My guess as to the time of day was proven, the glow of sunset lay on the pavement and wall out there. And night is ever the friend of the fugitive. As yet I had no thought as to what I would do when I was out of Osokun's stronghold, free in an unknown countryside. One step at a time was all my mind and will could encompass.

Before me was another door wide open on the courtyard. I could still hear the muffled quarreling behind, but now I tried to pick up sounds ahead. There was a sharp, high noise which I recognized as the squeal of a kas—but no man's voice.

I gained the deep recess of this door and peered out, sword once more in hand. To my left was a roofed space in which kasi were stabled, their triangular heads with the stiff, upstanding stocks of black hair tossed now and then. But there were ragged bits of leaves hanging from their jaws and I thought they had just been given their fodder.

For a moment I debated the chance of securing one of those mounts, but regretfully decided against it. Mind seek worked better with animals, even with alien species, than with humanoids, that was true. But to concentrate upon controlling a beast which might be unruly would require too much of me now. I would be safer, I was sure, depending upon myself.

The bulk of the building from which I had come cast a long shadow ahead. I could not see the outer gate, but I tried to reach a place in deeper shadows between two bales of kasi fodder and succeeded.

Now my field of vision was far better. To my right was the wide gate, well barred. Above that was a kind of cage and in it I detected movement which flattened me low against the bales. There was a sentry there. I waited for the shout, perhaps a crossbow bolt to find me, some sign I had been sighted. For I could not believe that I had escaped notice. When moments passed and no discovery came, I began to think that the sentry on duty there had eyes only for what lay outside these walls, not what chanced within.

I planned out a route which took me well along, first the bales of fodder, and then the end of the stable between me and that lookout. I moved slowly, though every nerve in me screamed for speed, feeling that a scurry might attract attention where creeping would keep me one with the concealing shadows. I counted the beasts in the stable as I passed, hoping to get some inkling as to the size of the present garrison. There were seven riding beasts, four of them used for burden. But that did not help, for this place might have a permanent unmounted garrison. However, the small number of mounts in a stable manifestly built to hold three, maybe four times that number suggested that there might only be a skeleton force in residence. And it also suggested that Osokun and his sword-sworn might well have gone.

There were two more of the high-placed sentry posts. But, though I watched them carefully, I caught no sign that they were manned. Then I ducked behind a half wall as tramping boots sounded loudly on the stones. A man came along. Though he wore the scale jerkin of a foot fighter, his head was bare of helm and he had a yoke across his shoulders supporting slopping buckets of water which he emptied into a stone trough that ran the length of the kasi stalls.

He went out with the yoke and empty buckets. But in my hiding place I fought down a sudden soar of spirit. For in those moments he had been ridden by so strong a desire that it reached me as a distinct message. Fear in him had given away to determination, a determination to act that was so strong I had been able to read it. Perhaps he also varied from his fellows in some quirk of mind which had laid him better open to my esper, for such variations exist, as we well know. And this was the third boon fortune granted me that day.

He was acting a part, I was sure, going about his duties but using them as a screen for his purpose. And the moment had come when immediate action was demanded if he would succeed. Carrying his yoke and the empty buckets, he strode openly along, while I slunk behind him, for what he wanted was my own wish.

There was a well in the yard beyond, and from the center core building extended a wing at a sharp angle about it as if the stone blocks threw out an arm to shelter the source of valued water. In the wing were more of the narrow slit windows and a door. The man I followed did not stop at the well. He gave a quick glance to right and left as he neared it. Apparently reassured, he sped straight to the door of the wing. I gave him a moment or two for lead and then followed.

This was a combined armory and storeroom. Weapon racks on the walls, gear piled in neat heaps, and the distinctive smell of grain and other food for man and beast. Behind one of the piles of supplies I saw the abandoned yoke and buckets. As I kept on the trail the mingled fear and will of my guide was a cord pulling at me. I came to another door half hidden behind a pile of grain bags, and that gave on a narrow stair, steep enough to make a man giddy to look down. There I paused for a space as I heard the boots of the one ahead, lest my own footgear make a noise he could hear. Wild with impatience I had to wait until all sounds had died away. And then I went slowly, aching with the effort of placing each foot, afraid my weakened body would betray me. Luckily that descent was not a long one.

At the bottom was a passage which ran only in one direction. Dark here, and I saw no gleam of light ahead to suggest that my guide used a lantern or torch. It must have been a way he knew well.

Nor could I hear him any longer. Then, along our mind link there was a burst of relief, as bright in my brain as a lantern would have been in my eyes. He had reached his goal, he was free of the fort to find what he believed to be safety. And I did not think he would linger at that exit.

So I put on what speed I could, staggering on at a half run to find the same gate. In the dark, I came up hard against sharp projections. But I did not fall, and was able after a moment to put out my hands to serve as eyes. Before me, according to touch, was another flight of steep steps, and up these I crawled on hands and knees, not certain I might take them otherwise.

I paused now and then to feel above my head for any sign of exit. At last I found a trap door which gave to my push. There was still not much light as I came out in a cave, or rather a heaping of rocks I did not believe to be natural, cleverly made to resemble nature as a cover for this door. In a land so constantly riven by petty wars such a burrow must have been necessary for each fort. To my mind this was less concealed at the other end than one might have thought needful.

For the time being my full concern was for getting out of sight of any wall sentry. The rocks covering the exit of the passage were, I saw as I edged along belly flat to the ground, only one such outcrop.

And I thought I could trace a pattern in them as if they marked the site of a much older and ruined fortress.

There was no sign of the deserter who had preceded me through the bolt hole, but I continued to move with caution. At last I took cover behind what could be the end of the ruins, much earth sunken and tumbled, and for the first time I surveyed the back trail.

The sky blazed with the particular wild color with which sunset was painted on this planet, sometimes so brilliantly that one dared not closely observe those strident sweeps of clashing shades. Under it the fort was a dark blot, already closed in by shadows which accented its grim aspect. It consisted of one inner building and the outer wall, and was even smaller than it had seemed when I was making my way out. I did not believe it was any holding, but rather a border post, a defense for the land it guarded. For one thing there were no dwellings or any cultivated fields ringing it. This was a camp for soldiers, not a place of refuge for farmers and townsfolk as any main castle keep would be.

There was a road by its main entrance, coming from a notch between two lines of hills, extending into the unknown level land. That road must tie it to both the center of the domain and the outer world, perhaps even Yrjar. And it was my guide.

My journey here had been such that I might just as well have been blindfolded all the way. I had no idea whether the port lay north or south from here, but it was certainly to the west. But I could not travel on the road. For the first time I began to think that all my good fortune in winning free from Osokun's keep had ended. I had the sword I had taken, but water, food, protection against any storm were lacking. And the energy which my will had fathered and which had sustained my ill-used body so far, was fast ebbing. Whether I *could* pull myself on was a question I was afraid to ask myself, because the answer was so plain.

Both the fort and the place of ruins where I emerged crested small hills. The passage which had brought me hither must have run under the gap of low ground between. Once I had put that high ground between me and the sentry post, I was in the clear. Then I got to my feet, determined to keep putting one before the other as long as I could, then to crawl, wriggle, do anything I could to keep moving.

Time became a phantom thing without measurement, save that which comes between one step and the next. I was favored by this much, the methods Osokun's questioners had used had caused great pain but had left muscle and body unimpaired for the effort I must now put forth. But I lapsed into a kind of stupor in which another portion of my mind took control, one which did not consciously know, plan, or live, but lay deep below all that.

Twice I roused enough to discover that I had wandered down to heel and toe along the smoother surface of the road, some hidden warning signal flashing possible danger. Both times I was able to stagger up again into the rough land where bushes and rocks gave me cover. Once I believe I was trailed for a space by some hunter of the night. But if that unseen creature was intrigued by me to considering me prey, it decided again and was gone.

The moon was bright, so bright its Rings were shining fire in the sky. Sotrath, that moon, held always two rings about it. But in a regular cycle of years came a time of three, which was a great portent for the natives. I did not look up to that wonder, and I was only thankful for the rays which made it possible to see the worst of the possible stumbling blocks before me.

It was near dawn when I passed through the gap between the hills, needing there to take to the road. My mouth was dry as if filled with ashes, acrid ashes which burned the tissues of tongue and inner cheek. Only my well-worn will kept me moving, for I feared that if I rested I could not possibly find my feet again, or even crawl. Somehow I must get past this place where the road was the only exit, into the open western country. Then, then I promised my body, I would rest in the first hole I could find.

Somehow I made it, the hills were behind me. I wavered off the open surface into the brush, pushing on until I knew I was indeed finished. There I fell to my knees with a last forward thrust that plunged my scratched and whipped body between two thick bushes. Then I lay still and what occurred immediately after I do not remember.

A river, a precious river of water wetting me, giving my parched body new life. But there was the thunder, the beat of rapids in the river. I dared not allow myself to drift on into a wild stretch of water, be beaten against rocks— Water—thunder—

I was not in any stream, rather did I rest on a hard surface which was secure and unmoving under me. I was wet, but the moisture came from above, falling in fierce curtains of rain. And thunder cracked indeed, but in the sky.

When I levered myself up from the ground, my tongue licking at the rain which spattered my face, I saw the flash of lightning along the hill crowns. It must be day again, but so dark a day that there was hardly more visibility than existed at twilight. For the moment I only raised my face to the rain, opened my mouth to it, sought to drink it in.

A thunderous rumble reached across the curtained sky, a wild split of lightning, almost as bright as a ship's tail flames—I looked through a small opening in the bushes at a party of mounted men riding as if driven by some storm whip eastward. They were cloaked and hooded and strung well out, with the mounts of the laggers laboring, threads of foam strung from their jaws. The whole aspect of the company was one of some overwhelming need for speed. As they passed my hiding place emotion washed over me from them— fear, anger, desperation—so strong that it was a blow for an esper mind. Under the muffling cloaks I could not see color or heraldic design, nor did any lord's travel banner crack over their heads. But I was certain this was Osokun riding to his den. And if it were not already, now the hunt would be up for me.

So stiff and sore was my body that I could barely get to my feet. My first wavering steps wracked and pained me. I had thought that I was tough and so honed by the life of a Free Trader that I was not to be easily worn by bodily discomfort. But now I moved again in a haze which wrapped me as close as if I were caught in the hunting web of a Tiditi spider-crab.

The storm creviced the ground with runnels of fast-running water, as if so much rain now fell from the skies that it could not sink into the soil but spun away on the surface. From these I drank from time to time, far past caring if they carried any alien element to injure me. But if I had water I lacked food, and the memory of the greasy mess I had so reluctantly eaten—when? a night ago, two nights?—haunted me, to assume the proportions of an Awakiian banquet with all the five-and-twenty dishes of ceremony. After a while I pulled leaves from the bushes and chewed upon them, spitting forth their pulp.

Time again had no meaning. How much of the day lay behind, I neither knew nor cared. The fury of the rain slackened. There was some slight clearing of sky, but not enough to dim the light—

Light? Suddenly I was aware that I marched steadfastly toward a light. Not the yellow of the lanterns I had seen in the fort or in Yrjar—no—

Moon globe—silver—beckoning— Once before there had been such a globe. A last wisp of warning in my mind faded quickly— moon globe . . .

Chapter 7

By the will of Molaster I have Singer's power, and having it so am I also bound to other things—the far sight, the long sight, the spinning of the Rings. And these be hard things to live with at times since the will within one can be set crosswise to all of them, and if that is done then the will of Maelen is always the loser. I, who desired only to remain at the great fair with my little people, rose from the first sleep of night knowing that a call had come, though I did not reckon the why and the wherefore. And in the cages I heard the whimpering cries of my little people, who are sensitive to the power, for its compulsion strongly touched also upon them, bringing uneasiness and fear.

My first thought was of them, putting my cloak about me, going to walk wand in hand up and down so that they could look upon me and forget fear. But when I came to the place wherein we had put the barsk, I saw that beast on its feet, with head down a little as if to spring, while its eyes were yellow fire and in them dwelt madness.

"There is a sending—" Malec came to me.

"There is a sending," I agreed. "But not from the tongues or the minds of the Old Ones. Unless they have called upon the power and that has answered not them but me!"

He looked to me gravely and made a gesture which in part denied my words. We are blood kin, though not to the second closeness, and Malec does not always see as I see. He acts many times to keep me from what he believes folly.

However, he could not deny a Singer who says she has caught a sending. So now he waited. And I took my wand between my hands and turned it slowly. For, now that my little people were soothed and their fear rose no more as a wall to bar the waves of power, I could so direct it. North, west, south—the wand did not move in my light grasp. But as I wheeled to the east did it right itself, pointing straight outward. In my fingers it was warm, demanding, so that I said to Malec:

"This is a debt-sending, and for me. Payment is required."

At a debt-sending one does not hesitate, for giving and taking must ever be equal on the scales of Molaster. This is even more true for a Singer than others, for only so is the power nourished and kept flaring bright.

Then I asked of him, "What of the off-worlder? And of Osokun, who has been planning plans of darkness?"

Malec shifted his feet upon the ground before he spoke. "Osokun can claim blood-kin to the second degree with Oslaph who—"

"Who has been chosen by temple lot this year to represent the lords upon the tribunal of the fair. And also, did not the off-worlder Slafid say his other kin, Ocorr, captains the guard. But surely neither can break all law and custom."

Then my certainty faded, for Malec did not speedily agree with me. I saw that he was troubled, though his eyes did not fall from mine, for he is of the Thassa and between us always there is truth and open dealing. So that I now said:

"There is that I do not know."

"There is. Shortly after midday gong the guards took the off-worlder, Krip Vorlund, to answer the claims of Othelm, the beast dealer. And the party were set upon by mounted men from beyond the boundary. When the skirmish was over the off-worlder was gone. It is believed that he is back with his kin, and the chief priest has ordered their trade booth closed and the Traders to remove themselves."

"You did not tell me this?" I was not angry, save with myself for believing that Osokun dared not move. For I should have read better in him that he was one to dare greatly without thinking overlong about the future consequences of any impulsive act.

"It was more rational to believe in his escape to his ship," Malec returned. "For it is very well known that the Free Traders care for their own. And they might not trust the justice of the court."

"Also that this was no concern of ours," I said a little sharply. "Perhaps it is not—of the Thassa. I know we are oath-bound not to interfere in the matters of the plainsmen. But this is a debt personal to me. And of you I ask one thing, by blood right, that you seek out the captain of the *Lydis*. And if it is true Krip Vorlund is not safe among his crew, you tell him all that has passed."

"We have not had an answer from the Old Ones," he objected.

"I take it upon me, by the scales of Molaster, the responsibility for this." And I breathed upon my wand so it shone silver-bright.

"And what will you do?" he asked, but I knew that he had already guessed my answer.

"I will go seeking what I must seek. But also it must be done with an excuse to cover my going. For now I do not doubt there will be eyes watching, ears listening, marking our coming and going. Thus—" I turned slowly and looked along the lines of cages, "we shall put up the van cart and in it I shall take Borba, Vors, Tantacka, Simmle, and"—I laid hand upon the barsk cage—"this one. Our excuse shall be that these ail and I fear they may spread some sickness among the others of our company, so it is best to withdraw them for a time beyond the crowded life here."

"Why this one?" he pointed to the barsk.

"For him that reason may be the truth. In the open country perhaps his mind will be at rest and he may be reached. Whereas here there is much to remind him of past torment."

I saw a shadow smile about Malec's lips. "Ahy, ahy, Maelen, ever do you hold to a wish, do you not? So still you think that you shall be the one, the first one, to add a barsk to your company?"

And I met his smile with my own. "I am patient, I am one with a strong will. And this I know, not guess, blood kin, I *shall* be the one to command a barsk. If not this, then another, someday, somehow."

I know that he thought this folly. But no one argues with another on whom a sending has been set, if that sending be one of debt payment. So he put the kasi to the wagon yokes and aided me to place those of our company I had chosen in the van, putting the barsk cage apart and screened. Weak as that creature was, still it continued to watch us and snarl whenever we approached, nor could my thought meet aught within its skull but the churning of madness.

We broke our fast together and summoned Otjan, the odd boy, to bring a priest who would take charge of our booth for an hour or so while Malec went on his errand to the *Lydis* and I turned east. Malec urged me to wait for his return, but in me swelled a feeling of urgency and I knew I could not do this, but must be on the move. For already I was sure in my mind that the off-worlder was not safely among his friends, but rather in dire danger elsewhere, or the debt by sending would not have come to burden me so sharply and without warning.

The van could not move swiftly, and moreover I must keep to its slowest pace while still in sight of the fair by reason of my excuse. For to tumble ailing animals would have been suspicious to any watcher. Thus, when all inside me urged speed and yet more speed, I set the kasi to an amble as I passed beyond the last line of fringe tents. I had believed that someone might question my going, though I had taken care to give my reasons to the priest and Otjan.

Those I had chosen to accompany me on this mission, though they now rode caged, were the keenest of mind, and the most aggressive of all our company. Borba and Vors were glassia of the mountain forests. They were in length the span of four hands placed end to end, and had long slender tails as long again as their bodies, their fur as black as a night of storm and no stars. They each had long paws with very sharp claws which they carried sheathed, but were like a sword blade to be used when the occasion demanded. Their heads were crowned with a tuft of gray-white stiff hair and this they flattened to their skulls when going into battle. By nature they were curious and fearless, willing to face enemies much larger than themselves—and ofttimes they won such battles too. They were seldom seen in the lowlands and thus could pass for animals we dared not lose.

Tantacka looked more dangerous than she was, though once roused her ire was a dogged, smoldering emotion which lasted long and made her more cunning in attack than her appearance suggested. She was plump of body, with a blunt-nosed face and small rounded ears, the merest stump of tail which she usually carried plastered down to her haunches. Twice as large as the glassia, she had power in her shoulders, for her favorite food in the wild was found only under rocks of size which her kind must uproot before dining. Her yellowish fur was so coarse that it resembled quills rather than hair. She was not a beautiful animal, rather clumsy, grotesque in appearance, but that added to her appeal when she gave her part of the show, for those watching marveled that such an apparently clumsy animal could do such clever things.

Simmle was of the same general species as the barsk, though her body hair was very short and tight to the skin. At a distance she looked to be not furred at all, but with a naked hide oddly marked, for across the even cream of her lower back and haunches were stripes of dark brown. Her tail was round and very thin, like the lash of a whip, her legs seemingly skin laid over bone with little flesh between, and the like upon her head, so that one could plainly see the ridges of the skull. Like Tantacka she was no beauty, but instead of clumsiness she gave the impression of speed and wiry endurance. And that was truth, for the venzese have long been used in the high plains for the coursing of game.

As I drove I felt their eager inquiry, their wonder at the meaning of our journey. To them I relayed my sense of danger, the need for wariness, to which they responded each in his own way. And, once well beyond sight of the fair, I brought each in turn out of the cage to sit beside me for a space, to look upon the country, to use his own senses for guide. For they had eyes to see what man's eyes do not, noses to lift from the breeze messages we do not note, ears to hear what we remain ignorant of—and these were in my service.

Simmle was uneasy, not because of what she sensed as she sat quietly beside me in the sunlight of the morning, but because of the barsk. To the rest he was no kin, near or far. And since they knew he was not free to harm them, they ignored his presence. But to Simmle he was enough like her own clan that she was ever aware of him, and I had to ease her fear, for madness is something so alien it breeds panic in those who come in contact with it.

On Yiktor there is madness, the brain does not think along smooth paths but slips out of pattern into chaos. And the mad man, the woman so afflicted, are deemed touched by Umphra, a primeval power. No one will harm such. When discovered they are put under restraint of the priests and taken high in the mountain to a certain Valley. And from memories of that Valley my mind ever flinches. To harm or kill the mad is to take into one's own body, believe the plainsmen, that illness which twisted awry its victim.

But animals that go mad are killed, and I think they are the more kindly used, being loosed so on the White Road where suffering and sorrow are naught, drawn so into Molaster's great pattern and keeping. I feared that I must deal so with the barsk, though still I was loath to take that final step. For as Malec had said, it had long been my wish to add this very rare and independent rover to our company. Perhaps I was vain of my own power and desired to add to the small fame I already had of one who worked well with the little people.

We forded the river, meeting with none other on the outward road from Yrjar than some belated fairgoers. And to the greetings of these I replied as one who had cares, twice saying that illness among my beasts drove me to this departure. But after midday I turned from the open road into a side trail which still led eastward, lest some passer-by would begin to wonder why I needs must go so far in my search for peace and quiet for my ill ones.

Before sunset we came to a meadow place by a stream, and there I made camp, loosing the kasi for grazing, my other ones to explore and enjoy their freedom. They relished this ability to nose about and lap from the stream, though none of them wandered far from the van, and in that the barsk remained curtained and alone.

After my companions were fed and bedded for the night and all was well, I looked upon the moon at its rising. Already the Third Ring was better defined. Another night or two and it would be bright—to be visible for some time thereafter. In my hands the wand caught its light and made it dazzle the eyes. I longed fiercely to try beam-reading, but since I was alone, and he who reads thus must in a manner of speaking depart from the body, lie entranced so that he may not easily awaken, I did not dare. But it was a hunger eating in me and I must rise and pace back and forth to quiet my nerves. Though I did dare again the use of the wand, it pointed firmly to the east.

At last I realized I must use the Qu'lak Song to summon slumber since the body must never be overridden by the mind, unless the need is very great. A Singer early learns that the temptation to forget the body is a strong one, and must ever be resisted. So I sang the four words and the five tones and opened my mind to rest.

There were twitterings and squeakings in the grass and I looked upon the mists of early morning. I released my little people once again while I prepared our food and put the kasi to the yoke. I fed the barsk and he lay quiet on his bedding. To the mind-touch he was weaker, growing lethargic as if the frenzy which had eaten him the day before had bruised and injured what contained it. And I wondered if this weakness was a good thing, to afford me a way of reassuring and perhaps leading those impulses back to stability. But my probe showed me that the time, if it would ever come, was not yet.

Once more we set out, though the trail we followed grew rougher and I feared I might reach a point the van could not pass and I would have to retrace my steps and seek out a side way. There was a kind of tension in the air which we all shared. I knew it for what it was, no warning of ill but rather the foreshadowing of what the Three Rings would bring to all who opened their minds rightly to the power. For at this time there was little limit on what might be assayed by the bold—though boldness is never enough when dealing with the power.

We were going into the hills and though this was not a country I was much familiar with, I knew that in this direction lay the holdings of Oskold. But I wondered at Osokun's rashness at bringing any captive here, unless the very boldness of such a move would, in a way, cover his tracks. None would believe that he would take a secret prisoner into the heart of his father's domain. But was Oskold himself a party to this? That set another design on the loom. For Oskold was seemingly a man of some intelligence and cunning. And if he were ready to defy law and custom, it would mean he held a mighty weapon in reserve with which to confound his enemies.

I remembered the half threat the off-worlder Slafid had made— that more was known about the Thassa than was right or safe for us. I hoped that our warning would stir the Old Ones into such countersteps as they could beam-read into taking. Rumor has always made much of us among the plainsmen. It is true that we are older in this land than they, that we were once great as they consider greatness, before we learned other ways to measure power and growth. We, too, built cities, of which only scattered stones abide in lonely places, knew rises and falls in history. Men progress, however, or they destroy themselves and sink back to their dim beginnings. By the will of Molaster did we progress beyond such matters. And to us now the quarrels and strivings of these newcomers were as the clamor of the little people, save that the little people are moved by simpler needs and go about their ways in more honest openness.

All through the day did the Abiding Influence of the Third Ring act upon us. From time to time my little people gave vent to their rising excitement with yells or barks, or whatever manner of sound was their normal speech. Once I heard the barsk, too, give tongue, but in a mournful, echoing howl full of mind-pain, which sent the rest of them dumb. I sent a sleep-wish to quiet him. Simmle gave me warning near midday of something coming, and I stopped the van to alight and followed her on foot through the yet frost-unkilled weeds and leafed brush to the top of a rise from which we could see the road east. A party came along it at a determined trot and their leader was Osokun. He did not ride in ordinary state, but headed a small squad with no display of banners, no way horn—as if he would pass through this wilderness with as little note as possible.

I watched them well out of sight before I returned to the van. My kasi were not meant for burst of speed, but only an unvarying pace. In a long haul they could beat and leave behind such swifter mounts as those of Osokun's men, but no spurt was in them and I must abide by that.

That night we reached the hills and I hid the van, went ahead to find a pass. But there was only one cut I could find which would take the passage of the van, where the road ran. I was very loath to return to that. Too open, the sort of place where any lord but the most foolish would have sentry posts. I loosed Simmle and she quickly found two—surely manned by guards selected for keenness of eye.

Here I could give when challenged no reason for my wayfaring. Danger or no, this night I must summon the power, for to run on headlong would be the sheerest folly.

I brought out Borba and Vors and sent them to seek what we needed, safety and solitude, not too far from the road. They were back well before twilight, pattering in from different directions. Borba had what was wanted. The van must remain some distance away from the spot, but there was concealment in a thicket of luk weed, which could be pulled and tangled about to hide it.

The kasi I freed to graze in the dell Borba led us to, setting upon them a no-stray thought, for there was plenty of water in a pool fed by a small falls, and fresh plaken growing knee-high in clumps. I could not shift the barsk cage, so I set the sleep thought deep for its inhabitant and took the others with me.

We ate of the supplies I had brought, for strength of body must back strength of mind in what I must do at moon-rise. Then I said "guard" to my little people and they melted into the shadows to obey.

I fed rest thoughts to my mind as best I could, though the Rings worked against such a pattern. Still, that would heighten my putting forth when the hour came. And when the moon found our hillside pocket I was ready.

With the wand I traced out the shield and go design in the level sand beside the pool, using white stones from the gravel of its bed to point the ends of the three curves. And the moon globe, mounted on a flat stone so that its rays shone over that area, gave all the light I needed. I began the Shield Song and sang it, watching the spiraling upward of the visible power from my stones. And then I came to the Go Plea and closed my eyes upon the outer world that I might better see the inner.

When one evokes the power with as little conscious guide as now I did, one accepts what is shown without hold or selection, thus learning in bits and pieces what must afterward be fitted together. So it was with me—for I was as if suspended in the air some distance above a small fort, no more than a portal sentry place. I looked down into that with the eyes of the mind, not those of the body.

Osokun I saw there, and also the off-worlder Krip Vorlund. And I saw what was done to the off-worlder by the orders of Osokun. Then there came a messenger riding, and Osokun and his men mounted and went forth in the dawn light.

The off-worlder I could not reach. Between us stood a barrier I might have breached with effort, but I felt that I had neither time at this moment nor dared I waste the strength such effort would cost me. I could see the spirit which dwelt within him and that it was strong and not easily vanquished. What I could do for him I could, moving certain forces this way and that so that he would be favored by fortune rather than hindered, though all initial effort must be his own.

Then I returned from that place which was not wholly one with Yiktor but shared it only in part. The dawn was very bright and my moon globe pale and wan. For the present I had my answer, not to go on, but wait where I was. And ofttimes waiting is by far the greater burden.

There passed a long day. We slept by turns, my little people and I. I longed to know how well I had wrought for him who lay in that fort across the land. But, though I be singer, I am not of the Old Ones who can aim their sight at command around half the world if the need arises.

I went to the van and tended the barsk. It awoke and ate of food, lapped at water, but only because my will held it to that nourishment. It was no longer savagely twisted of mind, but now apathetic. It would not care for its own needs had I not set it to such action. Malec was right, I thought sorrowfully, there was naught to do save set it free on the White Road—yet I could not bring myself to that. It was as if some command I could not understand had been laid upon me.

Night came, but past its middle the moon was veiled, dark clouds gathered and spun wide nets to choke the stars, those suns that nourish worlds we cannot see. And I thought again of what it would mean to walk alien worlds, see strange animals and people, learn ever more about all the wonders which are the gem-dreams of Molaster. And I sang a little, not one of the great power songs, but such words as lift the heart, strengthen the will, give meat and drink to the spirit. My little ones came to me in the darkness of the night, and I eased their hearts and turned outward their thoughts.

There was a storm threatening before dawn, so no real dawn broke the dismal hold upon the hills. We found a small place in the wall of our dell where we could wait under an overhang of stone, and huddled there together while thunder strode drumming from height to height, the lash of lightning urging it on. I have seen such storms in the uplands of the Thassa, but not heretofore so close to the plains.

In such torments of the sky, time and man are lost, the power to think grows dim. There was the warmth of furred bodies close about me and I crooned to soothe them. For so much I was glad, that I could busy myself so to put aside my own unease.

At length the worst of that assault from sky upon earth died away. I was moved then by a message of the power, not a clear sending, just a suggestion weaving in and out of mind-pattern. With my little ones I went to the poolside and there rescued the moon globe from a stone now encircled by rising water. I went down the dale to a place where the grass was less thick and there were outcrops of stone. On one of these I set up the moon globe, alight once more as if it could serve as a beacon. But for what, or whom, I was not yet sure. The belief grew in me that he whom I sought would be so drawn, providing such fortune as I had spun for him had been of tight enough thread.

Simmle growled and rose to her feet, showing her teeth in a snarl. Borba and Vors lifted their heads, crests flattened, ready to do battle, while Tantacka shifted her weight from left to right and back again on her broad pawed forefeet, rumbling deep in her throat so her warning was more vibration than audible sound.

Down the slope wavered a figure, pulling itself onward by grasping bush and sapling, going to the knees, yet always rising doggedly to advance, until at last it fell and slid limply down into the circle of moon-globe radiance, mud encasing much of its length. I stooped and gripped a shoulder, exerted my strength to turn over that flaccid body.

The face was mud-spattered, cut, bruised, swollen, yet the one I had expected to see. The off-worlder had won out of Osokun's hold and through the hills. Now I was ready to repay my debt—but how? For it was well like he had come from one danger into another equally as great. We stood on the border of Oskold's land where none would gainsay his orders—or rather I stood, and Krip Vorlund lay in a swound now so deep that I could not probe it. Like the barsk, he slept and perhaps was the better for fleeing the here and now. And so passed much of that day.

Chapter 8

There was a singing, low and sweet, a croon which sounded in my ears as the wind which the space-borne so seldom feel on their bodies. And from whatever place Krip Vorlund had gone into hiding, I was pulled back to be one again, body and spirit locked together. When I opened my eyes to look about me, it was upon a strange company. Still, their strangeness did not truly amaze me; it was as if I had expected to see each and every one of them—girl's face with silver hair escaping about it from the hood of a cloak, furred muzzles with bright animal eyes glistening inquisitively about them.

"You are—Maelen—" My voice surprised me, for it was a hoarse croaking.

She of the hood nodded. "I am Maelen." But she spoke absently and her head turned as if she stared beyond in search of something she feared to see. All the other heads swung also, and from them came snarls and growls, low and rumbling, each differently pitched. My drowsy content vanished, apprehension awoke.

Her hand lifted and light glowed along that which she held between her fingers, the wand. She put this with care on the flattened palm of her other hand. I saw, though she did not touch it, the rod stir of itself and turn to point in the same direction her eyes sought.

As if by a signal, the furred ones vanished into the gloom beyond the borders of the lamplight in which I lay. Now Maelen took up again the wand and pointed with it to the moon globe, which died into nothingness. She leaned closer over me, her weather cloak out in wide wings tenting us both.

"Quiet!" Her order was a mere puff of breath.

I found I was listening, straining to hear whatever her ears also sought. There was the sighing of the wind, the splashing of water not too far away, other sounds of the open—nothing more—save the rising pound of my own blood in my ears.

So we waited for a space I could not measure, save it seemed very long. Then once more she spoke, perhaps to me, perhaps only voicing her thought.

"So—they hunt."

"Me?" I whispered.

"You." I did not need confirmation of that.

"Listen now," she continued swiftly. "There are more than just Osokun's sword-sworn—these come from before and behind. And—" she hesitated, "I do not see how we can get through the net they weave for our taking."

"It is not your trouble—"

Her finger tips pressed upon my lips, cool and strong. "Mine the debt, man of the star lanes, mine the payment, so say the scales of Molaster—the scales of Molaster," she repeated. Then after a pause, she whispered again, "should I give you another skin, Krip Vorlund, for the undoing of the enemy?"

"What do you mean?" It seemed to me, although the cloak about us cast a dark pool of shadow, I could see her two eyes a little above me as sparks of frosty light, much as a beast's eyes will shine in the night if caught by a torch's ray.

"To my mind has come the answer of Molaster." She sounded bewildered, the confidence I had always seen in her shaken. "But you are not Thassa—not Thassa—" Her voice trailed away into a moment of silence. Then she spoke with her old assurance. "So be it, if you choose, so be it! Hark well now, off-worlder. I do not think we have a chance to elude those who search these hills. By their thought-throws I read they would have your death and that speedily if they come upon you."

"That I can believe," I told her dryly. "Have you time to get away? I may not be a trained swordsman but—"

I think she found that amusing, the sound she gave might have been a tiny laugh. "Brave, oh, brave star rover! But we have not come to such straits yet. There is another path, though a very strange one, and you may think being cut down by the blades of Osokun's men better than the walking of it."

Perhaps I read challenge into what was only warning, but I reacted stubbornly to her words. "Show me this path, if you think it means escape."

"There is this, you may change bodies—"

"What!" I struggled to sit up, pushed against her so that we both overbalanced and struck the ground.

"I am not the enemy!" Her hands thrust against my chest, punishing old bruises and making me wince. "Another body is what I said, and what I meant, Krip Vorlund."

"And this body I now wear?" I could not believe that she was serious.

"Let Osokun's men take it and welcome."

"Thank you!" I retorted. "Either I lose my life in my body, or they kill my body and leave me outside somewhere." The utter folly of what I said made me laugh a little hysterically.

"No!" Maelen retorted. She had pulled her cloak away and we sat facing each other in the twilight. I could see her face, but it was hard to read her expression, though I believed she was in earnest and meant exactly what she said.

"They will not harm your body, once you have gone from it. They will believe you under the cloak of Umphra, and to harm such beings brings instant and lasting misfortune on any man. Even at sword-oath no man, lord, or fighter would hurt those touched by Umphra."

"So they would let my body go?" I decided to humor her. My mind was in an odd state, nothing about this adventure had any reality by the standards I knew. I began to think it was one of those vivid dreams which now and then visit a sleeper, plunging him into an inner state of awareness so that he believes he is awake, not sleeping, as he undertakes impossible feats. It was beginning to seem, in this real dream, that perhaps all things were possible.

"Your body would not be tenantless, for two spirits will pass from one housing to another. For a space only need this be, as we can then retake your body and once more exchange."

"Because they would leave it here?" I continued, willing to go along with the fantasy.

"No, they would take it to the Temple of Umphra. And we would have to follow, even to the Valley of the Forgotten." Her head turned away and I had a feeling that what she said had some meaning for her which had nothing to do with me.

"And where would I be while we went hunting my body?"

"In another body, perhaps even better fashioned for what might have to be done."

This was a dream, of course. I no longer questioned that it might be anything else. Perhaps it was all a dream—my escape from the fort which had been so oddly favored by fortune, the nightmare journey through the hills and the storm, my coming here. Perhaps the dream extended even further—I had never been kidnaped from the fair, I lay safely now in my ship bunk and dreamed all this. And an odd curiosity awoke in me. I wanted to know how far this dream would take me and what new and weird action would come next.

"Let it be as you wish," I said, and I laughed, for I knew that neither this, nor the waking hours of my life were real.

She looked at me again. Once more I fancied I saw those sparks in her eyes.

"Truly you come of a strong race, star rover. Perhaps, though, seeing much along the space lanes leaves one with a loss of astonishment and a capacity for accepting what may or must come. But it is not because I wish it so, this must be *your* desire."

"Then it is." I humored her in my dream.

"Stay you here and rest." Her hands on my shoulders pushed me back to lie as I had when first roused to this part of my dream. I lay there wondering what would come next. Would I be waking in my bunk on the *Lydis*? One's dreams are boring to listeners, but this was so strange a one that if I could remember it once I roused I would tell it. Still I rested on the grass and saw sky above, smelled woodland scents and heard wind and the splash of water.

I closed my eyes and willed myself to wake. But it was an art beyond me, for the dream continued as vividly as ever. Something stirred beside me, I turned my head and opened my eyes. There was a furred head there, eyes peering at me intently. The fur was dark save for a crest of gray which stood erect, giving the animal the appearance of wearing a helm of dark metal surmounted by a standing plume, not unlike those of the sea rovers of Rankini.

Sea rovers of Rankini ... my mind strayed, floated ... but surely they had not been part of a dream, this or any other. I *had* stood with Lidj on one of their floating trade rafts and exchanged steel harpoon points for Aadaa pearls. Rankini, Tyr, Gorth—worlds I had known. I strung them from memory as one would slip beads along a string. Now they were spinning around those worlds ... whirling ... whirling. ... No, I was whirling dizzily, memory fled, and close after it all awareness.

"Ayee, Ayee—run on four feet.
Scent well the wind's messages—
Be wise and be fleet—
Strong and fair.
Arise and greet the moon.
By Molaster, and the Law of Qu'eeth,
By two power, into four power.
Up, runner of the high places!
Greet the sun after night,
For this be the dawn of your birthing!"

I opened my eyes. Then I screamed, for the world I looked upon was distorted, a matter of odd shapes, shades—so altered that terror walked there for me. But no scream did my ears record, rather a howl with naked fear in it.

"Fear not, the change is good, good! I had hoped only, but it is good! In all parts did you travel and arrive."

Did I hear that with my ears, or did it form only in my brain?

"No—no!" I tried to shriek, which I had not done when Osokun's men had worked to bring cries from me. But again came only a kind of barking.

"Why do you fear?" The voice sounded puzzled, even annoyed. "I tell you, it is even as I have said, the exchange went well. And just in time. Simmle says that they come. Lie you still."

Lie still? Exchange? I tried to put my hand to my head which still whirled. But no hand moved, though flesh and muscle obeyed the commands of my brain. I looked again. There was a paw covered with red fur, attached to a long thin leg, and that leg to a body—and the body—I was in that body! But no, this was not true, it could not be! I struggled wildly as in a nightmare. Awake, just let me awake! A man could go mad in such a dream. Awake!

"Let me out!" I might have been a child shut into a terrifyingly dark cupboard. But no words, only a yipping came from my jaws. I realized dimly that this panic was indeed driving me into a darkness from which there might not be any return at all. I fought then, as I have never had reason to fight before—not any outward enemy, but the terror which was imprisoned with me in this alien body.

I felt a touch on my head and jerked away, looked into animal eyes set in a cream-tan animal face. From sharply pointed jaws a tongue issued to lick me.

Reassurance was relayed by my heightened senses from that touch. And somehow it drew me back from the brink of madness. I blinked, tried the better to see the face of my companion, and found that this small concentration did make a difference. The distortion was fading, adjusting. I could see clearer with every second. The licking went on and the comfort soaked into me.

Stand up—I wanted to stand up. I wavered, staggered. To rise to four feet was not the same as standing upon two. I lifted my head. Scents, my nose drowned in scents; so thickly did they assault my nostrils that it was as if all possible odors had been sprayed into one ship's cabin and I was locked therein. I choked, thought that I could not breathe. But I did and the scents began to carry messages which I only partially understood. I tried to creep as a man would go on all fours, and tottered a step or two. The animal that had licked my head shouldered against me in support until I managed to stand without wavering. To look about me from this new angle was another thing to be learned, and I had by no means mastered it when there was a disturbance behind me.

The animal at my shoulder snarled, and I heard answering rumbles from the bushes a little beyond. Menace and danger read so sharply in those growls that I pushed around and raised my head to the highest to see who came.

Distortion remained, changes in size bewildered me. Again the scents were overpowering. But I was able to make out Maelen, her back to us, the long folds of her cloak sweeping the ground, confronting a group of men. Two were mounted and held the reins of riderless kasi, three advanced on foot, swords sharp and bright in their hands.

I felt lips wrinkle back from the teeth now mine, an unconscious reaction to the odor of men. For I now discovered that emotions were part of some scents, and here were to be felt anger, cruel triumph, and danger. The snarl of the animal that flanked me grew louder.

"—come for him—"

What had been a gargle of meaningless sounds sorted out into words. Or was it that I read those words as they filtered through the mind of Maelen, who displayed no surprise or dismay.

"What you have made of him, that is here."

She turned her head as if to point out what they sought with her eyes. Someone sat, or rather lolled, upon the ground. Slack lips hung loose with a thread of spittle spinning from the lower. I blinked, closed my eyes tight, and willed not to see what was there. But when I opened them again, it remained the same.

How many men ever look upon themselves, not in a mirror's surface, but as if their bodies have a life apart from their intelligence—their essence? To my belief such was impossible. Yet I stood now on four legs and looked through alien eyes to see and scent what was—*me!*

Maelen went to that sprawling body, put her hands to its shoulders, urged it up. But it seemed that my husk was just that, a husk which had naught left to animate it. It lived, yes, for I could see the breast through the ragged tunic rise and fall with great shuddering breaths. As she pulled and tugged to get it up it moaned and whined. I howled and one of the swordbearers started, swung around to eye me.

"Be quiet, Jorth!" Maelen's words were in my head, and I guessed she spoke to me, not to the shambling thing which she had at last standing, though she had to support it, for it appeared to want to drop to earth again.

Her order was enforced by the beast beside me, who nipped delicately at my ear and from whom came a telepathic warning.

Maelen led the body—somehow I could no longer think of it as *my* body—a few stumbling steps forward. And the men stared at the drooling, witless thing, stirring uneasily.

"Your work, sword-sworn?" Maelen demanded of them. "So did this one come to me, and you know who I am."

It would seem that they did, with awe and a little more than awe—fear. I saw two of them make gestures toward her as if to ward off ill fortune.

"Thus do I lay upon you your debt, men of—of—" she looked at them intently "Oskold. This one is under the cloak of Umphra, do you deny it?"

One by one, if reluctantly, they shook their heads. Those with the bared swords sheathed them.

"Then do you with him what must be done."

I thought, from the looks they shared, that they would object. But if they were so inclined her manner quelled such protests. One of them led out a kas and between them they got the thing that was no longer a man up on the beast's back and there made fast. Then they turned and rode away into the very early sun, which came from behind a cloud to illumine the dell.

"Why? What?" Yaps from my mouth, but she must have read my thoughts, for once they were gone she came swiftly and knelt before me, putting her hands out to hold my head firmly while she looked into my eyes.

"Our plan is working, Krip Vorlund. Now, give them a small lead, and we follow!"

"What?" I tried to think, not to make beast sounds. "What have you done to me, and why?"

Now she stared again into my eyes, her attitude one of puzzlement. "I have done as you desired, star rover, given you a new body and taken care to save the old, that you might not bubble forth your life's blood from rents their swords would make. So—" she shook her head slowly, "you did not believe that this could be done, even when you said aye to the doing! But it is done and lies now on the scales of Molaster."

"My—that body—can I get it back? And—what—what am I now?"

She answered my second question first. There was a small overflow of pool like unto a shallow plate of water. To this I was guided by her hand on the nape of my neck. Over it she passed her wand, and the water was still and calm so that I looked into it as I might a mirror. I saw an animal head, with a thick mane between the ears and running down the shoulders, red fur with a golden note—

"The barsk!"

"Yes, the barsk," she said. "And the body—they will take it, as they must or else face certain darkness now and ever after, to a place of refuge. We will follow and, once in the Valley of Forgetting, we shall be safe from Oskold. For those were Oskold's men, which means that much of this country is a death trap, or would be if you still abode in your former shell. Safe from Oskold you may once more be yourself and then move as you see fit."

She spoke the truth as she knew it. I had one last lingering thread of hope.

"This is a dream," I said to myself, not to her.

Again her eyes met mine and in them, as well as in the words she spoke, was that which cut the thread for me.

"No dream, star rover, no dream."

"And now," she rose. "We shall go, but not too fast on their heels lest suspicion be roused. Oskold is no fool and I think that Osokun has plunged his father, through his recklessness, into deep folly. I have saved you by the only method I knew, Krip Vorlund, however ill it may be to your eyes."

So I followed her out of the dell in the guise of an animal who owed her allegiance. For now I discovered that though the barsk body held the essence of a man, yet also was I now attuned in a new way to the form I wore, and more than just in the way I faced the world. Those four who trotted with me were not a company of servants following a mistress, but something more—companions of varied natures allied with another species who understood them and in whom they placed supreme trust.

We came to one of the vans such as I had seen in the yard of the show, the interior of which held cages. My companions went confidently forward and jumped in, pawed open the unfastened doors of the cages and settled themselves therein. But I stayed on the ground, growls rumbling in my throat. Cage—I was in that moment far more man than beast, and I had had enough of cages in Osokun's keep.

Maelen laughed softly. "Well enough, Jorth—so I have named you. For that means in the ancient tongue 'One-who-is-more-than-he-seems,' and was once granted as a battle name to Mimber of Yithamen when he went up against the Night Valks. Share my seat if you will, and I shall tell you of your name-hero and how he wrought."

There was nothing farther from my mind at that moment than the desire to listen to the folklore of Yiktor while riding blindly into a future which yet seemed so beyond belief that only by determined will could I consider it. Yet I mounted the seat beside Maelen and there sat upon my haunches, studying the world through eyes which still gave me strange reports.

But I began to see that there was more than the wish to beguile me out of considering my plight which moved Maelen to tell her tale. For as she continued to speak mind to mind, her powers to communicate and mine to receive were heightened and strengthened. Perhaps the esper I had used in my human body still worked in my favor. And, too, I found her story of value. Through its fabric was interwoven much of Yiktor—not the present, but an older, far more complex civilization which had once rooted here and of which the Thassa were the last survivors. There was much she said beyond my understanding, references to events and people unknown, such hints only making me wishful to go through the doors they represented and see what lay on the far side.

The van followed no path, taking the most open way across a wilderness country. We were on the eastern slopes of a range of hills forming a barrier between Oskold's holdings and the plains of Yrjar. But to return to the port in my present guise was the last thing I wished. Maelen continued to reassure me that our eventual goal was the mysterious place of refuge in the higher hills to which my body was being escorted. She explained that the natives believed mental disorders to be a visitation of certain powers, and those harboring them were sacred, to be placed as speedily as possible in the custody of priests trained in such care. But we dared not follow too closely to this place, she warned me several times over, lest they suspect some trickery.

"How did you—how did you make me thus?" I asked at last.

She was silent for a space and when she replied, her thoughts were guarded and remote.

"I did that which I long ago took oath not to do. For this I shall answer in another time and place to those who have the right to demand it of me."

"Why did you?"

"I was debt-laid," she replied still more remotely. "It was through me that you came into this misfortune, thus I must level the scales."

"But you did nothing—that small matter of the beast seller—"

"That, but also this. I knew that you had an enemy, perhaps more than one, and I did not warn you. Rather did I say that as Thassa the concerns of others were naught, save where they touched me. And for this I must also answer."

"Enemy?"

"Yes." And she told me of how Osokun had come to her with the man from the Combine ship, Gauk Salfid, and how they had suggested she attract a Free Trader into a net they would set. Although she had not done openly as they wished, she now believed that she had served their purpose because of curiosity. Thus had she begun the chain of events which had led to my kidnapping.

"That is not true. It was chance only until—"

"Until I made the moon-weave for you?" she interrupted. "Ah, that seems to you now the greatest of interference. But perhaps you will discover it the least as the future opens before us, then passes behind us. What I have done is a thing private to the Thassa." Then she stopped and I felt her thoughts withdraw and I could not touch her, for a barrier grew between us. Her body sat there, but her eyes were really turned inward and she had gone where I could not follow.

But the kasi forged onward as if she had set some direction in their minds and they kept on as a navigator would hold to his chart, at a speed which might be slow but which held steady. Above us the sun was warm and bright. Then I set myself to learning my new body, that I might inhabit it competently as long as I must—though still I could not rid myself of the belief that this was a long dream haunting the mind of one safe in his own place and person.

Chapter 9

Two days we traveled so, camping at night in hidden thickets. I became more and more a part of the body I wore, and I learned that there are some compensations, lessons to be learned, by one who travels four-footed and looks upon the world through animal eyes. Maelen fell into moods of abstraction now and then, but between these she talked much, either relating legends or else pointing out features of the country and speaking of her own life as a wanderer there. But, I came to note, she did not often mention her people in the here and now, only as they were in the past. Also there were questions I asked that she adroitly avoided answering. I came to make it something of a business to try to trap her and I think she knew what I would do and as cunningly slipped past me.

On the morning of the third day as we climbed into the van she was frowning slightly.

"From here," she said, "we come into the land of villages and men. And to cloak our purpose we shall call upon the skills of the little people."

"You mean—give shows?"

"Yes. The road to the Valley is such that there are no side ways. Also we may learn of those who have gone before us."

It was almost a shock to think of my body having ridden this road ahead, a sensation difficult to put into words. Maelen continued to promise me that those escorting that mindless thing would be careful to keep the spark of life within it, that, according to their superstitions, any neglect would result in a fate such as they would avoid at all costs.

"And I will be part of your entertainment?"

She smiled slowly. "If you wish. A very great part if you agree. For to my knowledge, and I assure you that is not small, no one has ever shown a barsk before."

"But you had hoped to?"

"Yes, I had hoped to."

"What happened to—to—"

"The spirit who wore your present body? It was failing. Another day, perhaps two, and I would have out of compassion sent it on the White Road."

"But in my body—now?"

"It is a feeble tenant. It does not suffer, only lingers for a time to keep the lamp lit until you return."

"This exchange—you must have done it before."

I had come out boldly with what I had tried to discover earlier. She looked at me.

"To each his own secrets, Krip Vorlund. I told you—this burden is mine, you will not be called to account for what has happened."

"But you will?"

"I will. Now let us consider what lies before us, not what may exist behind a mountain range or two. By midday we shall arrive at Yim-Sin, the road to it lies there—" We were coming down a bank to a road into which the kasi turned, heading upward from the plains.

"In Yim-Sin there is a temple of Umphra," Maelen continued. "There we shall be quartered and, if possible, learn of Oskold's men—though they may have taken the other road on the eastern side of the mountains. This night we shall give a performance. So now let us study what a barsk may do to astound the world."

I was willing to fall in with her plans, for this was the case of depending upon a navigator in the deeps. To the one with the proper knowledge one leaves the ordering of the ship. Together we set up a performance, suggesting the act of a well-trained animal. When we came to a place where terraced fields, now mainly cleared by harvest, made steps on the hillsides, Maelen paused and I withdrew from my usual seat beside her to the traveling cage like the rest of the four-footed company.

They drowsed, for two of their species were nocturnal in normal life, and the other, Tantacka, was a lazy animal when well fed with no need to forage. I found that my new body had habits, too, which were emerging. And I curled up nose to tail and slept a little as the van trundled along.

The scents of the open gave way to other odors, acrid, nose-tickling. I heard voices as if people were gathering around the van, running beside it—high shrill voices of children. Maelen must be bringing us into Yim-Sin. It was, she had told me, a farming village, with the addition of two inns and a temple for the accommodation of those bound for the Valley. Ofttimes those who had relatives there made the journey to look upon them. It was also true that the priests of Umphra sometimes wrought miracles and cured certain of their charges, so not all who went there were hopelessly lost.

While the fields of this up-and-down country were not wide or rich, yet they rooted a vine-grown crop which produced wine favored in the cities. The villagers were prosperous enough, at least their overlords were. But hereabouts there were absentee landlords and there would be only bailiffs and overseers in the two castle holdings along the road we traveled.

I tried to understand the cries, but the words were of a country dialect, not the speech of the Yrjar merchants. Yrjar—suddenly I wondered what had happened there after my kidnaping. Had Captain Foss taken his case to the fair authorities? Some of those authorities or their subordinates must have conspired in my disappearance for it to have happened at all. Had they taken Lalfarns too, or killed him?

Why had I been so important to risk so much on my capture? Surely Osokun must have known I could not give him what he wanted. Nor might Foss have traded the price demanded for me. Maelen had provided one small clue to what might be a greater coil—the part Gauk Slafid played. But the life-and-death struggle between Free Trader and Combine had been all in the past. Why this move now? I had read all the tapes of the old days and the struggle had been a bitter one, carried from planet to planet. Now the Combines dealt mainly with the inner-system worlds and sometimes dabbled in politics on those, to their hurt or gain. What could possibly interest them on Yiktor?

The van came to a halt and the smell of the town—or better described for barsk nostrils—the stench of the town was thick. I longed to peer through the curtains and see our surroundings. But I now wore a skin around which far too many legends of peril and death had been woven.

Borba and Vors uncurled from fur balls and came to peer out of their cages. Simmle whined a greeting to which my barsk vocal cords responded at a lower pitch. Their thoughts reached me as broken bits of expression.

"March-march—"

"Thump-thump—" That was Tantacka.

"Up and down."

So did they foresee their parts in the coming performance. They appeared to look upon their stage appearances as amusement to be anticipated and enjoyed.

"Many smells," I tried my own return.

Simmle barked. "Man smell—many men."

"March-march," chorused the glassia, "good—good!" Their small cries scaled up to a shrill squeaking.

"Food," grunted Tantacka, "under rocks—food." She snorted and went back to doze.

"Run." Simmle was wistful. "Run out in the fields—good! Hunt—good! Together—we hunt—"

Instinct of my body answered her. "Hunt—good!" I agreed.

Maelen opened the back flap of the van and climbed in. A man of the plainspeople, wearing a black robe which was crosshatched on back and breast with white and yellow, came with her. He was smiling and chatting in the village dialect, but, through Maelen, the sense of his words filtered to me.

"We are indeed fortunate, Freesha, that you have chosen this season for your return! The harvest has been good and the people plan a festival for thanksgiving. The Elder Brother wishes to make a happy time for all. He will open the west court for you and will pay all fees, so that your little people may give joy to all with their cleverness."

"The Elder Brother is indeed a maker of happiness and a force for good in this so-blessed village." Her reply sounded formal. "Does he permit that I loose my little people that they may stretch their legs in freedom?"

"But certainly, Freesha. Aught you may need is at your call—the third-rank brothers will serve you." He raised his hand. Fastened to thumb and forefinger were two flat pieces of wood and these he clicked loudly together. Two more heads crowded into view at the tail of the van. The closely clipped hair, the Hand of Umphra branded into their foreheads, marked them as priests, though they were only boys.

They were smiling broadly, and apparently well pleased to serve as Maelen's assistants. She opened Simmle's cage and the cream-coated venzese came out, swinging her tail eagerly, while Maelen fitted her with a show collar flashing small gems. Borba and Vors were so accoutered and loosed, and then Tantacka, to whose collar was added a kind of frontlet of richly embroidered red cloth, pointed forward between her ears. It would seem that the animals were old friends as the young priests greeted each by name, but with a gravity which suggested that Maelen's little people were far more than mere animals. Then she put her hand to the latch of my cage and the senior priest leaned forward as if to see me better.

"You have a new friend-in-fur, Freesha?"

"I have indeed. Come forth, Jorth."

As I passed around the door she opened, the priest's eyes went wide and his breath hissed between his teeth. "A barsk!"

Maelen was busy putting about my neck the collar she had sewn at our last camp, a strip of black with mirrorlike stars glittering in a scattered trail along it.

"A barsk," she agreed.

"But—" His astonishment had become half protest.

Maelen straightened, her hand still resting lightly on my head.

"You know me, Elder Brother, and my little ones. This is a barsk in truth, but Jorth is no longer a flesh eater and haunter of trails, but our comrade-in-fur, as all others who travel in my shadow."

He looked from her to me and then back again. "Truly you are one who accomplishes strange things, Freesha. But this is yet the strangest of all—that a barsk should come to your call, suffer you to lay hand upon his head, that you should name him and make him of your company. But if you so speak—that it will not give way to the evils of its kind—then shall men believe you. For the gifts of the Thassa are like unto the laws of Umphra, fixed and unchanging."

Then he stood aside and I went with Maelen, leaping down from the tail of the van. The young priests hesitated and drew a bit apart, their amazement more open even than that of their superior.

They allowed us to precede them. The other animals came to join us, Simmle beside me, aiming a quick lick at my cheek as I fell into step with her. We went out of the courtyard in which the van had halted into another walled space through a double-leafed gate, only one half of which was open for us. The inner area was paved with black stone veined with yellow, and empty, save along the walls where trained vines and trees grew from beds of earth bordered by fitted stone. At the far left was a fountain, the water boiling out of a stone-head into a pool.

One of the animals headed for the pool and lapped from its bounty. The water was cool, tasting good. Tantacka dipped in not only her blunt muzzle but also forepaws, flipping them up to send showers of drops flying in all directions.

I sat back on my haunches to look around. At the other end of the area were three broad steps which led to a columned porch, and in that was another door, intricately carved with a sprawling design I could not figure out. That gave entrance to a building which I thought must be the center portion of the temple. There were no windows to break the sweep of wall, only more carved panels, in alternating white and yellow stone, to pattern the black of the walls.

Maelen directed the boy priests who carried some boxes from the van to set them along the steps, and I noted that they continued to glance at me with some awe. When they had done, Maelen dismissed them with thanks and sat down on the lowest step. I lost no time in joining her.

"Well?" There was only one thing I wanted to know—had she gained any news of Oskold's men and that which they were transporting.

"They have not passed this way," she answered me. "Nor was I sure they would. If they needed to apprise their lord of what had happened they would have gone eastward and thus come on the other road which leads to the Valley."

"You seem very sure they want to get to this Valley."

Maelen put her hands to either side of my barsk head and raised it so she could better look into my eyes.

"Accept this, star rover: of the ways of the people of Yiktor I do know much. They are set to patterns which they do not break, not when there is naught to endanger them. Rest assured Oskold or his men will not alter *this* pattern. One way or another they shall bring that which belongs to you to the Valley."

"Ah, Freesha, so it is true."

The voice behind us rang in my ears as if Maelen spoke and I was startled, for this was the first time I had "heard" so as to understand except through her intermediacy. I jerked out of her hold and snarled involuntarily as I looked up the steps.

A man in priestly robes stood there. He was old, bent a little, leaning on a support which was more staff of office than cane, for it was almost as tall as his age-bared skull. His face was open, yet that of a man who had seen so much of sorrow that he would be colored with its gray wash to the end of his days. Only now he smiled, and in his smile was the sweetness of one to whom compassion was the greatest of virtues.

"You have brought a marvel indeed." He came down a step and in turn Maelen sped to join him, setting her arm under his in support. That aloofness which stood always between her and the plainsmen vanished and there was respect in her tone as she made answer.

"I bring a barsk, yes, Eldest Brother. Jorth, show your manners!"

Thus the first of the tricks we had worked out together was shown to the guardian of the temple as I bowed my head thrice and then barked my deepest. And gently, with the same smile, the priest inclined his head to me in answer.

"Go with the love and care of Umphra, brother of the upper ways," he said.

The beliefs of the Free Traders are few, and we seldom express them, even among ourselves. At ship's swearing, or when taking a permanent life companion, or when accepting a foster child into one's household—yes, we have oaths and powers we call upon as witness. I think that all living things with intelligence recognize THAT WHICH LIES ABOVE AND BEYOND. They must or be ever lost and driven by their inner fears and doubts beyond the endurance of their spirit. We give respect to gods of other worlds, for they are but man-distorted images of that which stands ever behind such faulty windows into the unknown. Now, in this man who had given his life to the service of such a god, I saw one who walked closely to the Great Truth as he saw it, and perhaps it was indeed a truth, if not one in which my people believed. Thus, forgetting the skin which covered me, I bowed my head as I would to those who have my respect.

And when I raised it to look once more in his face, I saw that his smile was gone; rather did he look at me very intently, as one might view some new thing which caught the full attention.

"What we know of the barsk," he said as if he spoke to himself, "is very little, and most of that, ill, having been sifted through the screen of fear. Perhaps there is much we should learn."

"My little people are not quite like those of their wild kin." Maelen spoke swiftly and I read both unease and warning in the half-thought she shot at me, a warning that this was one who had some of the inner sight and whose suspicions must not be aroused.

Thus I barked and snapped at an insect buzzing overhead and then went to join the others at the pool, hoping I had done my best to cover any lapse I had unwittingly made.

Maelen lingered with the priest and they spoke together in a murmur which did not reach my ears. Also she had shut off mind-communication with me and this I did not like. But I dared not try to listen in that manner either.

In the early evening we gave our show to all the villagers who could crowd into the court, repeating it twice so that all could see, using the porch of the temple for our stage, the boy priests helping Maelen arrange the few properties we used. They did this with such practiced skill that I guessed this was not the first time this had happened, though why Maelen would have come this way before, I did not know.

The acts were less elaborate than those which her other troop had presented at the fair. Now Tantacka sat on her haunches and thumped a drum to which Borba and Vors danced and marched. Simmle leaped over a series of ascending bars, prancing on her hind legs, answered questions from the audience with barks, played a small musical instrument by pressing on large keys with her forepaws. And I sat up, bowed, and did the other small tricks we had planned. I think my appearance alone would have been enough, for the villagers were startled. I wondered more and more at the fearsome reputation my host body held in this country.

When we had done we went back to our cages, and for once I did not demur at being so housed. I was as thoroughly weary as if I had labored man-fashion throughout a day.

But I had discovered that a barsk's sleep was not like that of a man. It did not last the night through, but was a series of short naps, between which I lay awake and alert, keenly aware through nose and ear of all that went on outside the curtains of the van. During one such wakeful spell I heard a stir in the fore part where Maelen had a couch she used in bad weather or when it was not possible to sleep in the open.

Light, so thin it seemed only a very pallid and weak reflection of her moon globe, filtered through a curtain slit. The latch of my cage had not been dropped. I was free to come and go, though I knew the danger of doing so in the village. Now I nosed open the door and moved to set my eyes to that slit.

On her bed place Maelen sat cross-legged, her eyes closed. One might have thought she slept, but her body moved from the waist slowly back and forth, as if in time to music I could not hear. Nor could I reach her mind, for when I strove to do so, I came against a tight barrier with the force of one running headlong into a fort wall.

Her lips were slightly parted and I caught a sound, the faintest whisper of sound issuing from them. She was singing—or was she? I could not be sure whether it was song, or some muttered invocation, even some plaint. Her hands rested on her knees, but between forefinger and forefinger her silver rod made a taut bridge, and it was from that the faint light beamed.

Around me, as I watched, the air held a kind of electric charge. My mane roughened and raised, there was a tingling along my hide, a prickling in my nose. We men of the ships have our kind of power and energies, but we never deny the fact that there are others elsewhere whom we do not understand and cannot control. For the art of controlling such may be a matter of birth and not of learning.

This was power, but whether she called it to her or whether she sent it forth, I did not know. And in that moment of my watching I was strongly aware she was alien, far more alien than I had believed.

She was silent after a space, and the tingling in the air began to ebb. Then with a sigh her head fell forward, and she jerked as one awakening, to place the now dim rod under her head as she stretched herself on the couch. The light was gone and I was sure she slept.

In the morning we left Yim-Sin, with the villagers cheering us out, shouting their desire for our return. We took a road which climbed and climbed. These were not hills we faced now, but rather mountains. The air was chill and Maelen wore her cloak, but when I took my place beside her on the seat I found my thick pelt needed no cover. The scents here were exciting and I found awaking in me time and again the strong desire to leap from my perch and run to the timbered slopes, in search of I know not what.

"We come now into barsk country," she told me with a laugh. "But I would not advise you to take advantage of your wish to see it better, Jorth. For, though some part of you is native here, you would speedily be at a disadvantage."

"Why do all look upon a barsk in your company as so strange and rare?" I asked.

"Because, though the barsk is known, in another way it is not. If that sounds to be a riddle, perhaps it is. Men of the high slopes, of whom there are few—though the Thassa haunt the mountain-caught clouds by choice—have slain the barsk, which in turn hunts them with cunning and patience. There are many legends about the barsk, Jorth, and it is credited with almost as much power as men set into the hands of the Thassa. Many lords have coveted a caged barsk, only to discover—if they are able to find one—it either gains its freedom and then takes dire vengeance upon man and herd, or else it wills itself to death. For it does not accept any curtailment of its freedom. The spirit which wore your body was so willing itself when the exchange was made."

I shivered. "And if that will succeeds?" I demanded.

Maelen hastened to reassure me. "It will not, there was a limit set upon it in the exchange. Your body will not die, Krip Vorlund—it will not be a discarded husk when you find it."

"Now," she shifted to another subject, "there is the watch post of Yultravan. But most of the people must be in harvest on the slopes. We shall not stop. But before the sentries see you, it would be well for you to be caged."

Reluctantly I climbed back and found my cage. Maelen exchanged greetings with two armored men who came from a small shelter beside the road. One of them lifted the curtain at the tail of the van to glance within, so I kept well in the back of the cage to escape notice. Again I thought they knew her as if she had made this journey before.

That night we camped in the open once more, and Maelen brewed a pot of liquid which gave forth such enticing odor that we all gathered around the fire to sniff longingly. I admit that I gulped my portion with no more manners than the real barsk might have displayed under the circumstances. Anticipation had ridden me during the day's journeying, for I knew that we were very close to our goal. But when I settled in my cage that night—Maelen deeming it safer for some reason that we all rest inside the van—I went immediately to sleep and this time did not waken.

We roused in the first of the dawn light and broke our fast on some crumbled cakes which were a mingling of grain and dried bits of meat. Then once more the van started upward. This time the slope was steeper, so that the kasi bent their shoulders to the yoke with visible effort. We stopped now and then to let them breathe, Maelen putting small weights she carried to block the backward roll of the wheels.

But we did not pause for a regular nooning, again sharing out cakes and lapping from bowls filled from Maelen's water bottle. It was midafternoon when we reached the top of the grade. Now the road descended through a cut between two heights. But what lay below was veiled by drifting mists, which only now and then parted to give a blurred hint of the depths.

"The Valley," Maelen said, and her voice was flat, wrung dry of emotion. "Stay with the van, we must keep strictly to the road. There are barriers and safeguards here which cannot be seen."

She gave the command to the kasi, and the van crawled on down into that place of mists and mystery.

Chapter 10

"Look with unclouded eyes upon your own desires," say the Old Ones when they speak among the Thassa. But one may believe all his thoughts clear, his motives open, and yet be moved by some hidden compulsion, as my little ones obey my wand when there is need for me to raise its power. Was my hidden desire awakened when I left Yrjar, virtuously telling myself and Malec that I went only to obey the law of the scales? If it was, then it was indeed deeply hidden.

Or did it spring to life after I had broken oath and sent the off-worlder from his own body into that of the barsk, that act sowing the seed? Or do any of us move, save by some design of Molaster's far beyond our understanding? To the Old Ones such an argument as that is blasphemy, for they hold that each is answerable for his own acts—though they sometimes take into consideration the motivation for those acts, when it is a strong one.

But the thought was already near to fruition in Yim-Sin, so that I was knowing and yet denying it. When the priest Okyen had speech with me privately, he had ill news and left me with despair and futile anger to chew upon. So when we traveled on, coming ever nearer the Valley where many hopes are buried, I was constantly under assault by temptation, even though I could not believe that naught but ill might come of it.

It was very difficult for me to occupy my mind with the plight of Krip Vorlund during those hours, and I determined that once we found what he sought, I would make the exchange speedily to lay this temptation. Nor would I trust myself to think upon the one who abode there and whose days were surely numbered.

We came down from the lip of the Valley, through the chill mists which cloud it, into that portion which is allowed to those from outside. I answered the off-worlder's questions as shortly as I could, still wrestling with myself. It was near sundown when we pulled into the outer court of the great temple, that which is for visitors. The guard priest came to greet us. I knew his face, but I could not set name to it—there is a kind of merciful forgetting allowed one at times—and this was the man who had greeted me here on a different occasion I tried not to recall. I asked to speak with Orkamor, only to be told he was busy and could not receive me. We took the van into the second courtyard and I released the kasi and fed and watered my little people. But Krip Vorlund asked me questions by mind-touch and some I could not answer.

We had lighted the moon globes by the van when a third-rank priest came to say Orkamor would see me. Krip Vorlund wished to go with me. He was impatient with all save finding and being united with his body. But I had to tell him that I must prepare Orkamor for what would happen and explain carefully, lest our story be thought wild raving. This he could accept.

Did it move stronger in me then, the belief that I need only act and much of the burden I had carried so long would be resolved? If it did, I still had the courage to resist.

Orkamor is not a young man and the burdens on him are a weighty load which grow heavier with the years, not lighter. Nor is he like the Thassa with their stronger, longer-lived bodies. So that each time I meet him, he seems to me even more shrunken, wasted, shadowy. Yet in him burns so strong a flame of will, and the need to answer need, that the spirit waxes while the fleshy envelope which holds it shrivels. After the first moments one sees only the spirit and not the man form that wears it.

"Welcome, sister." His voice was tired that night, thin and fluting as if it, too, had been used too much and too long.

I bowed my head above my wand. There are few the Thassa give full reverence to, besides their own Old Ones. But Orkamor deserves greatly of all Yiktor.

"Eldest Brother, peace and good." I made the Three Signs with my wand.

"Peace and good," he returned, and this time his voice was stronger, deeper, as if he battled away weariness with his will. "But we need no sooth-words between us, sister. I cannot tell you all is well."

"I know. I came through Yim-Sin."

"Was it well to come, sister? There is naught you can do, and sometimes surveying a wreck sorrows the heart past ever lifting of the cloud. It is better to remember a loved one walking in pride, than without pride or even manhood left."

My hands tightened on my wand, and I knew he saw me do that, but with Orkamor I did not care; he has seen worse self-betrayal in his time.

"I have come on another matter." Resolutely I thrust aside what he confirmed, and continued. "This—"

Quickly I turned to the matter of the off-worlder, telling the story to Orkamor simply. I could do this because he was who and what he was and would not read aught into my actions to make him think me more or less than himself. The priests of Umphra and the Thassa are not so un-kin as we are with others who dwell in the plains. When I was done he stared at me, but there was no great astonishment in his face.

"The way of the Thassa is not the way of mankind," he said.

"Tell me something I do not already know!" All that I had borne since Yim-Sin flared out in my sharp speech. And then, when I would have asked pardon, he waved it aside.

"Yes, you must have thought of the cost before you did this, sister. Those of your calling do not move lightly. This off-worlder was worth that much to you?"

"There was a debt."

"Which, if he knew all the consequences, he would not have demanded any payment from you. Now I must also say—there has been no charge brought hither by the men of Oskold."

I was not greatly disturbed. "If they returned to seek Oskold's leave— We came by the fore road, and though the van moves slowly that path is shorter."

"What if he is not brought, sister?"

I looked to the wand I twirled in my fingers. "They cannot—"

"You hope that they will not," he corrected me, and now there was sharpness in his voice. "By all you have told me, Osokun broke fair law in taking this man. He involved his father when he imprisoned the captive in a border fort. It was a man wearing Oskold's livery who came hunting him to the death in your camp. It may be that they think to kill him, hide his body, and leave it to their enemies to prove their crime. Would you not think thus, were you Oskold at this hour?"

"Being Oskold, with a plainsman's mind, perhaps I would. But not one who was—"

"Who was under Umphra's cloak?" Orkamor did not need to read my mind to follow my thoughts. "Having broken one law, it is always easier to break another."

"They broke man's law at the fair, but would they dare to break Umphra's law?"

"You are thinking as a Thassa." He sounded more gentle now, as one who must reason with an alien. "You have few Standing Words, and your moral precepts are so secure that they are seldom threatened. But, sister, what of your own actions under the Moon of Three Rings?"

"I have broken law, yes, and I will answer for it. Perhaps the reason for the deed will outweigh the deed. You know the judgment of my people."

"Yet you broke it with open eyes, though not in fear for yourself. Fear is the great lash the powers of darkness use to torment all men. If fear be great enough, then no law of man or god can stand against it. I have heard of Oskold. He is a strong man, though hard. He has but one heir, Osokun, and this has been that youth's bane. For his father favors him too greatly. Do you think that Oskold will tamely accept the outlawry of his son?"

"But how could he hope to conceal—"

"What men may say they know, and what they are able to prove are two different matters. And the full proof of Osokun's ill doing is the body of the off-worlder."

"No!" I should have seen this, of course. Why had I been so blind to logic?

"My sister, what did you really want?" Again Orkamor reached into my mind and sought what I did not want to see light.

"I swear—by the breath of Molaster, I swear—I did not—" I broke then, heard myself babbling, and strove to win control once more.

Orkamor looked at me steadily and made the truth, or what was now the truth, plain to both of us.

"And did you think, sister, that such could be? I tell you, it is not the body that makes a man, but what dwells within it. You cannot fill an empty frame and expect the past to come alive and all be as it once was. The Thassa can do much, but they cannot so give life to the dead."

"I did not mean it so!" I denied that once-hidden thought, now open in my mind. "I saved the off-worlder's life—they would have cut him down without mercy."

"And which would he have chosen, had all been made plain to him?"

"Life. It is a part of most to cling to life at that final Question."

"And now you will offer him life again, under new terms?"

I could, it would be so easy. Krip Vorlund had been in shock when he realized he was Jorth. Offered a human body again, would he hesitate—if it were proven his own body was beyond recall? Beyond recall—I stiffened against temptation.

"I will make no offers until I am sure that all has gone so awry." I promised.

"But you will tell him this now?"

"Only that his body has not yet reached the Valley. For that may be the truth, may it not?"

"We can always lean upon the mercy of Umphra. I shall send a messenger down the western road. If they are on the way, we shall be prepared. If not, there may be some news—"

"Thank you, Eldest Brother. Is it permitted that I—I—?"

"Do you really wish this, sister?" Kindness, great compassion, once more warmed his voice.

For the moment I could not decide. Was Orkamor right—that I should not see the one in the inner chamber, harrow my heart by looking upon—I shrank from that journey which was only a few steps, yet for me marked a distance like that between the stars which Krip Vorlund knew. Krip Vorlund—if I saw, then could I hold to my resolve, put aside desire?

"Not now," I whispered.

Orkamor held up his hand in blessing. "You are right, sister. And may Umphra arm you with his strength. I shall dispatch the messenger, do you have dreamless sleep."

Dreamless sleep! A kind wish, but not for me this night, I thought as I returned to the van. The off-worlder would want news. A part of the truth was all I had to offer him. Truth—perhaps the rest was not truth but surmise, perhaps Orkamor's messenger would meet the party we sought and all would come right after all—for Krip Vorlund. There are many rights in any world, and some may stand for others' wrongs. I must push away such thoughts.

I was right about the off-worlder and his questions. He was distraught when I said that the party from Oskold had not yet arrived, only small part reassured by the idea of the messenger sent down the western road. I dared not use mind-talk too much, lest I reveal in some way my new knowledge of myself. So I pleaded great weariness and went to my couch, lying there for half the night, hearing him shift and turn in his cage.

Morning came with the dawn call of the priest from the peak of the temple tower. I listened to those singing notes which, though not of the power of Thassa, yet had in them power of their own kind. For in this place where sorrow and despair could so well lay a black blanket over all, yet Umphra's servant sang of hope and peace, and compassion. And by so little was my own day lightened.

I brought out the little people and let them free in the courtyard, while two of the third-rank priests, who were hardly more than children, came gladly to bring us food and water. Krip Vorlund sat close to me, and ever as I looked up I found his eyes watching my every move, as if by such close surveillance he could trap me.

Why had I thought that? Such ideas out of nowhere sometimes carry the germ of truth.

"Krip Vorlund—" To use the name Jorth now, I believed, would add to his suspicion. He must continue to think of himself as a man only temporarily dwelling in a barsk body. "Today perhaps—"

"Today!" he assented eagerly. "You have been here before?"

"Twice." What was it that loosened my tongue then, made me tell him the truth? "There is one abiding here who is claim-kin to me."

"Thassa!" He seemed surprised, and I read that he looked upon my race with some of the awe which the plainsmen feel toward the Thassa.

"The Thassa," I said bitterly, "share much of the troubles of all men. We bleed if one raises sword or knife against our flesh, we die, we suffer many ills. Do you think we are impervious to that which ails others?"

"Perhaps in a way I did," he admitted. "Though I should have known it was not so. But what I have seen of the Thassa led me to think they were not akin to the rest of Yiktor in much."

"There are perils which are ours alone, perhaps, just as you have those which are peculiar to your people also. What are the dangers faced by space rovers?"

"More than I have now time to tell," he returned. "But your kin— the one who shelters here—is there nothing which can be done—"

"No!" I cut him short. To explain the why and wherefore of him who dwelt in the hall of Umphra, I could not. It hovered too close to his own present plight.

Among us those who would become Singers must undergo certain tests which reveal whether or not they have the proper gifts. And Maquad had been struck down during that time, not through any fault of his own, but because of one of those fell chances which are random shot by fate. We had surrendered what still lived into the hands of Umphra, not because we feared what he had become, as most of the plainsmen fear the deranged, but because we knew that here what life was left to his husk would be gently tended. For the Thassa no longer have fixed homes.

Once we had our halls, our cities, our rooted places. Then we chose another road and it was no longer necessary for any of us to claim a certain place for kin-clan being. There are old sites in hidden places, where we gather when there is need for council or on one of the Days of Remembering. We wander as we will, living in our vans. And thus to care for such as Maquad now was something we could not easily do. He was not the first we surrendered unto Umphra, though those had luckily been few.

"When will we know about—"

I roused out of my thoughts. "As soon as the messenger returns. Now, come, I would have you meet Orkamor."

"Does he know?"

"I have told him as was necessary."

But the man in the barsk body did not rise to follow as I stood, and to my surprise I read in him an emotion which I could not understand—shame. So strange was this to any Thassa that my amazement grew.

"Why do you feel thus?"

"I am a man, not a barsk. You have seen me as a man, this priest has not."

I could not yet understand. It was one of those times when two who seem to have put aside the alien separation of their backgrounds are pulled sharply apart by their pasts.

"To some men on Yiktor this would matter, to Orkamor it does not."

"Why?"

"Do you believe that you are the only one on this world ever to put on hide, run on four feet, test the air with a long nose?"

"You—this has been done before?"

"I—yes—also others. Listen, Krip Vorlund, ere I became a Singer and one able to company with my little people, I also ran the hills for a time in a different body. This is part of our learning. Orkamor knows this, so do others whom we visit now and then. At times we exchange parts of our learning. Now—I have told you something which you could use against the Thassa, tossing it as one might toss a firebrand into a standing yas crop to our ruin."

"And you—*you*—have been an animal!" There was first shock in his thoughts, and then, because he was a man of intelligence and of a mind more open than the planet-bound, he added, "But this is indeed a way to learn!" And I sensed that he lost then some of his uneasiness, so I thought I should have said the like to him earlier. Yet I also realized that I said it now only because there might be need for some hope should Orkamor's fears be true. Only—he must not look upon Maquad, nor know that story for the present.

We went into the inner hall of the temple and through that to the small garden where Orkamor rested his frail body, if not his compassionate mind. He sat there in a chair fashioned of hrata wood, deep-set in the earth so that the wood lived again and put forth small twiglets and branches, making a snug shield against the wind for one sitting there.

It was a place of deep peace, that garden, as was needful for the use to which it was put. For here not only came Orkamor to be renewed in spirit, but also he brought those for whom the world had ended when someone they loved had arrived to abide with Umphra thereafter. There are places where the power we all recognize under different names manifests itself in a way to inspire awe and even terror. Very few are there where it lays a comforting hand upon the afflicted. This was such a place and all who entered there were the better for it.

Orkamor turned his head and looked at us. He smiled rather than spoke his welcome. We went forward to stand beside him.

"The day is new, for us to write upon as we will," he repeated a sentence from the creed of Umphra. "So fair a tablet should draw the best from us." Then he spoke to Krip Vorlund. "Brother, Yiktor gives you much to write upon these days."

"That is so," the off-worlder replied in thought.

Orkamor had the inner language. He could not have been who and what he was without it. Few of his race, though, have developed that gift.

"It is given to any man to learn all he can during his lifetime, no limit set upon that learning. Only to refuse knowledge is our choice, and he who does so cuts himself off from much. I have never spoken with an off-worlder before—"

"We are as other men," Krip Vorlund replied. "We are wise and stupid, good and evil, living by this code or disregarding that one. We bleed from wounds, laugh at jests, cry at deep hurts—do not all men whether they walk this world or that?"

"True. And this would be more true for those who, as yourself, see more than one world so they may make comparisons. Will you humor an old man, planet-bound, and tell him something of what lies beyond our skies and marches with the stars—"

Orkamor did not look at me, but I understood his dismissal. Why he would have the off-worlder to himself, I did not know, and it disturbed me somewhat. But that I put aside, since I could think no harm in Orkamor and perhaps it was only as he said, that curiosity moved him to do so. He was so much apart by reason of his calling that one forgot at times to remember he was also a man and had a man's interests.

I nerved myself then to do what I could not face the night before—seek out Maquad. Of that there is no need to speak. To drag the sorrows of the past out of memory and relive them is a weak and useless thing. But I marveled anew at what they did in this place for those without hope.

At nooning I came again into the courtyard where I had left the van. My little ones napped in the shade of a tree, but roused and came to me. Krip Vorlund was not with them. And I wondered, for I did not believe that Orkamor could talk away all morning, the press of his duties was too heavy.

Then I called to one of the priests who brought us food and water. But he had seen nothing of the barsk and told me Orkamor was in the meditation chamber where he might not be disturbed.

Now I was worried. While the priests of Umphra will raise no hand against any living creature, there were others who might not think in their reaction to the sudden appearance of an animal. I was returning to the van when a secondary priest came in, his face bearing a frown.

"Freesha, there is a message from the western road, sent by a winged one. Those whom you seek never passed the gate town."

I gave my thanks mechanically, only a small part of my mind reacting to his words. The disappearance of Krip Vorlund was my major concern.

"The barsk—" I began, though why this priest, who had no contact with the supply duties of the temple, would know, I did not guess.

"It was here, when I came seeking you before." He looked around as if he might be able to conjure that red-furred body out of the ground by eye-search alone. "I remember I remarked to Brother Ofkad, for never have I known a barsk to walk with man before."

"How long ago was that, brother?"

"Two bell strokes before nooning. The gong spoke even as I left to seek you elsewhere."

So long a time! I went to Simmle, spoke to her by mind. She barked quickly, in some excitement, and ran to the gate.

"It would seem, brother, that my barsk has gone elsewhere. I must seek him."

I had warned Krip Vorlund before we entered the Valley of the traps it might contain for those who did not know its ways, or stay within the open ones. Why he had left the temple, I could not guess. Surely nothing that had passed between him and Orkamor could have led to this utter folly. Simmle could follow any trail he had left with ease, but a barsk might cover much ground in the time lapse the priest had mentioned—always providing he had not fallen into any of the trapped ways.

Simmle and I had reached the outer gate of the temple when I heard a hail from behind and turned impatiently to see the young priest who had charge of the guesting court.

"Freesha, they say you seek the barsk."

"Yes."

"It cannot be far gone, for it was drinking from the bowl when the messenger came. It is odd—" He hesitated.

"Yes?" I was impatient to be gone.

"It was—it was almost as if the barsk were listening to what we said. It barked when I noticed it. And when I turned again it was gone."

Could the off-worlder have understood them? The temple priests among themselves spoke the high tongue—and with it mind-touch —until often their speech was sometimes but a word or two, the rest all thought.

"What did you say that the barsk appeared to listen to?"

He did not quite meet my eyes then. "He—Older Brother—asked where you were. I answered that you were in the inner apartments with the protected one. We—we spoke a little of that one. And then the Older Brother said that you awaited those who were bringing a stricken one, but they were not coming. After that he went hence and when I looked—the barsk was gone."

Had—could Krip Vorlund have been rash enough to go looking for his body? But why had he so rushed forth and not come to me?

I waved Simmle on—

"Find him, girl." I gave her the order which sent her racing ahead, and I followed, bewildered, shaken, wondering what had chanced in that short time when I had sought my own sorrow and forgotten about the purpose which had brought me here.

Chapter 11

I lay on the earth and around me the smell of it, of the things that grew, roots set deep in its substance, and of the life that walked it, burrowed through it, was thick, teasing, testing. How far was I now from the Valley, how long the road I skulked along, I did not know as I lay and licked sore paws. I was now more Jorth than Krip Vorlund.

Man? Was there any longer a man who had once been Krip Vorlund? The priests of Umphra reported no party out of Oskold's territory with the husk of a man. Why, then, had I been brought to the Valley? What purpose had I been meant to serve for Maelen's desire, not mine? When I heard the priests talk among themselves suspicion had leaped into life, and I thought with new understanding of my interview with Orkamor in the garden of peace.

We had talked of worlds beyond, but always he wanted to know of the men who sought out such worlds, of what made them become star rovers. And it seemed to me that he had been trying to learn what manner of man would become a barsk to save his life—as if, by such a chance, I had taken a step from which there might be no return, and if I would accept such a fate for all time.

When Maelen spoke of the exchange, there had been a kind of logic to it. She knew the dangers, ah, how well she knew them. For the priests I had overheard not only spoke of my missing body, but also discussed Maelen and what brought her to the Valley, not once but again and again. There had been another who had run in a beast's body, at her bidding perhaps. And there had been no return exchange. So the man's body husk now dwelt in the Valley, and of the beast they did not speak. Or was that unfortunate one caged among her little people?

That perfectly trained company—were they all, or most, once men and women, not animals? Was that how the Thassa recruited their beast shows? Perhaps the name they had given to their performers—"little people"—was entirely apt.

She had long wanted to add a barsk to the company, she admitted that. And I had walked into her trap with the naïveté of a trusting child. Or had she brought to bear on me some of her power when my mind had been bewildered? What mattered now was not what had happened and could not be changed, but what might still be done. My body—my man's body—where was it? If it still lived at all— And to find out I must search Oskold's land. What I would do if I found it, I had no idea. But for the present the burning need to find it possessed me utterly, past logical reasoning. Perhaps I was no longer quite sane—

Hunger and thirst were dim urges stirring now. I scented man, the odors of a farm holding. And, wincing as I rose on my sore pads, I slipped through the underbrush. How much of the beast served me, I did not know. Man's knowledge might be an awkward leash upon my hunting skill. In dim twilight, as I stole from shadow to shadow along a wall of loosely piled stone, I was drawn by the messages my nostrils caught and classified.

Meat—saliva dripped from my tongue, my belly growled its emptiness—the scent of meat.

I crouched between two bushes, peering underneath them to an open farmyard. A kas stood stamping heavy hoofs. There were also four of those domesticated animals—forsphi—whose long-fleeced coats provided the raw material for the weaving of a highly weather-resistant cloth. They appeared uneasy, turning their long necks, bending their heads at queer angles, to survey the wall near which I crouched. And one of them voiced deep, coughing grunts of alarm. Just as I scented them, so must they also have picked up my presence.

But what I sought was not one of those, half again as large as I. A fowl picked an erratic path much closer to my hiding place. It was a long-legged creature with a sharply pointed bill which it repeatedly stabbed into the ground. I tensed as it neared. Unlike the animals, it appeared not to have any sense of danger. I burst from my bush and charged it. The bird whirled with a speed which I had not thought possible, and I felt a sharp and piercing pain above one of my eyes. Only a quick flinch saved me from another attack and I fled, blood blinding me on the left, aware that only happy chance had saved my sight.

The clamor of the animals rose as I ran back along the wall and into such cover as I could find. I ran a long distance before my sore paws and laboring lungs forced me to a halt.

Barsks were supposedly wily hunters. But I was not a barsk, I was Krip Vorlund.

I had one advantage not shared by my man body, the night did not blind me. The dark might be my day, which it probably was for a barsk. And before morning I fed, ravenously, certainly not daintily, on a reptilian creature I pawed out from between two stones in a stream bed. Then I found a hollow between a fallen tree and a rock and slept, waking now and then to lick my paws and hope that they were not too raw to carry me onward.

It was better, I decided, to switch traveling by day when I might be sighted to night, which was the natural time for barsk prowling. So I dozed throughout the light hours and limped on when the moon was high.

The Three Rings about that lunar disk were very bright tonight. My barsk head went up and, before I could subdue the impulse, I bayed—my deep cry echoing oddly until it sounded, even to me, more than just that of a night runner saluting the sky rider. There was something in that splendid display which drew and held the eyes, and I could understand why those of Yiktor attributed psychic powers to the rare phenomenon.

Three-Ringed moon meant power—but there was only one power I wanted and that was to regain my own body. I returned to the stream and hunted again, with slightly better results, for this time I flushed a warmblooded animal I surprised drinking at a pool. As Jorth I feasted, thrusting man-memory away during that meal. Then I drank my fill and started across country in search of a road which might be my guide.

I came upon an east-west path running through the woods. For a wide space on either side of the thoroughfare underbrush and saplings had been cut back, leaving open space. I kept just within this cover going west.

Oskold's land did not appear to be thickly settled, at least not in this section. Before dawn I passed, giving it wide berth, another fort such as the one I had been imprisoned in. But this one had a settlement by it, though the houses, or rather huts, were very roughly built as though meant to be only temporary shelters.

It was an encampment, I thought, barracks for more men than the fort could house. Sentries walked beats on the eastern side, and there were several lines of riding kasi pegged out, not grazing free. I believed Oskold's forces were alerted, as if to repel some invasion. I passed too close to a kas, which snorted and then gave voice to a roar, making its comrades highly vocal in turn. Men shouted and lanterns flashed along the hut lines. I slipped away hurriedly.

If the outer limits of the domain were empty land, prairie uncut by the plow, the same was not true of the country into which the road now led me. And it had been wise to change from day travel to night. After leaving the camp, I skirted before dawn a village of some size, slinking through the fields which sustained it. Harvest had bared most of the land. But as I skulked by a farmhouse, I was startled by a sharp yapping and read in that the warning of a long-domesticated hound-hunter. Other animals took up the alarm until the village rang with their cries, and I saw once more lights on, heard a shout or two aimed at the wildly baying yard dwellers.

The reaction of the people of Yim-Sin and the words of Maelen had assured me that a barsk was a rare and dreaded creature. Suppose I was sighted, or some farmer turned loose hounds to hunt the strange disturber? To go on into thickly settled territory could be suicidal folly. I paced up and down within the thicket I had chosen for the day's layup. And I heard myself whining a little at my thoughts. But somewhere—somewhere in Oskold's land was the answer to the fate of my man body, and that I *must* know!

After my experience, I dared not hunt at another farmyard. But wild life was scarce and shy hereabouts, and my hunger drove me at last to a walled field. Tonight there was no bright display of three rings in the heavens, rather clouds massed there. And that veiling gave me extra courage to attempt once more an attack on domesticated prey.

The creatures in the field were fodo; I had already sampled what they had to offer in the dried meat Maelen carried. They were small enough, about the size of Tantacka. Perhaps long ago some common ancestor had been theirs, though generations of domestication and supervised breeding had made the fodo much heavier of body and shorter of leg, doubtless thicker of wits also. The only trouble was that they chose to huddle together for sleeping, and a charge at the whole herd might well spoil my hunt.

I prowled around the wall, testing the air carefully for the scent I had come to identify with the yappers of the farmyards. The wind swept toward me, carrying only the rich odor of the sleepers. Had I a partner I thought it would be easy. One of us downwind could have stampeded the fodo to the waiting jaws of the other.

In the end I decided that my fleetness was my best weapon and I ran downwind. I had very little time to wait. The snorting heap of sleepers pulled apart, rose grunting. I charged and seized upon a squealer, dragging it with me in spite of its struggles. Getting over the wall so burdened was difficult, but hunger is a mighty drive and finally I managed it, as well as the return journey to a mass of rocks and brush along the river which provided me with a fort, though I had no mind to be besieged there.

I ate enough to satisfy my hunger. Then I prudently waded downstream, thus hoping to destroy any trail which an outraged farmer might bring his hounds to sniff out. A bridge spanned the river, and under its arch I came ashore and licked water from my fur.

While still so busied I heard the pound of hoofs echoing hollowly. Crouching in the shadows I lay low. There were two sets of hoof beats—each heading from opposite directions, and the speed with which they came spoke of dire necessity. I thought that the riders would pass close to where I lay, and I listened for any greeting which might explain their haste.

The beat lessened; I believed that both riders must be reining in their mounts. I dared to hold my head higher, creep to the end of the bridge, hoping I might hear something of importance. I did not know any dialect save that of Yrjar—though the thoughts of the priests of Umphra had been as clear as words spoken in Basic. But I could hope for neither advantage now.

The riders had stopped. I could hear the heavy blowing of the kasi, and now the sound of men's voices. The words—no—those were only a meaningless series of sounds such as any human speech might be for a true barsk. Though—fiercely I stretched my esper to tap thoughts.

". . . sends for aid . . ."

Surprise, some anger. ". . . dares . . . after this . . . dares!"

Desperation, a burst of it so intense as to be almost a mind-blow. ". . . must . . . is hunted . . . the off-worlders . . . they have demanded full outlawry."

"No use. Our lord has returned their man . . . he has offered to pay blood guilt . . . that is all he can do."

It would seem that the emotions of the two on the bridge were so high that their thoughts broke through to me more and more clearly, as a hearing of their words.

". . . refuge . . . must have refuge . . ."

"Madness!" The second messenger was emphatic. "Our lord is already gainsaid in council, those of Yimik and Yomoke turn on him. We have all the border to hold. If he brings in outlaws, then who will ride to defend him?"

"Let him decide—"

"Let him! You shall hear the same words. If the off-worlders have the power of Yu behind them, then outlawry can spread. They have the right to refuse blood-guilt price and ask for the other. What they have back now is no man—or do you name him so? You have seen him—"

There was no answer to that in words, only anger, fear. Then the cry of a man to urge his mount to the utmost. And one kas, that going west, beat out in a wild galloping. But the other rode, at not so harsh a pace, for the western border.

I dropped my head to my paws, hearing only the gurgle of the river. A man may lie in words, but his thoughts tell the truth. Now I had learned, so by chance, what I had come to seek—that my body was no longer in Oskold's land, but returned to my shipmates. For that the messengers had been concerned with my case I did not in the least doubt.

Yrjar was now my goal. The port—they would take my body to the *Lydis* where our medico would do what he could for that lifeless hulk. Suppose I did, by some miracle, reach the port and the ship, and even my body—what could I do? But Free Traders are open of mind. Maelen was not the only Thassa at the fair—there was the man Malec. Could I reach him, use him for explanation? Perhaps he might even make the exchange. So many doubts and fears between me and success, most of them formidable ones. But hope was all I had to cling to, lest I be swept away and drowned—man forever swallowed in beast.

Back then to the east, through the hills, down to the plains of Yrjar, where a barsk would be as conspicuous as a scarlet cloak flapping in the breeze. Yet that I must do.

I drank of the water curling before me, my throat suddenly as dry as if I had not drunk for a day or more. And there was a trembling in my legs, a shiver along my spine. Still there was no retreat. Then I waded into the water and finally swam along the center current, heading yet farther to the south before I came ashore on the eastern bank.

There was no longer need to follow the road and so meet any perils traveling thereon. The hills, dark and rolling across the sky, were guideposts enough. Beyond them lay the plains which cradled Yrjar, and the port. I sped through open fields, or trotted through forested places. I discovered that, though barsks were said to haunt the heights, yet their oddly small bodies and almost grotesquely long legs were meant for swift travel on the level. By sunrise I was well into the hills.

I passed at dawn that self-same fort where all my misfortunes had begun. Here, too, was extra garrison in evidence, men gathered in camp outside the walls. I made a wide circling to avoid their kasi lines.

As I ran I considered what I had learned from the messengers. He who had ridden westward, doubtless to Oskold's chief hold, had been bearing a cry for help—from Osokun and his men? It was said Oskold cherished his heir, but by the reaction of the second messenger some end had recently come to that. Oskold had offered blood-guilt price for my body—in other words he had attempted to settle by the one legal means on Yiktor the dispute between his son and the Free Traders, by offering Captain Foss the price of a crew member. Blood-guilt price could be offered for one killed inadvertently and without malice in time of peace. It was seldom accepted, almost never when the victim possessed close kin of the arms-bearing age, for blood feud was considered the more honorable solution. But if the victim left only females or boys too young to war within the required bonds of kinship, then the price could be accepted and the transaction recorded in the Temple at Yrjar.

Perhaps, because I was an off-worlder, as were the crew of the *Lydis*—who stood for my kin—the offer had been made with some hope of acceptance. But I wondered at Oskold's returning my body at all. It would have been more logical for him to dispose quietly of that damaging piece of evidence against his son and then defy anyone to prove what had happened. Did their fear of the insane hold them so in thrall?

At any rate it was apparent that Captain Foss had demanded full punishment and Osokun had been outlawed. The disgrace had lapped over, so that old enemies of Oskold saw an opportunity to drag down father as well as son. And Oskold's land was close to a state of siege. I wondered whether Oskold would turn rebel against all law and custom by sending assistance to his son. If so, would Oskold's sword-sworn continue to support him? Loyalty between lord and man was a firm bond, withstanding death and torture, as many a ballad told in detail. But it worked two ways, a lord had to be as loyal to those who had given him leige-oaths. And such sheltering of his son for his own purpose might, I believed, count as open break-oath, endangering his men past reason.

Yrjar—I tried to picture the city in my mind. I found it hard to count the days since I had been kidnaped from the fair, and I could not even be sure that the fair was still in progress. What if—I put on a new burst of speed—what if the *Lydis* had lifted off-world? That thought was so appalling I could only push it from my mind lest I yield to the terror it evoked in me.

If the *Lydis* still stood on the port apron, would Malec still also be at the fair? If not—how—I licked my still tender paws and growled softly. Then I realized that the barsk might be gaining on the man. Was that what had really happened to him whom the priests of Umphra sheltered for Maelen? Had he gone in beast body so long that the animal had conquered, and had fled to the high hills with no longer any ties with man? I could have thrown back my head and howled, as I had bayed the moon with no human reason. But I stifled that in my throat.

Griss Sharvan—he had been with me at the show—he had seen the return of the barsk, he had heard my story of what happened. And he might be open-minded if a barsk came to him now—be able to provide some contact. We all had esper powers, some more than others. Lidj—Lidj was the best aboard the *Lydis*—could I only get close enough. No, Krip Vorlund was far from beaten. In these hills I might move by day as well as by night—

I dug some small burrowing creatures out of the mold and ate, though they were only enough to stay the first edge of my hunger. And I climbed steadily up and up through the frosty air which bit at my laboring lungs. Patches of snow hurt my tender feet. I licked the snow and so gave my thirsty body a measure of moisture, though I thought often of the river where I had drunk so deeply and sweetly.

By midnight I found a pass which was no more than a knife edge of crevice, and was on the down slope to the plains. But fatigue drove me into hiding and the sleep I must have.

The sun was warm on my maned back when I awoke and looked about me through eyes slitted against the light, testing the breeze. Man scent, rank and strong. I flattened in my small patch of shadow, listened, used my nose.

There was the faint scrape of one hard surface against another, such as a boot sole might make slipping on rock. Whoever passed to my right and below was taking infinite precautions to go silently.

I wriggled forward, my head flattened against my forefeet as I tried to peer below. A man—no, men, for I saw another beyond the one so close to me—were creeping uphill. They had pulled over their scale shirts and surcoats roughly woven hooded cloaks, which were oddly patched with color. I believed that any eyes less keen than those of an animal would have found it near to impossible to sight them from a distance unless they were moving. A scouting party of Oskold's enemies?

It was of no consequence unless they found me, and now I began a retreat of my own, edging back into the brush before getting to my feet and moving undercover left and down from their advance. Twice I froze, keeping stone-still while more of the disguised party inched past. What their goal might be I could not guess, for I had seen no fort or post on this side of the hills. But their determination was plain to read.

Again I must turn south, for the creepers on the hill came from a larger party camped in the lower lands. All I had to guide me was the knowledge that Yrjar was somewhere to the west.

I lay up finally, waiting for night. And under a three-ringed moon I put on a burst of speed. So the hours of darkness passed while I alternately ran and walked, until my feet grew so painful that I had to rest. For a while I stood in a pool and there I also broke my fast, for a feathered creature, overlooking my presence because of my lack of movement, ventured too close. It was good eating, the best I had had since the fodo, and I cracked bones for the last taste of it.

Then I holed up in a thicket. But not long did I have to sleep. My head swung up and I listened, for this time sound, not scent, came first. Those were farm hounds and they hunted. Also whatever fled before them was coming in my direction.

As a man I had been hunted through these hills by Osokun's followers. Now as a beast was I also to know the chase. And there is a terror which comes from the sound of hounds on one's track. I held steady, listening, for I thought that I was not their quarry.

Then a slender-legged creature burst from the brush very close to me, passing in great leaping bounds. I recognized it for one of the wild ruminants of the plains, considered an excellent addition to the menu and usually hunted in numbers in the fall season so their flesh could be dried for winter storage.

This one had not been chased long and was running easily. But the pack was eager, too, and only a yip or two marked their coming, for they were running mute on a warm scent.

Again I moved south, angling away from the path the runner had taken. If I was lucky the hounds would be so intent upon their present game they would not pick up my scent. Or, if they did, was a barsk so formidable they would refuse to follow my trail?

The only trouble was that I neared open country. Not only were there no rocks or brush, no copses promising shelter from the sighting by a human hunter, but the fields had been harvested, leaving only stubble. And against that gray-yellow my own red coat must of necessity show plainly and in bright relief.

I caught the scent of water and remembered that a small stream ran from the pool where I had bathed my feet. Suppose I used that for my roadway, would it confuse my trail? What knowledge I had of such matters came only from tapes I had scanned for my amusement. And such hunting reminiscences, compiled from a man's point of view, might be very faulty indeed when applied to my present plight.

However, I could see no better answer, and waded into the stream to follow its course. But I had not gained much distance when a loud clamor from the place where I had lain sounded real menace. And I guessed the worst. The hounds had picked up my scent and, by some frown of fortune, had decided I was the better sport.

It was sheer panic which led to my downfall. I ceased to think. Like the plains animal that had fled, I ran, intent only upon leaving behind me that pack. And the rigors of my traveling had sapped my strength, so that though I strained to cover the ground, I knew that I could not draw far enough ahead. I leaped a wall, ran across a field and—

There was no longer ground under my pounding feet. I was in the air . . . falling . . . falling . . .

Chapter 12

Sand flew up about me, my body jarred against the earth with a force which both drove the air from my burning lungs and dazed me. Then I heard, if dimly, the wild chorus of the hounds, and struggled to rise. My vision was blurred, but slowly it cleared enough to show me that I was imprisoned in a steep-walled pit. A man with fingers and toes to cling to the irregularities of those walls might have climbed out. For four paws with blunt nails it was an impossibility.

I threw back my head and howled. And that cry, rendered more resonant by the earthen funnel which held me, brought silence for a moment or two to the slavering pack now ringing the opening above. Excited by the chase though they were, none ventured to leap down and join me, but took out their hatred in their cries.

Then some of them were brushed roughly aside and I saw, from the angle at which I must hold my head, men looking down at me. The first shouted in open amazement and the others stared wide-eyed. One of them raised a crossbow and I wondered if I could possibly dodge any shot, penned as I was. But he who stood beside the archer struck down the weapon with an angry order.

For a time I lay panting while the hounds and one of the men kept watch; the others had gone. Then there was a thud, and a mass of cords landed on and about me. I jumped to my feet, which was just what they wanted. For the net was jerked tight in an instant and I found myself helplessly entangled in its folds, being hoisted out of the pit.

The hounds leaped for me, to be beaten off by their masters as I was dumped, net and all, into a farm cart. So bound, I was transported to a farm and pitched into a dark shed.

About me the smell of animals, the acrid stench of man was thick. I panted, my lolling tongue and mouth ash-dry. Water—just a few drops to lick— But no one came near the shed as the hours wore away.

The shock of my landing in the pit remained in aches throughout my body, but the need for water became an all-demanding obsession. At last I tried feebly to use mind touch, of which I had been afraid, lest superstition lead to my instant death.

There were minds about me, yes. But though I tried with all my failing energy to implant in one of them my need for water, my harmlessness, there were none I could hold long enough to make my wants known.

I fell into an apathetic state, unable to keep fighting a lost battle. And so they may even have thought me dead when they did come at last, how much later I had no means of telling, save that it was dark outside when they pulled out the net and slung the package which held me into a cart once more. We passed a small pond and the smell of water roused me enough to whine, to raise my head. Then a blow sent me into unconsciousness.

Day now, bright sun hurt my eyes. And my ears were deafened by a clamor of shouts which I could not understand. The cart stopped and two men stood by its lowered tailboard, looking in at me.

"Water—" I tried to shape the word, but what came from my gaping jaws was a hoarse and despairing whine. One of the men leaned closer and when he spoke it was in the dialect of Yrjar which, very long ago, I too had spoken.

"Barsk—ten tokens—"

"Ten scale tokens?" exploded the other. "When, counterman, do you ever see a barsk here? And a live one—"

"Barely so," the first commented. "I will say perhaps he remains so until sundown. And that hide—it is cut—Even cured I could get nothing for it as fur."

"Twenty—"

"Ten."

Their voices became a drone, they wavered behind a misty curtain which now dropped before my eyes. I was very willing to drift into a beckoning dark which promised comfort and no more torment.

But I was roused to life again as the net was pulled from the cart and I was carried into a darker place, where the stink of ill-kept animals was ripe and heavy. Once before—my memory was like a spark to be extinguished forever—once before I had smelled just that stench. When? How?

Iron grip about my throat, hurting, choking— Feebly I tried to snap, to pull away. But instead that pressure impelled me into a small dark place, and then left me in cramped confines as a lid was slammed down. Two holes in the side gave small eyes of light, very little air. There was some straw, evil-smelling, for I was not the first captive to bide there. And the smell was not only of other bodies, but of minds also, filled with fear and hate, thickened by despair.

I tried to curl up my aching body, pillowed my head on my forefoot, seeking what small relief there could be in retreating from memory, from thought, from all around me. So I existed, or lingered; I did not live.

There was no water. Sometimes I thought or dreamed dimly of water, of how I had walked down those streams with the wavelets curling about my legs, sleeking my fur. And then it seemed that it had all been only a dream and there had never existed any world beyond this stifling box. There was no time, only an eternity of torture.

A snap overhead, the box top was raised to let in air and light. I think I tried to lift my head, but something heavy struck across my neck, pinning me to the noisome floor. And I could not see who stood surveying me.

"—near dead. You would offer *that* to my lord?"

"A barsk. When do you see a barsk alive hereabouts, Freesh?"

"Alive? Near dead, as I have said. And the hide—that is worth nothing either. You ask fifty tokens? You are fit for the Valley if you hold to that, fellow."

The pressure was gone from my neck, an instant later the lid slammed down to leave me once more in a prison. "Near dead—near dead—near dead—" The words buzzed in my ears. "Barsk—near dead—"

A barsk was an animal. I was not an animal, I was a man—a man! They must know, must let me out. I was a man not an animal! That life spark which had flickered close to extinction in me a moment earlier flared up again. I tried to brace my weakened body against the walls of the box, to attempt to fight my way to freedom. It was no use. Muscles twitched, but there was no strength left in me.

"A man—a man!" I could produce no sound but a faint whine. But my thoughts shrieked to the world outside the box. "A man dies here—not an animal but a man!"

And with lightning swiftness a thought, clear and forceful, locked with mine. I clung to it as one loosed from a ship's hull in space flight during repairs would cling to his lifeline.

"Aid—for a man who dies—"

"Where?" came the demand so clearly that its very force brought answering energy to my mind.

"In a box—in a barsk body—a man not an animal—" I tried to hold that lifeline of thought which seemed to slip through the hold of my mind, as though the gloves on a ship-space line were greased and could not hold. "A man—not an animal!"

"Think, keep thinking!" An imperative order. "I must have a guide, so think!"

"Man—no animal—" But I could not hold, the line was slipping from me fast. Making a supreme effort, I tried again. "Man—not barsk—in a box—in—I not know where—but in a city."

Yrjar? Was that city Yrjar?

"In a box—as a barsk—a barsk—Not barsk—man!"

It seemed that I could not breathe, that the dark of space enfolded me too tightly, crushed me—

"Man—I am a man—" I clung to that, fighting hard. But the dark was here and in it I spun away to nothingness.

"Here!"

Through the dark again came that thrust of answer, swift and sharp to stir me. But I could not listen, there was nothing left but the dark and an end of all struggle.

Light, far off, and voices which meant nothing. Then my head between two hands, raised. Dimly I could see a face.

"Listen," the order ringing in my brain. "You must help me in this much. I have said you are one of my little people, that you are a trained beast. Can you prove it?"

Prove it? I could prove nothing, not even that I was a man, not one who ran four-footed and killed with fangs in the dark.

Water poured across my swollen tongue, into my jaws, three times before I could swallow. Then again those hands cupping my head, the eyes meeting mine, reaching into me.

"Jorth—obey!"

That had once meant something, but I could not remember. Someone had called me by that name and—

I bowed my head, tried to raise my forepaws. There were broad steps and a man in a black-and-yellow robe who had once watched me. So, I must bow, and do all we had planned together. We? Who?

"My animal—"

"That is no proof, Freesh."

"I return what you paid for him. Or do I call the street guard?"

Still those hands holding up my head. And once more water in my mouth, so I could swallow. With it came a measure of life. But the hands grasping me did not loosen.

"Be strong, we shall go soon."

Voices above my head washing back and forth. Then arms about me, carrying me out into greater light, where I whined and closed my eyes against the glare. He who bore me laid me down on a soft mat and I sprawled there, unable to help myself. Under me the surface shook, moved, I heard the creaking of wheels, their grating over stone pavement.

On went the wagon, and the odors of the town stuffed my nose. I did not try to look about me, to expend that much energy was beyond my strength. Rattle, grate, rattle— The cart came to a stop.

"—trained animal—"

Plop of a footboard being pulled down and put up again. The cart moved on. Fresher air, a breeze. Another stop, and someone dropped from the driver's seat to the bed of the wagon, knelt beside me. My head was raised and once more liquid poured between my jaws. But this was not only water, it carried a stinging addition. I opened my eyes.

"Maelen—" I thought that name. But this was not the Thassa woman who had plunged me into this desperate venture, but the man who had been with her at the fair. Memory returned like a faint picture much faded by exposure and the overlay of harsh events.

"I am Malec," came his answer. "Now rest, sleep, and have no fears. We have won a space of free time."

The meaning of his words did not wholly register with me as I did as he bade and slept—though this was not the stupor of approaching death.

There was a fire not too far from me when I awoke once more. And the leaping flames of that were very reassuring. Fire and man, his old comfort and weapon, so long linked in our minds with safety that our spirits lift ever when we look into it.

Beyond the fire was another light, and seeing that I growled—and was startled to hear that sound. For I had momentarily been Krip Vorlund when I roused, and it was a shock to find I still wore the guise of Jorth.

My growl was answered from the shadows, where the full light of the fire, the beams of the moon globe did not reach. And my barsk nose, once more keenly in action, told me there were other life forms, many of them, around me in the half gloom.

A man came into the firelight, a kettle in one hand, a long-handled ladle in the other. I watched him pass along a line of bowls set out on the ground, into each measuring a portion of the kettle's contents. And so he came to me.

"Malec of the Thassa," I said mind-fashion.

"Krip Vorlund, from off-world."

"You know me?"

He smiled. "There is only one man who runs as a barsk."

"But—?"

"But you put on fur when I was not present? You have used Thassa power, my friend. Did you think that such would not be known?"

"*I* did not use it!" I countered.

"Not in that way of thinking," he agreed readily. "But it was used for your advantage."

"Was it?" I demanded.

"Was it not? Do you think you would have lived past your discovery by the sword-sworn of Oskold had Maelen not wrought for you as best she could—time allowing?"

"But the rest—"

He sat down upon his heels, so that now, I, up on my haunches, was a small bit taller. "You believe that she used you for her own purposes?"

I gave him the truth. "Yes."

"All races have that which they swear unbreakable oaths upon. So can I swear to you that what she did that night, she did wholly for you, the saving of your life."

"That night, perhaps, but thereafter? We went to the Valley—my body was not there, but she had another—"

He did not appear surprised. I do not believe I ever saw one of the Thassa show that emotion as men of other races do. But there was a moment of silence between us, before he continued:

"What *do* you believe?"

"That there were dangers beyond what she told me. That she had her own reason for wishing me in the Valley and that was not to *my* good, but hers."

Slowly he shook his head. "Listen well, off-worlder, she did not send you into any danger she had not already tasted. And had you not gone your own road, you would not have been in such a plight as I found you. No Singer among the Thassa takes on the calling of power until he or she has worn, for a space, the guise of fur or feathers. Maelen had taken this way before your star ship ever rocket-blasted the port apron of Yrjar."

"And that one in the Valley?"

"Did I ever say it is not a dangerous road to walk?" he demanded. "We do not slay the living things in the ranges, but that does not mean death holds aloof there. Maquad took upon him beast form, and a plains lord who went hunting without our leave shot a fatal bolt. It was one chance in ten thousand, for we did not know any walked our holy ground and we were not warned until too late. As for you, do you not think that Maelen will pay for her use of our power to aid a stranger? She believed truly what she told you, that Oskold's men would deliver your body to the temple and that all would be well. Had you remained there—"

"But my body is in Yrjar."

"Yes. And now we must make new plans, and I will not deny to you that they must be made in haste. Your friends will not understand and in their ignorance may try cures which will instead kill."

I shivered as along my spine sped a cold chill. "Yrjar—we must go—"

"Not so. We have just come from Yrjar. I was able to bring you forth from the city only by saying that I would take you beyond any inhabited place. Maelen knows, or will know shortly, where you are.

She will come hither, and then go to your captain, tell her story—we shall see if he is a man who will believe strange tales. Then we must plan to smuggle you into the port so Maelen can undo what has been done. And of this whole business"—he was frowning now— "I do not know what the Old Ones will think, for it has broken Standing Words, and put into the hands of those who do not share Thassa blood a secret weapon, should enemies desire such."

"You mean that the plainsmen do not know you can so change bodies?"

"Yes. Think you—they are men who do not have knowledge of the spirit, only of body and mind. Tell the ignorant among them that there are those living on this world who can make a man into an animal, an animal into a man, and then—do you foresee what could happen?"

"Fear drives men to kill."

"Just so. There would be such a hunt as would bathe the Quiet Places in blood. Already we know that this is spoken of us—by that off-worlder Gauk Slafid, who strove to use such knowledge as a bargaining lever. Whether he gained this information from Osokun or others of Yiktor, we do not know. I hope he did not—at least not from Osokun, or Maelen's singing would not have saved you. The sword-sworns would have killed you that night, both barsk and man. Nor has any hint of it among the plainsmen since come to me. Now our Old Ones search for it by thought. We could be walking a thin edge of crumbling earth along the rim of a great gulf."

"There is fighting, Oskold's neighbors turn against him. If one lord is embroiled with another, then do you not gain time?" I told him of what the messengers had said and what I had seen in the hills.

"Yes, his neighbors see a chance to whittle away at Oskold, but think you how quickly he would seize upon such a story to launch them, away from his throat, at the Thassa! This could be a rallying cry to put the lord who gave it at the head of a united army. That is why I believe Gauk Slafid kept that knowledge to himself. For, if Osokun had known of it, that knowledge would have served him much better than any foreign weapon. He might have headed a 'holy war' against a common enemy uniting the land under him."

"If you can change me back, I will be off-world and willing to swear no man shall ever hear of it from me."

He surveyed me grimly. "The Old Ones would make sure no loose tongues would wag. I agree that the sooner we make the exchange and get you from Yiktor, the better. At present Osokun and his sword-sworns are outlawed. They can live only by raiding, and that with every man's hand against them. Sooner or later a combined force will track them down and finish them. I do not know if Oskold could be bought by any plea from his son to give even secret support. But, if he were so minded, he would have to do it *very* secretly, lest his own men declare him oath-broke and leave him. Outlawry is no light thing and those who aid any outlaw come themselves at once under the ban. It needs only three freeholders to swear to this to condemn a man. Oskold will have enough to occupy him with these invaders."

"And we wait now upon Maelen." I returned to what was to me the main matter. Quarrels of feudal lords had no part in my future, or so I believed.

"We wait upon Maelen. She goes then to your captain at Yrjar. As I said, much will depend upon how open a mind he has. Perhaps you can give her some message which will reveal the truth to him, some incident from your shared past which none on Yiktor can know. Then, if he accepts her story, we can plan further."

Free Traders were open-minded. They had seen too much on too many worlds to say that this or that might never happen. But this was so unique, could belief be stretched so far? Malec's suggestion was a good one. I set myself to thinking of some identifying story Maelen might use on my behalf.

When time becomes a factor in one's life, then it can wield a whip as sharp as those of the slave drivers of Corfu. Malec had his duties with the animals, but I had only those thoughts which worked sharp as thorns into my mind, keeping me pacing back and forth beside the fire. Whatever drink and food Malec had given me since my release must have carried a stimulant as well as nourishment, for I felt alive in every part of me—something I had not really done since I left the Valley on my futile quest.

He had done with his duties for the animals and came back to sit before the fire, turning down the moon globe. At last I sat beside him, wishing to be taken away from all the ifs and maybes which rode me.

"Why do the Thassa choose to run as animals?" I asked him abruptly.

He looked at me, his large eyes seeming even larger in his pale face. "Why do you choose to spin from world to world, calling none your home?" he counterquestioned.

"It is a way of life to which I have been born and bred. I know of none different."

"Now you do," he pointed out. "We are the Thassa, who have also been born and bred to a way of life. Once we were a different kind of people, akin to those now living in the plains. Then there came a moment of choice, we were shown another path to be explored. But all things cost and for taking this new road there was payment. It meant uprooting ourselves and turning from all which seemed safe and secure. No more would walls enclose us, we must gather close-knit to our kind. We set aside one life to gain another. Now, as these plainsmen see us, we are wanderers, people without roots. They cannot understand why we do not want what seems treasure and the future to them; they hold us apart. And because they have seen from time to time a little of what we gained by our choice, they hold us also in awe. We share all life as they do not— No, not all life—as yet we cannot share some things—the pushing growth of a tree, the putting forth of new leaves with the season, the coming of fruit. But we can take on a bird's wings and learn the sky after the manner of the feathered ones, or put on fur and become four-footed for a space. You know many worlds, star rover, but none do you begin to know as the Thassa know Yiktor and its life!"

Malec fell silent. His eyes turned from me, to rest upon the flames which he fed now and then from a pile of wood beside him. Now he no longer spoke with his thoughts, a wall stood between us. Though he did not wear the rapt look I had seen on Maelen's face, yet I believed he was close to that state of otherness which I had seen hold her that night in the van.

Night air fed many messages to my nose. After a time I went into the shadows about the camp, sniffing my way. Many of the little people slept in their cages, but others awoke and kept sentry. I do not think anything could have crept undetected upon that camp.

Maelen came before dawn. I smelled her scent before I heard the creaking of van wheels. There was a chittering behind me which was both greeting and signal. Malec struggled out of his blanket roll by the now dying fire and I joined him; we stood together as she came into the half light of the camp.

It was to me she looked. I do not know what I had expected, rebuke perhaps for my folly in leaving the Valley—though I refused to think it folly, judging by what I had known, or suspected, at the time. After all, how could the Thassa begin to understand what their accepted customs could mean to another?

But only weariness showed on her face—as one who had stood a long, unrelieved watch of duty. Malec held up his arms to aid her from her seat, and she came into them with a sigh. Before I had always seen her strong; now she was altered, though how I did not know.

"There are riders in the hills," she said.

"Oskold is beleaguered," Malec returned. "But come—" He supported her to the fire, stirred its dying flames to feed it more wood. Then he put into her hand a horn he filled from a small flask. She sipped slowly, pausing between each mouthful. Then, cupping the horn against her breast, she spoke to me.

"Time passes, Krip Vorlund. With the dawn I am for Yrjar."

I think Malec would have protested, but she did not glance at him. Instead she stared now into the fire and drank all the horn held, sip by careful sip.

Chapter 13

It was a bright morning, such as brings the strong wine of wind to refresh nose and throat, a dazzling shaft of sun, the feeling in both man and animal that it is good to be alive. Before the sun had touched the ground where Malec had set our camp, Maelen mounted the riding kas her kinsman readied for her, and started west. I longed to run beside her. The good sense which kept me behind was more prison than any cage bars that morning. We watched her out of sight, and Malec walked among the cages, opening each door so that the occupant could come or go at will.

Some still slept as balls of fur. Others blinked and roused, but only a few came out. Simmle shouldered past the door and bounded to me, uttering sharp yelps of welcome, her rough tongue ready in caress. But Malec dropped his hand upon her head and straightway she looked up to him, her tail drooping. She glanced from right to left, whined, and then trotted into the bush.

"What is it?" I asked of the Thassa.

"Maelen said there are men in the hills. They may not all be intent on raiding Oskold. Somewhere the outlaws run."

"You think they might attack?"

"They need food, much else, if they are to survive. And there is only one way to get supplies, and that is to take them by force. We do not carry much to tempt them, but desperate men will fight for crumbs."

"The animals—"

"Some would be merely meat for the spit to such a party. Others would be killed, because men who are without hope kill for the sake of killing. If there comes trouble the little people can take to the land and be safe."

"And you?" He was making preparations as if he expected just such a raid soon. At his belt hung the long knife which was a part of normal apparel all over Yiktor. He had no sword, nor had I seen a crossbow in camp. Now he smiled.

"I, too, know the countryside as few of those who might so descend upon us. When our sentries give warning—then will the raiders find an empty camp."

Simmle was a sentry, I guessed.

"And you, if you will—" Malec continued.

Why not? As Simmle had done I went into the bushes, putting nose, eyes, and ears at his service. A few moments later I looked back at the vans. There were four of them—the lighter, smaller one which Maelen had taken, the three Malec must have brought from Yrjar. But who were the drivers for two of those? Save for the animals he was alone. Puzzled, I wondered about that—unless the kasi that had drawn them had followed behind the one he drove.

Though the cages had been set in a circle about the campfire, which still gave off a few lazy spirals of smoke, the rest of the gear had not been unpacked. I watched Malec go from wagon to wagon, busy himself in the interior of each for a space. Perhaps he was repacking contents for a longer pull.

As I had on my journey across Oskold's land, I skulked from bush to bush, going into higher land. We were, I decided, in the fringe of the hill country. Although why Malec had brought us into what might well be dangerous territory, I could not guess. I kept on climbing until I found a ledge on which grew concealing brush.

Though the branches had lost most of their leaves, still I thought I was well masked by the growth; from this point I could see the camp, plus a good slice of the country about it. There was no road leading to here. But the tracks of the vans were still visible in crushed grass and earth and there was little chance of hiding that trail for the present.

Malec was invisible within one of the vans, nor, as far as I could see, had many of the animals issued from their cages. The scene was one of drowsy peace and quiet, lulling to watch. The wind had died down, little scent carried to me. I continued to test with my nose. Simmle must be prowling to the south; perhaps there were other guards, stationed to the west.

The sun climbed into a cloudless sky, bringing almost summer warmth as can happen in midautumn months. Malec emerged from a van, a yoke across his shoulders, buckets dangling from its ropes. He went down to the stream, which I could see only as a flicker of sun on water here and there.

Then—Simmle barked fiercely, once. I squeezed from under my brush shield. A puff of wind upslope had brought me warning. I leaped from the ledge into a lower thicket, wriggled through its spiky grasp. That one war cry from Simmle and then nothing— nothing but the scent and sounds which perhaps a human ear could not have caught, but which to barsk hearing were as loud as a fanfare of horns. I slipped through the cover, heading to camp, dropped to my stomach, and crept under the nearest van.

Malec wavered up the slope from the stream. Yoke and buckets were gone. He stumbled and slipped, one hand pressed to his breast, the other outflung, fingers moving vainly as if he tried to grasp some support which was not there.

He went to his knees before he reached the circle of the cages, and then sank slowly forward. From between his shoulders, dancing with his heavy gasps of breath, stood the shaft of a crossbow bolt. His hands pushed into the soil, and then his efforts ceased and he fell forward on his face, quiet and spent.

As if his struggle had been a signal, those in the cages burst forth and fled, voiceless and swift. They were gone, hidden perhaps to any man's eye, but not to my nose or ear.

I crept on, though such a mode of travel was hard for my barsk body. There was someone coming up the bank from the river, trying to move quietly, but with little success, from my point of view.

Continuing on under the shadow of the van, I began a circuit of the campfire. Malec had not moved, but his assailant was very cautious. Perhaps the other did not know that the Thassa had been alone save for the animals. I tried to reach Malec through mind-touch. He was still alive, but there was no consciousness to pick up my message.

I reached the end of the van. There were the cages, but I did not know if they were sufficiently high to hide me. Or dared I play a bewildered animal out in the open? As I hesitated, a tan streak ran to my left. Simmle! What was she doing?

She did not pause by Malec, but angled down in the direction of the one who scouted toward the camp. I got to my feet and flashed after her. I still had not seen her quarry when he screamed. A moment later I nearly fell over the furiously fighting tangle of man and venzese. He was crying out, trying to hold snapping jaws from his throat with both hands.

I jumped and tore, and Simmle got the grip she fought for. In those seconds I was more barsk than man, in me boiled a red rage I would not have believed I could house.

There was a shout, something whizzed so close to my shoulder that I felt the burn of its passing. Simmle still worried her victim and now I leaped a second time, striking against her, bearing her to the ground with my weight.

"Loose!" I beamed that thought order at her. "Loose—come!"

Again a bolt struck close. The smell of blood was fuel to my beast rage, but I fought against that emotion.

"Loose—come!" I had opened my jaws to seize upon Simmle when she dropped her hold and looked at me, eyes red and gleaming. She growled as one who warns another from legitimate prey.

"Come!" Again I launched myself against her and this time my plunge sent her sprawling away from the body. She growled, but got to her feet as a bolt struck where she had lain but a second before. She snapped viciously at where it stood quivering in the ground, and bounded with me up the slope.

They continued to shoot after us and I zigzagged, hoping Simmle would follow my example. We came into the camp only a few feet from Malec, who lay just as I had seen him fall. Simmle dipped her head to nose him and then sounded a shuddering howl.

"On!" I urged her. She swung around, showing her teeth as if to launch at me. Then some of the red light dimmed from her eyes and she ran with me, shoulder to shoulder, between the vans to the country beyond.

I had no idea where the other animals had vanished to, though I caught their mingled scent and thought they had taken this same route. I was not even sure how many there were, or of what different species.

"Up!" I ordered Simmle. She had swung around and paused, facing back toward the camp. Her usually sleek hair was rough along the spine, and her head was down between hunched shoulders, stained fangs exposed as her muzzle wrinkled in a snarl. She took a step or two down our back trail. Then she turned again and led me in a wild race into the brush.

We worked our way well up into the heights before we halted and lay panting, watching the camp. There were men there now, kicking at the cages where the doors swung open, thrusting swords into the interiors of the vans as if to hunt out anything which might be hiding there. From Maelen's they tumbled boxes, breaking open their fastenings to find supplies of the meat-and-grain cakes. All in sight seized upon these eagerly, wolfing them down with the greed of men who had missed many meals.

They had dragged Malec's body to one side, bundling it out of the way under one of the vans. Two of the men walked along the line of the kasi where those animals snorted and pulled at their ropes, kicking out at any who approached too near.

The empty cages appeared to fascinate some of the men. They pushed them over as if unable to believe that they were bare of occupants, as if this rough handling would dislodge what must be within.

Into the disordered camp now rode a small party of three. One man supported another in the saddle of his mount, while the third came behind, as if to cover a rear attack. Now it was my turn to snarl. He who was being so tended I had last faced in the border fort. These were Osokun's outlaws who were making themselves free of the camp, and some time recently their leader had met with rough handling. His right arm was bound across his chest and his face was white and drawn. He was a sorry ghost of the cocky lordling who had tried to dictate terms to Free Traders.

The spoiling of the vans continued as the men sorted through the contents of boxes and baskets. Food appeared to be their first concern and they ate hugely, before putting all that was left into saddle bags. Some then went in a southwesterly direction and returned leading riding kasi. A few of the animals limped and all showed signs of hard and too long riding.

But the men were in no hurry to leave the camp. They lifted Osokun from his mount and put him on the divan they pulled from Maelen's van. One of the men who had supported him heated water on the fire, busying himself with the tending of his leader's wound. It would seem, however, that Osokun was no longer in command, for the orders of another man set the plunderers to work righting some of the mess they had made. He bent on one knee by the van under which they had rolled Malec's body and made a slow, careful study of their victim. Then, by his orders, the others pulled forth the Thassa and carried him off into the brush.

Beside me I felt Simmle's tense muscles, I heard her almost soundless growl.

"Not yet," I thought to her, "not yet—"

Whether I could hold her, I did not know. But I was considering our plight. Maelen had gone to Yrjar and had said that time was short. She would speed in both going and returning. And from present signs the outlaws were not planning to leave the camp soon.

Instead they were fast restoring to the vans all they had dragged out of them, pitching in the plundered containers, but getting them out of sight. Another man was going around among the empty cages, not only righting them in their original positions, but even latching their doors. When they had done, the officer looked around and nodded. As far as I could see, they were setting up the camp to look undisturbed.

This could mean only one thing. They believed that in Malec they had not gotten all of the Thassa, and they were setting a trap for the others. Did they know of Maelen? Had they perhaps trailed her the day before, and waited now to seize her?

I tested the air. Many of those scents I knew. If the little people had fled, none had gone far. Already my nose located perhaps ten or twelve within a short distance of the place where Simmle and I crouched. I tried to open my mind to them and suffered a slight shock. Not only were the animals all there, but they were united in purpose as I could not think normal beasts of such diverse species could be. Flight was not in their minds, but battle was.

"No!" I struggled to deny that thought from mind to mind. But they withstood me. I was not Maelen or Malec, or any leader they acknowledged.

"Not now!" I tried to change, but I despaired of getting through to them. In the daylight, with the men below armed and alert, the furred army would have very little chance. "Maelen—"

In my mind I built up a picture of Maelen as I had seen her in her power, all ruby and silver, directing her little people on the stage. "Maelen!" I thought at them. "Remember Maelen!"

Simmle whined very, very softly—she remembered. But the others, could I reach them so? I almost shut out the world of sight, sound, smell, held only to the world of the mind, picturing Maelen, trying in turn to learn their response to that picture.

"Maelen!"

They were responding! I tamped down relief and excitement as I sensed that response, concentrated on what I must give them now.

"Maelen comes—"

Upsurge of excitement.

"Not yet—" I hastened to repair what might have been a fatal move. "But soon—soon—"

Some questioning now.

"Soon. Below—they wait for Maelen—" I was fumbling, trying hard, conscious that I might make a mistake which would send them in the very direction they must not go.

Anger now, rising hotly.

"We must find Maelen, before she comes!" I built up as best I could a mental picture of her as I had last seen her—but this time riding toward the camp, not away. "Find Maelen before she comes."

It was like a sea wave rippling downslope as that thought flooded from one small mind to the next. Then I knew they were moving out, not toward the camp and the enemy below, but to circle wide of that danger spot and head into the plains westward.

I lay where I was, continuing to watch the camp. Though I had no experience of warfare, I believed I was interpreting the enemy action aright. Osokun had been taken into Maelen's van, his nurse and guard stowing away there with him. The rest of the men hid in the vans or under them, save for one who was busy watering and feeding the kasi. One other, after conferring with the officer, disappeared westward, a scout I thought.

Now I spoke to Simmle. "Stay, watch."

Her lips wrinkled back from her fangs.

"Stay—watch—"

Her first objection faded, she growled.

"Not fight, watch—Maelen comes."

Her agreement was blurred, not the sharp return *I* would have received from Maelen, Malec, or a human. I could only hope that she would remain in the same humor while I was gone.

The scout was my present objective. I crept out of cover, needing to make a wide detour around the camp. Surely those in hiding there must have been puzzled as to what had happened to the vanished animals. They would be on the lookout for four-footed as well as two-footed travelers.

I had not seen any hounds with the outlaw band, and out in the open country I believed that none of us need fear any man unless we foolishly courted detection. So when there was a goodly slice of woodland between me and the camp, I dashed on at the pace which came natural to this long-legged body, and cut west. It was my intention to work back toward the hills, crisscrossing the way any scout must come, taking him unawares and far enough from the others to hide the deed.

Twice my path crossed that of others of Maelen's band and each time I asked concerning the scout, only to receive negative answers. But I lingered long enough to impress upon them the urgent need for secrecy until they could find their mistress.

It had been almost noon when Malec had been struck down. With the best of success, I did not believe we could expect Maelen to return before two days passed. And I hoped those setting the trap in camp would grow discouraged before the end of that time. The strategy I had used to take the animals out of danger would be successful, unless they lost patience and returned.

Taking out the scout might be profitable in two ways, I reflected, as I continued my personal search. If their man did not return, then they might either send someone to look for him—affording another prey—or else they would conclude they were in danger and retreat.

I came down to the river and there I saw the traces of how they had come upon us, for the signs of their riding were there. Drinking my fill, I pried one of the under-stone dwellers loose from his hole and snapped him up. There was no time for a true hunt, and food was fuel which the body must have.

Twilight closed in as I crossed and recrossed, running by scent as well as by eyes and ears. The passing of the enemy troop was easy to pick up though it was hours old. But why I found no trace of the scout began to worry me.

Then I remembered that one scent among all those others occurred again and again—that of a kas. I had dismissed it as a trace of the first party, yet sometimes it was so strong as to seem fresh, and a whiff of it brought me now to a closer investigation. A patch of soft soil gave me a mark needing explanation. It smelled strongly of kas, but the print left there was of no kas hoof, instead of a shapeless splotch which bore no resemblance to any animal track I had seen.

I put my nose well down into the depression, drawing a deep breath into my lungs. Kas, so strong that it almost entirely hid all else. But under the kas was another scent, and beside that yet another. I crouched low and sniffed again. Hunter's wiles I did know as my man body would not have. There was kas, as strong as a stench, and under it some herb, and inside still—man. Suppose a man, seeking to elude those to whom scent was a powerful aid, would rub himself with an herb to deaden his natural odor, and then put on an outer covering steeped in kas? That could be the answer to my riddle and it was one I accepted. But to follow this kas—

Still doubting my ability to use barsk instincts, I went on. Perhaps the rest of our company had been befooled so. Back there Osokun, or the officer now in his place as leader, had a clever mind, and was using it to counter just what I had been doing.

Kas—I began to run the trail from that unclear footprint. It was strong, rankly so, but I had to puzzle out other odors from time to time, not daring to run on kas trace alone, for now and then it crossed early traces of the same beasts, perhaps the outlaw mounts.

The dusk gathered in. Still the kas trail pointed west, now in more open country where there was very little cover, and where any man, pausing to scout his back trail, could see a follower, I sat down upon my haunches, sending out a mental call—

My first answer came from the north. I recognized the hard-to-hold, in-and-out pattern of either Borda or Vors.

"One smells kas, is not. Where?" I attempted to send my message.

"No kas?" it was inquiry.

"Kas smell but not kas," I repeated.

"No—" That reply was emphatic.

Again I sent my call and had faint answer. "Kas but not kas?"

"Kas—yes—"

I turned south. Perhaps I was on a false trail, but I must check it. But I was to discover that he whom I hunted was a master at this game. For I soon came upon the reek of kas strong and clear again.

And my satisfaction at finding it was so great that I ran swiftly into the growing dark, trailing by nose, which was just what my quarry expected. I had drawn a deep breath before I realized my danger.

Smarting fire filled my nose, and the shock was so great I leaped straight up into the air, then pushed my nostrils into stubble and sand, pawing at my tormented flesh. The vile smell so clogged my whole head that my eyes teared.

I dragged myself across the ground, pushing my nose into the earth, scraping at it until my blunted nails tore the skin. I could smell nothing except the stink which now seemed a part of my own flesh. And that made me so sick that I rolled over and over, rubbing first one side of my head and then the other against the ground, until I was forced to raise myself and vomit.

There was a period until my wits began to work again. Either he who I trailed suspected he was being tracked, or else he had just used a general precaution. But he had flooded his path with some sickening liquid which had deadened my very important sense of smell. My eyes still watered and the tingling in my nose was a torment. But I had eyes and ears, and perhaps the aid of others.

Again I sent out a call. There were three answers from nearby.

"Kas—not kas—man—evil smell—"

Prompt agreement from all three, apparently the smell had reached them. But from farther off, Borba:

"Man comes—"

Once more I rubbed my head against the earth. My eyes watered, but not so much I could not see. And this night was made for barsk activity, no shadow was as dense for me as it was for human eyes. I stood behind a rock, listening, watched, put aside the misery in my nose. Undoubtedly a real barsk or other animal would have been thrown off by that weapon. It was the misfortune of Osokun's scout that he did not now come to face a true barsk.

He moved slowly, and he was not a true man outline at all, rather a shapeless bulk, his kas-hide disguise hanging loosely about him. I readied myself—

Now and then he paused for long moments, probably trying to pick out some landmark.

Perhaps a barsk attacks with sound. I did not as I flashed forward, striking at that portion of the approaching rounded shape which I believed to be my best target. And cunning as he had proven himself to be, I took him by surprise.

Chapter 14

I made the kill after the pattern Simmle had set me, then lay back panting on the ground beside the thing which had so recently breathed, walked, and been a man. Dimly I wondered that I did not feel the burden of my deed—it was as if in this I was far more barsk than man. That I had killed was a fact, but one which did not move me. We of the Traders use weapons in defense, but we do not carry war with us, preferring ever to find a way around a difficulty. I had seen men die before I planeted on Yiktor, but mainly from natural causes and accidents. And, when it had been otherwise, it had always happened in quarrels among aliens or strangers which were of no concern to the Traders, nor which involved any close to me.

But in this killing I was involved as perhaps those of my blood had not been involved for eons of time. Yet I did not care, save that I was in a manner satisfied with a job ably done. And there stirred in me a small fear that perhaps the longer I remained a beast, the stronger would the animal become, until there would run only Jorth on four feet, and he who walked on two would vanish.

This was no time to let fear stir me from what must be done, however, and I resolutely pushed aside that disturbing thought, to consider what action lay immediately before me. Should I leave this scout where he was, to be found by those who might come seeking him? Or would it be more baffling, and therefore upsetting to them, to have him vanish utterly?

"Dead—dead!" Out of the bushes came one of the long-nosed, big-eared animals I had last seen dancing to the drums on Maelen's stage at the fair, and mounted on its back was one of the ring-tailed riders. They both peered down at the scout and from them came a wave of satisfaction.

"Dead," I agreed and licked my paws, rubbing my nose still clogged by that choking stench.

The big-eared beast sniffed at the body and signaled repulsion before it retreated. I looked at the remains and decided to leave all as it was. The ground where we had struggled was churned by many prints, and regarding those I had a new idea.

"Make foot marks," I beamed at the two who had joined me. I set my forepaws deliberately where the soil was softest, to leave a readable print. Both creatures looked at me in surprise, and their query was open to read.

"Leave signs—all against men," I tried. I could never be sure how well they understood. Perhaps it was only when my suggestions matched their own wishes that they would obey. But I was very doubtful concerning ideas.

They both stared down at the earth where I had made those signature prints. Then the smaller one jumped from the back of his fellow and planted both forepaws, the digits well spread, directly beside the marks I left. He stood up on hind legs to view the result, his head slightly on one side. The prints looked like those of small human hands.

The big-eared one shambled over and walked back and forth, his long-toed feet making a web pattern, before the smaller one remounted. I examined the ground. Now let those others find the scout. The record about him would give them a few thoughts. Three creatures of very different species looked to have shared the pulling down of the man. If the enemy could be led to believe that all the animals from the camp had turned against them, we could make them look twice at every lurking place behind bush or tree, have them hear attack in every leaf rustle. Of their own accord no such dissimilar company of beasts would combine against a common foe; it was not their nature. But the Thassa had powers which the plainsmen already held in awe. The outlaws had been desperate enough to kill Malec. Perhaps now they would believe that not only natural but supernatural powers were allied against them. And for men already on the run, such knowledge would give a whip toward complete breakdown.

We left together, making for a space no effort to hide our going, but rather leaving plain tracks of three who traveled in company. After a time we began to conceal our trail, so that to any human tracker it would seem we had vanished into thin air.

Dawn found us in a dell where a spring bubbled. There were rocks among which we sheltered. My companions dozed, as did I, but we could wake in an instant to anything which was not ordinary. We were well to the east of the camp and, as nearly as I could tell, somewhere along the way Maelen must use on her return. But how soon we might expect her I did not know. My nose was still clogged, and with that foul odor ever about me, I could not test any breeze.

It was an odd day—the sun was cloud veiled, but there was no hint of rain, rather a misty hiding of the horizon. There was the feeling that beyond the limit of one's sight was a significant and perhaps dangerous shifting, that one could not depend upon what was reported by one's eyes. And I wished at that moment that at least one of our company was equipped with wings, that we could have a spy whose vision of the country would be wider and better than our own.

But if there had ever been any birds or flying creatures among the Thassa little people, I had never seen them. So our sight was limited. What did happen during the day was an increasing contact with the rest of the scattered company. They linked minds at times so that fragmentary reports sped along a line wide enough, I hoped, to cover the whole front Maelen might cross in her return to the hills.

There were paired combinations such as the two who shared my refuge in the dell, the big eared animals and their riders. Apparently these partnerships did not exist only on the stage, but held continually. Borba and Vors, Tantacka, the ones who had drummed and some I could not identify, all reported. Simmle must have remained at the camp as I had asked, for I did not pick up any answer from her.

We did not venture further into the plains. It was better to reserve our strength by waiting for Maelen. I discovered during that day, as I tried to hold and read those minds, that the little people did not equate the Thassa with the plainsmen, whom they looked upon as natural enemies to be avoided and regarded with suspicion and wariness. The Thassa, however, were accepted wholeheartedly as kin and trustworthy companions. I remembered what Maelen and Malec had said—that the Thassa who would be Singers dwelt as animals for a space. What form had Maelen worn when she had so run the hills? Had she been one with Vors, or Simmle, or these with whom I now companied? Did one have a choice or was one assigned? Or was it chance, as it had been with me because the barsk ailed and was available?

Twice during the day I roved out into the open country as stealthily as I could, seeking for any traveler. And on my second trip I sighted a mounted company heading toward the hills. But they were a troop riding under some lord's banner, armed men mustering perhaps—and they were some distance to the south. I knew they would sight none of us.

Impatience came with nightfall. We sought food, prowling up and down the line we had assigned ourselves. I found my luck was such as to keep my belly empty, for I could not scent any game. But water was not lacking and I learned that to go hungry does not cripple one.

There came the middle part of the night and with it a ripple of message. "One comes!"

Only one person, I thought, could awaken that response in those with whom I shared this vigil.

"Maelen!" I sent an imperative mind-call into the night.

"Coming." It was dull, a whisper, if such communication can be so judged.

"Maelen." In contrast my sending was a wordless shout. "Trouble—take care, wait—let us know where you are."

"Here—" Louder, a beacon to which we gathered from brush and grass.

She sat there in the moonlight on her hard-ridden kas. In contrast to the clouded day, the night was clear and the Three Rings burned in a glory of light. Her cloak was about her shoulders, the hood pulled over her head so that we could see no woman, only a dark figure on a stumbling mount. I ran into the open with my ground-covering leaps.

"Maelen—trouble!"

"What?" Again her send was a whisper, tired, as if strength had ebbed from her and she kept going by will alone. Now fear nipped at me, and I sped to her.

"Maelen, what is wrong? Have you been harmed?"

"No, but what has passed?" Her question was stronger, her body straightened.

"Osokun's men raided the camp."

"Malec? The little people?"

"Malec"—I hesitated and could find no way to tell it better—"is dead. The others are with me here. We have been waiting for you. They have tried to make the camp into a trap for us."

"So!" The weariness had gone out of her. She made of that word the whistle of a whip lash. "How many of them?"

"Perhaps twelve. Osokun is wounded, another has taken command."

For me anger has always been a hot and burning thing, but the wave of emotion which washed from her to touch me now was cold, very cold and deadly. Also it was very deep, and I flinched as I might have dodged a blow from her hand.

Moonlight became silver sparks as it struck the wand she held out. The light appeared to drip from that rod, until it held my eyes, made me dizzy. And she sang, first in a low murmur, but the words, the notes entered into one, became a tingling along the veins, nerves, muscles; and then louder and louder, to fill one's head, driving out all save a will and purpose that caught us up and welded us all into a single weapon which fitted her hand as perhaps no sword has ever suited the plainsman who bore it.

I saw that silver wand move and I marched in obedience to it, with all the others of that furred company, as Maelen and her sword-sworn took the field. Of that journey back to the hills I do not now remember anything; for, as those with me, I was filled with a purpose which crowded out all else, save the necessity for satisfying the hunger that Maelen's singing had set in me. And the answer to the hunger was blood.

There came a moment when we lay in hiding and looked down upon the camp. To our eyes this was deserted save by the kasi that stamped and nickered at their lines. But our other sense made it plain that those we hunted were still there.

Again Maelen sang, or else the echo of her earlier song moved in me. She got to her feet and started down the slope toward the vans. Back and forth before her she moved her wand. It had been burning silver in the moonlight. Now, though it was day, yet still it was bright, dripping fire from its tip.

I heard a shout from the camp. And then we were in upon them.

These were men used to dealing with animals they considered inferior beings, to be hunted, slain, tamed. But animals that had no fear of man, who combined for the slaying of men—these were so opposed to nature as our enemies had always known it that the very strangeness of our attack unnerved them in the beginning. Always Maelen sang. In us her song was a willing, a sending—what it might have been to the outlaws, I do not know. But I remember two men at least who dropped their weapons and rolled upon the ground, mouthing senseless cries, trying to cover their ears with empty hands. And such were easily dealt with. We were not all lucky, we could not be, but we did not know that until the singing ended and we stood in a camp we had taken at cost.

I was as one awakened from a vivid, frightening dream. I saw the dead, and one part of me knew what we had done. But another awakened from sleep and pushed aside such memories. Maelen stood there, not surveying the bodies, but rather staring straight ahead, as if she dared not look upon the havoc spread around her.

Her hands hung limply at her sides and in one of them was the wand. But it no longer shimmered with life; it was dull and dead, while her pale face was ashen gray, her eyes turned inward.

I heard a whimpering cry and toward her came Simmle, dragging herself along the ground, a great wound welling blood across her hindquarters. Then I heard other cries and whines as those who had battled, and were still living, tried to reach their mistress. But she did not look at them, only stared ahead.

"Maelen!"

Fear welled in my mind. Was it only a husk of womankind, or Thassa-kind, who stood there unheeding?

"Maelen!" I put into that mental cry all the strength I could summon.

Simmle whimpered. She had pulled herself to Maelen's feet, stretched out her head to rest it upon a dusty boot.

"Maelen!"

She stirred, almost reluctantly, as if she had no wish to return from that place of nothingness which had held her. Her fingers loosened and the wand fell from her grasp, rolled into the mud of blood and dust, a dead thing. Then her eyes came alive as she looked upon Simmle.

With a cry as desolate as any uttered by her animals, she knelt and laid her hand on the venzese's head. And I knew that she was safely back with us again. For a time then it was a matter of tending the wounded, seeing what could be done for what was left of the company. There were no outlaws left alive, but also too many of the little people were gone.

I dragged a bucket down to the river and filled it with water, brought it back once, twice, for Maelen's use while she wrought with her simples and herbs for the easing of the wounded. And on the third such trip my nose, recovering at last from the assault by stench, told me of danger—man scent, strong, recent, going off into the bushes. I put down the bucket and went to nose out that trail, though I had not gone far before the summons came via mind-touch for my return.

With a nagging suspicion that I had better follow that trail and soon, I returned. Someone had escaped the battle by the vans, and with a crossbow even one man could lie upslope and pick us off at his ease. Full of this I ran back to camp and Maelen, but before I could report my find she spoke:

"There is that I must tell you—"

"Maelen, there were—" I began to interrupt.

Almost imperiously she refused to listen, continued. "Krip Vorlund, I bring ill news from Yrjar."

For the first time in hours I returned to the plight of Krip Vorlund. And I was startled by the wrench needed to bring my thoughts back from Jorth's concerns to Krip's.

"The captain of the *Lydis* appealed to fair law when you were taken by Osokun's men. One of your shipmates was struck down and left for dead, but recovered to tell of what happened, identified the clan pattern he saw. Then it was a matter for the Overjustice, and a party went under claim-banner to Oskold's, where they found your body. They took it back to Yrjar, believing Osokun's treatment had broken your mind. The medico of the *Lydis* said that only off-world could they find the proper aid. Thus—" She paused, eyes meeting mine. Yet in hers there was nothing, for they looked beyond me, seeking something more than Krip Vorlund, or Jorth. "Thus," she began again, "the *Lydis* went from Yiktor with your body on board. This is all I could learn, for there are strange troubles abroad in the city."

Inside me somehow I knew she spoke the truth. For a long moment or so it had no meaning, nor did I listen to what else she was saying—it was as if she spoke some other language.

No body! The thought began to beat inside my head, growing louder and louder, until I could have screamed with the rhythm of the thumping. But as yet it was only a beating, not something I understood. Now she no longer looked into any far distance, but to me. And she tried, I believe, to reach through the beating to my mind. Only nothing she said meant anything. I was not Krip Vorlund, I would never be again—I was Jorth—

I heard sounds, I saw Maelen through a scarlet haze, her eyes wide, her lips moving. Her commands were far away, muffled by that beating. I was Jorth, I was death—I would hunt—

Then I was on the trail I had found in the bushes by the river. Hot and rich, the scent filled my nose. Kill—but to kill one must live a little longer. Be not too reckless, a barsk was cunning, a barsk was—

A beast with centuries of beast craft to call upon in mind. Let Jorth be entire. I withdrew, skulked apart as the remnants of what had once been a man, watching the going of the beast on the age-old business of the hunt. Three different scents I nosed out, one from the other. No kasi—these men fled afoot. And around one hung a sickliness which told of injury. Three, heading back into the hills.

They would be watching for a tracker, yes. This was a matter in which to use all skill. Nose here, nose there, watch ahead for aught which could be an ambush. Perhaps the cunning of man was still joined with that of the beast.

It would seem that they could not climb the steeper slopes. Perhaps the hurt one was too great a burden, for the trail followed the easiest footing. I found once where they had paused and there was a blood-stained rag I nosed disdainfully. But they kept doggedly on the march, heading toward the border of Oskold's land. Now I searched for other scents—those of the invaders I had seen in these hills. I was not of any mind to be robbed of my prey.

And ever there was a plucking at my mind from behind, though I held a barrier against that, refusing to open to call. I was Jorth and Jorth hunted, that was all that was real—just as perhaps Jorth would cease to be before another day. But if Jorth did so die, it would not be alone.

Up and up. I came to a place where two saplings had been hacked from their roots, and thereafter I followed only two sets of tracks, not three. Two carried the third, and their pace was much slower.

Now I left the trail, for we entered a gully between two sharply slanted rises, and I believed those I trailed would stay in the bottom of that cut. But I did not go at a blind gallop, rather did I slip from one cover to the next. Nor did I bury my nose on any close scent, remembering the trick the scout had played upon me.

Night came and still I caught no sight of them. I marveled a little at their ability to keep ahead, burdened as they were—unless they had left the camp before, not during, our attack, and so had more of a start than I had judged. The moon was with me, throwing into sharp relief the landscape, veiling part in shadows which cloaked my advance.

Then I saw them. The two on their feet leaned against a large rock outcrop. Even as I sighted them, one slid down that support and sat, his head drooping on his chest, his hands falling limply between his outstretched legs. The other breathed in great gasps, but kept on his feet. While on a rude stretcher lay the third, and from him came small whistling moans.

Two were done, I decided, but that other who still stood—him I watched carefully. He moved at last, fell to his knees, and brought forth a small flask he held to the mouth of the man on the stretcher. But that one flung up his arm and struck outward, uttering a harsh, excited cry. The flask hit the boulder and burst, leaving a dark trickle on the rock. He who had held it gave a hoarse grunt, tried to reach the fragments, then raised his head and looked about wildly as if hunting something in the wilderness about them to relieve his misery.

All this time the man who sat had not moved. But now he shook his head slowly from side to side as if trying to clear it of some clouding mist. Then he pulled back to his feet, bracing himself against the rock. The moonlight fell now across his face, and I saw that he was the one who had guarded Osokun's rear when he and his companion had brought their wounded lord into the Thassa camp. I had not wondered about the identity of the three I had followed; somehow I had known from the first whom I would find here. Nor did it astonish me to see that I knew this one from an even earlier time, when he had done his lord's will in the narrow cell of the border fort.

Krip Vorlund—who was Krip Vorlund—what call had he on Jorth the barsk for vengeance? It did not matter. These were my kill—

So much did I consider them my prey that I came into the open without any more use of cunning, and gave a war cry in the deep-chested growl of my kind. He that lay upon the stretcher would be helpless. The other two—let them fight for their lives. It was better that way.

I sprang for the man now standing. I do not think his fatigue-dulled mind and ears had really carried the message of my presence before my weight struck him full in the chest, crashed him to the ground, my fangs aiming true.

Easy—easy prey!

I snapped and tore, then was up, facing the other. He had steel, bright and clear in the moonlight, waiting in his hand as he half crouched between me and the stretcher. He shouted—battle cries? Calls for assistance? What did it matter—they were not for my ears and would matter to no one.

But the blade did, and we wove a pattern between us like the intricate design of some formal dance. I made him ever turn and twist and in the end that was my advantage, since his fatigue deadened his limbs with chain weights. At last my jaws closed upon the wrist of his sword hand. And that was the beginning of a swift end.

Panting from that dance of death, I turned upon the stretcher. He who had been carried on it was sitting up. Perhaps fear had overridden his weakness of body for those seconds, giving him a return of energy. I saw his hand move, a flash of light spun through the air, then came a blow between neck and shoulder as the knife bit hard and deep. But since he had not killed me outright, he had not saved himself.

Thus it was that I lay at last among my dead, and thought that here, too, died Jorth the barsk, who had once been partly a man. This was a good ending for one who had no hope of returning along the strange path leading to this time and place.

Chapter 15

Scales of Molaster. Days ago—nights and moons, days and suns, since I started on that strange path to adjust the scales of Molaster. But now they were as unbalanced as ever, and instead of doing good my efforts had wrought evil; I marveled dully that so much ill could be rooted in hope of good. I thought that Molaster was gone from my life, and that I was one who was lost and drifting on a tide I could not breast. Perhaps I had believed too much in myself and my own powers, and this was my punishment.

I stood in the camp among the dead, the enemy and my own little ones. And I looked about me, knowing that all this had sprung in part from my own acts, for which I must be the first to answer. Perhaps it is true, as some argue, that we are but the play pieces of great forces and are moved hither and thither for purpose not of our reckoning, certainly not of our desires. But, though such a belief is quieting to one's heart, putting aside guilt, yet it is not to be held by one who has known the discipline of a Singer. Thus did I refuse it now.

My spirit wept for my little people, and for Malec, though I knew that the White Road is not to be regretted for those we hold in close fellowship. It is sometimes far harder to remain in this life than to pass through the gate and into the way which leads elsewhere. We cannot allow ourselves to mourn for those who are gone; they have but discarded the old dress to put on a new.

So, too, for my little people. But those who still suffered, ah, for them did I also feel pain, fever, misery. And for another must I also bear the burden of life—he who had fled from the camp with such a threat riding him as to drive any man to death. Him I must find, if I could, for to him was I deeply in debt.

Also did I suspect that which was even worse, that my inner desires had willed just such an ending. And, if such powerful wishes be beamed, then they influence action to come. Although I had not sung this into being, could I be sure that I had not unconsciously twisted the future to serve my heart's longing? I knew that I had one escape to offer the man who had been Krip Vorlund from off-world, and, if he agreed, then—

I spoke to my little people soothingly, telling them what must be done. And I sang over my rod of office, though it was still day and not night, for I could not wait for dark. Then I set out food and drink for those who had been my companions for so long. Afterward I sat beside Simmle, telling her where I must go and why. The first streamers of sunset were in the sky when I went into the wilderness.

Had it not been for the power of my wand, I would not have kept to the trail. But when Krip Vorlund had entered into Jorth's body, the rod had wrought it, and it would seek him out for me as long as he walked the earth of Yiktor. I carried with me a shoulder sack of supplies, for I did not know how long I must journey, though a feeling in me said it could not be far.

Deliberately I refrained from trying to reach him by thought. Either he would shut his mind tight against me now, or else such a sending might distract him in a moment when he needed all his cunning for his own salvation. This much I knew—he had not run blindly away from the truth, but rather he had gone to seek battle. It might well be that he did not mean to survive such an encounter.

We have always known that when we take on the forms of the little people, we also take on a measure of their natures. And when a man was in the state of mind Krip Vorlund was, he would react to the most savage in his new form. Of all the animals the barsk was the most cunning, intelligent, and fierce, those three qualities having kept its species so long apart from all other life on Yiktor. Only because the beast had been so disordered by its treatment had I been able to work with it before the coming of Krip Vorlund to my upland camp.

Thus I could believe that the creature I now sought was for a time a savage hunter. And whomever it trailed must be some fugitive from Osokun's band. Osokun's body had not been found with the slain, perhaps he was the bait now. And with him, how many others? I had not known the number of raiders. While all we had surprised in camp were now dead, there could be more.

On toward the borders of Oskold's holding that trail led. Night came and with it the moon, which is ever favorable to the Thassa. Now I sang—not words to draw power from about me, but an inner questioning that kept the rod steadily pointing. And I did not tire, for through the rod flowed what fed my spirit.

When one sings one does not think, except for the purpose of shaping the notes. So I went with only one need in me—to find him who had been lost. For if Molaster favored me in even a very, very small way, there might yet come good from all this pain and ill.

The ground was rising, though all about me was in shadow. No longer was I fully of the world of which it was a stable part. Moon and shadow warred, first one and then the other seizing a strip of ground. I went swiftly, for the taking of one step and then the other does not matter to one who walks by song and rod.

Thus I came in the gray of dawn into a valley where death was a rank odor in the air, a feeling to daunt the spirit. I saw the bodies of three men. Two I had not looked upon before to my remembrance, but the third was Osokun. And as I approached where he lay on a rude stretcher as if he had been so borne to this place, I saw him whose need had drawn me here.

I thought-quested, believing that I might find the silence of body death. But, no! Flickering, yes, but still trapped was the spirit! By so little was I in time.

Thrusting my rod into the stained soil, I gave a flash of thanks to Molaster, and then set about looking for wounds on that red fur, so close to the color of the blood I feared to see.

There was only one which mattered. Driven deep was a short belt-sword which still stood in the wound. I began to work as I never had before. With my little ones the need had been rooted in love and pity, but now I must save a spirit, lest the last chance for either of us be lost. And I fought off death with my two hands, my knowledge, and the power of song.

We do not usually fight death to the last barricade. It is not meet among the Thassa to be so jealous of another's freedom as to deny him admittance to the White Road when he is already a step or two along it. To draw back the wayfarer is to blight his future. But this was a matter which was not for the Thassa to decide. And I have yet to find another race which shares our acceptance of the Great Law in the same way. To some species, I know, death was total extinction by their belief, and so they regarded it with horror which darkened most of their lives. I did not know how Krip Vorlund looked upon death. But I believed that he had a right to make his choice, was he to be numbered among those who saw death as an enemy rather than a gate. Thus I wrought as I would not have for one of my own.

The spirit was in him, but how long it would remain, or I could hold it, I dared not guess. In the hours of early morning I sang again, this time aloud, and drawing upon all the power I could summon. And under my hand that faintly beating heart grew, so I dared to believe, a thread more strong. Finally I picked up that limp body. It was lighter than I had feared, and I felt the bones under the skin, as if for a long time Jorth had been on short rations.

Back we went through the hills and all that way I sang, and held, and sang, fighting the battle to keep the one I held to the ways of earth. When we came to the camp, I found my little ones glad to see me, breaking in upon my concentration with their cries, their thoughts. I laid Jorth down beside Simmle. She still lived, which I had not thought possible. I tended her wound again, but looking upon it I knew that life such as would be left to her would not be enough.

Then I took her head between my two hands as we had often sat. And I asked her the Question. For a long moment we sat so, and then she gave me the Answer. Around us the rest of the company whimpered and cried a little. For the little ones are not Thassa, and it takes great courage for them to make such an Answer, their belief not being ours.

Now I made memories for Simmle, all the best ones, and let her wander in them, while all the pain of her body was gone. And she was happy and content. When she was most happy and content I gave release according to the Answer. But in me a sword was thrust, for memory is sour as well as sweet, and this one added more to my burden.

I wrapped the husk of Simmle, the part which was no longer of any matter to us, certainly not to her who was free. And I put it among the rocks. Jorth slept deep in that place where, if there was to be any healing, it could begin. And of the others none were so hurt they would not mend.

Then I looked about the camp, knowing that I must be off to find what assistance I could, and that speedily. For where Osokun had come others might follow. Having broken my fast and that of my little people, I fell to the labor of preparing to move out.

One of the vans I must abandon and from that I brought what was most needed. Those who had despoiled our belongings had taken much, but I loaded in what was left of food and healing supplies. My little peoples' cages I set in two of the vans, making comfortable those riding in them. I put Jorth on an open pad of mats just behind the seat in the first of the vans. Then I ordered the kasi to move out, one van following the other, for those behind needed no driver; they would come in my wake.

The sun was paler, for the season was close to winter. To each part of the year its own magic. Some judge autumn a time for sorrow, for so much which is alive in the warmth seems then to die and vanish from the earth, and the coming of winter is dreaded. But each season has its own life and energies, and none can say that this or that one is not good because it fails in comparison in some parts with the others.

To the Thassa winter is a time of rest, of gathering in—both physically in clan groups and inwardly in spirit, a time of judgment and study. And this year I, Maelen, might face the justice of my race in a way not known for generations. But, though autumn faded, it was not yet gone from the land. And though the life spark in Jorth was faint, still it continued to abide.

Twice I saw mounted men ride in bands far off. But if my small train of wagons excited any comment among them, they did not seek me out. Perhaps it was better that we went our way openly by day, for the Thassa were always strange to the plainsmen and known to be wanderers. Whereas a journey by night would have aroused their suspicion.

The kasi, having had a long rest in camp and being well fed and watered, were good for many hours of slow but steady moving, and I intended to press on past the usual limits of a day's journey. I would have to, for time was not my friend but a threatening enemy.

We paused from time to time that I might visit my little people and look to those who were hurt. What I missed most now was Simmle's presence beside me. She had been more to me than any of the others—because we were linked by that old exchange, having once been paired body to body, mind to mind. For that relationship there are no real words to explain. To me there would never be another like unto her. If I had been the one to go before, she would have felt the same emptiness.

I wondered, whenever I turned to look upon Jorth, whether, if his body would be his once again and the barsk spirit returned to its rightful envelope, this off-worlder would find himself united to other life forms in a fashion such as no one of his race or species ever had been before.

We moved on, back up along the Valley trail. Now I thought of the Old Ones. What had come of the message Malec and I had sent from Yrjar? It had never been answered, he had told me that. There would come a time, which I could not and would not escape, when I must go before the assembly and speak of all I had done, give the reasons thereto. But I did not believe I had an excuse they would deem strong enough to stand against the weight of their anger.

I shut out such musings from my mind, for dark thinking attracts only ill fortune. Instead I built what I could for good by singing, choosing a growing song, as growing is close-kin to healing and what may root one is also part of the other. As the kasi pulled steadily toward Yim-Sin, I sang for both Jorth and my little people. In such singing all energy is bound into a single will-wish and all else slips away, as is needful.

On we rolled. Night came and I saw in the dark the glow of fire against the sky, marking some violence of man to man. Oskold's land lay behind the hills; we were now in the plains. Either he had carried war against the invaders, or the first quarrel had spread, involving many more. And I thought of the rumors I had heard in Yrjar that off-worlders meddled in the wrangling of lords, and that the *Lydis* had really gone off-world to escape some danger here.

In times of war among the plainsmen, the Thassa follow ever the old rule, drawing back into the high country and the safe places. So I thought other wagons would be moving through this night. But I did not try to use mind-touch to learn if that were so. I sang, nursing a small flicker of life, healing where healing was needful.

Perhaps because we moved under the Moon of Three Rings the singing held more power than ever before. I knew this was true as I turned on my seat and used the rod, drawing in the air above the skin-and-bones body of the barsk, sending strokes up and down without touching hide or hair, changing all power into one use. My wrist grew tired, my mouth dry, my throat sore.

I put aside the rod and leaned over. What had been a flicker of life now held steady. I was too tired to give thanks, save wordlessly, but now I knew that this lost one would live. And with returning life must surely come acceptance of what I had to offer.

We paused beside the turn into the main road to Yim-Sin. I loosed those of my little people who wished to be free and tended the rest. Borba came to me with a message that brought me into the road.

My nose could not pick up the story written there for most of my company. But there was no hiding from the eye that a large mounted party had passed this way. And, while I cannot use my nose to advantage, I can pick other subtleties from the air. Peril and anger had ridden this way and not long before us. To go on would be to face danger.

Yet I had no choice. What did these others hunt ahead? All men knew that this road led only to the Valley, and that was a place to be shunned, save for those whom fate had sent. I could not believe any raiders would voluntarily take this way.

There was only one reason, which hinted at such recklessness and disregard for custom as to suggest madness among the men who chose it. The Valley had two entrances: one from the west, which was the road where we now stood, another from the east, where a trail came through Oskold's land. Had some one of his enemies, moved by insane hatred, decided to lead his men into the Valley and hence again down that other road, striking so into the heart of Oskold's territory?

For a leader so to outrage custom was almost unbelievable. Yet in time of war madness, much is done which afterward wondering men look back upon, unable to believe that such was so. Men driven by an unbridled desire to triumph over their enemies are released into a kind of callosity to do whatever they are moved by happenstance along the way.

I thought of the peace of Umphra and those who had guarded it for years upon untold years, and how they would not believe anyone would trouble them. They would be as insects under the sole of some unheeding giant's boot.

But what I suspected might not be so. And I had no other road. So I tended my company, and we rested until moonrise. This night I needed the moon, it was a draft to lift my spirit, to provide me with energy.

It came, unveiled by any clouds. But the moon was not too bright to hide the splotch of fire above. I looked at that, my lower lip caught between my teeth. For I believed it spurted forth at Yim-Sin. And such red flowering comes only from the plant of war. That which I feared must surely be!

I put the kasi back into harness and took to the road. On its smooth surface we made better time. Time for what? To run into the red ruin of the sacking of Yim-Sin by crazed men? I had my own kind of weapons, but they were not for such battles.

To turn aside from this road would shortly be easy enough. There was a certain point ahead from which I could reach the high country and safety. If all Yiktor had gone mad—then it would be well for those still sane to gather together and keep in safety, letting the rest destroy themselves.

Behind me I heard what my ears had been waiting to report—a sound of feeble movement on the mats. I looked down. His eyes were open, but as yet no sign of intelligence sparked within them. A small new fear pricked me—had Jorth indeed won and the man been done to nothingness? This had sometimes occurred, though it was rare, when a man could not withstand the stress of beast nature.

I used mind-call. "Krip Vorlund!"

I made that as sharp as a summons to arms, with all the skill of such communication that I possessed.

Still those eyes were dull, naught dwelt within them. It was almost as if I now looked at the barsk I had taken from Othelm, an animal so deeply sunk in misery that it had withdrawn from life.

"Krip Vorlund!" Once more I forced that summons into his mind.

His head moved, as if he were trying to avoid some blow. Truly he had retreated, his mind now almost as far from me as his vital force had earlier been.

"Krip Vorlund!" I raised the rod, caught the moonlight on its length, guided that down to strike upon the head of the barsk.

Out of him came a cry of pain and terror, a wailing such as I had never heard from any animal. And my little people answered him in their own ways. He was trying to pull himself up. But I put my hand on his shoulders, being careful not to touch near his wound, and with the weight of that kept him lying flat.

"*You are Krip Vorlund.*" I made of each of those words a crossbow bolt, shooting them into his mind, setting them so firmly they could not be dislodged. "You are a man—a man!"

He was looking at me now, with a beast's eyes right enough, but there was a difference in them. He did not try to answer; left alone he would retreat again. I could not allow that, for I might not be able to draw him into life a second time.

"A man," I repeated. "And while a man lives, lives also the future. I swear to you—" I put the blazing rod between us and saw his gaze go from me to it and then back again, "I swear to you by the power which rests in this—and for me that is an oath binding past either life or death—that all is not yet lost!"

Was he alert enough to accept those words, understand them, and, understanding them, would he believe?

I could do no more in this time and place, the remainder rested solely with him. And what did I know of what moved this off-worlder and would set him on this road or that?

For a long, long moment I feared I had lost, that he understood but rejected belief.

"What remains—?"

His mind-speech was very faint; I could hardly catch it.

"Everything!" I hastened to hold, strengthen our contact.

"And what is everything?"

"For a space a new body—a man's body. So housed you can make your way unchallenged into Yrjar. Then you can either follow your ship into space or find a way to summon it back for you." Would he accept this?

"What body?"

This much encouraged me, his mind-touch was growing stronger. He was no longer rejecting contact with me as he had at first.

"One awaiting us—"

"Where?"

"In the hills." I hoped that I spoke the truth. I must believe that I spoke the truth or all was lost. He stared into my eyes.

"I think—you mean—this—" Again his contact weakened, but not this time by will; rather his body was failing him.

"I do. But you are sore hurt, you must sleep."

More than by my reassurance, I thought he was then ruled by weakness, the need for putting aside any decision or immediate action. He rested his head once more on the mat and closed his eyes as the van trundled on. He slept.

But for me there was no sleep. I could not take into danger with me those other small lives this far linked to mine. Once I had used them, or rather accepted their assistance. Those left must be made safe. I would not look upon another Simmle. When we reached the turnoff into high country, we would come to a parting of the ways. I could set a pattern in kasi minds which would keep them moving at their own speed for a day or two. Then—well—if no Thassa picked up the distress signal I would also loose, they could take to the wilds and a measure of safety. It was the best I could do for them now.

All followed as I had planned. I remained in the light van and sent the other two off by a pattern I impressed on the draft kasi. That would fade in a matter of hours, but the other small device I had triggered would keep them wandering in the general direction of the high country and would alert any Thassa to their aid. They were in their cages, but those were not latched and I left food and drink available.

I watched the vans out of sight and then I returned to my own seat. Jorth still lay in deep sleep. The two kasi pulling us were the best of our company, suited to hard going. I looked up at that fire glow. It was dimmer and there was light in the east. We would move on into the dawn of another day, into what peril, I did not try to guess.

Chapter 16

Like all the Thassa, I have ever loved the heights above the plains, where sometimes the breath clogs in the throat and there is such a dust of both country and man as to thicken the mind and slow thought. I do not know from whence my race came. The past stretches long and long, and is far lost in misty beginnings. Sometimes at in-gatherings we speak idly of this, speculating about this and that. It has been said among us that we are perhaps not even of Yiktor, but born of another world, in our time as new to this planet as the off-worlder riding with me. But if that is so, our coming is now so far behind us that not even any faint legend remains.

While we were still dwellers under roofs, our cities were of the mountains not of the plains, and that is why we made no difficulties over land when the plains dwellers came overseas to settle here. For they sought the lowlands as we the high places.

Now as the van climbed toward Yim-Sin, almost insensibly my heart grew a little lighter, as must any wanderer's coming into a land which welcomes him. Yet this time fear also rode with me. Had Simmle still shared my life, she could have scouted ahead, being my warning eyes and ears.

The sun climbed, but was much hidden by the peaks of the hills and we had neither its full light nor its warmth. I ate and drank as we went, but I no longer sang. For in me the power was much lowered by all the calls I had made upon it during these past few hours, and there might be need ahead for a weapon of some force. The signs of the troop which had preceded us could still be read.

Along the curves of the hills were the terraced vineyards, the leaves on the vines withered and purplish, proving the harvest well past its peak. Down from the crest land came no good wind to rustle through them, rather one carrying the reek of burning. I no longer doubted what was to be found at Yim-Sin.

The smoke still coiled lazily from some heaps of ashes; and from places where the harvest had been stored came oily clouds. I wet a scarf and tied it about nose and throat, but my eyes smarted.

Umphra's temple alone stood unfired. But the great gate hung askew from its hinges and on it were marks of a battering ram. I stopped the van to listen. Very faintly from out of that inner court I heard a muffled plaint, not loud enough for true crying. About me I did not look too closely. Death had walked here and not as a friend. I climbed down from the van and went into that place beyond the broken gate.

It was plain what had happened. Yim-Sin had been taken by surprise, but a handful of her people had managed to reach here, hoping for a sanctuary not to be theirs. I searched for life, for the crying had stopped. And I found it in a child whom I took up in my arms, one who looked upon me vacantly and neither shrank from nor invited my hold.

Bestowing her in the van apart from Jorth, lest intelligence return to her and she be frightened by such a companion, I went again into Umphra's temple.

Senseless had been the slaying and destruction, as if those who had wrought it had been only shells of man with far worse than any human spirit within those shells. But that is how man can be when he thrusts aside all controls upon the kernels of cruelty and evil which dwell within him. I am a Singer, and to win my power I faced many dire trials and tests. I am of the Thassa, a people now pledged to a form of peace. What I saw that day in Yim-Sin was beyond all experience, and I came forth sick and shaking, unable to believe that this had been wrought by any who were still to be termed men.

If Yim-Sin had fared so, then what had happened in the Valley? But the Valley had safeguards, intended to protect, even from themselves, those who dwelt there. Would those safeguards have turned outward to save them from this?

I went back to the van and gave orders to the kasi. Then I took into my arms the girl-child I had found still alive, and to her I sang a small song to give her sleep for a time and open the deep place within her as refuge for her terrified spirit. When I laid her back within the van, Jorth raised his head and looked at us.

"What has happened?"

I gave him the truth of what I had found here and told him that death might now run before us.

"Why? Who?"

"Neither can I tell you. My only guess is that some enemy would come upon Oskold by way of the Valley."

"But I thought that the Valley, its roads, was sacred, untouchable."

"In war the gods are forgotten or outraged. It is often so."

"But would the plainsmen do such a thing just for a chance at a sneak attack upon one lord?" he persisted.

"I have thought that also, but I have no answer. There were fires out on the plains last night. I can only believe that this is not merely an invasion of Oskold's land but a conflict which has spread far more widely, perhaps already laps with fire and blood across the whole land. For what I have seen here there is no sane reason. Outlaws might act so, but there is no outlaw band large enough to take a town—and with Osokun and his men dead, who are the outlaws?"

"But we go on—to the Valley?"

"I have sworn to you an oath," I replied wearily. "What I can do to restore to you something of what has been taken, that I shall do. And the answer is in the Valley."

"You propose to give me Maquad's body?"

I was not surprised at his words. He was not stupid, and the fitting of one thing to another to make the right sum was not difficult. "Yes, if you agree, Maquad's body. In that you can go to Yrjar, I with you. We can tell your tale, your ship may be signaled, they will return."

"Many ifs in that," he commented. "Tell me, Maelen, why should you give me Maquad's body?"

"Because," I said dully, "it is the only one possible."

"No other reason? Not that you wish Maquad to live again?"

"Maquad is gone. Only that which held him has life still—after a dim fashion."

"Then you separate man from body, you Thassa." I did not know just what he was trying to say.

"You are Krip Vorlund," I returned. "Do you feel yourself less Krip Vorlund because you now dwell in another outer casing?"

He was silent, considering this. I hoped it was the right answer to direct his thinking. If he believed the body did not matter as much as that which was within it, then the exchange would not be so hard for him.

"Then to you, your people, it does not really matter what body you wear?"

"Of course it matters! I would be one lacking in wits to declare it otherwise. But we believe that the inner part is far greater than the outer, that it is our true identity; the other only clothing for the eyes and sense. Maquad's outer casing still lives, but that which was Maquad is gone from it and us. I can offer you his former dwelling place so that you can once more be a man—"

"A Thassa!" he corrected me.

"And is that not the same?"

"No!" his denial was sharp. "We are far different. As Jorth I have learned that a residue of the original inhabitant, as you would say, still dwells in this body and that it can influence me. Will it not be the same if I try another switch? Will I not be Krip-Maquad rather than Krip Vorlund?"

"Does barsk or man rule in Jorth?"

"Man, I hope—now—" But his answer was a little hesitant.

"Would not then Krip Vorlund be Krip Vorlund no matter what body he dwells in?"

"But you are not sure—"

"Is anyone," I burst out then, "to be sure of anything in any world under any sun?"

"Except death."

"Is death then a surety for you off-worlders? Do you believe that is just an end and not a beginning?"

"Who can tell?" he made answer. "Perhaps we can not demand any unqualified reply to any question we are moved to ask. So, you offer me a body more akin to my lost one. You say, take this and go to Yrjar, tell your story, and ask for the return of that which is yours. Yet it would seem that we must deal not only with our own affairs, but with a war lying between us and Yrjar."

"Think, Krip Vorlund, have I ever promised you that this would be an easy thing?"

"No," he agreed. "Nor can you either promise me a body—if those we trail now have used the Valley as they used Yim-Sin."

"The Valley has safeguards the village did not. It is able to protect those who dwell there, and it may be there is a good defense against these raiders as well. I have offered you the best I can, Krip Vorlund. No one, man or Thassa, can do more than that."

"Agreed. What will you do with this child?"

"If the Valley is still intact, Umphra will care for her. If not, she goes with us."

For the first time, he appeared to note the loss of the rest of our company, for he asked:

"Where are the animals?"

"I have sent them to where I hope my people will find them. If not, they will be free to roam as they choose."

For a while he was silent, and then he said, "Both our lives have been changed by that walk we took together in the fair of Yrjar. I would not believe this story had I not lived it."

"Stuff for the weaving of a legend," I agreed. "I have heard it said that if you dig far enough into any old tale you will unwrap at least one small kernel of onetime fact."

"Maelen, what was Maquad to you?"

I was off-guard and perhaps he had sensed that. The sudden shot brought the truth from me.

"He was the life companion of my sister by birth, Merlay. When—when he went from us, I thought she might follow. She still turns her face from the fullness of life."

"Tell me, would that alliance be again in effect did Maquad return?" His second demand was as sharp as the first.

"No. You would wear Maquad's body, but you are not Maquad. Looking upon you, however, she might be moved to accept the truth and awake once more from dark to light." There it was, my poor frayed wish spoken into words at last.

"But would your people know I was not as I seemed?" He appeared not to have heard the ending of my speech.

I smiled wryly. "Do not think you can hide your true identity from any Thassa, Krip Vorlund. They would know you at meeting. And, I must tell you this also, they will not approve of what we would do. I defy all our Standing Words when I give to you Maquad's dwelling, even for a short space of time. They cannot prevent that act, but it is one I must answer for in time to come."

"Then why—?"

"Why must I do it? Need you ask that, off-worlder? This tangle is of my snarling, mine must be the unraveling. I am pledged by the strongest oath of my people to see that you have all aid within my power. I cannot tell why this has been so set upon me. But one bears the burdens sent by Molaster, one does not question them."

He asked me no more, and I was glad that he meditated upon his own thoughts. For I was busy in my own mind. I had told him the exact truth. He would wear Maquad's body and he would not be Maquad. But just as the beast influences a little the human indweller, so would the shell of Maquad influence him. And this off-worlder was sensitive with esper power.

Maquad had been a Singer of the second degree. He had been searching for knowledge to lead him higher when he was slain in four-footed guise. The animal of his exchange had been young, not used before, and so it lapsed after a period of violence into a cataleptic state which no mind-send could reach. But the beast portion had not, could not, reach all of the human brain, just as the human could not entirely possess the animal. There was a residue left in Maquad, if not the same Maquad of his memories, or more— Even the Old Ones do not know the full extent of changes so wrought. In all our history there was never a case of a human's return to a human or Thassa body not his own. Suppose, just suppose, that in Maquad's body that residue would awake and influence— I could not be sure, but even a part-Maquad might brighten Merlay's days for a space, draw her back to us again!

I stared out past the kasi and the road, and saw neither animals nor way but only her face and the change which might come to it were Maquad—or part-Maquad—to walk with her for a time! Although if what I longed for did not come, still I would abide by my oath—we would ride to Yrjar and try to change what might be unchangeable.

Also I thought of the Valley and what might be happening there this day. By all signs those who had finished Yim-Sin must have reached there by now, and the time space between us lengthened as we climbed so slowly. We passed the sections where sentries had once stood to ask the business of wayfarers. There were no sentries and I did not pause to seek them. I was not minded to hurry our ascent, to arrive while a battle might still be in progress. The Valley safeguards would make no distinction between friend or foe. And who knew—perhaps some measure of sanity would return to the raiders aloft.

The child slept and perhaps Krip Vorlund did also, for he lay quiet, his head pillowed on a forepaw. Nor did he speak to me again. We made a nooning in the wilderness where only the road broke the land. There water bubbled in a mountain stream and I loosed the kasi to graze and rest.

"No sign yet?" The off-worlder asked when I brought him a bowl of the water.

"None save they came this way. But who they are, or why they do this—" I shook my head.

"Your powers," he commented, "appear to have their limits."

"As all do. You have mind-send. But do you also teleport or the like?"

"No. There are those who can, but I have yet to meet one. Only I had thought that the Thassa—"

"Could perform stranger acts than that? Sometimes, but the site *and* the time must fit the pattern. Given both I might beam-read and get a half view of the future, or rather *a* future."

"Why a future? Do futures change?"

"They do, because they depend upon decisions, and does a man remain always subject to the same thoughts, hour after hour, day after day? What seems right and meaningful at this moment may not be so later. Therefore the future in the broad sense, yes, that can be read. But our relation to the future changes through our need to face this crisis or that. I could tell you the fate of a nation, but not of the individual men of that nation."

"But you might tell the fate of the Valley?"

"Perhaps, given the right time, which I am not. For that is beyond my grasping."

"And soon we may learn for ourselves," he said. "When I first met you in that dell—how long ago was it? I have since lost all numbering of days."

I shook my head. "Days bearing numbers are not the concern of the Thassa. Long ago we ceased to deal with such. We remember what has chanced, but not this day or that."

Had he been man at that moment, I think he might have laughed.

"You are so right, Freesha! Enough has happened to me on Yiktor that days have certainly ceased to count in number. But when I came to your camp fresh from Osokun's fort, I thought I was caught up in some vivid and unpleasant dream. And to that belief I am inclined to return now and then. It would explain what has happened so much more easily than to think that waking I have lived—am living—this."

"I have heard that off-world there are methods of inducing such dreams. Perhaps you have tried such and so are ready for such a belief. But if you have been dreaming, Krip Vorlund, I am awake! Unless I am a part of your dream—"

He ate from my fingers the meat cake I crumbled, then drank from his water bowl. The child stirred and moaned.

"You put her to sleep." That was more statement than question.

"Thus she could not remember, or fear."

I took her up in my arms now and put to her lips a small cup wherein I had mixed water and the juice of healing herbs. In her sleep she drank, and then her head turned on my shoulder and she passed into deeper slumber.

"Maelen, are you wed? Do you have a child?"

I thought suddenly, in all this strange adventure we were sharing neither of us had asked such a question of the other, nor had we cared what had passed before.

"No. I am a Singer. While I sing, I have no life companion. What of you, Krip Vorlund? I had heard that the Traders have families. Is it with you as it is with the Singers, that you can be but one thing at a time?"

"In a manner." He told me of the life of his people, wedded to many stars and not one alone. They had life companions, but only when they had reached a certain rank within their companies. Sometimes a planet woman might accept Trader life for the sake of a man; but that a Trader abandon his ship for any world because of a woman was unthinkable.

"You are like unto the Thassa," I said. "For you, to be firmly rooted in one place is to die. We sweep across the earth of Yiktor and her seas at our will. We have certain places such as your space cities where we gather when there is need. But for the rest—"

"Gypsies."

"What?" I asked.

"A very ancient word. It means a people who live ever traveling. I think there was a nation of such once, very long ago, and worlds away."

"So the Thassa have their like across the void. I spoke once of a ship and my little people, and the visiting of other worlds."

"Such might still be done. But it would cost more tokens than lie even within the temple treasury of Yrjar. And such a ship must be built on another world after much study and experimentation. A dream indeed, Maelen, for no one would have such treasure as to bring it to life."

"What is treasure, Krip Vorlund? Does it not take different forms from world to world?"

"It is what is rare and valuable on each particular planet. Rarity plus beauty in some cases, rarity plus usefulness in others. On Zacon it is knowledge, for the Zacathans look upon learning as their treasure. Bring to them an unknown artifact, a legend, something which hints at a new sentence in the history of the galaxy, and you have brought them treasure.

"On Sargol it is a small green herb, once common on forgotten Terra, utterly irresistible to the Salarki, who would willingly exchange gems for it. And those same stones on another planet—one no longer than the nail of your smallest finger, Maelen—will allow a man to live as a lord of Yiktor for five years or more. On Hasku it is feathers, sprokjan feathers. I can recite you the list of treasures for a quarter of the galaxy, as they pass through our warehouses."

"So, to each world a treasure, and it varies so that what seems a fortune on one planet will on another be worth nothing—or perhaps more?"

He laughed inside his mind and even the barsk jaws fell apart in a faint likeness to a smile.

"Usually less rather than more. Gems—those are best, for gems and things of beauty speak to more than one people and species as worth taking and keeping safe."

"This world wherein such a ship as would carry my little people might be built, what manner of treasure do they there prize?"

"All that is high wealth. They are an inner planet and the men there are satiated with the best of a hundred worlds. What they have to sell, their ships, draw all the treasures they will accept. It would have to be something very rare, perhaps never seen before, or so large an amount of trade credits as would wipe out the contents of half our warehouses."

I laid down the sleeping child, making her comfortable, but setting a barrier between her and the barsk again, so that if she woke she would not see that animal. Then I brought the kasi back to their duty. Once more we traveled the road. But I thought now and then of the nature of treasure and how different worlds rated it. I knew what the off-worlders took off Yiktor and I guessed such cargo passed as ordinary things. We had gems, but they were not such rare objects that off-world traders struggled to buy them. I decided that Yiktor might be termed, in the eyes of such experts, a relatively poor planet.

The Thassa did not, as the plainsman, try to gather portable wealth. When we had more of any one thing than we needed, we left the surplus at one of the ingatherings for those who lacked. Our beast shows brought us many tokens, but we did not build up reserves from them. For we considered them a form of training for both animal and Singer. They also gave us more reason for a roving life.

But to lay up any treasure and guard it—that is foreign to us. And if we had done it in the past, before we left our cities, we had forgotten it.

As we began once more our slow journey to the Valley, I asked of Krip Vorlund, "What is your greatest treasure? Gems? Or some other rare thing?"

"Do you mean mine personally, or what is so regarded by my people?"

"Both."

"Then I shall answer you with one word, for with both me and and my people it is the same—a ship!"

"And you gather naught else besides?"

"What we gather, and it is as much as we can of the treasures others want, it is only that we may finally spend all we have so garnered for a ship of our own."

"And how many of you ever achieve such?"

"Perhaps as many as find lordships on Yiktor. The struggle is as hard, though in another way."

"You—do you believe you will ever have this treasure?"

"No one willingly loses any dream, even when the point of being able to realize it is past. A man, I think, continues to hope for good fortune until he dies."

We camped that night, but not for the whole space of darkness, only for a few hours. I watched the moon rise, but I made no move to draw its power—not then. One cannot store it too long, and to tap it and be forced to loose it before using it to any advantage is a stupid waste. So I did not raise my rod, nor did I sing outwardly or inwardly. All that I did was to aid the kasi with thought power when and where I could.

The moon hung low when we came to the lip of the descent into the Valley. And, as was always true at nighttime, the mist covered thickly, hiding whatever might lie below. From where I sat I could see no change, no sign that any danger had passed this way. But my sight was very limited.

I heard the barsk stir, looked back to see he struggled to get to his feet. I restrained him with an outflung hand.

"We are above the Valley. Lie you still, rest while you may."

"You are going down?"

"I shall take precautions." I brought out my rod. The moon was not at its height, but it was there. I began a deep song, an inward chant, and the kasi started down into the Valley.

Chapter 17

When I first awoke and knew that I was still alive, tended by Maelen and once more in the Thassa van, it seemed that the dream in which I had been caught had come full circle. There was an acceptance in me, the kind with which one faces incongruities met in a nightmare, wherein nothing surprises. But I came to learn during the following hours that this Maelen was one I had not met before. I now saw Maelen not unsure, but rather as one to whom duty had become the lead star of life. And, in spite of my own need to know what must be faced, I could never press past certain boundaries she held.

As we descended into the mist-cloaked Valley, she kept the van to the exact center of the road. I read in her mind that those precautions or defenses which she had spoken of could well be our undoing even though we came in peace. That they had been the bane of those we trailed was a hope we shared.

Another worry nagged at me. Though my mind was alert, yet the body housing it was weak and would not obey my commands. Were we to be attacked I could offer nothing, not even in my own defense. I could lift my head, stretch my legs as I lay upon the mat. But if I drew a deep breath pain followed and there was a languor, which came and went, to disturb me. Maelen had healing powers, that I knew, but would they succeed with the wound in my breast—? There was good reason to believe that Osokun's blade *had* bitten too deep, and that survival in my present body did not mean recovery.

I had gone to seek death when I had trailed Osokun and his sword-sworn, the shock of the news Maelen brought from Yrjar sending me into that temporary madness. But there is planted, at least in my own species, a stubborn resistance to the end of existence. And now a small measure of hope bulwarked what spirit I had. The alternative Maelen suggested had possibilities. Equipped with a Thassa body, I could indeed return to Yrjar. The Traders shared a consular representative on the planet; I had met him when the *Lydis* landed. I could go to Prydo Alcey, state my case, let him send a message to Captain Foss. It ought to be easy to frame some message such as only Krip Vorlund could send to certify my identity. Then, with my own body returned, another switch and I would be truly myself.

Of course there were many pitfalls between this present moment and that to-be-wished-for result. And several might lie directly before us. I tried to move, to lift my heavy head and loose-muscled body so that I might see over the driver's seat. But I could accomplish nothing and lay panting and weak, alarmed at my state. It was only when I lay so that I became aware that Maelen was engaged in more than merely directing the kasi down the road. There was an aura about her which tugged at mind-send powers. I was lying now so that I could watch her profile, her half face stern and set. Her hair was not piled in elaborate rolls as it had been at our first meeting, but bound about her head smoothly as to form a silver helmet. And the arabesque of ruby and silver which had then been on her forehead was gone. Now her eyes were half closed, the lids well down as if her gaze turned inward, or on other things than the sights of this world.

But there was such a brightness on her face as to dazzle me a little. Was it the moon against her very fair skin, or did some of it come from within, the reflection of power stored there? Always before I had seen the human in the Thassa; now she was more alien than any of the animals with whom I had shared life and battle these past few days.

"Taking precautions," she had called this. "Arming" was the name I would set upon it. I dropped my heavy head. I could no longer see her; yet the consciousness of her, how she sat, what she did, was so with me that it was as if I continued to watch her.

There grew up about us a new sensation as the van rumbled on—a kind of warning. It was as if some scout on a distant hill waved away our advance. As we did not heed that warning the uneasiness grew sharper, feeding into the mind a shadow of foreboding which became steadily blacker. Whether this was one of the defenses of the Valley, I could not tell. But apparently it did not affect Maelen, or swerve her from our advance.

I heard the child stir uneasily beyond the blanket, making small sounds of distress. But whether she slept and dreamed ill dreams, or waked to find them reality, I did not know. For I was ridden now by my own distresses. Lassitude in me was growing. At moments it was clear where I was and what was about me, at other times I swung out into a void of nothingness where the resulting giddiness frightened what sense I had left. And I could not tell whether the mists which fuzzed my sight when I tried to fasten on some part of the van were of the real world or born of my increasing weakness.

The journey was endless. Time vanished, or rather the measurement of it did. I lay in the van and heard the whimpering of the child—I was gone—as if I rested on a shuttle racing back and forth weaving a future which eluded me.

Around, the air throbbed and beat—in time to the swing of the shuttle which bore me? No, this was a pulsation which broke that rhythm, anchored me in the van. Then I heard a sound which was part of that beat, a chant, I thought. It did not come from Maelen, but from the Valley, and it grew louder with every forward step of the kasi.

Oddly enough that beat of sound, of power, strengthened me as if it poured back into my slack body the essence which had ebbed since Osokun's knife had sought my life. I lay, feeling that wash into me. Some ebbed again, yes, but each receding wave left a residue behind to hearten me. I was no longer only holding on grimly to what life I had, I was once more able to think beyond my body and my own concerns.

Once more I struggled up and looked at Maelen. Her head was thrown back now, her hands raised before her. Between her two palms, pressed together, was her wand. It seemed to spin, throwing off sparks of silver which struck her head and breast and then vanished. And she was singing—not like the chant which still filled the air, but very high and sweet, notes which pulled at me.

Somehow I braced my forepaws hard against the floor of the van, and managed to raise myself. Now my eyes were level with the seat on which she sat. I glimpsed the world below; it was still night, or very early morning. The moon was no longer bright, but ahead, down, there were other lights to be seen.

That was not the yellow-red of fires, nor the blue shade of the lamps I had seen in Yrjar. Rather these were moon globes as Maelen carried, only they were not fixed but moved about as might lanterns.

And it was from that place of lights that the chanting arose, stronger and deeper. I dragged myself farther up until, in spite of the pain it cost me, I could place one foreleg across the seat, resting my head upon it. Maelen did not notice me, she was still wrapped in her singing.

Two men carrying moon globes came to meet us. I saw the white-and-yellow-patterned black robes of priests. But they did not greet Maelen or try to halt us, only stood aside one to right, one to left, and were silent as we passed between. Their faces remained impassive and they continued to chant words I did not understand.

We passed more of the priests of Umphra engaged in tasks along the road. I sniffed the stench of burning, and beneath that barsk nostrils picked up also the reek of blood. No, the Valley had not escaped the doom which had come to Yim-Sin. Yet I believed the doom had not been as complete here as it had been in the village.

The kasi turned without any outward sign of control from Maelen and we went through the gates. The portal which had hung there was splintered and scored, and in it bristled bolts from crossbows. The mist was now the smoke of destruction. We entered the first temple courtyard.

For the first time Maelen moved, raised the wand until its brilliant shaft pressed against her forehead. The light which had spun from it was gone and, as she dropped her hands once again, it was a simple rod. Her eyes opened.

A priest came to us. There was a bandage about his head, and he carried his right arm in a sling.

"Orkamor?" Maelen asked him.

"He sees to his people, Freesha."

She nodded gravely. "Evil has been wrought here. How great that evil, brother?"

"Much that was long and long in building has been broken." His voice was somber, his face drawn, with the deep-set eyes of a man who has been forced to witness the destruction of what had been very much a part of him. "But the foundations have not been destroyed."

"And who did this? They did worse in Yim-Sin."

"That they told us. As to who they were—men who have fallen under a darkness grown from seed brought from elsewhere. They have not, however, prospered in their wickedness."

"They are destroyed?"

"They destroyed themselves. For they did not heed the safeguards. Only, behind them they have left ruin."

"Those—those whom Umphra holds under his cloak—" she began, almost timidly. "How fare those, elder brother?"

"Him you hold in your heart-hand, Freesha, survives. Others— some Umphra has at last loosed upon the White Road."

She sighed. Her wand lay across her knees, her hands rubbed her forehead.

So Maquad was still alive; I clung to that much. My lassitude was creeping back. I could not find it in me to care greatly that her plan had not been swallowed after all. The pain in my breast gave me a sharp twinge, and I slipped from my half sprawl across the seat to huddle on the mat once again. It was as if my last small reserve of strength left me.

Light—shining into my face so that it smarted through the small slits between my nearly closed eyelids. . . . I tried to turn my head away from that light, but I was held to it and I breathed in vapor which was sharply aromatic, clearing my head. I opened my eyes and found that I now lay in a room and Maelen bent over me, a bowl in her hand holding a golden liquid. From this rose the fumes which had summoned me back.

With her was another, and that old, benign face I knew. Once, a very long time ago, we had sat in a quiet garden and talked of life beyond the star which was Yiktor's sun, of how men carried out their destinies in many strange places. This was Orkamor, servant of Umphra. I tried to say his name.

"Younger brother"—his words formed in my mind—"is this your wish, truly your wish, to put off the body you now wear for another?"

Words—words—but, yes, that was my wish, of course it was! I was a man—a man! I claimed a man's body. And that rose in me as no mere desire, but as a demand which was centered with all the strength I could now summon.

"Be it as you will, then, sister, brother—"

Orkamor receded from my vision as if he floated away. Once more Maelen leaned above me, holding the bowl that its reviving fumes might clear my brain.

"Say this, Krip Vorlund, word for word: 'I wish this by the power, to put aside fur and fang, to walk again as a man!'"

"I wish—this—by—by—the power, to put aside—fur and fang—to walk—to walk again as—a man!" Triumphantly I finished that plea, wishing I could shout it aloud from some mountain top for all the world to hear.

"Drink!"

She held yet closer the bowl of aromatic liquid. I lapped at its contents eagerly. It was as cool water from a mountain stream. I had not realized how I thirsted until I swallowed. It was good—good—I drank until the bowl was emptied, until my tongue found no lingering drop.

"Now—" She put aside the bowl to bring forward one of the moon globes. And though the room had seemed light to me, yet did that lamp make it brighter.

"Look into this," she bade me. "Loose, look and loose—"

Loose? Loose what? But I set my eyes upon the globe. It was a world of silver such as one might see rise up on the visa-screen of the *Lydis* as she made planet-fall in a new system—a silver world reaching out—drawing one . . .

Who wanders on silver worlds, and what do they see there? Out of some depth that thought came to me. But this was waking not dreaming. Yet still I would not open my eyes to see, for there was a difference now and some wary part of me wished to explore that difference slowly.

I drew in a deep breath, waiting for my nose, for the barsk senses to tell me all they could. But it was as if those senses had been deadened, shriveled. There were scents, yes, the perfume of some growing thing, and others, but all weak compared to those I had known.

As yet I had not tried to move. But when I had breathed so deeply, that pain which had become so much a part of me—it was gone! Now I opened my eyes. But—distortion! Colors were less sharp in some ways, stridently screaming in others. I blinked, trying to make my surroundings return to normal. But they did not. It required effort to focus, to make my eyes once more my obedient servants. Once—once before this had happened—Memory stirred in me.

I stared ahead. There was a wide surface, a wall, and in it a window. Beyond that branches waved in the pull of the wind. My mind readily supplied names for all of these, recognized what my eyes reported, even though they saw everything differently. I opened my mouth, tried to lick sharp fangs with my tongue. But the tongue which moved there was not long, it swept across teeth—these were not the tearing implements of a barsk.

My—my paws? I ordered a foreleg into my range of vision, somehow not daring yet to raise my head. There was an arm moving slowly upward for me to see—a hand—fingers which curled when I ordered— Arm—hand—? I was not a barsk— I was—a man! Abruptly I sat up and the room, still somewhat distorted in my sight, swung giddily. And I was alone within it. But I raised human hands, two of them, to stare upon and I looked down at a human body! The flesh was pale, so pale it made me a little uncomfortable to look upon it. That was not right— I should be brown, very brown. I huddled on the edge of the bed where I had lain, looked searchingly at the length of my new body, at its pallor, the thinness which was close to emaciation.

Then I dared to raise my hands, to explore by touch my face. It was human right enough, though by touch alone I could not estimate its difference from the Krip Vorlund who had been kidnaped from the Yrjar fair. I wanted a mirror. I must see!

Stumbling a little, for it was a strain to walk erect once more after running for so long on all fours, I got to my feet. I inched one of those bare feet forward in a step, my hands out to balance me as I teetered from one foot to the other. But as I reached the window and then turned, my confidence in such a method of progression returned. It was as if I revived an old skill forgotten for a space. I looked about for the furred body which was Jorth, but it was gone— nor did I ever see it again.

The room was very small, the bed occupying much of its area. There was a door in the opposite wall and a coffer which also served as a table, judging by the cup and flagon set out upon its lid. From the window the wind swept in cool enough to send me shivering, and I tottered back to the bed to pull its upper covering off to wrap about me. I still longed to see my face. Judging by my body I was Thassa—Maquad—

But to my surprise I found in me some regrets for those senses which had served Jorth so well, but which were barsk. It would appear that the Thassa had limitations which matched those of my original self.

With the bedcover as a cloak about me I went to the coffer, thirst moving me to investigate the cup there. It was empty, but the flagon which shared its tray was not and I poured slowly the golden liquid.

That was cool, satisfying, and in my body spread a new sense of well-being, of unity with this new habitation. I heard a low cough and looked up at the priest with the bandaged head, whom I had last seen as he greeted Maelen. He inclined his head and crossed over to lay his burden on the bed, clothing, gray with touches of red, such as the Thassa favored.

"The Eldest Brother would speak with you, brother, when you are ready."

I gave him thanks and began to dress, far more sure about my movements now. When I had finished I guessed that I must look like Malec.

Malec! Another thrust of memory, and with it anger. Malec had brought me out of the hell of that barsk in Yrjar—and what had been his end? I had known so little of him, and I owed him so much.

Although my new belt held a long-bladed dagger, there was no sword, and certainly no wand such as Maelen carried. Yet in me was the desire for a weapon to fit my hand when I thought of the killing of Malec.

There was no mirror, I could not see the whole of the guise in which I now walked. But when I went out of that room, I found one of the boy priests waiting for me. He limped as he led the way, and in his face was the same emptiness of shock and fatigue as had marked his superiors. Also, in this place was still the smell of fire, though not as strong as Jorth had scented it.

We came into that same small garden where Orkamor had received me once before. And again he sat in the tall chair of sprouting wood, though the leaves on it now were sere and withered. There was a stool there, too, and on it Maelen, her shoulders drooping, her eyes sunken and dull, marking one who has expended a great effort to her own ill advantage. In me was the impulse to go to her, take those listless, limply lying hands in mine, and rouse her. Strange had she seemed to me in Yrjar when I had seen her confident, and strange had she been during all our journeyings; but now no longer. She seemed only as one who had claims upon me and who was worn and tired. But she neither looked up nor welcomed me.

Orkamor's eyes met mine, reaching in and in as if he meant to search out every thought, no matter how deeply buried it lay in my brain. And that searching was as keen as if he sought for a flaw he knew lay there. Then he smiled and raised his hand, and I saw there was a great, angry-looking bruise across its back, and one of his fingers was splintered and stiffly bound. But the gesture he made was of welcome, and, more than welcome, of happy surprise.

"It is done, and done well."

He did not speak aloud, and his words must have rung in Maelen's brain also, for she stirred, her head coming up a little, turning slowly, her eyes to rest upon me at last. I saw surprise and a kind of wonder in them, which astonished me in turn. For if she had wrought this change for me, why should the results amaze her?

She spoke to Orkamor. "Is this well done, Eldest Brother?"

"If you mean, sister, have you accomplished as you wished—yes, it is well done. If you mean will it lead to more complications, then I cannot answer you yes or no."

"The answer"—if thought could be a whisper, then was hers now—"is mine now. Well, what is done is done, and what must be done— With your permission, Eldest Brother, we will ride forth to see the end of all this."

Still she had not spoken to me, and now it was as if she did not want to look at me again. For after that first measuring stare, she turned her head away. I was curiously chilled, as if I had put out a hand in greeting, only to have it refused, myself ignored. And yet I could not make any move to draw her attention again.

We went inside to find food and drink. Maelen ate as one who must fuel an engine for running. And I did the same, discovering my body welcomed what I gave it. But still she was behind a wall I could neither breach nor climb.

I judged it midday when we came out into the courtyard of the temple. There was no sign of the van, but two riding kasi awaited us, journey cloaks across their saddle pads, bundles of provisions hanging ready. I would have aided Maelen to mount, but she was too quick for me, and I went to my own kas. Could it be she shrank from any contact in aversion?

We went through the devastation in the Valley. There were fire-blackened ruins, other signs of the fury which had hit to cripple, but not totally to destroy. Maelen pushed ahead along the road to Yim-Sin. It was plain she was in desperate haste to fulfill the rest of her plan, to return us both to Yrjar and resolve, as far as she could, the tangle fate had snarled about us.

Nor would she look at me during that upward climb, even touch thought with me. Was it so revolting to her that I now wore the body of one who had been close-kin and who might be now deemed doubly dead? I chafed at that. Nothing of what had happened to me had I asked for.

But I had, memory responded. Twice I had asked through some Thassa ritual for these changes. And twice perhaps they had saved me from death. For the first time I wondered who would inhabit the body I now wore when and if I finally regained my own. Would Maquad indeed die then, totally and finally?

Since the pace Maelen set took us much farther than the former speed of the van, we were well out of the Valley before sunset. By sunrise we might again see the ruins of Yim-Sin. Then across the plains to Yrjar— But what was happening on those plains? And because I must look a little into the future, I forced myself on my companion.

"What could the servant of Umphra tell you about what might be happening on the plains?"

I think that her thoughts were so far away in another direction that it took her a few seconds to return to the here and now and my question.

"Those who came from the west," she answered, "were strangers. It seems there is a new enemy abroad in Yiktor, more ruthless than any plains lord has ever dared to be. And that force comes from off-world."

"But the Traders—" I was too astonished to grasp it quickly.

"These are not Traders like unto the men of the *Lydis*. These newcomers fight to carve themselves a rooting in our soil, gather to themselves power, build their own kingdom. Some of the lords they have already overwhelmed, having worked secretly for a time to sow dissension among their people; others they have gathered to them with promises of much treasure to be later shared. They have set one against another, stirring ever the cauldron of war with that spoon which will make it boil the most furiously. I do not know what we shall find now in Yrjar. I do not even know if we can reach the city. We can only try."

What she said was not too enlightening, and not at all promising. It sounded as if this had been longer building than we had suspected— To plunge into a land where every man's hand was raised against his neighbor was daunting. But the port was at the outskirts of Yrjar, and there lay my only chance of reaching the *Lydis*.

Yrjar lay some distance away, and as I chewed upon what Maelen had said, the journey appeared to double. Were we wise to take the road at all now?

That thought was already shaping in my mind when the summons came. It was sharp and strong, as ringing as any horn call. But it did not reach me through my ears.

There was an after moment of silence, then once more the pealing, demanding order we could not disobey. I heard a small cry from Maelen, of protest—

Then, before we willed it, we had turned our mounts to the right, out of the road into the wilderness of the northern ridges, answering a call which body and mind must obey—the horn-in of the Thassa, which sounded only in times of great import.

Chapter 18

What I had seen of Yiktor had been much like any other world of its type—plains backed by hills, covered with vegetation varying in shade. But Yrjar, the fort of Osokun, Yim-Sin, the temples of Umphra, had their counterparts on many planets and were also familiar to me in part. Where we rode now was very different.

The horning set such bonds upon us that we could not have disobeyed its order. And we rode on and on, ever north, always into higher country. The rises here were not softened by any growth of trees, or even slightly veiled by brush and shrubs. Only small patches of grass, now killed by the first breath of winter, broke the general desolation of the stone.

For this was truly a desolate country. I have visited planets burnt off in some nuclear war of such antiquity that it antedated the coming of my own species into space. That is ruin to daunt the heart of any who look upon it. But this was even more alien than that. It was a vast loneliness which rejected life as our kind knows, a stark stripping to the bones of Yiktor itself.

Yet there was life here. For when we rode deeper and deeper into this wilderness of naked stone and sand, we saw traces of those who had gone before us, tracks left by vans, hoof prints of riding kasi.

It was as if we lay under some spell, for we did not speak to each other, neither did I have any desire to turn back to the plains and what had once seemed my pressing business there. Night came.

From time to time we dismounted, rested our kasi, ate of the supplies in the bags, walked up and down to ease our own bodies, only to remount and take up the trail once again.

At dawn our road wound between two towering cliffs. I thought that at some immeasurably early time in Yiktor's history this must have been the bed of a great river. There were sand and gravel and tumbles of boulders which looked water worn, but no living thing, not even so much as a single tuft of withered grass. And that river bed brought us into a huge bowl, also ringed by heights. If we had come up the river, now we entered a lake bed.

Here for the first time had man, or some intelligence, broken the austerity of the wilderness. Cut back into the cliffs about the lake bed were a series of wide openings, each bordered with carving which had once been chiseled deep, but now worn away to faint, unreadable tracings.

These cliff dwellings had inhabitants, for there were vans drawn up before them, the smoke of fires drifted into the morning air. Animals wandered about. But men, or Thassa, were missing. Maelen took the lead, for once we entered the basin the compulsion which had kept me ever by her side lifted. She guided her mount to a picket line, slid from its back, and straightway loosened her saddle pad, freeing it. The kas shook its head and then lay down and rolled in the sand, snorting vigorously. And mine, as I stripped it, did likewise.

"Come." For the first time in hours she spoke to me.

I dropped my saddle pad beside hers and we went across the valley, heading for the midpoint of the opposite wall. There was a rock doorway easily twice the size of the others flanking it. I marveled at the vast labor its carving had demanded, but I could not detect any meaning in the patterns which were outlined, for they were far too badly eroded.

Where were the Thassa? All I could see were animals and vans. But as we approached the cliff door I had my answer. From it came a sound which was more than mere chanting. It partook also of the movement of the air in a way I do not have any words in off-world vocabulary to describe. I fell into the rhythm of it unknowingly and then realized what I did. Beside me I heard Maelen's voice raised in song.

We passed from the light of the valley under that heavy portal into a hall. It was not dark, globes hung high over our heads and we walked through moonlight, although a few feet outside the sun struck hot across the rock.

And the Thassa were there in numbers I could not count. Before us there was a pathway open to the very center of the place, and down that Maelen went; I, less surely, a step or two behind her. Always that singing rang in our ears, beat in our blood, was a part of us.

So we came to a space where there was an oval dais or platform raised a few steps above the surface of the floor. And on that stood four of the Thassa; two were men, two women. Although they were firm of flesh, bright of eye, yet about them was such an aura of age, authority, and wisdom as to set them apart, even as their present positions set them bodily above the rest. Each carried a wand. But these were not the relatively short rods such as Maelen bore; rather did they top their holders' heads when one end was planted firmly on the floor. And the light which shone from these shafts rivaled and paled the moon globes.

Maelen did not mount the two steps to join them, but stood in the open just below. And when I hesitantly came up beside her, I saw that her face was closed and bleak; yet still she sang.

They all sang until it seemed to me that we did not truly stand on firm rock, but rather that we wavered back and forth in the currents of an ocean of sound. I felt that I did not look upon Thassa but upon other people—or spirits. My vision of them was never complete; rather were they shadows of what might be the truth.

How long did we stand so? To this day I do not know, any more than I can dimly guess the meaning of what was happening. I think that by their united will as a people they built up certain forces, and from those they drew what they needed for their purposes. This is a very fumbling explanation of what I involuntarily joined during that day.

The song was dying, fading away, in a series of slow, sobbing notes. Now it carried with it a vast burden of sorrow, as if all the private griefs of an old, old people had been distilled through centuries, and each small ultimate drop of despair preserved for future tasting.

It was not for other ears, that end-song of the Thassa. I might wear Maquad's body, and in some small ways respond to Thassa ways, but I was not Maquad and now I put my hands to my ears to shut out the song I could no longer bear. I felt tears on my cheeks, sobs burst from my chest, although those about me gave no outward sign of the unbearable grief they shared.

One of the four on the dais moved. A wand swung out and pointed to me. And then I no longer heard! I was free of the cloud I could not bear. So it was until the song was done.

Then the second of those commanding that assembly moved. This time the wand pointed to Maelen. From her fingers her own symbol of authority freed itself, to fly to the greater rod as iron might be drawn to a magnet. She gave a little gasp and put out her hand as if, too late, she would have caught her errant wand. Then both hands fell to her sides and she stood motionless.

"What is your tale in this time and place, Singer?"

The question, which resounded in my head as well as in hers, was not voiced aloud, but was none the less plain.

"It is thus—" She began our story, telling it simply and clearly. None of them interrupted her while she spoke, nor commented on any part of our incredible experiences. When she had done, she on the dais whose wand had entrapped Maelen's spoke:

"This, too, was in your mind, Singer; that there was one of your blood-clan who knew heart hunger, and that if the semblance of the one for whom she hungered be returned, perhaps good might come of it."

"Is this not so?" the man to the right of the speaker asked.

"In the beginning, I do not think so. Later—" Maelen's hand rose and fell in a small gesture which I read as resignation.

"Let that other who is so concerned stand forward," summoned the woman.

There was a stir and from the right came a Thassa woman. Although I could not read age among them, I believed that she was perhaps even younger than Maelen. She held out her hand to Maelen, and their fingers interlocked in both greeting and deep affection.

"Merlay, look upon this man. Is he the one whom you have mourned?"

She turned slightly to look at me. For a moment there was a kind of awakening in her face, a light in her eyes, as one might look when fronting a miracle. Then that light was gone, her face veiled and still.

"This is not he," she murmured.

"Nor could ever be!" the other woman on the dais said sharply. "As well you know, Singer!" And her sharpness was keener yet as she spoke to Maelen. "Standing Words are not to be altered, Singer, for any personal reason. You have sworn oaths, do you now admit yourself forsworn."

The other man on the dais, moved now, raising his wand and swinging its tip lightly through the air between the three and Maelen.

"Standing Words," he repeated. "Yes, we lean upon Standing Words as our anchors and supports. Yet it seems to me that this sorry coil was begun through Standing Words. Maelen"—he was the first to speak her name and I thought there was some compassion in his tone—"first saved this man because of a debt. Nor is she responsible thereafter for much which happened. Therefore we lay upon her that she do as she has thought to do, return with him to Yrjar and there undo what has been wrought through her powers."

"Which she cannot do," said the sharp-voiced woman, and I read satisfaction in her speech. "For have we not had news of what will happen to Maelen the Singer if she is seen there?"

Maelen raised her head to look at the other in open surprise.

"What mean you, Old One? What danger lies in Yrjar?"

"The off-worlders who have raised fire, shed blood, and loosed the barsks of war have said that Maelen enchanted Osokun and drove him mad, and that they will have her dead—many believing them."

"Off-worlders? What off-worlders—and why?" For the first time I broke into what had seemed none of my affair, only between Maelen and the rulers of her people. But off-worlders—what *was* behind all this?

"Not of your breed, my son," the man who had spoken for Maelen replied. "But rather that one who sought out Maelen before the beginning of all this and wished her to be his tool, and those for whom he carried a sword in this matter. It would seem that you and yours have some powerful enemy off-world, who have now brought the quarrel to Yiktor."

"But—if you mean the Combine men—" I was startled. "I have no personal enemy among them. Long ago their kind and mine warred, that is true. But of late years our differences have been settled. This is madness."

One of the women on the dais smiled sadly. "All war and slaying is madness whether it be between man and man, or man and animal. But for whatever reason these bring their fight to the plains, it is true they have set a price on Maelen. Perhaps they fear she knows too much of them to venture into Yrjar—"

"As Maelen," spoke the girl who stood hand in hand with my companion, "perhaps not. As Merlay—?"

The eldest man considered. Then he shook his head, almost regretfully. "There is the matter of time. Already the Third Ring begins to fade from the night sky. And only under it may an exchange of Thassa with Thassa hold true. You would not survive more than four days."

"It need not be so," continued Merlay, "if the exchange is not made here, but in the hills which border the plains. Then to Yrjar—four days will suffice."

Maelen shook her head. "Better I go in my own body than risk yours, sister. I pay my own debts."

"Have I said that you do not?" countered Merlay. "I only ask that you follow wisdom and not folly. You have said, Mylrin," she appealed to the leader, "that Maelen has a right to bring this venture to the proper ending. There are those in Yrjar who knew that Maquad and I were life companions. If we go together, will we be suspect? This is the best way."

At length it was decided that she had the best plan. I was not consulted. In fact, at that moment, I was thinking too much about the off-worlders. According to Maelen, Salfid had been mixed up in Osokun's intrigues from the first. He had threatened to tell of the Thassa body-changing to force Maelen and Malec to his aid. But as far as I knew he was no more than a very junior officer on a Combine ship. Why would any Combine wish to war here on Yiktor? They had done the like on other primitive worlds in the past, we knew gory stories of that—so that they might fish in troubled waters when both sides were exhausted. But Yiktor, as far as I knew, had no resources so rich as to tempt them to risk attention from the Patrol.

I was puzzling over this when we started back on the trail. Maelen and I, Merlay, and two of the Thassa men were mounted on the pick of the riding kasi. We covered the distance at the best pace the animals could keep. But it took four days of hard riding to reach a nook in the lower plains for the camp we wished.

That night we slept and through the next day we rested also, for that which must be done between Merlay and Maelen required bodies not strained to the edge of endurance. In the meantime I tried to discover what I could about the off-worlders. When they knew my concern the others discussed it with me, but among us we could light on no reason why Yiktor was a target for such interference.

"Treasure," Maelen said. "You spoke of treasures which are many and diverse. You said what is worth perhaps a man's life or a country's freedom on one world may be nought, less than a child's toy on another. I do not see what treasure we have here which could bring upon us disaster from the stars."

"Nor do I," I agreed. "You have told me there was nothing new and startling displayed at the fair. And all wares there were already known to the Free Traders. We could make a profit on a cargo from Yiktor—or we would not come—but only a reasonable one, not one to attract a Combine into one of the old-time raids."

"Mathan," one of the Thassa guards said to his fellow, "when we ride hence again, it might be well that we do not say 'This is not of our life, let the plainsmen do as they will about it.' For it might be that our whole world will be involved and it *will* be our concern."

"There is the off-world consul in Yrjar." I clung to my last hope of learning the why and wherefore of all that had happened since the *Lydis* had planeted here. "He must have the answer, or a part of it!"

On the second night the Thassas wrought their magic. This time I was no part of it, but was sent to await the one who would come out of the small tent they had set up to veil their actions. And when she did, booted and cloaked, ready to ride, we were off for the plains together, while the others remained.

The signs of war were here, though we took as covered a route as we could. I began to wonder if we could get through to Yrjar. We might well arrive to find the city under siege. She who wore Merlay's body, but was Maelen, did not agree with my pessimism. Yrjar had always been a kind of neutral meeting place, even when the fair was not in progress. And if the uprising was indeed inspired by off-worlders, they would make sure first of keeping the spaceport free. Warfare on Yiktor had always been more a matter of raids, hit-and-run attacks, rather than lengthy sieges to reduce well-fortified places. There was small profit in that, and loosely organized fighting units quickly lost patience.

Luckily we would not have to go into the walled portion of the city in order to reach our goal. For the building which housed the consul was on the edge of the port field. So we swung south to avoid the main roads into Yrjar and came in on the field. There was only one ship there—an official courier, and I noted that it was set down unusually close to the consular buildings. For the rest the port was deserted. We came in warily, tired from two long days of riding since we had left the camp in the foothills. Our kasi were close to done and we would have to have new mounts if we rode forth again—or rather Maelen, in her guise as Merlay, would. For if all went well, my only exit from Yrjar would be by ship.

We reached the edge of the field without any challenge and I did not like the silence, the feeling of being the only living things abroad in a forsaken world. With caution we worked our way to the gate of the consular compound and then were challenged, not by any guard, but by a force beam. The whole building must be englobed!

I slapped my palm against the voice box on the outer post, though a Thassa palm against that would mean nothing to the lock, and then I stated to the speaker that I had urgent business with Prydo Alcey. For a long moment, a very long one, I thought I might either be talking to an empty office, or else I was such a suspicious figure that I could expect at any moment to be crisped by a beamer. But then the plate lit up and I saw the face of the consul, knew that he must view me in return.

When I stated my business I used the Trader tongue, and now he looked out of the plate in amazement. He turned his head and spoke to someone over his shoulder, then he looked back to me.

"Your business?" He used the speech of Yrjar. But I answered in Trader tongue.

"Urgent, and with you, Gentle Homo!"

I thought he was going to deny me, for the plate went dark and he made me no answer at all. But a few seconds later the door of the inner court opened and he stood there, backed by two guardsmen. With the force shield in place, however, they were certainly safe enough from any weapon known to Yiktor.

"You are—?"

I decided to answer with the truth and hoped the apparent lie would spark his curiosity enough to let me tell the whole of it.

"Krip Vorlund, assistant cargomaster, Free Trader *Lydis*."

He stared and then gestured. One of the guards slapped the wall, and the sheen of the force shield was gone—for a moment. But both guards now held beamers on us as they motioned us in. We rode our stumbling kasi into the courtyard and I heard a swish as the screen went up behind us.

"Now," Alcey said quietly, "suppose this time you begin with the truth."

All men who travel the star lanes must develop the ability to accept weird things beyond the normal edge of belief. But I think that the consul of Yrjar found my story more bizarre than any he had heard before, except that, Thassa though I looked, I was able to supply so many off-world details that he had to admit only one who had served on a Trader could have given them. And when I had done he looked from me to Maelen and then back again.

"I saw Krip Vorlund when he was brought in—what was left of him. Now you arrive and tell me this. What do you want?"

"Get in touch with the *Lydis*, let me send a message. I can provide details which will prove the truth."

He smiled then, and it was the type of smile to dry up any flow of speech.

"You have my permission to signal off-world anything you wish, Vorlund, if you can."

"If I can?"

"I am, as you might have guessed from your welcome, no longer a free agent on Yiktor. There is a blanket satellite operating on short orbit up there—" He pointed to the ceiling over our heads.

"Blanket satellite! But—"

"Yes, but—and but—and but! A hundred planet years ago this might have been a reasonably normal situation. Now—it comes as somewhat of a shock, does it not? The Korburg Combine, or at least some agents stating they represent that Combine, have landed and believe they have the situation well in hand. I tried to get off a courier last night and was warned there was a stop-circuit set up. Because I have seen other evidences of their ruthlessness in operation here, I did not take the chance."

"But what do they want?" I demanded. As he had said, a hundred years ago such piracy would have been usual, but now! The appetites of the big Combines and Companies had long been curbed by the Patrol; there were drastic answers to such action.

"Something," Alcey returned. "Just what has not been made entirely clear. So your problem"—he shook his head—"now becomes a relatively minor one, except of course for you. There is this—" he hesitated. "I may not be doing right to tell you this, but you should be prepared. I saw your body when it was returned here. Your medico, he was not sure you could make it, but the *Lydis* had been warned out privately by one of their local merchant contacts. They agreed to carry a message from me to the nearest Patrol post. We had only hints and rumors then, but enough to know they must lift ahead of time. And you—or your body—could well not have survived that lift. The medico protested it on your behalf."

I glanced down from meeting his eyes to the hands resting before me on the table top. Long thin fingers, ivory skin, strange hands— but they did my will, moved at my command. What if—if he was right in his foreboding that the Krip Vorlund taken away in the *Lydis* was dead, now perhaps spaced in a coffin suit after the manner of my people, so to lie among the stars for all eternity?

Beside me Maelen stirred. "I must be going," she said, and her voice was faint, very weary. So she recalled my thoughts—the change between her and her sister could not last much longer. With every passing moment their danger grew.

"But you do not know what Korburg wants here?"

"This much. There have been recent changes in the Council, especially as it touches the government of some inner planets. This world might provide a refuge or way station—temporary, of course, but perhaps necessary for some Veep when a coup on his home world has failed, a place from which he could come back with an army trained here.

It sounded unlikely, but his preparation for guessing right was better than mine. It remained clear that there was no hope at present of reaching the *Lydis*. If Captain Foss had made it to the nearest Patrol post—Then it would only be a matter of time before they would visit Yiktor. On the other hand Maelen had very little time left. And we would be safer to return to her people to wait out the struggle. I asked for a recorder, and with both of them listening taped a message which I thought would identify me to all on board the *Lydis*. Then I told Alcey what I would do and he agreed.

The consul furnished us with fresh mounts, though they were not as wiry and mountain-trained as the two who had carried us to Yrjar. At nightfall we rode from the port. This time we were not so lucky in escaping notice, for we were trailed and only Maelen's power acting on the mounts of the pursuers let us pull ahead. The singing left her further drained and she urged us to greater speed, lest she fail before we found the camp.

Toward the end of that nightmare journey I carried her before me in my arms, since she could no longer sit on her animal. We put on a last burst to come to the secluded ravine between two steep hills where we had left the others. The tent was there, rent and crumpled on the ground. And half entangled in the folds lay one of the Thassa.

"Monstans!" Maelen broke from my hold and stumbled toward him, falling to the ground by his side, yet struggling up to look into his still, white face. She caught his head between her hands, bent to set her lips to his, sharing her breath with him.

I saw the tremor of his eyelids. The whole front of his tunic was stained scarlet, but somehow he had held on to the last dregs of his life force until our coming.

"Merlay"—it was a whisper in our minds, not any words shaped by those pallid lips—"they have taken her—think she—is—you—"

"Where?" Our demand was as if in one voice.

"East—" So much had he done in our service, but no more. The life he had held to swept out of him in one small sigh.

Maelen looked to me. "They seek my life. If they believe that they now have me—"

"We can follow." I had to promise that. And, for good or ill, I knew I would keep my word.

Chapter 19

I saw thereafter how determination of will can carry one beyond the limits of body strength. For she whom I had brought before me drew upon such will to send her on from the destroyed camp.

"Mathan?" I searched about for some trace of the other Thassa before I left the body I had wrapped in the tattered tent. Maelen sat on her saddle pad, both hands pressed to her face. Now she spoke, her voice muffled by her fingers.

"He has gone ahead."

"A prisoner also?"

"My power fades so fast. I cannot say." She dropped her hands to look upon me. Her eyes were dull. It was as if even as I watched, life ebbed from her. "Tie me," she begged. "I do not know how much longer I can ride."

I did as she wished before we left the ravine, following a trail the raiders had made no effort to conceal. There were many kasi tracks and, while I could not be sure, I thought that more than a dozen riders had passed this way.

The way we took was not a road, yet it had been used before, and it pointed through the hills ever westward toward Oskold's hold. Maelen made no effort to guide her mount, which nevertheless followed closely the one I rode. She once more shaded her face with her hands, and I thought that now she shut out the world both physically and mentally, so she could either reach or hold some tie which would pull us to what we now sought.

Night became day and we found a camp where there were embers of a fire still warm to the touch. Maelen's head now hung forward heavily on her breast, her arms limp at her sides. She roused only to much urging from me. But I got water between her lips, saw her swallow as if that act were both painful and difficult. More than a little liquid she refused.

It was strange to see one I had come to accept as having more than human powers become so dependent. But her half-open eyes focused on me after I had made her drink, and there was knowledge and recognition in them.

"Merlay still lives—they take her to some overlord—" Her voice was the merest thread of whisper.

"And Mathan?" I held to the hope that the other Thassa had escaped death or injury, that he might eventually join us in whatever frail attempt we must make to free Maelen's body from the raiders.

"He is—gone—"

"Dead!"

"Not—so. He has gone to call—" Her head fell forward again and her too slender body swayed in the bonds which held her on the kas. I could not rouse her again. Thus I stood in the deserted camp of the enemy and wondered what was to be done. Manifestly Maelen could not continue, and to go on alone was rank folly. Yet neither could I abandon the trail.

"Ahhhhhh—" Half sigh, half crooning cry from Maelen. I hurried to her again. But, though that sound continued from between her lips, still she did not come out of the stupor.

There was a rustling in the bushes. I whirled, the Thassa sword-knife fitting in my hand awkwardly, since it was a weapon new to me. From the branches, down-drooping and still hung with leaves, came an animal—an animal? No—more than one, and not from just one side. Nor was the beast that had first pushed a fang-fringed muzzle through the vegetation a pattern for the rest. No, here were the Borba and Vors, and their like Tantacka, here was the like of— Simmle— More and more of them!

And the beast who led that silent, purposeful advance was one new to me, long and lithe of body, feline in its movements, with a prick-eared head, and—and eyes with the spark of human intelligence in them!

"What? Who?" I tried to beam an inquiry at their leader.

"Mathan!" The identification was sure.

Those others, were they also Thassa? Or some of those whom Maelen had sent into the wilderness? Or companions of other beast masters and mistresses?

"Part and part," Mathan gave me answer.

He loped soft-footed to Maelen's kas, stood upon his hind legs to look upon her.

"Ahhhhh—" Again that cry from her. But she did not open her eyes or look at him and that company. For a company—no, a regiment!—it was.

More and more rustling in the brush, heads out into the open, animal eyes regarded me narrowly.

"She cannot ride any farther," I told Mathan.

Furred head turned, round eyes met mine. "She must!" With his teeth he caught one of the ties which kept her on the pad, gave it a sharp tug. "This will hold. She *must* come!"

If he had passed some command to that army, I did not hear it. Now they flowed past Maelen and went westward and were swallowed up in the cover. Of their number I could not be sure, save there were more of them than I had ever seen gathered together before. But the feline Mathan paced just before us as we rode on. I tried to stay beside Maelen to steady her. She slumped forward now, lying against the kas's neck, wholly oblivious of us and the road.

There was a coming and going of animals, occasionally some would return and look to Mathan. I was sure that messages passed between them, but I could not pick up any information. We had progressed well into the hills, taking a way which did not lead to any gap but up steep ascents, where I dismounted and walked beside Maelen. There was no sign of any trail here, and several times we inched along a knife-edge advance. I dared not raise my eyes from the footing, lest I turn giddy.

At last we came out on a level space. Snow lay here, and fine flakes of it stung my nostrils, were glitter points in the air. If the plains had not yet quite felt the last of autumn, here winter already licked at the land. I fastened the cloak tighter around Maelen; she stirred beneath my hand. I felt a shudder run through her thin frame, heard her gasp and then cry out. She struggled against my hold, sitting up as she had not for hours, to look at me, at the rocks and snow, with eyes which were first wild and unseeing, then had recognition in them.

"Maelen!" The voice she used was shrill, carrying enough to bring an echo. There was a deep growl from the beast with Mathan's eyes. And too late she put her hands to her lips as if to stifle that cry.

She who had been so drained and helpless was now erect, as if strength flowed into her in great waves. There was even a delicate flush on her cheeks, more color than I had ever seen on Maelen.

Maelen? It was clear to me now—this was not Maelen. Merlay had returned to her own body. But before I could say that, or ask the reason, she nodded to me.

"Merlay." She gave me the answer I had guessed. Maelen's time had run out, the exchange had been made without any ceremony or outward sign.

"And Maelen?" My words, Mathan's thought sped together.

"With them." She shivered and I knew it was not from cold, though the wind was a breath of frost.

She looked about, from peak to peak, as if searching for some landmark. Then she pointed to one to the right, yet well ahead.

"They camp on the far slope there."

"For how long?" Mathan demanded.

"I do not know. They wait for someone, or some message. They hold Maelen by the orders of a leader I never saw. But I do not think we have much time."

Again a growl from Mathan's throat. He was gone in a flash of gray-tawny fur, and I knew that all those others he commanded in his strange regiment were running with him. Merlay looked to me.

"I am no Singer. I have no power to aid us now, save that I may be your guide."

She urged the kasi on in Mathan's wake, and I after her. For these few moments I wished I had again the barsk body, that I might run behind the Thassa warrior. The lope of a sure-footed animal in this maze of rock and fall would have been far swifter than our constrained walk. My impatience was a goad. I had to exert full control or I might have overridden her.

Now and then she glanced at me, and each time she looked quickly away again. It was as if something drew her eyes, searching ever for what was not there, and each time being met by loss. I thought I could guess what pulled and then repelled her.

"I am not Maquad."

"No. Eyes can deceive, they are the gateways for illusion. You are not Maquad. Yet am I glad in this hour you wear what was once his.

Maelen is caught in coils not altogether of her spinning, the heart can betray the mind many times over."

I did not really understand her words, but it did not matter. For I had one bit of knowledge. I might be Thassa only in outward appearance, yet I did not believe at this moment I could follow any other road, to any other end, than that which lay before me. Was I still Krip Vorlund, asked a doubting thought not far buried? As I had partaken of the nature of Jorth the barsk, sometimes losing man within the animal, so might I not also join with the residue of Maquad lingering in his husk? And if I actually returned to take on the body of Krip Vorlund once again—though that seemed remote now—would I be only Krip Vorlund thereafter?

"Why do they want Maelen? And how did they find you?"

The second question she answered first. "Not by chance—they trailed us. But whether they first came upon our tracks by chance and followed—that I do not know. As to why they want Maelen—that, too, is hard to read. They wish to lay upon her, as we heard, a measure of blame for what they have done. I think that they plan to use her somehow to win Oskold to them, or to open some door in the western lands where he may still be paramount lord. This much I can tell you: those who hold her have their orders to do just that, no more. He who comes will decide—"

Once more we climbed, and slipped, and climbed again where no trail ran, but where the kasi appeared able to pick footage. We were under the shadow of the peak she had indicated. Around us there was no rustling of brush, no sign any animal army marched with us, save that here and there a paw print left a sharp signature.

Merlay left her saddle pad. "The kasi can go no farther. We make our own road from here."

And a steep and perilous way that was. At times we had mere holds for fingertips and toes, but still we fought for inches of advance. We rounded a rocky outcrop and so came to the other side of the rise. The snow had stopped, but it was followed by a still cold which bit at a man's lungs with every breath he drew. And we came together in a niche to look down into the purplish depths of the eastern foothills of Oskold's land.

Night was coming fast. I wished I had Jorth's eyes to read through shadows. The ground before us was as rough as that we had just covered. And to descend it in the dark promised trouble. But we had no time to linger. Merlay pointed.

"There!"

No tents or vans, but a fire, yes. It would appear that those there did not care if they attracted attention. I tried to pick out a spot on the slope where they could have stationed a picket to scout pursuit. Shadow slipped from shadow—mind-touch— This was Borba coming up to us.

"Come—" His head swung to indicate a path and we crept behind him. Thus we came down as silently as we could. And in that coming we passed a pool of dark. A hand, lax-fingered and very still, protruded from it, palm up and empty. Borba's lips wrinkled and he snarled as he passed that hand and what lay behind it.

We came off rock and into soil rooting small trees of a ragged timber line. From here we could not see the beacon of the campfire, must depend upon the small furred guide. I no longer possessed Jorth's sense of smell, but perhaps the Thassa were better equipped with noses than my own race. For I picked up whiffs of animal odor, enough to tell me that though we neither saw nor heard them, Mathan's force lay in waiting about us. Then a larger shape rose out of the ground at our feet and I caught the thought of the Thassa leader:

"A party comes to the camp. Hasten!"

We moved to the dark side of a rock. Beyond, the fire shot higher, gave more light, as it was fed energetically by two men. I counted eight in plain sight. They were all, to my eyes, like any sword-sworn I had seen in Yrjar. I could not read the emblems on their cloaks or surcoats.

"Whose?" I mind-beamed to Mathan.

"Oskold's there—there—there—" He indicated three. "The rest— I have not seen that device before."

The sound of a horn, sharp and clear, cut the small noises of the camp. There was silence for a second and then shouts of welcome.

"Maelen?"

"There!"

Merlay answered my question. What I had taken for a roll of sleep covering lay, unmoving, well into the firelight.

"They fear her—to look into her eyes," Merlay whispered. "So they have tied cloaks about her lest she turn them into animals. They have been told that she will do this, that we all shall do this."

I did not hear Mathan growl, but I felt the vibration through the fur-clad shoulder pressed close to mine.

"Can we get to her—" I had begun when another party tramped into the firelight. The flames glinted and flashed from ornamentation on cloak and helm. And he who led them was older than the rest.

"Oskold." Mathan's thought identified him.

Their voices carried, but the words were in the inland tongue and I did not understand. I tried to read the thoughts behind them. There was triumph, satisfaction, anger. Yes, emotions were easier to pick up than words.

One of the fire-feeders stooped and jerked at the bundle which was Maelen, pulling her upright. Meanwhile another stepped forward to grasp the covering about her head and shoulders and pull it loose. Her silver hair shook free, and then she raised her head with a toss which cleared that silver veil from her face; she stood head up and unbending to front Oskold.

"'Ware, lord, she will make you beast!" One of his companions laid hand on Oskold's arm to pull him back, the intensity of his thought readable to me.

Oskold laughed. His hand, covered with a glove reinforced across the knuckles with metal strips, swung up to strike Maelen full in the face. She crumpled down.

So it was Oskold who gave us our signal. The raging fury which now boiled out of the dark and the tree shadows leaped, tore, screamed, growled, shrieked in that moment after Maelen went down. I heard the cries of men, the tumult of the beasts, but I headed for Maelen.

I was no swordsman and my sword-knife was a poor weapon, but I reverted to Jorth's rage in those moments when the flames became a red curtain in my mind, drowning thought, leaving me only one purpose in mind. This was as it had been when I had gone after Osokun and his men—

She was under my hand—still—no life in her, her face up to the sky, the red ruin that blow had wrought on flesh and bone made plain. And I crouched above her, snarling as any of the furred ones who fought about me.

As it had been with the outlaws who had killed Malec and taken our camp, so it was now with these. For there is a kind of horror in such warfare which the minds of men find impossible to comprehend. To have waves of animals break about them unnerved some from the start, fighting men though they were. Others rallied, killed, some standing their ground; others fought a rearguard action to withdraw, always harassed, pulled down, overrun.

For me there was but one in that enemy company. And knife in hand, I made for him. In spite of the surprise of our attack, at least one of his guards had come to Oskold's side, fending off with his shield two rushes from a pair of venzese who sprang to snap and bounced back to wait another chance.

I tripped over a body and sprawled forward, almost into the heart of the fire. Then my hands, bracing me up again, closed on a beamer—something I had not expected to find there, but which fitted into my palm as familiarly as a long-worn glove. I did not even try to get to my knees; I lay and pressed the firing button of a weapon which had no right to be there.

The ray it threw was a thrust of eye-searing fire. No shield could stand against that, no, nor man either! I had wanted to let Oskold feel my hands upon him as he went down, but I took the means fate sent me and used the off-world arm. Once, twice—Oskold might be on the ground now but there were others of his following— There was a sputter and the ray died, its charge exhausted. I hurled it from me into the fire and crawled back to Maelen.

Above that fearful wound her eyes were now open and she saw me, knew me—of that I was sure. I caught her up and went back into the dark, to that rock where Merlay had been. I staggered a little when I reached that poor shred of cover, so I had to lean against the chill stone. Merlay was still there, but she did not touch what I held, only laid her hand upon my shoulder. A flow of strength was channeled so from her to me.

This was a battle, and it was fought, and men died and animals died, but for me it was a nightmare which I cannot well remember. Only at last there was quiet, and we came once more to the fire. For it seemed ours was the victory. Yet it might well be that it was also defeat—

I laid Maelen down on the robes Merlay spread to receive her. Still she looked at me and at Merlay, and at the animals who came to her, and last of all to the feline Mathan, who staggered into the fire shine with a wound in his side. But her thoughts did not come to me. Only her eyes told me she still lived.

Suddenly I could not look into them any longer, but got up and walked blindly away, stumbling among the dead. One followed me and sprang to catch my dangling hand between sharp teeth. I glanced down at Borba. A split ear dripped blood, but undaunted eyes met mine.

"Come."

Because nothing mattered now, I went as he wished and we threaded among bushes until we came to where there was a line of picketed kasi. Someone moved ahead of me there, slowly, so slowly I thought he might be wounded. Borba hissed and pulled at my hand, urging me on. The figure, fumbling with a lead rein, swung around to face me. In this lack of light I could not see his face, but that he was a fugitive from the camp, I knew. I leaped for him. Under my weight he collapsed, though he struggled feebly. I struck an off-world blow, felt my slender Thassa hand go numb. But the one under me was still. I hooked fingers into his collar and pulled him with me into the firelit open.

"Krip Vorlund!"

It was not recognition but summons. I left my prisoner lying and went to the three who waited on me. Mathan lay with his head resting on Merlay's knee, and Maelen—I could not bring myself to look upon her.

But it was her mind-call which had brought me. I went down on my knees and took her two hands into mine. They gave me back no pressure, no sign that more than her eyes lived. Beside her something moved with a whine. Vors—was it Vors or another of the same breed crouched there?

Merlay stirred, Mathan raised his head. There was firelight here, but over us hung the moon. And that Third Ring which had been so bright, so sharply defined when this whole mad venture began, was now only a misty haze, soon to disappear.

"Moon!" A thought—a whisper of a whisper— "Mathan—moon!"

Her hands were very cold in mine, there was nothing which could ever warm them now. Suddenly the glassia beside her cried out, a kind of keening.

Mathan's head rose higher. There was a rumble from his throat, but it was no beast growl. Rather it was singing, a singing which entered my head, my blood, traveled through me. Then I heard Merlay take up that song, which she could not initiate, but which she could second. And Maelen's eyes held mine, searched into me, somehow touched a part of the body I wore which had never been open to Krip Vorlund. So I believe I sang, too, though I am not sure.

We sat there in the fine haze of the fading moon Ring and helped sing Maelen out of death into a new life.

When I again looked with full consciousness around me, the hands I held were those of a husk which the spirit had deserted. And resting on my arm, warm and living, was a small furred head. I dropped the hands of death to gather close warmth and life.

The prisoner I had taken by the kasi lines looked at me when we brought back his senses to him, but did not know me. I knew him well, though, for there was little change in him since that afternoon when he had suggested my meeting with Maelen. Gauk Slafid.

He tried to make a bargain with those of us he believed to be Thassa. Such stupidity I did not understand, unless being made prisoner in such a fashion muddled his wits for a time. Then he mouthed threats, telling us what would happen to all the Thassa unless we instantly set him free and made abject terms with those behind him. And here, too, perhaps fears prompted his ravings. But we heard enough so that I might guess the rest.

Alcey had hit upon the beginnings of it. Yiktor had been closely studied for years by men who needed, as part of their plans, a primitive planet as a base and supply depot. And, playing politics, the Korburg Combine had waded into waters so deep they must aid these exploiters or drown.

The Thassa had been thought to constitute a threat, so a grand crusade against them had been planned. It had been planned to unite the lords under one leader into an army which could later be directed as the exploiters saw fit. But the ancient feuds and rivalries had not made this smooth working, and they chose to use Maelen's involvement with Osokun to whip up that crusade.

What would come of it all, who knew? But at this moment Gauk Slafid was one piece removed from the game board. And I believe the realization of that ate into him acidly, so he mumbled on and on, refusing to face the wreck of his own ambitions.

We took him back with us into that strange dead-lake valley in the hills. And there we all stood before the Old Ones. Slafid they wasted little time upon, giving him to me to take to the port to face the judgment of his own species, saying he was of my blood and mine the responsibility for him.

But then they came to the judging of Maelen under their own law. And I was not allowed to question, or to speak thereupon, for they let me know at once that I only abode there by their favor. When I rode from that place, a guard of Thassa going with me, I carried a furred one who was not Vors, but another.

For this was their judgment—she was to abide in the body given her freely by one who loved her, that her spirit have housing—to remain so until moon and stars drew a pattern in her favor, according to some obscure reckoning of their own. And while so she was to be with me, whom, they said, had been her victim—though to this I did not agree.

With Slafid, who had now lapsed into sullen silence, we came to Yrjar. There he talked again, to officers of the Patrol come at the message borne by the *Lydis*. So was that off-world conspiracy finished, at least as far as Yiktor was concerned. That planet left to lick its wounds and sort some order out of chaos.

I sat at last with Captain Foss and those from the *Lydis*. And I looked past them to a mirror on the wall of the consul's inner chamber. Therein I saw a Thassa. Inside that body, though I might be altered a little, I was still Krip Vorlund. Thassa ways were not mine. Not being truly of them I could not live their life. They would open their vans, their tents to me (Mathan, once more in human-guise, had asked me to join his clan), but among them I would be as a cripple stumping on one foot, using but one hand, seeing with but one eye.

All this I said to Foss, but the final decision lay with him and the others, according to our custom. For the casing which had brought Krip Vorlund to Yiktor was gone, cast into space when it had "died" weeks earlier. Now I waited to hear whether Krip Vorlund was indeed dead, or whether he would be allowed to return to life.

"Free Trader," Foss mused. "I have seen many things traded in my time, and on many worlds, but this is the first time I have seen an exchange of bodies. You say these Thassa look upon their outward flesh and bones as we would upon a suit of clothing, to be changed when the need arises. Does that also stand for you?"

I shook my head. "My own body, yes—but no other. I am Thassa to look upon, not Thassa in powers. I will remain as you now see me."

"Good enough!" Lidj brought his hand down in a mighty blow on the top of the table between us. "You pulled your weight before. Standing in another body will not change that. Are we agreed?"

He glanced at Foss, at the rest of them. And I read their verdict before they spoke it. Inwardly, I wondered if I had done right in asking to return. In me somewhere lay a small part of Jorth, and of Maquad. I perhaps wore more than just the body. But if they thought me Krip Vorlund, I would try to be him again fully. And, looking out upon the port and the waiting *Lydis*, I knew I must throw away all doubts. Jorth and Maquad were less than nothing beside what was waiting out there for me. I was Krip Vorlund, Trader, and that was all—it must be all!

Yet more than just another body did I take out of Yiktor. A small furred person shared my cabin and my thoughts. Many times I do not see her as she is, but as she was. She came by free choice and the will of the Thassa.

Time stretches far between the stars, and fortune makes many turns for good or ill. There are treasures and treasures. Perhaps one shall fall into our hands and paws. And we shall have our ship, and our company of little people to travel the trails of space. Who can tell? I am Krip Vorlund of the *Lydis*, and already they forget that I look different. But I do not forget who lies beneath the skin of Vors and will walk two-footed someday. We shall both see Yiktor again— and if it lies then under Three-Ringed Sotrath—who can foresee what may happen?

Exiles of the Stars

Chapter 1

KRIP VORLUND

There was an odd haze in the room, or was it my eyes? I cupped my hands over them for a moment as I wondered, not only about trusting in my sight, but about this whole situation. For the haze might be the visible emanation of that emotion anyone with the slightest esper talent could pick up clearly—the acrid taste, touch, smell, of fear. Not our own fear, but that of the city which pulsed around us like the uneven breathing of a great terrified animal.

Sensing that, I wanted to run out of the room, the building, beyond the city walls to such security as the *Lydis* had to offer, where the shell of the Free Trader which was my home could shut out that aura of a fear fast approaching panic. Yet I sat where I was, forced my hands to lie quietly across my knees as I watched those in the room with me, listened to the clicking speech of the men of Kartum on the planet Thoth.

There were four of them. Two were priests, both past middle life, both of high standing by the richness of their deep-violet over-mantles, which they had not put aside even though the room was far too warm. The dark skin of their faces, shaven heads, and gesturing hands was lightened with designs in ceremonial yellow paint. Each fingernail was covered with a claw-shaped metal sheath set with tiny gems, which winked and blinked even in this subdued lighting as their fingers, flickering in and out, drew symbols in the air as if they could not carry on any serious conversation without the constant invocation of their god.

Their companions were officials of the ruler of Kartum, as close to him, they averred in the speech of Thoth, as the hairs of his ceremonial royal beard. They sat across the table from our captain, Urban Foss, seemingly willing enough to let the priests do the talking. But their hands were never far from weapon butts, as if they expected at any moment to see the door burst open, the enemy in upon us.

There were three of us from the *Lydis*—Captain Foss, cargomaster Juhel Lidj, and me, Krip Vorlund, the least of that company—Free Traders, born to space and the freedom of the starways as are all our kind. We have been rovers for so long that we have perhaps mutated into a new breed of humankind. Nothing to us, these planet intrigues—not unless we were entrapped in them. And that did not happen often. Experience, a grim teacher, had made us very wary of the politics of the planet-born.

Three—no, we were four. I dropped a hand now and my fingers touched a stiff brush of upstanding hair. I did not have to glance down to know what—who—sat up on her haunches beside my chair, feeling, sensing even more strongly than I the unease of spirit, the creeping menace which darkened about us.

Outwardly there was a glassia of Yiktor there, black-furred except for the tuft of coarse, stiffened gray-white bristles on the crown of the head, with a slender tail as long again as the body, and large paws with sheathed, dagger-sharp claws. Yet appearances were deceiving. For the animal body housed another spirit. This was truly Maelen— she once a Moon Singer of the Thassa—who had been given this outer shape when her own body was broken and dying, then was condemned by her own people to its wearing because she had broken their laws.

Yiktor of the three-ringed moon— What had happened there more than a planet-year ago was printed on my mind so that no small detail could ever be forgotten. It was Maelen who had saved me—my life if not my body, or the body I had worn when I landed there. That body was long since "dead"—spaced to drift forever among the stars—unless it be drawn some day into the fiery embrace of a sun and consumed.

I had had a second body, one which had run on four legs, hunted and killed, bayed at the moon Sotrath—which left in my mind strange dreams of a world which was all scent and sounds such as my own species never knew. And now I wore a third covering, akin to the first and yet different, a body which had another small residue of the alien to creep slowly into my consciousness, so that at times even the world of the *Lydis* (which I had known from birth) seemed strange, a little distorted. Yet I was Krip Vorlund in truth, no matter what outer covering I might wear (that now being the husk of Maquad of the Thassa). Maelen had done this—the twice changing—and for that, despite her motives of good, not ill—she went now four-footed, furred, in my company. Not that I regretted the last.

I had been first a man, then a barsk, and was now outwardly a Thassa; and parts of all mingled in me. My fingers moved through Maelen's stiff crest as I listened, watched, sucked in air tainted not only with queer odors peculiar to a house of Kartum but with the emotions of its inhabitants. I had always possessed the talent of mind-seek. Many Traders developed that, so it was not uncommon. But I also knew that in Maquad's body such a sense had been heightened, sharpened. That was why I was one of this company at this hour, my superiors valuing my worth as an esper to judge those we must deal with.

And I knew that Maelen's even keener powers must also be at work, weighing, assaying. With our combined report Foss would have much on which to base his decision. And that decision must come very soon.

The *Lydis* had planeted four days ago with a routine cargo of pulmn, a powder made from the kelp beds of Hawaika. In ordinary times that powder would have been sold to the temples to become fuel for their ever-burning scented fires. The trade was not a fabulously handsome payload, but it made a reasonable profit. And there was to be picked up in return (if one got on the good side of the priests) the treasures of Nod—or a trickle of them. Which in turn were worth very much indeed on any inner world.

Thoth, Ptah, Anubis, Sekhmet, Set; five planets with the sun Amen-Re to warm them. Of the five, Set was too close to that sun to support life, Anubis a *frozen* waste without colonization. Which left Thoth, Ptah, and Sekhmet. All those had been explored, two partly colonized, generations ago, by Terran-descended settlers. Only those settlers had not been the first.

Our kind is late come to space; that we learned on our first galactic voyaging. There have been races, empires, which rose, fell, and vanished long before our ancestors lifted their heads to wonder dimly at the nature of the stars. Wherever we go we find traces of these other peoples—though there is much we do not know, cannot learn. "Forerunners" we call them, lumping them all together. Though more and more we are coming to understand that there were many more than just one such galaxy-wide empire, one single race voyaging in the past. But we have learned so little.

The system of Amen-Re turned out to be particularly rich in ancient remains. But it was not known yet whether the civilization which had flourished here had been only system-wide, or perhaps an outpost of a yet-unclassified galactic one. Mainly because the priests had very early taken upon themselves the guardianship of such "treasure."

Each people had its gods, its controlling powers. There is an inner need in our species to acknowledge something beyond ourselves, something greater. In some civilizations there is a primitive retrogression to sacrifice—even of the worshipers' own kind—and to religions of fear and darkness. Or belief can be the recognition of a spirit, without any formal protestation of rites. But on many worlds the gods are strong and their voices, the priests, are considered infallible, above even the temporal rulers. So that Traders walk softly and cautiously on any world where there are many temples and such a priesthood.

The system of Amen-Re had been colonized by ships from Veda. And those had been filled with refugees from a devastating religious war—the persecuted, fleeing. Thus a hierarchy had had control from the first.

Luckily they were not rigidly fanatical toward the unknown. On some worlds the remnants of any native former civilization were destroyed as devilish work. But in the case of Amen-Re some farsighted high priest in the early days had had the wit to realize that these remains were indeed treasure which could be exploited. He had proclaimed all such finds the due of the god, to be kept in the temples.

When Traders began to call at Thoth (settlement on Ptah was too small to induce visits), lesser finds were offered in bargaining, and these became the reason for cargo exploitation. For there was no local product on Thoth worth the expense of off-world shipping.

It was the lesser bits, the crumbs, which were so offered. The bulk of the best was used to adorn the temples. But those were enough to make the trip worthwhile for my people, if not for the great companies and combines. Our cargo space was strictly limited; we lived on the fringe of the trade of the galaxy, picking up those items too small to entice the bigger dealers.

So trade with Thoth had become routine. But ship time is not planet time. Between one visit and the next there may be a vast change on any world, political or even physical. And when the *Lydis* had set down this time, she had found boiling around her the beginnings of chaos, unless there came some sharp change. Government, religion, do not exist in a vacuum. Here government and religion—which had always had a firm alliance—were together under fire.

A half year earlier there had arisen in the mountain country to the east of Kartum a new prophet. There had been such before, but somehow the temples had managed either to discredit them or to absorb their teachings without undue trouble. This time the priesthood found itself on the defensive. And, its complacency well established by years of untroubled rule, it handled the initial difficulty clumsily.

As sometimes happens, one mistake led to a greater, until now the government at Kartum was virtually in a state of siege. With the church under pressure, the temporal powers scented independence. The well-established nobility was loyal to the temple. After all, their affairs were so intertwined that they could not easily withdraw their support. But there are always have-nots wanting to be haves—lesser nobility and members of old families who resent not having more. And some of these made common cause with the rebels.

The spark which had set it off was the uncovering of a "treasure" place which held some mysterious contagion swift to kill off those involved. Not only that, but the plague spread, bringing death to others who had not dealt with the place at all. Then a fanatical hill priest-prophet began to preach that the treasures were evil and should be destroyed.

He led a mob to blow up the infected site, then went on, hot with the thirst for destruction, to do the same to the local temple which served as a storage place for the goods. The authorities moved in then, and the contagion attacked the troops. This was accepted by the surviving rebels as a vindication of their beliefs. So the uprising spread, finding adherents who wanted nothing more than to upset the status quo.

As is only too common where there has been an untroubled rule, the authorities had not realized the seriousness of what they termed a local outburst. There had been quite a few among the higher-placed priests and nobles who had been loath to move at once, wanting to conciliate the rebels. In fact there had been too much talk and not enough action at just the wrong moment.

Now there was a first-class civil war in progress. And, as far as we were able to learn, the government was shaky. Which was the reason for this secret meeting here in the house of a local lordling. The *Lydis* had come in with a cargo now of little or no value. And while a Free Trader may make an unpaying voyage once, a second such can put the ship in debt to the League.

To be without a ship is death for my kind. We know no other life—planetside existence is prison. And even if we could scrape a berth on another Trader, that would mean starting from the bottom once again, with little hope of ever climbing to freedom again. It would perhaps not be so hard on junior members of the crew, such as myself, who was only assistant cargomaster. But we had had to fight for even our lowly berths. As for Captain Foss, the other officers—it would mean total defeat.

Thus, though we had learned of the upsetting state of affairs within a half hour after landing, we did not space again. As long as there was the least hope of turning the voyage to some account we remained finned down, even though we were sure there was presently no market for pulmn. As a matter of routine, Foss and Lidj had contacted the temple. But instead of our arranging an open meeting with a supply priest, they had summoned us here.

So great was their need that they wasted no time in formal greeting but came directly to the point. For it seemed that after all we did have something to sell—safety. Not for the men who met us, nor even for their superiors, but for the cream of the planet's treasure, which could be loaded on board the *Lydis* and sent to protective custody elsewhere.

On Ptah the temple had established a well-based outpost, mainly because certain minerals were mined there. And it had become a recognized custom for the hierarchy of the church to withdraw to

Ptah at times for periods of retreat, removed from the distractions of Thoth. It was to that sanctuary that they proposed now to send the pick of the temple holdings, and the *Lydis* was to transport them.

When Captain Foss asked why they did not use their own ore-transport ships for the purpose (not that he was averse to the chance to make this trip pay), they had a quick answer. First, the ore ships were mainly robo-controlled, not prepared to carry a crew of more than one or two techs on board. They could not risk sending the treasure in such, when tinkering with the controls might lose it forever. Secondly, the *Lydis,* being a Free Trader, could be trusted. For such was the Traders' reputation that all knew, once under contract, we held by our word. To void such a bond was unthinkable. The few, very few, times it had happened, the League itself had meted out such punishment as we did not care to remember.

Therefore, they said, if we took contract they knew that their cargo would be delivered. And not only one such cargo, but they would have at least two, maybe more. If the rebels did not invest the city (as they now threatened) too soon, the priests would continue to send off their hoard as long as they could. But the cream of it all would be on the first trip. And they would pay—which was the subject of the present meeting.

Not that we were having any wrangling. But no man becomes a Trader without a very shrewd idea of how to judge his wares or services. Thus to outbargain one of us was virtually impossible. And, too, this was a seller's market, and we had a monopoly on what we had to offer.

There had been two serious defeats of the government forces within a matter of ten days. Though the loyal army still stubbornly held the road to the city, there was no reason to believe that they could continue to do so for long. So Foss and Lidj made the best of their advantage. There was also the danger of an uprising in Kartum, as three other cities had already fallen to rebels working from within, inciting mobs to violence and taking advantage of such outbursts. As one of the priests had said, it was almost as if a kind of raging insanity spread from man to man at these times.

"Trouble—" I did not need that mind-alert from Maelen, for I could feel it also, an ingathering of darkness, as if any light was swallowed up by shadows. Whether the priests had any esper talents, I did not know. Perhaps even this aura of panic could be induced by a gifted enemy at work. Though I did not pick up any distinct trace of such interference.

I stirred; Lidj glanced at me, picked up my unspoken warning. Those of the *Lydis* had learned, even as I, that since my return to the ship in this Thassa body my esper powers were greater than they had once been. In turn he nodded at the priests.

"Let it be so contracted." As cargomaster he had the final decision. For in such matters he could overrule even the captain. Trade was his duty, first and always.

But if the priests were relieved, there was no lightening of the tension in that chamber. Maelen pressed against my knee, but she did not mind-touch. Only I noted that her head tuft was no longer so erect. And I remembered of old that the sign of anger or alarm with the glassia was a flattening of that tuft to lie against the skull. So I sent mind-seek swiftly to probe the atmosphere.

Straight mind-to-mind reading cannot be unless it is willed by both participants. But it is easy enough to tune in on emotions, and I found (though at a distance which I could not measure) something which sent my hand to the butt of my stunner, even as Maelen's crest had betrayed her own concern. There was menace far more directed than the uneasiness in this room. But I could not read whether it was directed against those who had summoned us, or against our own ship's party.

The priests left first with the nobles. They had guardsmen waiting without—which we had not. Foss looked directly to me.

"Something is amiss, more than just the general situation," he commented.

"There is trouble waiting out there." I nodded to the door and what lay beyond. "Yes, more than what we might ordinarily expect."

Maelen reared, setting her forepaws against me, her head raised so that her golden eyes looked into mine. Her thought was plain in my mind.

"Let me go first. A scout is needed."

I was loath to agree. Here she was plainly alien and, as such, might not only attract unwelcome attention but, in the trigger-set tension, even invite attack.

"Not so." She had read my thought. "You forget—it is night. And I, being in this body, know how to use the dark as a friend."

So I opened the door and she slipped through. The hall without was not well lighted and I marveled at how well she used the general dusk as a cover, being gone before I was aware. Foss and Lidj joined me, the captain saying, "There is a very wrong feel here. The sooner we raise ship, I am thinking, the better. How long will loading take?"

Lidj shrugged. "That depends upon the bulk of the cargo. At any rate we can make all ready to handle it." He spoke in code into his wrist com, giving orders to dump the pulmn to make room. There was this much the priests had had to agree to—they must let us, at the other end of the voyage, take our reckoning out of the treasure already stored in the temple on Ptah. And a certain amount must be in pieces of our own selection. Usually Traders had to accept discards without choice.

We headed for the street. By Foss's precaution our meeting had been held in a house close to the city wall, so we need not venture far into Kartum. But I, for one, knew that I would not breathe really easily again until my boot plates rang on the *Lydis's* entry ramp. The dusk which had hung at our coming had thickened into night. But there was still the roar of life in the city.

Then—

"'Ware!" Maelen's warning was as sharp as a vocal shout. "Make haste for the gates!"

She had sent with such power that even Foss had picked up her alert, and I did not need to pass her message on. We started at a trot for the gate, Foss getting out our entry pass.

I noticed a flurry by that barrier as we neared. Fighting. Above the hoarse shouting of the men milling in combat came the *crack* of the native weapons. Luckily this was not a planet which dealt with lasers and blasters. But they had solid-projectile weapons which made a din. Our stunners could not kill, only render unconscious. But we could die from one of those archaic arms in use ahead as quickly as from a blaster.

Foss adjusted the beam button of his stunner; Lidj and I did likewise, altering from narrow ray to wide sweep. Such firing exhausted the charges quickly, but in such cases as this we had no choice. We must clear a path ahead.

"To the right—" Lidj did not really need that direction from Foss. He had already moved into flank position on one side, as I did on the other.

We hurried on, knowing that we must get closer for a most effective attack. Then I saw Maelen hunkered in a doorway. She ran to me, ready to join our final dash.

"Now!"

We fired together, sweeping all the struggling company, friend and foe alike, if we did have friends among those fighters. Men staggered and fell, and we began to run, leaping over the prone bodies sprawled across the gate opening. But the barrier itself was closed and we thrust against it in vain.

"Lever, in the gatehouse—" panted Foss.

Maelen streaked away. She might no longer have humanoid hands, but glassia paws are not to be underestimated. And that she was able to make good use of those she demonstrated a moment later as the side panels drew back to let us wriggle through.

Then we ran as if the demon hosts of Nebu brayed at our heels. For at any moment one of those projectile weapons might be aimed at us. I, for one, felt a strange sensation between my shoulder blades, somehow anticipating such a wound.

However, there came no such stroke of ill fortune, and we did reach the ramp and safety. So all four of us, Maelen running with the greatest ease, pounded up into the *Lydis*. And we were hardly through the hatch opening when we heard the grate of metal, knew that those on duty were sealing the ship.

Foss leaned against the wall by the ramp, thumbing a new charge into his stunner. It was plain that from now on we must be prepared to defend ourselves, as much as if we were on an openly hostile world.

I looked to Maelen. "Did you warn of the fight at the gate?"

"Not so. There were those a-prowl who sought to capture you. They would prevent the treasure from going hence. But they came too late. And I think that the gate fight, in a manner, spoiled their plans."

Foss had not followed that, so I reported it to him.

He was grimly close-faced now. "If we are to raise that treasure— they will have to send it to us. No man from here goes planetside again!"

Chapter 2

KRIP VORLUND

"So, what do we do now? We're safe enough in the ship. But how long do we wait?" Manus Hunold, our astrogator, had triggered the visa-plate, and we who had crowded into the control cabin to watch by its aid what happened without were intent on what it could show us.

Men streamed out onto the field, ringing in the *Lydis*—though they showed a very healthy regard for her blast-off rockets and kept a prudent distance from the lift area near her fins. They were not of the half-soldier, half-police force who supported authority, though they were armed and even kept a ragged discipline in their confrontation of the ship. However, how they could expect to come to any open quarrel with us if we stayed inside, I could not guess.

I had snapped mind-seek; there were too many waves of raw emotion circling out there. To tune to any point in that sea of violence was to tax my power near to burn-out.

"They can't be stupid enough to believe they can overrun us—" That was Pawlin Shallard, our engineer. "They're too far above the primitive to think that possible."

"No." Lidj had his head up, was watching the screen so intently he might be trying to pick out of that crowd some certain face or figure. Hunold had set the screen on "circle" as he might have done at a first set-down on an unexplored world, so that the scene shifted, allowing us a slow survey about the landing site. "No, they won't rush us. They want something else. To prevent our cargo from coming. But these are city men—I would not have believed the rebels had infiltrated in such numbers or so quickly—" He broke off, frowning at the ever-changing picture.

"Wait!" Foss pushed a "hold" button and that slow revolution was halted.

What we saw now was the gate through which we had come only a short time ago. Through it was issuing a well-armed force in uniform, the first sign of a disciplined attack on the rebels. The men in it spread out as skirmishers to form a loose cover for a cart. On that was mounted a long-snouted, heavy-looking tube which men swung down and around to face the mob between them and the ship. A fringe of the rebels began to push away from the line of fire. But that great barrel swung in a small arc, as if warning of the swath it could cut through their ranks.

Men ran from the mass of those besieging us—first by ones and twos, and then by squads. We had no idea of the more complex weapons of Thoth, but it would seem that this was one the natives held in high respect. The mob was not giving up entirely. But the ranks of the loyal soldiery were being constantly augmented from the city, pushing out and out, the mob retreating sullenly before them.

"This is it!" Lidj made for the ship ladder. "I'd say they are going to run the cargo out now. Do we open to load?" Under normal circumstances the loading of the ship was his department. But with the safety of the *Lydis* perhaps at stake, that decision passed automatically to Foss.

"Cover the hatches with stunners; open the upper first. Until we see how well they manage—" was the captain's answer.

Minutes later we stood within the upper hatch. It was open and I had an unpleasantly naked feeling as I waited at my duty post, my calculator fastened to my wrist instead of lying in the palm of my hand, leaving me free to use my weapon. This time I had that set on narrow beam. Griss Sharvan, second engineer, pressed into guard service and facing me on the other side of the cargo opening, kept his ready on high-energy spray.

The barreled weapon had been moved farther out, to free the city gate. But its snout still swung in a jerky pattern, right to left and back again. There were no members of the mob left in front of us within the now-narrowed field of our vision, except several prone bodies, men who must have been picked off by the skirmishers.

Beyond, the gate had been opened to its furthest extent. And through that gap came the first of the heavily loaded transports. The Thothians had motorized cars which burned liquid fuel. To us such seemed sluggish when compared to the solar-energized machines of the inner planets. But at least they were better than the animal-drawn vehicles of truly primitive worlds. And now three of these trucks crawled over the field toward the *Lydis*.

A robed priest drove each, but there were guards aboard, on the alert, their heads protected by grotesque bowl-shaped helmets, their weapons ready. Between those, we saw, as the first truck ground nearer, more priests crouched behind what small protection the sides of the vehicles offered, their faces livid. But they arose quickly as the truck came to a halt under the swinging lines of our crane, and pawed at the top boxes and bales of the cargo. It seemed that they were to shift that while the guards remained on the defensive.

Thus began the loading of the *Lydis*. The priests were willing but awkward workers. So I swung out and down with the crane to help below, trying not to think of the possibility of a lucky shot from the mob. For there was the crackle of firing now coming from a distance.

Up and down, in with the crane ropes, up—down. We had to use great care, for though all were well muffled in wrappings, we knew that what we handled were irreplaceable treasures. The first truck, emptied, drew to one side. But the men who had manned it remained, the priests to help with the loading of the next, the guards spreading out as had the skirmishers from the gate. I continued to supervise the loading, at the same time listing the number of each piece swung aloft, reciting it into my recorder. Lidj by the hatch would be making a duplicate of my record, and together they would be officially sealed in the presence of the priests' representatives when all was aboard.

Three trucks we emptied. The load of the fourth consisted of only four pieces—one extra-large, three small. I signaled for double crane power, not quite sure if the biggest crate could be maneuvered through the hatch. It was a tight squeeze, but the men there managed it. When I saw it disappear I spoke to the priest in charge.

"Any more?"

He shook his head as he still watched where that large crate had vanished. Then he looked to me.

"No more. But the High One will come to take receipt for the shipment."

"How soon?" I pressed. Still I did not use mind-touch. There was too much chance of being overwhelmed by the raw emotion engendered on a battlefield. Of course the *Lydis* was such a fort as could not be stormed, but I knew the sooner we raised from Thoth the better.

"When he can." His answer was ambiguous enough to be irritating. Already he turned away, calling some order in the native tongue.

I shrugged and swung up to the hatch. There was a stowage robo at work there. My superior leaned against the wall just inside, reading the dial of his recorder. As I came in he pressed the "stop" button to seal off his list.

"They won't take receipt," I reported. "They say that there is a High One coming to do that."

Lidj grunted, so I went to see to the sealing of the holds. The large crate which had been the last was still in the claws of two robo haulers. And, strong as those were, it was not easily moved. I watched them center it in the smaller top hold, snap on the locks to keep it in position during flight. That was the last, and I could now slide the doors shut, imprint the seal which would protect the cargo until we planeted once more. Of course Lidj would be along later to add his thumb signature to mine, and only when the two of us released it could anything less than a destruct burner get it out.

I stopped in my cabin as I went aloft. Maelen, as was usual during cargo loading, lay on her own bunk there. Her crested head rested on her two forepaws, which were folded under her muzzle as she stretched out at her ease. But she was not sleeping. Her golden eyes were open. At a second glance I recognized that fixity of stare—she was engaged in intense mind-seek, and I did not disturb her. Whatever she so listened to was of absorbing interest.

As I was backing out, not wanting to trouble her, the rigid tension broke. Her head lifted a little. But I waited for her to communicate first.

"There is one who comes, but not he whom you expect."

For I thought of the high priest coming for the receipt.

"He is not of the same mind as those who hired our aid," she continued. "Rather is he of an opposite will—"

"A rebel?"

"No. This one wears the same robe as the other temple men. But he does not share their wishes. He thinks it ill done, close to evil, to take these treasures from the sanctuary he serves. He believes that in retaliation his god will bring down ill upon all who aid in such a crime, for such it is to him. He is not one who tempers belief because of a change in the winds of fortune. Now he comes, because he deems it his duty, to deliver the curse of his god. For he serves a being who knows more of wrath than of love and justice. He comes to curse us—"

"To curse only—or to fight?" I asked.

"Do not think of the one as less than the other! In some ways a curse can be a greater weapon, when it is delivered by a believer."

To say that I would scoff at that is wrong. Any far rover of the sky trails can tell you that there is nothing so strange that it cannot happen on one world or another. I have known curses to slay—but only on one condition, that he who is so cursed is also a believer. Perhaps the priests who had sent their treasure into our holds might so be cursed, believe, and die. But for us of the *Lydis* it was a different matter. We are not men of no belief. Each man has his own god or supreme power. Maelen herself had him she called Molaster, by whom and for whom she fashioned her way of life. But that we might be touched by some god of Thoth I could not accept.

"Accept or not"—she had easily followed my thought—"believe or not, yet a curse, any curse, is a heavy load to carry. For evil begets evil and dark clings to shadows. The curse of a believer has its own power. This man is sincere in what he believes and he has powers of his own. Belief *is* power!"

"You cry a warning?" I was more serious now, for such from Maelen was not to be taken lightly.

"I do not know. Were I what I once was—" Her thoughts were suddenly closed to me. Never had I heard her regret what she had left behind on Yiktor when her own body had taken fatal hurt and her people, in addition, had set upon her the penance of perhaps years in the form she now wore. If she had any times of longing or depression, she held them locked within her. And now this broken sentence expressed a desire to hold again what she had had as a

Moon Singer of the Thassa, as a man would reach wistfully for a weapon he had lost.

I knew that her message must be passed on to the captain as soon as possible and I went up to the control cabin. Foss sat watching the visa-plate, which at present showed the line of empty trucks on their way back to Kartum. The snouted weapon still sat just outside the gate, its crew alert about it as if they expected more trouble.

"Hatch closed, cargo sealed," I reported. Though that was only a matter of form. Lidj was in the astrogator's seat, slumped a little in the webbing, as he chewed thoughtfully on a stick of restorative slo-go.

"Maelen says—" I began, not even sure if I had their full attention. But I continued with the report.

"Cursing now," Foss commented as I finished. "But why? We are supposed to be saving their treasures for them, aren't we?"

"Schism in the temple, yet," Lidj said in answer to the captain's first question. "It would seem that this High Priest has more than one complication to make life interesting for him. It is rather to be wondered at why this was not mentioned before we accepted contract." His jaws clamped shut on the stick.

The visa-plate pictured new action for us. Though the trucks had gone through the gates, the guards there made no move to fall back. However, there was a stir at that barrier. Not more of the army, rather a procession which might have been honoring some feast day of the god.

We could see plainly the dull purple of priestly robes, brightened by dashes of vivid crimson or angry bursts of orange-yellow, as if flames sprouted here and there. We could not hear, but we could see the large drums borne by men on the outer edges of that line of march, drums being vigorously beaten.

"We have that on board which might be as fire to a fuse," Lidj remarked, still watching the screen, chewing at his slo-go. "The Throne of Qur."

I stared at him. One hears of legends. They are the foundation for much careless talk and speculation. But to see—actually to lay hands on the fabric of one, that is another matter altogether. That last, the largest crate we had hoisted aboard—the Throne of Qur!

Who had been the first, the real owners of the treasures of Thoth? No one could set name to them now. Oddly enough, though the remains found were obviously products of a very high civilization, there had never been discovered any form of writing or record. We had no names for the kings, queens, nobles, priests, who had left their possessions so. Thus the finders, of necessity, had given the names of their own to the finds.

The Throne had been discovered all alone, walled away in a section by itself at the end of a blind passage in one of the early-located caches. The adventurer who had bossed the crew uncovering it had been not a native to Thoth, but an archaeologist (or so he claimed) from Phaphor. He had named his discovery for a deity of his home world. Not that that had brought him luck, perhaps the contrary. For such christening had offended the priests. The adventurer had died, suddenly, and the Throne had been speedily claimed by the temple, in spite of the fact that the priesthood had earlier sold excavation rights. For that find had been made in the days before the complete monopoly of the priesthood had been enforced. To uncover the Throne he had given his life, as he must have known, for he had made a vain attempt to reseal that side passage, perhaps hoping to smuggle the Throne away. Only it was far too late for that as soon as it was found.

The Throne had been fashioned for one of a race who had physically resembled us. The seat was wrought of a red metal, surprisingly light in weight for its durability. Guarding this were two side pieces, the tops of which furnished arms, and those reared as the heads of unknown creatures, all overlaid with scales of gold and burnished green, with eyes of milky white stones. But it was the flaring, towering back which was its chief marvel. For it seemed to be a wide spread of feathers so delicately fashioned of gold and green that they might once have been real fronds. And the tip of each feather was widened to enclose a blue-green gem, a full one hundred of them in all by count.

But the real peculiarity of the piece, apart from the skill and wonderful craftsmanship, was that those blue-green stones and the milky ones set in the arms were, as far as anyone had been able to discover, not only not native to Thoth but unknown anywhere else. Nor were their like set into any other object so far found on this planet.

Once revealed, the Throne had been moved to the temple in Kartum, where it formed one of the main attractions. Since a close inspection was allowed only after endless waiting and under strict supervision, not much had since been learned of it—though images of it appeared on every tape dealing with Thoth.

The procession by the gate moved out toward the *Lydis*. And those bright red and yellow touches were now seen as wide scarves or shawls resting about the shoulders of the center core of marchers, strung out behind a single man. He was tall, standing well above those immediately about him, and so gaunt that the bones of his face were almost death's-head sharp. There was no softness in that face, nothing but deeply graven lines which spelled fanaticism. His mouth moved as though he were speaking, shouting, or chanting along with the drums which flanked him. His eyes were fastened on the *Lydis*.

I was aware of movement beside me—Maelen was there, her head strained at an angle to watch the screen. I stooped and picked her up that she might see more easily. Her body was more solid, heavier, than it appeared.

"A man of peril, a strong believer," she told me. "Though he is not like our Old Ones—yet he could be, were he properly schooled in the Way of Molaster. Save that such as he have not the open heart and mind that are needful. He sees but one path and is prepared to give all, even life, to achieve what he wishes. Such men are dangerous—"

Lidj glanced over his shoulder. "You are right, little one." He must have picked up her full mind-send. To my shipmates Maelen was all glassia, of course. Only Griss Sharvan had ever seen her in her Thassa body, and even he now seemed unable to connect animal with woman. They knew she was not in truth as she seemed, but they could not hold that ever in mind.

The procession of priests formed a wedge, with their leader at its tip—a spear point aimed at the ship. We still could not hear, but we saw the drummers rest their sticks. Yet the lips of the tall priest still moved and now also his hands. For he stooped and caught up a handful of the trampled, sandy soil. This he spat upon, though he looked not at it, but ever to the ship.

Having spat, he rolled it back and forth between his palms. And now and then he raised it higher, seemed to breathe into what he rolled and kneaded so.

"He curses," Maelen reported. "He calls upon his god to curse that which would take from Thoth the treasures of the temple, and all those who aid in the matter. And he swears that the treasure shall be returned, though those who take it will then be dead and blasted—and for its return he shall wait where he now stands."

The priest's lips no longer moved. Two of his followers pushed forward, one on either side. They whipped from beneath their cloaks two lengths of matting, and these they spread upon the ground one over the other. When they had done, though he never looked once at them but only to the *Lydis*, the priest knelt upon that carpet, his hands crossed upon his breast. Nor did he afterward stir, while his followers, drums and all, withdrew some paces.

Now from the gate came a small surface car which detoured around the kneeling priest in a very wide swing. And it approached the *Lydis*.

"Our take-off authorization." Lidj climbed from his seat. "I'll go get it—the sooner we lift the better."

He put the uneaten portion of his slo-go back into its covering, stowed it in a seam pocket, and started from the cabin. With take-off sure to follow soon, we all scattered, making for our posts, ready to strap down. Maelen I aided into her upper berth, laced the protective webbing which she could not manage with her paws, then dropped into my own place. As I lay waiting for the signal I thought of the kneeling priest.

Unless we did make a second trip to pick up more cargo, he was going to have a long wait. And what if we did return, having made our first delivery to Ptah? Would such a return prove him so wrong that he would not only lose his followers but be shaken in his own belief?

"Let us return first—" Maelen's thought came.

There is no betraying intonation in thoughts as there sometimes is in voices. Yet there was something— Did she really believe some ill luck would come to us?

"The Scales of Molaster hang true and steady for those of good will. Any evil in this matter is not of our doing. Yet I do not like—"

The signal for blast-off cut across that. She shut her mind as one might shut his mouth. We lay waiting for the familiar discomfort as the *Lydis* headed up and out—not to the stars this time, but to the fourth planet of the system, a pale crescent now showing in the western sky.

Since we did not go into hyper for such a short trip, we unstrapped as soon as we were on stable speed. Also we were now in free fall, a condition which is never comfortable—though we had been accustomed to it practically from birth. Maelen did not like it at all and preferred to spend such periods in her takeoff webbing. I saw that she was as comfortable as might be under the circumstances and then pulled my way along to Lidj's quarters.

But I found, to my amazement, that my superior was not alone. Though he had discarded the robe and cape of his calling, the shaven head of the man lying on the cargomaster's own bunk was plainly that of a priest. We had not been prepared for any passenger; at least I had not been informed of one. And it was so seldom that a Free Trader carried any but a member of the crew that I looked quickly to Lidj for enlightenment. The priest himself lay limp, held by take-off webbing still, appearing totally unconscious.

Lidj waved me outside the cabin and followed. He pulled shut the sliding panel to seal the cabin.

"A passenger—"

"He had orders we had to accept," Lidj informed me. I could see he had little liking for the matter. "He not only brought a warning, to rise as soon as we could, but authorization from the high priest for him to see our cargo to its destination and take charge there. I do not know what pot has boiled over down there—but our Thothian charterers wanted us away as fast as rockets could raise us. At least we can do with one extra aboard, as long as he is going no farther than Ptah."

Chapter 3

MAELEN

I lay in my assigned resting place in this ship and fought once again my weary battle, that battle which I could never share with another, not even with this outlander who had fought a like one in his time. I who was once Maelen, Moon Singer, and (as I know now) far too arrogant in my pride of deed and word, believing that I alone had an accounting with fate and that all would go according to my desire.

Well do we of the Thassa need to remember the Scales of Molaster, wherein the deeds of our bodies, the thoughts of our minds, the wishes of our hearts, will be weighed against truth and right!

Because I had been so weighed and found wanting, now I went in other guise, that of my small comrade Vors. And Vors had willingly given me her body when my own had failed me. So I must not belittle or waste the great sacrifice she had made. Thus I willed myself to endure and endure and endure—to fight this battle not once but again and again, and again and again.

I had chosen, as a Moon Singer who must learn to be one with other living things, to run the high places of Yiktor in animal guise, and had so fulfilled my duty. Yet that had been always with the

235

comfortable knowledge that my own body waited for my return, that this exile was only for a time. While now—

Always, though, I was still Maelen—myself—ME; yet also there was an occupying part which still held the essence of Vors. Much as I had loved and honored her for the great thing she had done for me, yet also I must struggle against the instincts of this body, to remain as much as I could only a temporary in-dweller. And always was the brooding shadow of a new fear—that there would be no escape ever, that through the years Vors would become more and more, Maelen less and less.

I longed to ask my companion—this alien Krip Vorlund— whether such a fear had ridden him when he had run as a barsk. Yet I could not admit to any that I carried such unease in me. Though whether that silence was born of some of my old pride and need to be mistress of the situation, or whether it was a curb which was needful, I did not know. It remained that I must play my role as best I could. But also I welcomed those times when it was given me to play some necessary part in the life of the *Lydis*, for then it seemed that Maelen was wholly in command again. So it had been that during those last hours on Thoth I had been able to forget myself and enter into the venture of the ship.

Yet I lay now and my thoughts were dark, for I remembered the priest who had ceremoniously cursed us. As I had told Krip, there is power in the pure belief of such a man. Though he had used no wand or staff to point us out to the Strengths of the Deep Dark, still he had called upon what he knew to encompass us. And—I had not been able to reach his mind; there had been a barrier locking me out as securely as if he had been an Old One.

Now I lay on the bunk, held snug by the webbing (for with all my shipboard life I have never been able to adjust well to free fall)—I lay there and used mind-seek.

Those of the *Lydis* were as always. I touched only lightly the surface of their thoughts. For to probe, unless that is desperately needed, is a violation to which no living being should subject another. But in my seeking I came upon another mind and—

I swung my head around, reached with my teeth for the lacing which held me. Then sane reason took control, and I sent a call to Krip. His reply was instant—he must have read my concern.

"What is it?"

"There is one on board from Thoth. He means us ill!"

There was a pause and then his answer came clearly.

"I have him under my eyes now. He is unconscious; he has been so since the ship lifted."

"His mind is awake—and busy! Krip, this man, he is more than all others we met on Thoth. He is akin, closely akin, to the one who cursed us. Watch him—watch him well!"

But even then I did not realize how different he was, this stranger, nor just how much we had to fear him. For, as with him who had cursed us, there was a barrier behind which he hid more than half his thoughts. And though I could not read them, I did sense peril there.

"Do not doubt, he shall be watched."

It was as if the stranger had heard what had passed between us. Perhaps he did. For there followed a swift subduing of the emanations of his mind. Though that could have come from a bodily weakness also. But I was on guard, as if in truth I walked a sentry's beat in the belly of the *Lydis.*

There is no night or day, morn or evening, in a ship. Which was something I had found hard to adjust to when first I came on board. Just as the narrow spaces of the cabins, the corridors, were prison-like for one who never had any home save the wagons of the Thassa, had always lived by choice beyond man-made walls. There was always an acrid scent here. And sometimes the throbbing of the engines which powered us from star to star seemed almost more than I could bear, so that my only escape was into the past and my memories. No night or day, save those which the Traders arbitrarily set for themselves, divided into orderly periods of sleep and waking.

Once the ship was in flight and set on course, there was little which had to be done to keep her so. Krip had early shown me that her crew did not lack occupation, however. Some of them created with their hands, making small things which amused them, or which they could add to their trade goods. Others busied their minds, learning from their store of information tapes. So did they labor to keep the ship from becoming their prison also.

For Krip—well, perhaps it was for him now as it was for me, and the body he wore influenced him a little. Because he was outwardly Thassa, he asked of me my memories, wanting to learn all he could of my people. And I shared with him freely, save for such things which could not be spread before any outlander. So we both escaped into a world beyond the throbbing cabin walls.

Now a little later he returned, ready for the sleep period. Was there any change in what I had learned about our passenger, he asked. Lidj had taken it upon himself, after my warning, to give the man a certain drug which was meant to ease lift-off and which should keep him in slumber for much of our voyage.

No, no change, I answered. And so accustomed had I become to the ship's pattern that, I, too, felt the need of sleep.

I was sharply awakened from my rest, as sharply as if a noose of filan cord had closed about my body, jerking me upright. I found myself in truth fighting the webbing which held me fast to the bunk, even as my mind steadied.

For a dazed moment or two, I could not guess what had so roused me. Then I knew that I no longer felt the ever-present beat of the engine, but rather there was a break in the smooth rhythm. And only a second later a shrill sound came from above my head, issuing from the intercom system of the ship—a warning that all was not well with the *Lydis*.

Krip rolled out of the lower bunk. Since we were in free fall his too-swift movement carried him against the other wall with bruising force. I heard him give a muttered exclamation as he caught at a wall rack and clawed his way back to where I lay. Holding on with one hand, he ripped loose my webbing.

Now that the first warning had awakened us, words came from the intercom, booming like a signal of doom.

"All off-duty personnel, strap down for orbiting!"

Krip paused, his hand still on my webbing, while I clung with my great claws to the bunk so I would not float away, unable to govern my going. Then he responded to orders, pushing me back, making me secure again before he returned to his own place.

"We cannot have reached Ptah!" I was still shaken from that sudden awakening.

"No—but the ship—"

He did not need to continue. Even I, who was no real star voyager, could feel the difference. There was a catch in the rhythm of the engines.

I dared not use mind-touch, lest I disturb some brain needed to concentrate on the ship's well-being. But I tried mind-seek. Perhaps it was instinct which aimed that first at the stranger in our midst.

I have no idea whether I cried out aloud. But instantly Krip answered me. And when he read my discovery his alarm was near fear.

I am—was—a Moon Singer. As such, I used the wand. I could beam-read. I have wrought the transfer of bodies under the three rings of Sotrath. By the grace of Molaster I have done much with my talent. But this that I now touched upon was new, alien, dark, and destructive beyond all my reckoning.

For there flowed from that priest as he lay a current of pure power. And I could slip along it, as I did, drawing Krip's thought with me, through the *Lydis*, down to something that lay below those engines which were her life—something in the cargo hold.

And that mind power released the force of what lay in hiding, which had been cunningly attuned to the thought of one man alone. So that there now emanated from that hidden packet a more powerful force than any thought, and a deadly one, acting upon the heart of the *Lydis* to slow the beat of her engines, make them sluggish. And in time it would bring about their failure.

I tried to dam that compelling force flowing from the mind of the priest. But it was as if the current of energy were encased in the Rock of Tormora. It could be neither cut nor swayed from its purpose. Yet I sensed that if it might be halted, then the packet would fail in turn. Learning that, Krip sent his own message:

"The man then, if not his thought—get to the man!"

Straightway I saw he was right. Now I ceased my fight against that current and joined with Krip to seek out Lidj, who should be nearest to the stranger. And so we warned the cargomaster, urging physical action on his part.

It came! That current of feeding energy pulsed, lessened, surged again—then sparked weakly and was gone. The vibration in the ship steadied for perhaps four heartbeats. Then it, too, flickered off. I could feel through the *Lydis* the surge of will of those in her, their fear and need to hold that engine steady.

Then came the return of gravity. We were in orbit—but where and—

My glassia body was not fashioned to take such strains. Though I fought frantically to retain consciousness, I failed.

There was a flat-sweet taste in my mouth; moisture trickled from my muzzle. That part of me which was Vors remembered blood. I ached painfully. When I forced open my eyes I could see only through a mist. But the roof of the cabin was steadily up and I was pulled to the bunk by a gravity greater than that of Thoth.

We had set down. Were we back on Thoth? I doubted it. Hooking my claws against the sides of the bunk, I was able in spite of the webbing to wriggle closer to the edge, look down to see how it had fared with my cabinmate.

As he pushed himself up his eyes met mine. There was a sudden look of concern—

"Maelen!" he said aloud. "You are hurt!"

I turned attention to my body. There were bruises, yes. And blood had issued from my nose and mouth to bedaub my fur. Yet all hurts were small, and I reported it so.

Thus we planeted, not on Thoth, nor on Ptah, which had been our goal, but on Sekhmet. Strange names, all these. Krip had long since told me that the early space explorers of his race were wont to give to suns and their attendant worlds the names of gods and goddesses known to the more primitive peoples of their own historic past. And where those worlds had no native inhabitants to use a rival name, those of the Terran explorers were accepted.

These of the system of Amen-Re were so named from legend. And Krip had shown me the symbols on the map edge to identify each. They had come from the very far past. Set, too fiery to support life, had the picture of a saurian creature; Thoth, that of a long-beaked bird. Ptah was human enough, but Sekhmet was represented in that company by the furred head of a creature which Krip knew and had seen in his own lifetime and which he called a "cat."

These cats had taken to space voyaging easily and had been common on ships in the early days—though now they were few. Only a small number were carefully nurtured in the asteroid bases of the Traders. A cat's head had Sekhmet, but the body of a woman. What powers the goddess had represented, Krip did not know. Such lore was forgotten. But this world she had given her name to was not of good repute.

It had heavier gravity than Thoth or Ptah, and was so forbidding that, though there had been attempts to colonize it, those had been given up. A few prospectors came now and then, but they had discovered nothing which was not present also on Ptah and much more easily obtained there. Somewhere on its land mass was a Patrol beacon for the relaying of messages. But for the rest it was left to its scouring winds, its lowering skies, and what strange life was native to it.

Not only had we set down on this bleak world—which act was a feat of skill on the parts of our pilot and engineer—but we were in a manner now prisoners here. For that energy which had played upon our engines had done such damage as could not be repaired without supplies and tools which the *Lydis* did not carry.

As for the priest, we had no answers out of him, for he was dead. Lidj, aroused by our warning, had struck quickly. His blow, meant to knock the Thothian unconscious, had not done the harm; rather it was as if the sudden cessation of the act of sabotage had recoiled, burning life out of him. So we did not know the reason for the attack, save that it must have been aimed at keeping us from Ptah.

What was left to us now was to make secure our own safety. Somewhere hidden among these roughly splintered hills (for this land was all sharp peaks and valleys so deep and narrow that they might have been cut into the planet by the sword of an angry giant) there was a Patrol beacon. To reach that and broadcast for help was our only hope.

Within the shell of the *Lydis* was a small two-man flitter, meant to be used for exploration. This was brought out, assembled for service. Over the broken terrain such a trip in search of a beacon which might lie half the world away was a chancy undertaking. And though all the crew were ready to volunteer, it was decided that they should draw lots for the search party.

This they did, each man drawing from a bowl into which they had dropped small cubes bearing their rank symbols. And chance so marked down our astrogator Manus Hunold and second engineer Griss Sharvan.

They took from the stores, making packs of emergency rations and other needs. And the flitter was checked and rechecked, taken up on two trial flights, before Captain Foss was assured it would do.

I had said that this was a planet of evil omen. Though I found nothing by mind-seek to indicate any menace beyond that of the very rugged nature of the surface and the darkness of the landscape. Dark that landscape was.

There are many barren stretches of waste on Yiktor. The high hill country, which is the closest thing to home territory the Thassa now hold, is largely what the lowland men term desert waste. Yet there is always a feeling of light, of freedom, therein.

But here the overpowering atmosphere was one of darkness. The rocky walls of the towering escarpments were of a black or very dark-gray stone. What scanty vegetation there was had a ghostly wanness, being of a pallid gray hue. Or else it nearly matched the rocks in whose crevices it grew, dusky nodules so unpleasant to look upon that to touch them would require a great effort of will.

Even the sand which rose in dunes across this open space where Captain Foss had brought us in for a masterly landing was more like the ashes of long-dead fires—so powdery and fine (save where our deter rockets had fused it) that it held no footprint. Clouds of it were whirled into the air by the cold winds—winds which wailed and cried as they cut through the tortured rock of the heights. It was a land which was an enemy to our kind and which made plain that hostility as the hours passed.

It was those winds which were the greatest source of concern for the flitter. If such gusts grew stronger, the light craft could not battle a passage over dangerously rough country.

Some rewiring and careful work on the com of the *Lydis* had brought a very weak suggestion of a signal. So our com-tech Sanson Korde was certain that there was a beacon somewhere on the land where we had set down. A very small piece of doubtful good fortune.

For me there was little enough to do. My paws were not designed to work on the flitter. So I set myself another task, prowling around among those grim rocks, listening with every talent I had—of body and mind—for aught which might live here and mean us ill.

Sekhmet was not devoid of animal life. There were small scuttling insects, things which hid in the breaks between stones. But none of them thought, as we measure mind power. Of larger creatures I discovered not a trace. Which did not mean that such could not exist somewhere, just that if they did they were beyond the range of my present search.

Though I picked up no spark of intelligent life, there was something else here which I could not explain—a sensation of a hovering just beyond my range of conscious search. It was a feeling I had never known before save in one place, and there I had good reason to expect such. In the highest lands of Yiktor the Thassa have their own places. Once, legend tells us, we were a settled people even as the lowlanders are today. We knew the confinement of cities, the rise of permanent walls ever about us.

Then there came a time when we made a choice which would change not only those alive to make it then, but the generations born to follow them—to turn aside from works made by hands to other powers, invisible, immeasurable. And it was the choice of those faced by such a splitting of the life road to take that which favored mind over body. So gradually it was less and less needful for us to be rooted in one place. Possessions had little meaning. If a man or woman had more than he needed he shared with the less fortunate.

We became rovers, more at home in the lands of the wilds than those which had held our forefathers rooted. But still there were certain sacred sites which were very old, so old that their original use had long since vanished even from the ancient tales. And these we resorted to on occasions when there was a need that we gather for a centering of the power—for the raising up of an Old One, or a like happening.

These sites have an atmosphere, an aura, which is theirs alone. So that they come alive while we abide there, welcoming us with a warmth of spirit as restoring as a draft of clear water is to a man who has long thirsted. And this feeling—of vast antiquity and purpose—was something I well knew.

But here— Why did I have something of the same sensation—of an old, old thing with a kernel of meaning, a meaning I did not understand? It was as if I had been presented with a record roll which must be learned, yet the symbols on it were so alien they sparked no meaning in my mind. And this feeling haunted me whenever I made the rounds of our improvised landing field. Yet never could I center it in any one direction so that I might explore further and discover the reason of its troubling. I felt it only as if it were part of the dry, grit-laden air, the bitter wind wailing in the rocks.

I was not the only troubled one, but that which occupied the minds of my companions was a different matter. That the priest had triggered the device which had brought about our disaster they knew. The device itself had been found, and in a surprising place. For a careful search had led them to the Throne of Qur. First they thought that what they sought would be within the crate which covered that. But that was not so. They fully exposed the Throne and discovered nothing. Then they began a careful search, inch by inch, of the piece itself, using their best detector. Thus Lidj had uncovered a cavity in the towering back. Pressure upon two of the gems there had released a spring. Within was a box of dull metal.

The radiation reading was such that he put on protective gloves before he forced it out of its tight setting, transferring it into a shielded holder which was then taken out of the ship to be put among the rocks where whatever energy it broadcast could do no harm. These Traders had traveled far and had a wide knowledge of many worlds; yet the workmanship of that box and the nature of the energy it employed were unknown to them.

Save that they agreed on one thing, that it was not of Thothian making, since it was manifest that the technology there was too primitive to produce such a device.

"Unless," Captain Foss commented, "these priests in their eternal treasure-seeking have uncovered secrets they are not as quick to display as the other things they have found. It is apparent that that hollow in the Throne was not lately added, but must have been a part of it since its first fashioning. Was this also left over from that time? We have a dead man, a secret which is dangerous. We have a weapon used at just the right point in our voyage to force us to Sekhmet. And this adds up to a sum I dislike."

"But why— We could have been left derelict in space—" Shallard, the engineer, burst out. "It was only by the favor of fortune we were able to make a good landing here."

Foss stared across the rocks and the shifting dunes of powdery sand.

"I wonder—on that I wonder," he said slowly. And then he turned to the two who had drawn the lots for the beacon search. "I am beginning to believe that the sooner we contact authority the better. Prepare to take off in the next lull of the wind."

Chapter 4

MAELEN

So did they wing off in the flitter. In that was a device which kept them in contact with the *Lydis*, though they did not report more than passing above the same landscape as we saw. However, Foss kept in contact with them by the com unit of the ship, and his unease was as clear as if he shouted his thoughts aloud.

That we had been sabotaged it was unnecessary to question. But the reason remained unclear. Had we been delayed before take-off on Thoth, that would have been simple. Either the rebel forces or that fanatical priest could have done so. Only this stroke had come in mid-flight.

Had we been meant to land on Sekhmet? The captain was dubious about that—such depended too much on chance. He was more certain the attack had been meant to leave the *Lydis* helpless in space. And the rest of the crew agreed with him. At least on-planet one had more of a fighting chance; we might not have been given even that small advantage. In either case the threat was grave, so that even before he gave his orders to Korde, the com-tech had opened panels, was studying the maze of wiring behind them. There was a chance that these elements could be converted to a super-com, something with which to signal for help if the voyage of the flitter failed. The Traders were well used to improvising when the need arose.

Night was coming—though the day on Sekhmet had been hardly more than pallid dusk, the cloud cover lying so thickly across the riven hills. And with that flow of shadows the cold was greater. So I bushed my fur, not consciously, but by instinct.

Krip summoned me back to the ship, for they planned to seal themselves within, using that as a fort, even as it had been outside Kartum. I made one more scout sweep—found nothing threatening. Nothing which I could point to and say, "This is danger." Yet—

As the hatch closed behind me, the warmth and light of the *Lydis* giving a sense of security, still I was troubled by that other feeling— that we were ringed about by— What?

I used my claws to climb the ladder which led to the living quarters. But I was opposite the hatch of the hold wherein sat the Throne when I paused, clinging to the rungs. My head swung to that closed door as if drawn by an overwhelming force. So great was the pull that I hunched from the ladder itself to the space by the door, my shoulder brushing its surface.

That box which had wrought our disaster was now safely gone; I had watched its outside disposal. But from this room flowed a sense of—"life" is the closest I could come to describing it. I might now be in the field of some invisible communication. There was not only the mental alert, but a corresponding tingle in my flesh. My fur was rippling as it might under the touch of a strong wind. I must have given forth a mind-call, for Krip's answer came quickly:

"Maelen! What is it?"

I tried to reply, but there was so little of which I could make a definite message. Yet what I offered was enough to summon them to me with speed—Krip, the captain, and Lidj.

"But the box is gone," Captain Foss said. He stepped to one side as Lidj crowded past to reopen the sealed hatch. "Or— Can there be another?"

Krip's hand was on my head, smoothing that oddly ruffled fur. His face expressed his concern, not only for what danger might lurk here, but in a measure for me also. For he knew that I could not tell what lay behind the door, and my very ignorance was an additional source of danger. I was shaken now as I had never been in the past.

Lidj had the door open. And, with that, light flashed within. There sat the Throne, facing us squarely. They had not recreated it as yet. Only the cavity in the back was closed again. The captain turned to me.

"Well, what is it?"

But in turn I looked to Krip. "Do you feel it?"

He faced the Throne, his face now blank of expression, his dark Thassa eyes fixed. I saw his tongue pass over his lower lip.

"I feel—something—" But his puzzlement was strong.

Both the other Traders looked from one of us to the other. It was plain they did not share what we felt. Krip took a step forward—put his hand to the seat of the Throne.

I cried aloud my protest as a glassia growl. But too late. His finger tips touched the red metal. A visible shudder shook his body; he reeled back as if he had thrust his hand into open fire—reeled and fell against Lidj, who threw out an arm just in time to keep him from sliding to the floor. The captain rounded on me.

"What is it?" he demanded.

"Force—" I aimed mind-speech at him. "Strong force. I have never met its like before."

He jerked away from the Throne. Lidj, still supporting Krip, did the same.

"But why don't we also feel it?" the Captain asked, now eyeing the Throne as if he expected it to discharge raw energy into his very face.

"I do not know—perhaps because the Thassa are more attuned to what it exudes. But it is broadcasting force, and out there"— I swung my head to indicate the wall of the ship—"there is something which draws such a broadcast."

The captain studied the artifact warily. Then he came to the only decision a man conditioned as a Free Trader could make. The safety of the *Lydis* was above all else.

"We unload—not just the Throne, all this. We cache it until we learn what's behind it all."

I heard Lidj suck in his breath sharply. "To break contract—" he began, citing another part of the Traders' creed.

"No contract holds that a cargo of danger must be transported, the more so when that danger was not made plain at the acceptance of the bargain. The *Lydis* has already been planeted through the agency of this—this treasure! We are only lucky that we are not now in a drifting derelict because of it. This must go out—speedily!"

So, despite the dark, floodlights were strung, and once more the robos were put to work. This time they trundled to the hatches all those crates, boxes, and bales which had been so carefully stowed there on Thoth. Several of the robos were swung to the ground and there set to plowing through the dunes, piling the cargo within such shelter as a ridge of rock afforded. And there last of all was put the Throne of Qur, its glittering beauty uncovered, since they did not wait to crate it again.

"Suppose"—Lidj stood checking off the pieces as the robos brought them along—"this is just what someone wants—that we dump it where it can be easily picked up?"

"We have alarms rigged. Nothing can approach without triggering those. And then we can defend it." The captain spoke to me. "You can guard?"

It was very seldom during the months since I had joined the ship that he had asked any direct service of me, though he acknowledged I had talents which his men did not possess. What I had I gave willingly, before it was asked. It would seem now that he hesitated a little, as if this was a thing for which I ought to be allowed to volunteer.

I answered that I could and would—though I did not want to come too close to that pile of cargo, especially the glittering Throne. So they rigged their alarms. But as they went into the ship again, Krip came down the ramp.

His adventure in the hold had so affected him that he had had to withdraw for a space to his cabin. Now he wore the thermo garments made for cold worlds, the hood pulled over his head, the mittens on his hands. And he carried a weapon I had seldom seen him use—a blaster.

"Where do you think you're—" the captain began when Krip interrupted.

"I stay with Maelen. Perhaps I do not have her power, but still I am closer to her than the rest of you are. I stay."

At first the captain looked ready to protest, then he nodded. "Well enough."

When they had gone and the ramp was back in the ship, Krip waded through the drifting sand to look at the Throne—though he kept well away from it, I was glad to note.

"What—and why?"

"What and why, indeed," I made answer. "There are perhaps as many answers as I have claws to unsheathe. Perhaps the captain is wrong and we were indeed meant to land here, even to unload the cargo. Only that dead priest could answer us truly what and why."

I sat up on my haunches, balancing awkwardly as one must do in a body fashioned to go on four feet when one would be as erect as one ready to march on two. The wind curled about my ribs and back in a cold lash, yet my fur kept me warm. However, the sand-ash arose in great choking swirls, shifting over the Throne of Qur.

Now I squinted against that blowing grit, my gaze fixed upon the chair. Did—did I see for an instant divorced from true time what my eyes reported? Or did I imagine it only?

Did the dust fashion, even as if it clung to an invisible but solid core, the likeness of a body enthroned as might be a judge to give voice upon our affairs?

It was only for an instant that it seemed so. Then that shadow vanished. The wind-driven dust collapsed into a film on the red metal. And I do not think Krip saw it at all.

There was nothing more in the night. Our lights continued to shine on the air-spun dust, which built small hillocks around the boxes. My most alert senses could not pick up any echo among the rocks or in the near hills. We might have dreamed it all, save that we knew we had not. A fancy that it had been done to force the cargo out into the open settled so deep in my mind that I almost believed it the truth. But if we had been so worked upon to render the treasure vulnerable, no one now made any move to collect it.

Sekhmet had no moon to ride her cloudy sky. Beyond the circle of lights the darkness was complete. Shortly after the ship was sealed again, the wind died, the sand and dust ceased to drift. It was very quiet, almost too much so—for the feeling that we were waiting grew stronger.

Yet there came no attack—if any menace did lurk. However, in the early morning something occurred, in its way a greater blow at the *Lydis*, at our small party, than any attack of a formless evil. For this was concrete, a matter of evidence. The flitter's broadcast suddenly failed. All efforts to re-establish contact proved futile. Somewhere out in the waste of hills, mountains, knife-sharp valleys, the craft and her crew of two must be in trouble.

Since the *Lydis* carried only one flitter, there was no hope of manning a rescue flyer. Any such trip must be done overland. And the terrain was such as to render that well-nigh impossible. We could depend now only on the improvised com in the ship. To gather volume enough to signal off-world, Korde must tap our engines. Also, for any such broadcast there would be a frustrating time lag.

As was customary among the Traders, the remaining members of the crew assembled to discuss the grim future, to come to an agreement as to what must be done. Because Free Traders are bound to their ships, owning no home world of earth and stone, water and air, they are more closely knit together than many clans. That they could abandon two of their number lost in the unknown was unthinkable. Yet to search on foot for them was a task defeated before begun. Thus caught between two needs, they were men entrapped. Shallard agreed that the *Lydis* might just be able to rise from her present site. But that she could again make a safe landing he doubted. All his delving into the engines did not make plain just what had hit her power, but important circuits were burned out.

Again, as was the custom, each man offered what suggestions he could. Though in the end there was only one which could be followed—that the off-world com must be put into operation. It was then that Lidj voiced a warning of his own.

"It cannot be overlooked," he told them, "that we may have been pulled into a trap. Oh, I know that it is just on the edge of possibility that we were meant to fin down here on Sekhmet. On the other hand, how many cases of actual looting of ships in space are known? Such tales are more readily found on the fiction tapes, where the authors are not bound by the technical difficulties of such a maneuver. I think we can assume that the cargo is what led to sabotage. All right—who wants it? The rebels, that fanatic of a priest? Or some unknown party, who hopes to gather in loot worth more stellars than we could count in a year—if they could lift it from us and transport it out?

"Once away from this system, it would be a matter of possession being nine-tenths of the law. Only here are the claims of the priesthood recognized as legal. You have heard of the Abna expedition, and the one that Harre Largo managed ten years back? They got in, found their treasure, got out again. The priests yelled themselves near black in the face over both, but the finds were legitimate, made by the men who ran the stuff out—they were not stolen.

"Then there are the laws of salvage. Think about those carefully. Suppose the *Lydis* had crashed here. That would cancel our own contract. Such an accident would open up a neat loophole which would be easy to use. Anyone finding a wrecked ship on an unsettled world—"

"That would only apply," cut in Captain Foss, "if all the crew were dead."

He did not have to underline that for us. A moment later he added: "I think we can be sure this is sabotage. And certainly this idea of a third party is logical. It could explain what happened to the flitter."

As he said, it all fitted together neatly. Yet, perhaps because my way of thinking was Thassa and not Trader, because I depended not upon machines and their patterns, I could not wholly accept such an explanation. There was something in what I had felt by the Throne of Qur, in that lowering feeling of being watched, which did not spring from any ordinary experience. No, in an indefinable way it was oddly akin to the Thassa. And I was sure that this affair was of a different nature from those of the Traders.

But because I had no proof, nothing but this feeling, I did not offer my suggestion. Those on the *Lydis* believed now that they were under siege, must wait for the unknown enemy to show his hand in some manner. And they voted to turn all their efforts to the broadcast for aid.

However, only two of them could provide the knowledgeable assistance Korde needed. For the others, Captain Foss had another task. That cargo now piled in open sight was, he decided, to be hidden as quickly as possible. Once more he disembarked the working robos, while Krip and I went out from the immediate vicinity of the ship in search of a good cache site.

There were plenty of possibilities in this very rough country. But we wanted one which would fulfill the captain's needs best—that being a site which could be sealed once the treasure was stowed. So we examined any narrow crevice, surveyed carefully any promising hole which might give entrance to a cave or other opening.

I was no longer aware of any current flowing between the Throne and some place beyond the valley. In the morning's early light that artifact, now shrouded in dust which clouded its brilliance, was only an inanimate object. One might well believe that imagination had supplied the happenings of the night before, except that it had not.

Had that emanation been a kind of beacon, informing others of our position?

If so, once they were sure, they could well have turned off that which made a magnet of the cargo. So, as we went, I mind-searched as well as I could, even though to beam-read properly and at a goodly distance I did not have what I needed most, my lost wand of power, plus the chance for complete concentration—shutting all else out of my mind.

We came at last to a ridge taller than those immediately around our landing site. And the light was brighter, the sullen clouds less heavy. Along the wall—

Some trick of the light, together with a filmy deposit of sand which clung in curve and cut and hollow— I rose to my haunches, straining back my short neck, longing for a better range of vision.

Because the dust and the light made clear something of those lines on the stone. I saw there a design, far too regular in pattern for me to believe that it had been formed by erosion alone, the scouring of the wind-driven sand.

"Krip!"

At my summons he turned back from where he had gone farther down that cut.

"The wall—" I drew his attention to what seemed clearer and clearer the longer I studied it—that pattern so worn by the years that at first it could hardly be distinguished at all.

"What about the wall?" He looked at it. But there was only open puzzlement on his face.

"The pattern there." By now it was so plain to me I could not understand why he also did not see it. "Look—" I became impatient as I pointed as best I could with a forepaw, unsheathing claws as if I could reach up and trace the lines themselves. "Thus—and thus— and thus—" I followed the lines so, in and out. There were gaps, of course, but the over-all spread was firm enough not to need all the parts long weathered away.

He squinted, his eyes obediently following my gestures. Then I saw the dawn of excitement on his face.

"Yes!" His own mittened hand swung up as he, too, traced the design. "It is too regular to be natural. But—" Now I sensed a whisper of alarm in his mind—as if something in the design was wrong.

It was when I looked again, not at the part closer to me, but moving back even farther to catch the whole of it, that I saw it was not the abstract design my eyes had first reported. What was really pictured on the cliffside was a face—or rather a mask. And that was of something neither human nor of any creature I knew.

But into Krip's mind flashed one word—"CAT!"

Once he had so identified it I could indeed trace a resemblance between it and the small symbol on the old map of the Amen-Re system. Yet it was also different. That head had been more rounded, far closer to a picture one could associate with a living animal. This was a distinctly triangular presentation with the narrowest angle pointing to the foot of the cliff.

In the area at the wider top there were two deep gashes set aslant to form eyes. Deep and very dark, giving one the disturbing impression that they pitted a skull. There was an indication of a muzzle with a lower opening, as if the creature had its mouth half open, while a series of lines made upstanding ears. There was nothing normal about the mask. Yet once it was called to my attention, I could see that it had evolved from a cat's head.

I had felt nothing but interest when I had seen the cat on the chart, a desire to see one of these animals for myself. But this thing—it was not of the same type at all.

The hollow which was the mouth held my interest now. And I went to explore it. Though the opening was so narrow that anyone of human bulk must crouch low to enter, I could do it with ease. In I padded, needing to know the why and wherefore, for so much effort had been expended in making the carving that I was sure it had a purpose.

The space was shallow—hardly more than half again the length of my glassia body. I raised one of my paws and felt before me, for it was too dark here to see. Thus I touched a surface which was smooth. Yet my seeking claws caught and ran along grooves, which I traced until I was sure that those marked divisions of blocks which had been carefully fitted into place.

When I reported this to Krip I was already sure of what we might have discovered by chance. While Sekhmet had never been known to house any treasure (perhaps it had never been well searched), we could have discovered such a hiding place. Though we had little time to prove or disprove it.

I tried to work my claw tips between the stones, to see if they could be so loosened. But it was impossible. When I scrambled out, Krip had his wrist com uncovered, was reporting our find. Though the captain showed some interest, he urged us now to carry out our original task and locate a place where the cargo could be cached.

"Not around here." Krip's decision matched mine. "If they— whoever they may be—do come looking, we need not direct them in turn to that!" He gestured to the cat's head.

Thus we turned directly away from that, heading to the northwest. So we came upon a crevice which the light of Krip's torch told us deepened into a cave. And since we had found nothing so good closer to our landing site, we selected that.

So rough was the terrain that the passage of each laden robo had to be carefully supervised. Foss wanted no cutting or smoothing of the way to the hiding place. It took us most of the remaining daylight hours to see all into the crevice. Once the cargo was stowed, rocks were built into a stopper, well under the overhang of the outer part of the crevice, where they might be overlooked unless someone was searching with extra care.

Then a small flamer, such as is used for ship repairs, was brought in and the rocks fused into a cork which would take a great deal of time and trouble to loosen.

Lidj made a last inspection. "Best we can do. Now—let's see this other find of yours."

We led them to the cliff face. It was difficult now, though they shone working lights on it, to see the lines which had been more distinct in the early morning. I thought perhaps the dust had largely blown away. Lidj at first professed to distinguish nothing. And it was only when he hunched well down and centered a torch into the mouth, located that inner wall of blocks, that he was convinced the find was not some far flight of imagination.

"Well enough," he admitted then. "What this may lead to"—he held the torch closer to the wall—"can be anyone's guess. Certainly nothing we can explore now. But who knows about later?"

However, I knew that beneath his outer calm he was excited. This was such a find as might return to the *Lydis* all the lost profit from this voyage—perhaps even more.

Chapter 5

KRIP VORLUND

"Men who go looking for trouble never have far to walk." Lidj leaned back in his chair, his hands folded over his middle. He was not gazing at me, but rather at the wall over my head. In another man his tone might have been one of resignation. But Juhel Lidj was not one to be resigned or lacking in enterprise in any situation, or so it had been so far during our association.

"And we have been looking for trouble?" I dared to prod when he did not add to that statement.

"Perhaps we have, Krip, perhaps we have." Still he watched the wall as if somewhere on it were scrawled or taped the answer to our puzzle. "I don't believe in curses—not unless they are my own. But neither do I know that that priest back on Thoth did not know exactly what he was doing. And, to my belief, he was playing some hand of his own. When the news comes that we are missing, then his credit will go up. The efficiency of his communication with their god will be proven."

"Temple politics?" I thought I followed him. "Then you believe that that is at the bottom of it, that we don't have to be worried about being jumped while here?"

Now he did glance at me. "Don't put words in my mouth, Krip Vorlund. Perhaps my suggestion is just another logical deduction. I'm not a theurgist of Manical, to draw lines on my palm with a sacred crayon, pour a spot of purple wine in the middle, and then read the fate of the ship pictured therein. To my mind there is the smell of temple intrigue in this, that is all. The question which is most important is, how do we get out of their trap?"

That brought back what was uppermost in our minds, the disappearance, if not from the sky of Sekhmet, at least from our visa-screen, of the flitter. This was, judging by the terrain immediately about us, a harsh world, and forced down on such, Hunold and Sharvan would be faced by a desperate choice—if they still lived. Would they struggle on, trying to reach the beacon, or were they already attempting to fight their way back to the *Lydis*? Perhaps it all depended upon how far they judged themselves to be from either goal.

The Traders stand by their own. Such is bred in us, as much as the need for space, the impatience and uneasiness which grips us when we have been too long planetside. It was only the knowledge that without any guides, we ourselves might wander fruitlessly and to no useful purpose, which kept us chained to the *Lydis* and not out searching for our lost shipmates.

"Korde can do it, if it can be done. There is a Patrol asteroid station between here and Thoth. If he can beam a signal strong enough to reach either that or some cruise ship of theirs, then we're set."

Patrol? Well, the Patrol is necessary. There must be some law and order even in space. And their men are always under orders to render assistance to any ship in distress. But it grated on our Free Trader pride to have to call for such help. We were far too used to our independence. I spun the case of a report tape between thumb and forefinger, guessing just how much this galled our captain.

"One thing on the credit side," Lidj continued. "That find which your furred friend turned up out there. If there is a treasure cache here, the priests cannot claim it. But we can."

He was once more staring at the wall. I did not have to mind-probe to know what occupied his thoughts. Such a find would not only render the *Lydis* famous, but perhaps lift us all to the status of contract men, with enough credits behind us to think of our own ships. Even more so since the find was made on a planet where exploration was not restricted, where more than one such could be turned up.

I had been thinking ever since Maelen had drawn my attention to those cliff-wall carvings. And I had done some research among my own store of tapes.

A Free Trader's success depends on many things, luck being well to the fore among those. So luck had been with us here, good as well as bad. But the firm base of any Trader's efficiency is knowledge, not specialized as a tech must have, but wide—ranging from the legends of desert rovers on one planet to the habits of ocean plants on another. We listened, we kept records, we went with open minds and very open ears wherever we planeted, or when we exchanged news with others of our kind.

"When Korde is through with this com hookup, do you suppose he could rig something else?" I knew what I wanted, but the technical know-how to make it was beyond my skill.

"Just what, and for what purpose?"

"A periscope drill." The term might not be the right one, but that was the closest I could come to describing what I had read about in the tapes. "They used such, rigged with an impulse scanner, on Sattra II where the Zacathans were prospecting for the Ganqus tombs. With something like that we might be able to get an idea of what is back in the cliff. It saves the labor of digging in where there may be nothing worth hunting. As on Jason, where the tombs of the Three-eyes had already been looted—"

"You have information on this?"

"Just what it does, not the mechanics of it." I shook my head. "You'd have to have a tech work it out."

"Maybe we can—if we have the time. Bring me that note tape."

When I returned to my cabin to get that, Maelen raised her head from the cushion of her forepaws, her gold eyes agleam. Though I saw a glassia, yet when her thoughts met mine it was no animal sharing my small quarters. In my mind she was as I first saw her, slender in her gray-and-red garments, the soft fur of her jacket as bright in its red-gold luxuriance as the silver-and-ruby jewel set between the winging lift of her fair silver brows, her hair piled formally high with ruby-headed pins to hold it. And that picture I held closer because somehow, though she had never brought it into words between us, she found comfort in the knowledge that I saw her as the Thassa Moon Singer who saved my life when I was hunted through the hills of Yiktor.

"There is news?"

"Not yet." I pulled down one of the seats which snapped up to the wall when not in use. "You cannot contact them?"

But I need not have asked that. Had she been able, we would have known it. Her gifts, so much the less compared to what they had once been, were always at our service.

"No. Perhaps they have gone too far—or perhaps I am too limited now. But it is not altogether concern for those of our company missing which lies in your mind now."

I clicked one tape cover against the next, hunting that which had the notation I wanted. "Maelen, is there any way to thought-see through the cliff—behind the cat mask?"

She did not answer me at once. She must have been considering carefully before she did.

"Mind-send must have a definite goal. If I knew of some spark of life there I could focus upon it. As it is—no. But—you have thought of some way?" She had been quick to pick that up from me.

"Something I heard of—a periscope drill. It might just work here, so we could learn if we have found a treasure cache or not. Yes, here it is." I snapped the tape into my reader, ran it along impatiently, seeking the pertinent section.

She shared my absorption in that the rather vague report which a fellow Trader, who had been chartered to supply the Zacathan expedition, had furnished me.

"It seems a complicated machine," she commented, not entirely with favor. Her reaction might have arisen from the Thassa distaste for machines and any need to depend upon them. "But if it works, then I can see it in use here. Also, I believe you are correct in your guess that if this is a treasure cache it will not be the only one to be found on Sekhmet.

"Krip, do you remember how once, long ago it now seems, we spoke of treasure and you said that it could be many things on many worlds, but that each man had his own idea of what it was? Then you added that what would be precious to you was a ship of your own, that that was what your people considered true treasure. Suppose this cache, or another, were to yield enough to give you that. What would you do with such a ship—voyage, as does the *Lydis*, seeking profit wherever chance and trade call you?"

She was right in that a ship was the Trader standard of treasure. Though it would take a sum beyond perhaps even the value of the cargo from Thoth to buy a ship for each member of the *Lydis*'s crew. And all finds would be shared. But a ship of my own—

Dreams can be dreamed, but to bring them alive calls for logic and planning. I was in training as a cargomaster and, as I well knew and admitted, a long way from being ready to take full responsibility for top rating even in that berth. I was no pilot, engineer, astrogator. What would I truly do if I had credits in my belt tomorrow which would buy me the ship of my daydreaming?

Again she followed my thoughts.

"Do you remember, Krip Vorlund, how you spoke when I told you *my* fancy—of taking my little people in a ship to the stars? Could such a treasure buy that ship?"

So she still held to *her* dream? Though perhaps it had now even less chance of realization than mine.

"It would have to be a treasure past all reckoning," I told her soberly.

"Agreed. And I have not gone a-voyaging these past months with a closed mind. The Thassa know Yiktor in width and length, but they know not space. I have learned that there are limits of which I was unaware when I claimed to be a Moon Singer of power. We are but a small people among many, many races and species. Yet to recognize that is a good beginning. With your delving machine do you go hunting, Krip—if the time is given you."

"Lidj thinks—" I told her what the cargomaster had said. But before I had finished, her furred head moved from side to side.

"Such a conclusion is logical. But there is this. Since I first took sentry duty here, I know we have been watched."

"What! By whom—from where?"

"It is because I cannot answer just such questions that I have not given a warning. Whatever it is which forces my unease, it lurks beyond the edge of my probe. I can no longer far-beam-read. The Old Ones took much of my power when they reft from me my wand. There only remains enough to warn. What is here only watches; it has yet made no move. But—tell me. Krip—why is it that a cat face is upon the cliff wall?"

Her sudden change of subject startled me. And I could not give her an answer.

"This is what I mean." Her thought-send was impatient. "The cat is an ancient symbol of Sekhmet, for whom this planet is named. That you told me. But—were not this sun and its attendant worlds given their names originally by some Scout of your people who landed here in exploration? Therefore the cat is an off-world symbol.

"Yet here we find it—or a pattern enough like it so that you say 'cat' at once when you trace it—marking something *not* left by settlers of your kind. Why did these unknown and forgotten earlier ones use the cat mask?"

I had not really thought of that before.

"It must be something left by the first settlers. Perhaps they tried to colonize Sekhmet before the other planets."

"I think not. I think this is far too old. How many years has this system been settled? Do you have such a record?"

"I don't know. If they were of the first wave, perhaps a thousand years, a little less."

"Yet I would judge that carving to be twice, maybe thrice that age. To erode stone so deeply takes a long time. At our places on Yiktor that is so. And the rest of the treasures are not of settler making; they were found by the first men to land. Still we have here a cat mask! Who, and how old, were the gods for whom this system was named—this cat-headed Sekhmet?"

"They were Terran and very old even on that world. And Terra took to space a thousand years ago." I shook my head. "Much history has been forgotten in the weight of years. And Terra is halfway across the galaxy from here. When such gods and goddesses were worshiped, her people had no space travel."

"Perhaps your species did not then go forth from their parent world. But did any visit them there? The races of the Forerunners—how many such civilizations rose and fell?"

"No one knows, not even the Zacathans, who make the study of history their greatest science and art. And nowadays even Terra is half legend. I have never met a space-farer who has actually been there, or one who can claim clear descent from its people."

"Fable, legend—in the core of such there exists a small kernel of truth. Maybe here—"

The com over my head crackled and Foss sounded a general message.

"Broadcast now possible. We are sending off-world."

Though whether that effort would avail us, who could tell? I took my tape and went back to Lidj, playing the pertinent portion for him and then again for Shallard. The latter did not seem very hopeful that he and Korde could produce any such instrument, but went off again at last to consult his own records.

Waiting can be very wearying. We set up a watch which did not involve either Korde, always on com duty, or Shallard. Maelen and I shared a term. We made only the rounds of the valley in which the *Lydis* had finned down, not venturing beyond its rim, however much we would have liked to explore near the cat mask or prospect about that for other indications that long-ago men, or other intelligent beings, had been there.

We saw no one, heard nothing; nor was Maelen able to pick up any thought waves to suggest that this was more than a deserted stretch of inhospitable land. However, she continued to affirm that there was an influence of some kind hanging about which puzzled and, I think (though this she did not admit), alarmed her.

Maelen had always been much of an enigma to me. At first her alienness had set a barrier between us, a severance which had been strengthened when she had used her power to save my life by the only method possible—making man into beast. Or rather moving that which was truly Krip Vorlund from one body to another. That the man body had died through mischance had not been her fault, hard as my loss had seemed to me at the time. She had given me the use of a barsk's body. And she had brought me to the one I now wore in turn.

Thassa I walked, though Thassa I did not now live. And perhaps that outer shell of Thassa moved me closer in spirit than I had been before to the Moon Singer, Mistress of Little Ones, that I had known. Sometimes I found myself deliberately trying to tap whatever residue of Thassa might linger in my body, so that I could better understand Maelen.

Three guises I had worn in less than one planetary year—man, beast, Thassa. And the thought ever lurked in the depths of my mind that each was a part of me. Maquad, whose body finally became mine, was long dead. As a Thassa undergoing instruction he had taken on beast form, and in that form he had been killed by an ignorant hunter from the lowlands, poaching on forbidden territory. In his humanoid form the beast spirit had gone mad after a space, unable to adjust—so that what remained was a living husk. I had displaced no one when I took that husk.

But the body which had been Maelen's—that had died. And only because Vors, one of her Little Ones, had offered her spirit a dwelling place had she survived. The Old Ones had condemned her to live as Vors for a time they reckoned by a reading of the stars which hung in Yiktor's skies. But when that time had passed—where would she find a new body?

That question troubled me from time to time, though I strove to hide it from her, having a strange feeling that such speculation would be forbidden, or was wrong to mention, until she herself might clear such uncertainty. But she never had. I wanted to know more of the Thassa, but there was a barrier still raised around certain parts of their lives, and that I dared not breach.

Now we stood together in the early morning, having climbed to the cliff top which was part of the valley rim. Maelen faced out, her head pointing in the direction the flitter had taken as it bore off into the unknown. The wind ruffled her fur just as it also curled about my thermo jacket.

"Out there—it abides," came her thought.

"What does?"

"I do not know, save that it lies there waiting, watching—ever. Or—does it dream?"

"Dream?" Her choice of word surprised me. Though I strove with all the esper talent I had to catch that emanation which appeared so clear to Maelen, I had never yet touched it.

"Dream, yes. There are true dreams which can be foreseeing. Surely you know that." Once more she was impatient. "I dreamed— that I know. Yet the manner of my dream I cannot recall—save in small snatches of light, color, or feeling."

"Feeling?" I sought to lead her on.

"Waiting! That is the feeling!" There was triumph as she solved a problem. "I was waiting for something near me, something of such importance my life depended upon it. Waiting!" She held to the last word as if it were part of an important formula.

"But the rest—"

"A place strange and yet not strange—I knew it and yet knew it not. Krip"—her head swung around—"when you ran as Jorth the barsk, did you not fear that in some ways the beast was becoming greater than the man?"

So did I at last learn her fear, as if she had described a vision of terror. I went to one knee and put my arms about that furred body, drawing it close. I had not thought that this fear would be hers, knowing that body change was a part of Thassa life. But perhaps she was no longer guarded by the safe checks they used on Yiktor.

"You think this may be true for you?"

She was very close to me, passive in my hold, yet still her mind held aloof. Perhaps she already regretted even that small reaching for reassurance.

"I do not know, no longer am I sure." Her admission was painful. "I try—*how* I try—to be Maelen. But if I become all Vors—"

"Then shall I remember Maelen for us both!" What I could offer her I did. And it was the truth! Let her slip back into the animal, yet I would make myself continue to see not fur but firm pale flesh, silver hair, dark eyes in a humanoid face, the grace, the pride, and the beauty of the Moon Singer. "And neither shall I let you forget, Maelen. Never shall I let you forget!"

"Yet I think of a failing memory—" If thought could come as a whisper, so did hers sink so low.

My wrist com buzzed, and I stripped back my mitten to listen to the click of code. Fortune was favoring us. Our off-world signal had raised an answer far sooner than our most optimistic hopes had dared suggest. There was a Patrol Scout coming in and we were now recalled to the *Lydis*.

The Scout set down in the night, braking rockets flaring in a valley near our own. Her crew would not try to reach us until morning, but in the meantime we beamed through to them a full report of all that had happened since our lift-off from Thoth. All except one matter—our find of the cat mask on the cliff.

In return the Scout had news of import for us. The rebellion on Thoth had flared high in Kartum, fed by a split within the loyalist party arising from the cursing of our ship. With priest turned against priest, and the solidarity of the ruling caste so broken, the rebels had found it easy to infiltrate and conquer. Those with whom we had had a contract were now dead. The rebels were demanding the return of the treasure. And there was talk that we had meant all the time to space with it as our spoil. We listened to this and then Foss spoke:

"It seems we now have another problem. Perhaps we did better than we knew when we cached the cargo here. Until we can sort out just who takes lawful custody now, let it remain where it is."

"It is contracted still for Ptah," Lidj pointed out. "We only cached it for fear of its possible influence."

"Our contract was given by men now dead. I want to know the situation on Ptah before we go in there—if the rebels have a foothold there too. Dead men don't own anything, unless you count their tombs. If the government is changed, what we have may be legally claimed elsewhere. To be caught on another planet with a cargo of uncertain origin can put a Trader out of business—perhaps permanently. Until we are sure of the present owners, we want to take no chances of being accused, as it seems we already are, of jacking it all ourselves. I am depositing second-copy contract tapes with the Patrol at once. That will cover us for a while. But we'll leave the cache as it is until we hear from the temple on Ptah."

"What about payment?" Lidj asked. "According to contract we were to take our pick *after* we set down on Ptah. We can't collect before delivery. And a dry run, with repairs unpaid for, is a setback we are not able to take now. We dumped cargo at Kartum to take this on."

"Interference claim—at least to cover repairs?" I ventured. "We can prove it was that box and the priest that brought us here. That ought to make a good claim—"

"Well enough," Lidj agreed. "But get to the fine points of stellar law and this can be argued out for years. If we pick up our pay at the end it will be too late to help us. We could be bankrupt or dead by the time the space lawyers got tired of clicking their jaws over it. We need that carriage fee. In fact, we have to have it if we are going to continue lifting ship!

"On the other hand, we dare not be accused of looting either. The best we can do at present is make a formal Claim of Interference, post our tapes, and ask for an investigation on Ptah—to be made by the Patrol. If they reply that everything is as usual there, are you willing to chance delivery?"

We agreed. I wondered a little at Foss's seeming reluctance to proceed without a solemn, signed crew agreement. Traders are always cautious, to a point. But Free Traders, especially on a Class D ship such as the *Lydis*, are not given to many second thoughts. We are of an exploring fraternity, willing to run risks in order to work among our own kind. Did Foss suspect something which was not clear to the rest of us? The fact that he even suggested that the ship not resume her voyage to Ptah after the necessary repairs was suspicious. Yet after we were alone, making a recorder copy of all matters pertaining to the contract, Lidj did not comment. And since he did not, I was silent also.

By early morning we had our tape ready as the Patrol flitter came gliding over the barrier of the valley wall and stirred up ashy sand in landing beside the *Lydis*. The two men who climbed out of the small flyer appeared to be in no great hurry to join Foss, who stood at the foot of our downed ramp. Instead one knelt in the sand, setting up an instrument. And the other watched him closely. They could have been conducting an exploring survey.

Chapter 6

KRIP VORLUND

There is something about the cloak of authority which tends to put even the citizen with a clear conscience on the defensive. So it was when we fronted the representatives of the Patrol. As law-abiding and inoffensive space traders, making regular contributions to planetary landing taxes, all papers in order, we had every right to call upon their help. It was just that they eyed us with an impassivity which suggested that to them, everything had to be proved twice over.

However, we had the box taken from the Throne of Qur carefully disinterred after they admitted that their own instruments registered emanations of a heretofore unknown radiation. It was surrendered gladly to their custody, along with the body of the priest, which had been in freeze. And we each entered testimony on the truth tape, which could not be tampered with.

With relief we knew they had not asked all the questions they might have. Our find at the cat cliff was still our secret—though we did tell of the cargo cache. Lidj, armed with all the precedents of space law, explained that once repairs were made, we intended to continue our voyage and deliver the treasure to the temple on Ptah—providing we were sure that the priests to whom it was officially consigned were still in power.

"We have no news from Ptah." The pilot of the Scout displayed so little interest in Foss's inquiries it was plain our present dilemma was of no concern to him. "Your repairs, yes. Our engineer has checked with your man. We want visa-tapes of the damage for our report. We can lift you and your engineer off to our space base, where you can indite under League contract for what you need."

Indite under League contract was a suggestion to worry one, though here we had no alternative. Once we had so indited we would be answerable not to the Patrol, but to our own people. Not to pay up within the stated time meant having the *Lydis* put under bond. There was so great a demand for ships (men waited for frustrating years for some stroke of luck which would give them even the first step on the ladder of spacing) that bonds weighed heavily on those who had to accept them. They could mean the loss of a ship. So we had no way of recouping, saving that of delivering our cargo to Ptah, hoping to collect. That—or the wild chance that the cat cliff hid something worth the labor of breaking in. We had no time now to build a probe, nor could we do that without giving away the reason.

In the end it was decided that Foss and Shallard would lift with the Scout. But an armed party of Patrol, plus their flitter, would remain on Sekhmet, their first order being to search for our missing men.

Since the Patrol flitter was a heavy-duty craft, armed and protected by every device known, it might have a better chance in a search. It carried a pilot, two gunners to man its shockers, and room for two more passengers. There was no drawing of lots this time. Before he took off for the Scout Foss spoke directly to me.

"You and Maelen will go. With her powers to search and yours to interpret—"

Of course he was right, though the Patrolman regarded his choice of what appeared to be an animal with open disbelief. However, though I gave no history of Maelen's past, I laid it out clearly that she was telepathic and would be our guide. Since no man may know all there is to be learned about alien creatures, they accepted my assurance of her worth.

For a full day after the Scout lifted with Captain Foss and Shallard, there was a storm lapping at the *Lydis*, raising the fine dust of the valley into an impenetrable fog, keeping us pent within the ship, the Patrolmen with us. There was no setting out in this murk, since we could not fly on any set beam but would be questing freely over an unknown area.

But on the second morning the wind failed. And though the ash-sand had drifted high about the fins of the ship and half buried the flitter, which was well anchored in what little protection the *Lydis* herself offered, we could take off. As we swung out over the knife-ridged country, the massed clouds overhead broke a little now and then, though the sunlight which came through was pale and seemed devoid of heat. Its radiance accentuated the general gloom of the landscape beneath us rather than dispersing it.

The pilot kept to the lowest speed, watching his instruments for any sign of radiation which might be promising. Maelen crouched beside me in the cramped cabin of the craft. It was seldom I was truly aware of her present form, but with the Patrolmen glancing at her as if she were a very outré piece of equipment, I was more conscious of her fur, her four feet, the glassia guise. And because I had heard her plaint of fear, that she might in time slide back too far into the animal to be sure of her identity as a Thassa, her unease was plainer to me. I myself had known moments when beast eclipsed man. What if my identity had been so lost?

Maelen was stronger, more prepared than I had been to overpower the flesh envelope she wore, since she knew well all its dangers. But if *her* steady confidence was beginning to fade—

She stirred, muscles moving with liquid grace under her soft fur. Her head pointed away in a quick turn.

"Something?" I asked.

"Not what I seek now. But—but there is that down there which is not of rock and sand."

I craned to look through the vision port. Nothing showed to my sight, but rocks twisted and eroded into such wild shapes could hide anything.

"Within—" she informed me. "But we are already past. I think perhaps another cache—"

I tried to memorize landmarks, though such seen from the air and from the ground were two different matters. But if Maelen was right, and her certainty of report suggested that she could be depended upon to be that, perhaps we had indeed come upon that which would redeem all debts we might incur through this trouble. A second cache! Was Sekhmet to prove as rich a treasure field as Thoth—perhaps more so?

However, Maelen reported nothing else as we flew in a zigzag pattern, cruising back and forth over the broken land. The country was bad for visual sighting. There were too many of those deep, narrow valleys which might have swallowed up a grounded or crashed flitter, hiding it even from air survey. And we knew only the general direction.

Back and forth, as all the rocks took on the same look—though we did pass over several wider valleys where there were stands of withered vegetation. One held a cup of water in the form of a small, dark lake rimmed with a wide border of yellow-white which may have been a noxious chemical deposit.

Maelen stirred again, pressing more tightly against me, as she stretched her head toward the vision port.

"What now?"

"Life—" she signaled.

At the same time our pilot leaned forward to regard more closely one of the many dials before him.

"Reading—faint radiation," he reported.

Though we were already at a low altitude, he dropped us more, at the same time cutting speed nearly to hover so we could search with care through the vision port. We were heading over one of the valleys, which was roughly half-moon-shaped. At the upper point of that were the first trees (if trees one might term them) I had yet seen on Sekhmet. At least they were growths of very dark foliage which stood well above bush level. But the rest of the ground was covered only with the gray tough grass.

"There!"

There was no need for anyone to point it out—for it was as visible as if painted scarlet. A flitter stood in grass as high as its hatch. But there were no signs of life about it.

The pilot had been calling on his com, trying to raise an answer. As yet he made no move to set down. I did not wonder at his caution. There was something about the stark loneliness of that valley, about the seemingly deserted machine so plainly in sight, which chilled me.

"Do you pick them up?" I asked Maelen.

"There is no one right here." By that she seemed to contradict her earlier report.

"But you said—"

"It is not them. Something else—" Her thought-send faltered, almost as if she were now confused, unable to sense clearly.

And my uneasiness, which had been triggered by the sight of the parked flitter, was fed by a suspicion that perhaps this was what Maelen had obliquely warned me of earlier, that she could no longer be sure of her powers.

"Snooper picks up nothing," the pilot reported. "I don't get any ident reading. By all tests there's no one aboard."

"Only one way to make sure," commented the Patrolman at the port-side defense. "Set down and look."

"I don't like it. Looks almost as if it were put out for someone to come and see it." The pilot's hand had not yet gone to the controls. "Bait—"

That was a possibility one could readily accept. Though who would be using such bait? With the Patrol insignia plain on our own craft, it would be top risk for anyone to spring a trap. Perhaps my faith in the force of the Patrol was right, for we did come down. Though both gunners stayed at their posts as we flattened the high grass not too far from the parked flitter.

The grass was not only close to chest-high, but tough and sharp-edged, cutting any hand put out to beat it down. Yet it also gave us a clue as to what might have happened to the two we sought. For the flitter was empty of any passengers. Not only that, but their supply packs were still stowed within, as if Sharvan and Hunold had never expected to leave the flyer for long.

Out from the trampled and crushed section of grass immediately around the hatch a trail led straight for the stand of trees. The path was deeply indented, as though it might have been made by the transportation of heavy cargo. Yet here and there along it tougher patches of stem and leaf were lifting again.

I searched the flitter carefully, triggering its report tape. But that repeated nothing more in its last recording than a description of what we ourselves had seen during our morning's passage over the broken lands. Then it stopped in mid-word, the rest of the tape as bare as if it had been erased. For this I had no explanation at all. Whatever had brought them to land here remained a mystery. Still, all the instruments were in working order. I was able to apply full power and raise to a good height in testing before I set down again. There had been no failure of the craft to force a landing.

As I made my examination one of the Patrol gunners and the pilot, Harkon, went for some distance down the trail leading to the trees. Maelen remained behind, hunkered down at the edge of the slowly rising grass. And as I emerged from the hatch I had one question for her.

"How long?"

She sniffed the ground in the trampled space, using glassia gifts now.

"More than a day. Perhaps as long as they have been missing. I cannot be too sure. Krip—there is a strange scent here—human. Come—"

A swing of her head beckoned me to one side and there she used the unsheathed claws of one forepaw to pull aside the tall grass. The tuft did not come easily and I put out my mittened hands to help. Then I found the vegetation had been woven into a blind, forming a screen about a space where the ground had been grubbed clear. Upon the patch of soil was the impression of a square which might have been left by a heavy box.

I had knelt to examine this depression as the Patrolmen returned. Harkon joined me. He held a small detect and I heard a revealing chatter from that.

"Small residue of radiation. Could be left from something like a call beam," he commented. Then he studied the woven grass curtain. "Well hidden—this could not have been spotted from above at all. They could even have produced engine failure and at the same time blotted out a distress signal—"

"But why?"

"You people have already claimed sabotage. Well, if your men had reached the beacon they could have spoiled any game to be played here. It was only by chance we picked up your space call, one chance in five hundred, really. Whoever is in hiding here could not have foreseen that. Or even that your com-tech had the knowledge and equipment to try it. If they have a reason to keep you pinned here, the first step would be to cut you off from the beacon. And they must believe that by taking your flitter, they have done that effectively. And as to who 'they' are—" He shrugged. "You ought to have some guess."

"Outside of jacks with inside knowledge about our cargo—no. But what about Sharvan and Hunold?"

I meant that question as much for Maelen as Harkon, and I thought she might have the more reliable answer.

"They were alive when they left here," she replied.

"No attempt made to conceal the trail. I don't think they believed anyone would be after them in a hurry," Harkon replied when I passed along Maelen's report.

"You have this much reassurance," he added. "The Free Traders' loyalty to their own is a known fact. They might keep your men alive to bargain with."

"Exchange." I nodded. "But we have had no offers—nothing. No one we could detect has been near the *Lydis*."

"Which is not to say that they won't show up with a ransom deal sooner or later."

I arose, brushing the dead grass wisps from my thermo suit. "Maybe not now. Not if they saw your ship land."

Yet jacks are not timid, not when they have such a rich take as the *Lydis*'s cargo to consider. The Patrol ship was a Scout, and it had gone off-world again. Three Patrolmen in an armed flitter, and the reduced crew of the *Lydis*— This might be the very time the enemy would select to make such a move, if they did have us under observation. I said as much.

"Well follow the trail to the woods anyway," Harkon answered. "If there's nothing beyond"—he shrugged again—"nothing to do then but wait for reinforcements. We can't stand up to a jack gang with only three men."

I noted that he apparently did not class the Free Traders as part of his fighting force. But perhaps to the Patrol any outside their own close company was not to be so considered. Just another of the things which made them less than popular.

We left one gunner on guard and tramped along the grass track once more, Maelen with me now, Harkon ahead, his fellow bringing up the rear. As we drew near that wood I saw that the growths could indeed be termed trees, but they lacked any attraction, their limbs being twisted and coiled as if they had once been supple tentacles flung out in a wild attempt to embrace something and had solidified in such ungainly positions. The leaves were very dark and thick-fleshed, and there were not many to a limb. But they were still able to form a heavy canopy which shut out that pallid sunlight and made the way ahead a tunnel of deep dusk.

But the path we followed did not enter there. Instead it turned left to run along the edge of the stand. Here there was little grass, but the gray soil showed scrapes and scuffs, being too soft to retain sharp prints. Having skirted the woods, the way came to the very point of the valley. Maelen, who had paced by my side, drew away to the sharp rise of the cliff.

She sat up on her haunches, her head swaying a little; she might almost have been reading some inscription carved on that rugged wall, so intently did she regard it. I took a couple of strides to join her, but I could see nothing, though I searched, believing that she must have come upon something such as the cat mask.

"What is it now?" I ventured to break her concentration.

For the first time she made no answer. Her mind was closed as tight as any defense gate barred to the enemy. Still she stared, her head turning a fraction right, left, right again. But I could detect nothing to keep her so scanning stone.

"What is it?" Harkon echoed my question.

"I don't know. Maelen does not answer." I touched the raised crest on her head.

She drew back from even that small physical contact. Nor did she open her mind or show that she was aware of me. Never before had this happened.

"Maelen!" I made of her name a challenge, a demand for attention. And I thought that even so I had not reached her. That fear she had implanted in me, the suggestion that she might surrender to her beast body, was sharp.

Then that swinging of the head, the unblinking stare, broke. I saw her red tongue flick out, lick her muzzle. Both her forepaws scraped upward along the sides of her head in a gesture which aped the human. She might have been trying to close her ears to some sound she could no longer stand, which was racking her with pain.

"Maelen!" I went to my knees. Our eyes were now nearly level. Putting out my hand, I caught those paws holding her head, urged her face a little around to meet my gaze. She blinked and blinked again—almost as one rousing from sleep.

"Maelen, what is the matter?"

There was no longer that solid barrier. Rather I was answered by a flood of confused impressions which I could not easily sort out. Then she steadied her chain of thought.

"Krip—I must get away—away from here!"

"Danger?"

"Yes—at least to me. But not from those we seek. There is something else. It has prowled at the edge of my thoughts since first we set foot on this dark world. Krip, if I do not take care there is that here which can claim me! I am Thassa— I am mistress—" I felt she did not say that to me, but repeated the words to herself to steady her control. "I am Thassa!"

"You are Thassa!" Straightway I hastened to say that, as if merely repeating my conviction would be a life line thrown to one struggling against dire danger.

She dropped her forepaws to earth. Now her whole body was shaken by great shudders, such as might result from violent weeping. I dared to touch her again, and when, this time, she did not repulse me, I drew her close for such companionship as that hold might give her.

"You are Maelen of the Thassa." I held my thought firm. "As you will ever be! Nothing else can claim you here. It cannot!"

"What is the matter?" Harkon's hand was on my shoulder, giving me a small shake as if to summon my attention.

"I do not know." I told him the truth. "There is something here that threatens esper powers."

"Harkon!" The other Patrolman, who had gone along the cliff, now stepped away from it. "Set-down marks here. A flitter—big one by the looks of them."

Harkon went to see; I remained with Maelen. She had turned her head, was nuzzling against my jacket in an intimacy she had never before displayed.

"Good—good to have you here," her thought came. "Keep so, Krip, keep so with me. I must not be less nor other than I am—I must not! But it is calling—it is calling me—"

"What is?"

"I do not know. It is like something which wishes help that only I can offer. Yet I also know that if I do go to it—then I am no longer me. And I will not be not-Maelen! Never while I live will I be not-Maelen!" The force of that was like a shout of defiance.

"No one but Maelen. Tell me how I can aid. I am here—" I gave her quickly what I had to offer.

"Remember Maelen, Krip, remember Maelen!"

I guessed what she wanted and built in my mind the picture I liked to remember best of all—of Maelen as I had first seen her at the Great Fair in Yrjar, serene, sure, mistress of herself, untroubled, proud of her little furred people as they performed before the awed townsfolk. That was Maelen as she would always be for me.

"Did you indeed see me so, Krip? I think you draw a picture larger and more comely, more assured, than I was in truth. But you have given me that to hold to. Keep it ever for me, Krip. When I need it—have it safe!"

Harkon was back. "Nothing more to do here." His tone was impatient. "We had better head back. They lifted in a flitter, all right, which means they can be anywhere on this continent. Can you pilot your own flyer?"

I nodded, but looked to Maelen. Was she ready, able, to return? She wriggled in my hold and I loosed her. Perhaps she was well pleased to be on the move again. She scrambled into the flitter, curled up in the second seat as I settled in front of the controls.

The Patrol flitter headed straight back toward the *Lydis* and I matched its speed. Maelen, curled still, seemed to sleep. At least she made no attempt at mind-touch. However, we were not to be long without a new problem. My com clicked and I snapped it on.

"Can you raise your ship?" was Harkon's terse demand. I had been so absorbed with Maelen I had not thought of sending any report to the *Lydis*. Now I pressed the broadcast button. There was a hum— the beam was open. But when I punched out our code call I got no answer. Surprised, I tried again. The beam *was* open; reception should have been easy. Surely with us out on search the ship's receiver would have been constantly manned. Still no reply.

I reported my failure to Harkon, to be answered with a stark "Same here."

We had set out in early morning, eating our midday meal of concentrates as we flew. Now began a fading of the pallid sunlight, a thickening and in-drawing of the clouds. Also the winds were rising. For safety's sake we both rose well above the rocky hills. There was no way we could be lost—the guide beam would pull us to the *Lydis*—but strong winds make a blind landing there tricky. A blind landing? It should not have to be blind. They would be expecting us, have floodlights out to guide us down. Or would they? They did not answer—would they even know we were coming? *Why* did I get no answer? I continued to click out the code call, pausing now and then to count to ten or twenty, praying for an answer which would end my rising suspicion that something was very wrong.

Chapter 7

MAELEN

It was hard to fight this thing which had come upon me in the valley where we found the flitter. Never had I been so shaken, so unsure of myself, of what I was—of *who* I was. Yet I could not even remember clearly now that which had flowed in upon my mind, possessing my thoughts, struggling to eject my identity. I know shape-changing, who better? But this was no ordered way of Thassa doing. This had been a concentrated attempt to force me to action which was not of my own planning.

As I crouched low now in the second seat of the flitter, I was still trying to draw about me, as one might draw a ragged cloak against the stabbing air of winter, my confidence and belief in my own powers. What I had met there I could not trace to its source and did not know—save that I wanted no more of it!

I was thus so intent upon my own misery and fear that I was not wholly aware of Krip's actions. Until his thought came piercing my self-absorption in a quick, clean thrust.

"Maelen! They do not reply from the *Lydis*. What can you read?"

Read? For a moment even his mind-send seemed to be in a different language, one beyond my comprehension. Then I drew

277

heavily on my control, forced my thought away from that dire contact in the valley. *Lydis*—the *Lydis* did not answer!

But at least now I had a concrete focus for my search. I was not battling the unknown. Though the ship itself, being inanimate, would not act as a guide to draw my search; Lidj would be best for that. I pictured in my mind the cargomaster, loosed my tendril of seek—

What I encountered was a blank. No—below the surface of nothingness there pulsed something, a very muted sense of identity. I have mind-sought when those I so wished to touch were asleep, even in deep unconsciousness produced by illness. This present state was like unto the last, save that it was even deeper, farther below the conscious level. Lidj was not to be reached by any seek of mine. I transferred then to Korde—with the same result.

"They are unconscious—Lidj and Korde—deeply so," I reported.

"Asleep!"

"Not true sleep. I have reported it as it is. They are not conscious, nor do they dream, nor are their minds open to under-thought as they are in true sleep. This is something else."

I tried to probe deeper, to awaken some response, enough to win information. But even as I concentrated I was—seized! It was as if I had been pushing toward a goal when about me rose a trapping net. This net had the same feel as that which had entranced me for a space in the valley. Save that this time it was stronger, held me more rigidly in its bonds, as if another personality, stronger, more compelling, had joined with the first to bind and draw me. I could see Krip and the flitter. I could look down at my own furred body, at my forepaws, from which the striking claws were now protruding as if I were preparing to do battle. But between me and that sane outer world there was building a wall of haze.

Maelen—I was Maelen! "Krip, think me Maelen as you did in the valley! Make me see myself as I truly am, have been all my life, no matter what body I now wear. I am Maelen!"

However, my plea must not have reached him. I was dimly aware of a crackle of words from the com, words which had noise but no meaning.

Maelen—with all my strength of mind and will I held to my need of identity, besieged by rising waves of force, each beating upon me stronger than the last. Dimly I thought this a worse peril because I *was* one who had been able to change the outward coverings of my spirit—something which made me the more susceptible to whatever abode here.

But—I was Maelen—not Vors, no one else—only Maelen of the Thassa. Now my world had narrowed to that single piece of knowledge, which was my shield, or my weapon. Maelen as Krip had seen me in his memory. Though, as I had told him, I had never been so fair, so strong as that. Maelen—

All beyond me was gone now. I closed my outer eyes lest I be disturbed from my defense. For how long I continued then to hold Maelen intact I do not know, as time was no longer broken down into any unit of measure. It was only endurance in which I feared weakening more than any bodily death.

That assault grew in strength, reached such a height that I knew if it advanced I could not hold. Then—it began to fail. With failure there came a secondary current, first of raging impatience, then of fear and despair. This time also I had held fast. That I could do so a third time with this strange power fighting against me, I doubted. And Krip—where had Krip been? What of his promise that he would stand with me?

Anger born of my great fear flared hot in me. Was this the true worth of what I might expect from him, that in my hour of greatest need he would leave me to fight a lone battle?

The influence which had tested me this second time was now gone, the remnants winking out as a lamp might give way to the dark. I was left so drained that I could not move, even once I had returned to an awareness of what lay about me.

Krip—he still sat at the controls of the flitter. But the flyer was on the ground. I could see from the vision port the fins of the *Lydis*, though the bulk of the ship towered far above us.

"Krip—" Weakly I tried to reach him.

Tried—but what I met was that same nothingness which I had encountered when I had sought Lidj and Korde! I pulled up on the seat, edged around to look directly into his face.

His eyes were open; he stared straight ahead. I reached out a forepaw, caught at his shoulder. His body was rigid, as if frozen, a piece of carving rather than blood, flesh, and bone! Had he been caught in that same net which had tried to encompass me, but more securely?

I began to fight again, this time to reach that which lay beneath the weight of nothingness. But I was too weakened by my own ordeal— I could not win to that secret place where Krip Vorlund had been imprisoned, or to which he had retreated. He sat rigid, frozen, staring with eyes I did not believe saw anything of the outer world. I scrambled off the seat, clumsily freed the catch of the door hatch with my paws.

Though the fins of the *Lydis* were bulky enough to show through the dark, the rest of the valley was well hidden in night shadows. I dropped over the edge of the hatch into the soft sand, which puffed up around my haunches, cushioning me by the edge of a dune. The hatch closed automatically behind me. Krip had not noticed my going, made no effort to join me.

Standing in the shadow cast by the flitter, I surveyed the valley. There was no boarding ramp out from the *Lydis*. She was locked tight, as we had kept her during each night on Sekhmet. Beyond the fins was the Patrol flitter. Around that was no stir. I padded through the sand to reach its side. There was a faint glow within, the radiance of the instrument panel, I thought.

Glassia can climb, but they are no leapers. Now I made a great effort, putting all I could into a jump which allowed me to hook my claws over the edge of the port, hang there long enough with a straining of my shoulder muscles for a look within.

The pilot occupied his seat with the same rigidity Krip displayed. His nearest companion was in position by the weapon, also frozen at his post. I could only see the back of the head of the second gunner, but since he did not move, I believed I could assume he was in a like state. Both the pilot and Krip had made good landings here, but now they seemed as truly prisoners as if they were chained in some dungeon in Yrjar. Prisoners of whom—and why? Still, since they had landed their flitters in safety, it was plain that the enemy did not yet want them dead, only under control.

That they would be left so for long, I doubted. And prudence suggested that I get into hiding while I could and stay so until I learned more of the situation. I might already be under surveillance from some point in the valley.

I began to test mind-seek—only to find it limited, so drawn upon by the ordeal I had been through that I dared not try it far. For the time being I was reduced to depending upon the five senses inherent in my present body.

Though it disturbed me to rely on the glassia abilities, I relaxed my vigilance and my control of my body, raised my head so that my nose could test the scents in the air, listened as intently as I could, tried to see as much among the shadows as my eyes would allow. The glassia are not nocturnal. Their night vision is probably but little better than a man's. But the contrast of the light-gray sand with the flitters and the tall bulk of the *Lydis* was enough to give me my bearings. And if I could reach the cliff wall, its rugged formation would offer me hiding in plenty. I squatted in the shadow of the Patrol flitter and mapped out a route which would give me maximum cover.

Perhaps I was wasting time; perhaps the valley was not under observation and I could have walked boldly enough. But that was too chancy. So I covered the ground with all the craft I could summon, alert to any sight or noise which could mean I was betrayed.

Then I found a crevice I thought was promising. It was so narrow that I must back into it. Within that I crouched, lying low, my head resting on my paws, taking up vigil to watch the ship and the two flitters.

As during that pallid day before, the clouds parted a little. There were stars to be seen, but no moon. I thought with longing of the bright glow of Sotrath, which gave such light to Yiktor, filling the night with blazing splendor.

Stars above me—or were they? For a beast, distances are altered, angles of vision changed. Not stars—lights! Those lower ones at least were lights, at one end of the valley. Three I counted. And in that direction was the spot where we had cached the cargo. With the crew and the Patrolmen caught now, were those mysterious others we suspected to be at the root of our troubles working to loot the treasure?

Having established the presence of the lights, I caught something else which came through the rocks about me—a vibration. Nothing stirred in the valley, there was no sign of any watcher. Perhaps whoever had set this trap had been so confident of its holding for as long as necessary that no sentry had been posted. I squirmed uneasily. I did not in the least want to do what I thought must be done—go to see if my suspicions were correct, that the cache was being looted—to see who was responsible. Stubbornly I hunkered in what seemed to me now to be a shell of safety, one I would be worse than foolish to leave.

I owed no allegiance to the *Lydis*. I was no Free Trader. Krip—
Krip Vorlund. Yes, there was a tie between us I had no thought or
wish to break. But for the rest— Yet Krip had as strong ties to them,
so I was bound to their fate whether I would or no. Could a glassia
have sighed, I would have done so then as I most reluctantly crawled
out of my safe little pocket and began to pad along at the foot of the
cliff, making use once more of every bit of cover.

When I had gone exploring with Krip we had suited our path to
the demands of his human body. But I knew I could take a much
faster way up and over the heights, since my powerful claws were
well fitted to climbing this rock riddled with cracks and crevices. I
worked my way around until I reached a spot which I thought
directly in line with those lights. There I began to climb. The rock
face was dark enough so that my black fur would not show against
its surface as it would have on the light dunes. As I had hoped, my
claws readily found and clung to irregularities which served me well.

I made better speed at this than I had skulking about on the
ground, and so managed to pull out on top of the ridge hardly
winded by my efforts. From this vantage point I could see my
suspicions were in part true. Three lights, giving from here a greater
glow of illumination, were at the point where Foss and the others
had thought they had so well hidden the cargo. Yet the effort of
breaking through the plug they had left there could not be an easy
one. I guessed from the vibration in the rocks, and a faint purr of
sound now to be heard, that some machine had been brought in to
handle that task.

So intent had I been on that distant work I was not at first aware
of what lay closer. Not until I moved a little aside and edged against
that beam— Shock struck me with the power of a blow. Had I met it
at a point of greater intensity I might actually have been borne back
to crash into the valley.

It was pure force, delivered with such strength that one could
believe such a beam should be visible. And it was mind force. Yet
this was a concentration I had never experienced, even when our
Old Ones merged their power for some needful action. That it had
to do with the blanked minds of the humans below, I had no doubt
at all. I was prepared now, wary, my defenses up, so that I could skirt
the danger and not be once more entrapped. And that I must find
the source, I also knew.

I did not want a second meeting with that deadly beam, yet I must somehow keep in contact in order to trace it. So I was reduced to flinching in and out on the edge, reeling away, shuffling on to touch again. Thus I came to a niche in the rocks. There was no light there, no one around; I summoned up enough mind-seek to make sure before I approached that pocket from the rear. It was very dark and whatever was in there was deeply set back in the niche.

Finally I had to pull my way to the top of the rock pile, since I had made sure that the only opening lay at the front. Crouched with my belly flat on the arch, I clawed myself forward. Then I bent my head down, hoping that the beam did not fill the whole of the opening, that I could see what lay inside.

It had seemed dark when viewed from a distance. But within the very narrow space was a faint glimmer, enough to reveal the occupant. I was looking, from a cramped, upside-down position, into a face!

The shock of that nearly loosed me from my precarious hold. I regained control, was able to concentrate on those set, grim features. The eyes of the stranger were shut, his face utterly expressionless, as if he slept. And his body was enclosed in a box which had been wedged upright so that he faced out over the valley. The main part of the box was frosted, so that only the section of cover directly over his face was clear. The face was humanoid enough, though completely hairless, without even brows or lashes. And the skin was a pale gray.

The box which enclosed him (I believed the sleeper to be male) was equipped with a front panel which might have been transparent had not the frosted condition prevailed, for it looked like crystal. This was banded by a wide frame of metal flecked here and there with small specks of color I could not see clearly.

At the foot of the box was another piece of equipment. And while the sleeper (if sleeper he was) resembled nothing I had seen before, what sat at his feet was familiar. I had seen its like employed only a few days ago in the *Lydis*. It was an amplifier for communication, such as Korde had rigged when he made the off-world distress call.

Seeing it where it now was left only one inference to be drawn. The mind-blast was coming from the boxed body, to be amplified by the com device. Also, its being here could have only one purpose— that of holding Krip, the Patrolmen, and presumably the crew of the

Lydis in thrall. Could I in some manner disconnect it, or abate the flow of current, they might be released.

About the boxed sleeper I could do nothing. I was not strong enough to handle the case—it had been too tightly wedged into that niche. My eyes, adjusting to the very faint light emitted from the frame, showed the rocks had been pounded in about the large box to pin it in place.

So—I might not get at the source of the mind-thrall, but the amplifier was another matter. I remembered well how cautiously Korde had adjusted the one on the *Lydis*, his constant warning that the slightest jar could deflect the line of force beam. But this was a task I had to push myself to. For, just as I had tired under my battle in the flitter with that which had tried to take over my mind, so now did my body send messages of distress through aching muscles, fatigue-heavy limbs.

I withdrew to the ground below and moved in cautiously from the side, creeping low and so hoping to elude the full force of the beam. Luckily it did not appear to sweep the ground.

Having made this discovery, I found it easy to wriggle closer. I could see only one possible way, and success would depend upon just how clumsy this animal body was. Backing off, I went to look for a weapon. But here the scouring winds had done their work far too well. There were no loose stones small enough to serve me. I padded along, nosing into every hole I saw, becoming more and more desperate. If I had to return to the floor of the valley to search, I would. But I still hoped.

Stubbornness rewarded me in the end, for in one of the hollows I found a rock which I worried at with my claws until it loosened, so that I could scrape it out into the open. When one has always been served by hands, it is difficult to use one's mouth. But I got the rock between my teeth and returned.

Once more I edged in as flat as I could, and with the stone between my teeth I hammered away at the top of the amplifier, until that was so battered I did not believe those who had left it could ever use it again.

I did not approach the box of the sleeper. But from that seeped a dank chill, like the worst blast of highland winter I had ever met on Yiktor. I believed that had I set paw to that frosted front, I might well have frozen a limb by that unwary touch. There was no change in the face, which could have been that of a carven statue. Yet the sleeper lived, or had once lived. Looking up at the entombed stirred a confused feeling in me.

Quickly I not only glanced away from those set features, but also backed out of the line of sight of the closed eyes. The other added presence I had sensed in the flitter—I felt a stirring of that. And the sensation caused such alarm in me that I loped away without heeding the direction of my going.

When I had my emotions once more under control, and that hint of troubling influence was gone, I discovered I had headed not back to the ship valley but toward the lights and the purr of sound. It might be well for me to scout that scene of activity. I hoped that now that the broadcast had been stopped, those in the *Lydis* and flitters would be free. And it could be to their advantage if I were able to supply information upon my return.

The strangers had no guards or sentries about. Perhaps they were so certain of that which they had put to work in the heights that they felt safe. And it was easy enough to slip up to a good vantage point.

Busy at the cache they were, with flares lighting the scene, brighter even than Sekhmet's daylight. Robos, two of them, were at work on the plug we had set to seal the crevice. But the Traders had done so good a job there that the machines were not breaking it down in any hurry. They had various tools, flamers, and the like fitted into their work sockets and were attacking the fused stone with vigor.

The robos of the *Lydis* were mainly for loading, although in extreme need they could be equipped with a few simple working tool modifications. These looked larger and different. They were being directed to their labor by a man holding a control board. And, though I knew little of such machines, I thought they seemed chiefly intended for excavation work.

As far as we of the *Lydis* knew, there were no mines on Sekhmet. And casual prospectors did not own such elaborate and costly machines. We had found traces of what might be treasure deposits here. Could these robos have been imported to open such deposits?

The men below—there were three of them—looked like any spacers, wearing the common coveralls of ship crewmen. They appeared completely humanoid, of the same stock as the Free Traders. The two who were not controlling the robos carried weapons, blasters to be exact, an indication that they could well be outside the law. The sight of those was warning enough for me to keep my distance.

I stiffened against the ground, my breath hissing between those fangs which were a glassia's natural weapons. A fourth man had come into sight. And his face was very clear in the flare lamps. It was Griss Sharvan!

There were no signs of his being a prisoner. He stopped beside one of the guards, watching the robos with as much interest as if he had set them to work. Had he? Was it Sharvan who had led this crew to the cache? But why? It was very hard for anyone who knew the Traders to believe that one of them could turn traitor to his land. Their loyalty was inbred. I would have sworn by all I knew that such a betrayal was totally impossible. Yet there he stood, seemingly on excellent terms with the looters.

From time to time the robo master made adjustments on the controls. I caught a feeling of impatience from him. And when that reached my conscious attention, I thought that the weakening of my power had passed. Which meant I might just dare to discover, via mind-probe, what Sharvan did here. Settling myself to the easiest position I could find, I began probe.

Chapter 8

KRIP VORLUND

It was very quiet; there was no *thrum* in the walls, no feeling of the usual safe containment which a ship gave. I opened my eyes—but not upon the walls of my cabin in the *Lydis*; instead I was facing the control board of a flitter. And as I blinked, more than a little bemused, recollection flowed in. The last thing I could remember clearly was flying over the broken ranges on my way back to the ship.

But I was not flying now. Then how had I landed, and—

I turned to look at the second seat. There was no furred body there. And a quick survey told me that I was alone in the flitter. Yet surely Maelen could not have landed us. And the dark outside was now that of night.

It took only an instant or two to open the hatch and stumble out of the flyer. Beside me rose the *Lydis*. Beyond her I could make out a second flitter. But why could I not remember? What had happened just before we landed?

"Vorlund!" My name out of the night.

"Who's there?"

"Harkon." A dark shadow came from the other flitter, plowed through the sand toward me.

"How did we get here?" he demanded. But I could not give him any answer to that.

There was a grating sound from the ship. I raised my head to see the ramp issue from her upper hatch like a tongue thrust out to explore. Moments later its end thudded to earth only a short distance away. But I was more intent on finding Maelen.

The sand around held no prints; I could not pick up a trail. But if the ship's ramp had been up, she could not have gone aboard. I could not imagine what would have taken her away from the flitter. Except her strange actions back in that other valley made me wonder if some influence had drawn her beyond her powers of resistance. If so, what influence, and why would it affect her more here? Also, I could not remember landing the flitter—

I flashed out a mind-seek. And an instant later I reeled back, striking against the body of the flitter I had just quitted, going to my knees, my hands against my head, unable to think clearly, gasping for breath—for—

By the time Harkon reached me I must have been very close to complete blackout. I recall only dimly being led on board the *Lydis*, people moving about me. Then I choked, gasped, shook my head as strong fumes cut through the frightening mist which was between me and the world. I looked up, able to see and recognize what I saw—the sick bay of the ship. Medic Lukas was by me, backed by Lidj and Harkon.

"What—what happened?"

"You tell us," Lukas said.

My head—I turned it a little on the pillow. That sickening wave of assaulting blackness mixed with pain ebbed.

"Maelen—she was gone. I tried to find her by mind-seek. Then—something hit—inside my head." It was as hard now to describe the nature of that attack as it was to remember how I had come earlier to land the flitter.

"It agrees," Lukas nodded. But what agreed with what, no one explained to me. Until he continued, "Esper force stepped up to that degree can register as energy." He shook his head. "I would have said it was impossible, except on one world or another the impossible is often proved true."

"Esper," I repeated. My head ached now, with a degree of pain which made me rather sick. Maelen, what about her? But perhaps to try mind-seek again would bring another such attack, and that dread was realized as Lukas continued:

"Keep away from the use of that, Krip. At least until we know more of what is happening. You had such a dose of energy that you were nearly knocked out."

"Maelen—she's gone!"

He did not quite meet my eyes then. I thought I could guess what he was thinking.

"She wasn't responsible! I know her sending—"

"Then who did?" Harkon demanded. "You stated from the start that she is highly telepathic. Well, this is being done by a telepath of unusual talent and perhaps training. And I would like to know who landed us here—since we cannot remember! Were we taken over by your animal?"

"No!" I struggled to sit up, and then doubled over, fighting the nausea and feeling of disorientation that movement caused. Lukas put something quickly to my mouth and I sucked at a tube, swallowing cool liquid which allayed the sickness.

"It was *not* Maelen!" I got out when I finished that potion. "You cannot mistake a mind sending—it is as individual as a voice, a face. This—this was alien." Now that I had had a few moments in which to think about it, I knew that was true.

"Also"—Lukas turned to Lidj—"tell them what registered on our receivers here."

"We have a recording," the cargomaster began. "This esper attack began some time ago—and you were not here then. It broke in intensity about a half hour since—dropped far down the scale, though it still registers. Just as if some transmission of energy had been brought to a peak and then partly shut off. While it was on at the top range none of us can remember anything. We must have awakened, if you can term it that, at the moment it dropped. But the residue remaining is apparently enough to knock out anyone trying esper communication, as Krip proved. So if it was not Maelen—"

"But where is she now?" I swallowed experimentally as I raised my head, and discovered I felt better. "I was alone in the flitter when I awoke—and no one can find a trail through that sand out there."

"It may be that she has gone to hunt the source of what hit us. She is a far greater esper than any of our breed," Lidj suggested.

I pulled myself up, pushing away Lukas's hand when he put it out to deter me. "Or else she was drawn unwillingly. She felt something back there in that valley where we found the flitter, she begged me to get her away. She—she may have been caught by whatever is there!"

"It is not going to help her to go charging out without any idea of what you may be up against." Lidj's good sense might not appeal to me then, but since he, Lukas, and Harkon made a barrier at the door of the sick bay I was sure I was not going to get past them at present.

"If you think I am going to stay safe in here while—" I began. Lidj shook his head.

"I am only saying that we have to know more about the enemy before we go into battle. We have had enough warning to be sure that this is something we have never faced before. And what good will it do Maelen, Sharvan, or Hunold if we too are captured before we can aid them?"

"What *are* you doing?" I demanded.

"We have a fix on the source of the broadcast, or whatever it is. On top of the cliff to the east-northeast. But in the middle of the night we aren't going to get far climbing around these rocks hunting for it. I can tell you this much—it registers with too regular a pattern to be a human mind-send. If it is an installation, which we can believe, working on a telepath's level—then there should be someone in charge of it. Someone who probably knows this country a lot better than we do. But we have our range finder out now—"

"And something else," Harkon cut in crisply. "I loosed a snooper, set on the recording pattern, as soon as Lidj reported this. That will broadcast back a pick-up picture when it locates anything which is not just rock and brush."

"So—" Lidj spoke again. "Now we shall adjourn to the control cabin and see what the snooper can tell us."

The Patrol are noted for their use of sophisticated equipment. They have refinements which are far ahead of those on Free Trader ships. I had heard of snoopers, though I had never seen one in action before.

There was a flutter on the surface of the small screen set over the visa-plate of the *Lydis*—a rippling of lines. But that continued without change and my impatience grew. All that Lidj had said was unfortunately true. If I could not use mind-seek without provoking such instant retaliation as before, I had little chance of finding Maelen in that broken country, especially at night.

"Something coming in!" Harkon's voice broke through my dark imaginings.

Those fluttering lines on the screen were overlaid with a pattern. As we watched, the faint image sharpened into a definite scene. We looked into a dark space where an arching of rocks made a niche. And the niche was occupied. It was the face of the man or being who stood there which riveted my attention first. Human—or was he? His eyes were closed as if he slept—or concentrated. Then the whole of the scene registered. He was not in the open, but rather enclosed in a box which, except for the space before his face, was opaque. That box had been wedged upright, so he faced outward.

At his feet was a smaller box. But this was broken, badly battered, wires and jagged bits of metal showing through cracks in it.

Harkon spoke first. "I think we can see why the broadcast suddenly failed. That thing in front is an alpha-ten amplifier, or was before someone gave it a good bashing. It's meant to project and heighten com relays. But I never heard of it being used to amplify telepathic sends before."

"That man," Lidj said as if he could not quite believe what he saw. "Then he is a telepath and his mind-send was so amplified."

"A telepath to a degree hitherto unknown, I would say," Lukas replied. "There's something else—he may be humanoid, but he's not of Terran stock. Unless of a highly mutated strain."

"How do you know?" Harkon asked for all of us.

"Because he's plainly in stass-freeze. And in that state you don't broadcast; you are not even alive, as we reckon life."

He glanced at us as if he now expected some outburst of denial. But I, for one, knew Lukas was never given to wild and unfounded statements. If he thought that closed-eyed stranger was in stass-freeze, I would accept his diagnosis.

Harkon shook his head slowly. Not as if he were prepared to argue with Lukas, but as if he could not honestly accept what he was seeing.

"Well, if he is in stass-freeze, at least he's tight in that box. He did not get there on his own. Somebody put him there."

"How about the snooper—can it pick up any back trail from that?" Lidj gestured to the screen. "Show us who installed the esper and the amplifier?"

"We can see what a general life-force setting will do." Harkon studied the dial of his wrist com, made a delicate adjustment to it. The screen lost the picture with a flash and the fluttering returned.

"It isn't coming back," Harkon reported, "so the life-force search must be at work. But as to what it will pick up—"

"Getting something!" Korde leaned forward, half cutting off my view of the screen, so I pulled him back a little.

He was right. Once more there was a scene on the screen. We were looking into a much brighter section of countryside.

"The cache—they're looting the cache!" But we did not need that exclamation from Lidj.

There were excavation robos busy there. And they had broken through the plug we had thought the perfect protection. Three—no, four—men stood a little to one side watching the work. Two were armed with blasters, one had a robo control board. But the fourth man—

I saw Lidj hunch farther toward the screen.

"I—don't—believe—it!" His denial was one we could have voiced as a chorus.

I knew Griss Sharvan; I had shared planet leave with him. He had been with me on Yiktor when first I had seen Maelen. It was utterly incredible that he should be standing there calmly watching the looting of our cargo. He was a Free Trader, born and bred to that life—and among us there were no traitors!

"He can only be mind-washed!" Lidj produced the one explanation we could accept. "If an esper of the power Krip met got at him, it's no wonder they could find the cache. They could pick its hiding place right out of his brain! And they must have Hunold, too. But what are they—jacks?" He asked that of Harkon, depending upon the authority of one who should know his lawbreakers to give him an answer.

"Jacks—with such equipment? They don't make such elaborate efforts in their operations. I would think more likely a Guild job—"

"Thieves' Guild here?"

Lidj had a good right to his surprise. The Thieves' Guild was powerful, as everyone knew. But they did not operate on the far rim of the galaxy. Theirs was not the speculation of possible gains from raiding on frontier planets. Those small pickings were left to the jacks. The Guild planned bigger deals based on inner planets where wealth gathered, drawn in from those speculative ventures on the worlds the jacks plundered. If jacks had dealings with the Guild it was only when they fenced their take with the more powerful criminals. But they were very small operators compared with the members of that spider web which was, on some worlds, more powerful than the law. The Guild literally owned planets.

"Guild, or perhaps Guild-subsidized." Harkon held to his point stubbornly.

Which made our own position even more precarious, though it would also account for the sabotage and the elaborate plan which seemed to have been set up to enmesh the *Lydis*, both in space and here. The Guild had resources which even the Patrol could not guess. They were rumored to be ready to buy up, or acquire by other, more brutal means, new discoveries and inventions, so that they might keep ahead of their opponents. The boxed esper with the amplifier—yes, that could well be a Guild weapon. And the mining robos we saw at work here—

I thought at once of that cat mask on the cliff, of Maelen's assurance that other finds existed. Suppose some enterprising jack outfit, ambitious and far-seeing, had made the discovery that Sekhmet had such finds. With such a secret as their portion of the partnership, they could get Guild backing. At least to the extent of modern excavation equipment, plus such devices as the esper linkage for protection.

Then one of their men on Thoth could have picked up the news of our cargo. And they might have prepared to gather that in as a bonus. The Throne of Qur would be worth any effort. I could not help but believe that was the answer.

But what other devices could they have? That which sabotaged the *Lydis* we still do not understand. And the esper was something entirely new. Nor were the Free Traders backward in hearing about such things.

"Look out!"

I was startled out of my thoughts by Harkon's cry. We could still see the scene of the cargo cache. The robos had started to bring out what we had stored there. But it was not that action which the Patrol pilot had noted.

One of the guards had turned about, was pointing his blaster directly at our screen. A moment later that went black.

"Took out the snooper," Harkon commented.

"Now they know—first, that their esper is no longer controlling us; second, that we have learned of their activities in turn," Lidj said. "Do we now expect an attack in force?"

"What arms do you carry?" Harkon asked.

"No more than are allowed. We can break our seal on the ordnance compartment and get the rest of the blasters. That's the extent of it. A Trader depends on evasive action in space. And the *Lydis* does not set down on worlds where the weapons are much more sophisticated than on Thoth. We haven't broken that seal in years."

"And we don't know what they have—could be anything," Harkon commented. "I wonder who took out that amplifier. Might that man of yours be operating on his own—the one you did not see?"

But I was as certain as if I had witnessed the act. "Maelen did that."

"An animal—even a telepathic one—" Harkon began.

I eyed him coldly. "Maelen is not an animal. She is a Thassa, a Moon Singer of Yiktor." The odds were that he had not the slightest idea of what that meant, so I enlarged on that statement. "She is an alien, wearing animal form only for a time. It is a custom among her people." I was determined not to go farther into that. "She would be perfectly capable of tracing the esper interference and knocking out the amplifier."

But where was she now? Had she gone on to the cache to see what was happening there? I did not know how the jack guard had picked the snooper off so accurately. They were programmed to evade attack. He could have been just as quick to dispose of Maelen, had he sighted her. They had probably been planeted on Sekhmet long enough to know most of the native wildlife, so they would have recognized her even in animal form as something from off-world, and been suspicious. I could imagine plainly the whole sequence of such a discovery.

If only I dared mind-search! But even though the amplifier was not of use, I knew I could once more bring upon myself that force I had experienced earlier. Until the stass frozen man—or thing—was rendered harmless (if he could be) I had no hope of tracking Maelen except by sight alone. And in the dark of night that was impossible.

"We can just sit it out," Korde was saying when I again paid attention. "Your ship"—he nodded to Harkon—"will be back soon with Foss. We have power enough to warn them once they come into braking orbit."

But Lidj was shaking his head. "Not good enough. The jacks must have been watching us all along, even if we could not detect them— they certainly possess a protective field which blanks out even esper when they want, or Maelen would have picked them up earlier. So they know about us and that we are waiting for help. They could move fast now—pack up and be off-world before we get reinforcements. After all, their base may be half this continent away, hidden anywhere. We've got to keep on their tails if we can. But it won't do any good to try another snooper. They will be watching for that now."

"We haven't one anyway," Harkon commented dryly. "For the rest; I would say you are right. There is also this—if we stay in or around your ship, they may be able to pin us down, blank out any com warning, hold us just as tightly as they did before. I say, leave the ship with a guard and a locked-up boarding ramp. The rest of us will take to the country. It is rough enough to hide an army. We'll work our way northeast, starting at the cache, and see if we can at least locate the general direction of their base. They won't be able to transport all they are pulling out of there without making a number of trips. Also—that esper is still up there. If we find him before they come to see what is wrong, we may just be able to shut him off, or do whatever needs to be done to hinder them in using him again. And what about this Maelen of yours—can you contact her, find out where she is?" He spoke directly to me.

"Not as long as that esper is broadcasting. You saw what happened when I tried that before. But I think she is near that cache. It may be that if I get close enough she can perhaps pick me up, though I can't be sure. She is far more powerful than I am."

"Good. That makes you our first choice for the scouting force." He certainly did not wait for volunteers. Not that I would not have been the first of those. But a Free Trader does not take kindly to any assumption of authority except from his own kind. And it was very apparent that Harkon considered himself without question to be the leader of any sortie we planned.

Lidj might have challenged him, but he did not. He went instead to break the seal on the arms locker. We took out the blasters, inserted fresh charges, slung on ammunition belts. E rations were in packets. And we had our thermo suits as protection against the chill.

In the end Korde and Aljec Lalfarns, a tubeman, stayed with the ship. Harkon's gunners from the flitter removed the charges from those crafts' defense to render them harmless and made ready to join us. It was still dark, though dawn could not now be too far away. We had a short rest and ate our last full ship's meal before we left.

It was decided we would try the more arduous climb up over the cliff, so we could find the esper and take action to insure he would not trouble us again. And climb we did, the blasters on their slings over our shoulders, weighing us back, making the climb more difficult, though the face of the stone was already rough enough. We had had to put aside our mittens in order to find handholes, and the chill of the rock bit deep, so that we must press on as quickly as we could before any numbing of our fingers could bring about disaster. I thought of Maelen's sharp-pointed claws and knew that this road must have been a fairly easy one for her. But her passing had left no traces.

We reached the top of the cliff, spread out in a single thin line as Harkon ordered. From this height we could see the lights at the location of the cache. The workers there made no effort to hide their presence. And, having been alerted by the snooper, they could already be preparing a warm welcome.

Our advance had been very short when my wrist com buzzed. "To the right," clicked the signal which brought me in that direction, picking my way more by feel than sight.

Thus we gathered at the niche we had seen from the snooper. The smashed amplifier had not been moved. It was apparent that those who had installed it there either had not arrived to check on it, or had abandoned it. I stepped closer, flinched. For the first time in my life I experienced mind-send not only in my brain, but as an invisible but potent force against my body.

"Don't go directly in front of it!" I said sharply.

At my warning Harkon edged in from one side, I from the other. There was no sign of life on that face. It was humanoid, yet it had an alien cast. I might have been looking at a dead man, in fact I would have said so, had I not felt that strong current of send. The Patrolman stepped back, yielding his place to Lukas. Now the medic put out his unmittened hand and moved his fingers, held an inch or so away from the surface of that case, as if he were smoothing it up and down.

"Stass-freeze to a high degree," he reported. "Higher than I know of in general use." He unsealed the front of his jacket, drew out a life-force detect, and held that at the level of the sleeper's chest, though we could not see the body through that opaque opening.

In the very dim light radiated by the box I saw the incredulous expression on Lukas's face. With a sharp jerk he brought the detect up level with the head, took a second reading, returned to heart level for another examination. Then he edged back.

"What about it?" Harkon asked. "How deep in stass is he?"

"Too deep—he's dead!"

"But he can't be!" I stared at the set face of the box's occupant. "The dead don't mind-send!"

"Maybe he doesn't know that!" Lukas gave a queer sound, almost a laugh. Then his voice steadied as he added, "He's not only dead, but so long dead the force reading went clear out of reckoning. Think about that for a moment."

Chapter 9

KRIP VORLUND

I still could not really believe that. A mind-send from a dead man—impossible! And I said so. But Lukas waved his detect and swore that it was working properly, as he proved by trying it on me and pointing to the perfectly normal reading. We had to accept that a dead body, linked to an amplifier, had managed to keep us in thrall until the machine had been smashed; that esper power, strong enough to upset anyone human (I could hope Maelen was beyond its control) who tried to use a like talent in its vicinity, was issuing from a dead man.

But the cache was still being looted. We dared not spend too long a time with this mystery when action was demanded elsewhere. The damaged amplifier was speedily disposed of, but we could not unwedge that box. So we left the strange sleeper there, still broadcasting, as he had—for how long? Though I was sure not from the same site.

The way over the cliffs was much shorter than the ground-level trail. We crept up, following all the precautions of those invading enemy territory, until we could look down at the cache. There the robos had emptied our hiding place. The glittering Throne stood in a blaze of harsh glory amid the boxes and bundles.

A flitter, perhaps double the size of our own, had grounded, was being loaded with the smaller pieces. The three jacks we had seen via snooper were studying the Throne. It was plain to see that that was not going to fit into the flyer, and its transportation must present a problem.

Save for those three there appeared to be no one else below. Sharvan had disappeared. But at the moment my own concern was for Maelen. If she had come here, was she hiding somewhere among these rocks, spying as we were? Dared I try mind-send again?

There was no other way of finding her in this rough terrain. Though one of Sekhmet's cloudy dawns was at hand and visibility was better than it had been when we had begun this trek. I made my choice for mind-seek, ready to withdraw that instantly if I so much as brushed the edge of any deadly broadcast. But this time I met none. So heartened, I fastened upon a mind-picture of Maelen and began my quest in earnest.

But I did not even meet with the betraying signal of a mind-block. She was not on the heights where we lay in hiding. Down in the valley near the cache then? Very cautiously I began to probe below, fearing to trigger some such response as I had before. They might well have a second sleeper at the scene of action as a cover.

I met nothing, and that in itself was kind of a shock. For all three of those I could see conferring about the Throne did not register at all. They were mind-shielded with a complete barrier against any probe. Perhaps because of the fact that they dealt with the sleeper, and only thus could they venture to use him. So there was nothing to be learned from them either. Nor did Maelen's answer come from the valley.

Having made sure of that, I began to extend my search—choosing south, the way from which we had come when we had first discovered this place. And, as my send crept on and on, I picked up the faintest quiver of an answer!

"Where—where?" I put full force into that.

"—here—" Very faint, very far away, "—aid—here—"

There could be no mistaking the urgency of her plea. But the low volume of the send was an even greater spur to action. That Maelen was in dire trouble, I had no doubt at all. And the choice I must make now was equally plain. The cargo had brought us here; it was the responsibility of the *Lydis*'s crew. We were eight men against an unknown number.

And there was Maelen—lost—calling for my aid.

The decision was partly dictated by my Thassa body, of that I am now sure. Just as I had once feared that Jorth the barsk was stronger than Krip Vorlund the man, so now Maquad of the Thassa—or that small residue of him which was a part of me—changed my life. Thassa to Thassa—I could not hold out against that call. But neither would my other heritage allow me to go without telling my own kind that I must.

Chance had brought me closest to Lidj. I crawled now until I could set hand on his shoulder. He jerked at my touch, turned to look at me. Dusky as this cloud-shrouded day was, we could see each other clearly.

"Maelen is in trouble. She is calling me for aid," I told him in a whisper which I meant to carry no farther than this spot.

He said nothing, nor did any expression cross his face. I do not know what I expected, but that long, level look was one I had to force myself to meet. Though I waited, he continued silent. Then he turned away to gaze into the valley. I was chilled, cold, as if the thermo jacket had been ripped from my body, leaving my shoulders bare to the winds.

Yet I could not bite back my words; there was that in me which held me to my choice. I turned and crawled. Not only from the side of the cargomaster, but from that whole length of cliff where the others crouched waiting for Harkon's signal to attack, if that was the order he would give.

Now I had to force from me all thought of those of the *Lydis*. I must concentrate wholly on that thread, so thin, so far-stretched, which tied me to Maelen. And a thin, far-stretched one it was, so tenuous I feared it would be severed and I would have no guide at all.

It brought me down from the cliffs. And I could not mistake landmarks I had memorized. This was the way to the cat mask. I reached a point from which I ought to be able to see that pale and ghostly vestige of ancient carving. But this morning the light, perhaps the lack of sand to cling in the right places, did not aid me. I could trace nothing but the hollow which was its mouth.

And Maelen's desperate call led me there. I wriggled forward on my belly, expecting she must lie there in the shadows. But the pocket was empty! Only her call continued—from beyond the wall!

With my mittened hands I pushed and beat against the blocks, certain that there must be some concealed door, that one or another of them would fall or turn to provide me with an opening. How else could Maelen have entered?

But the blocks were as firmly joined as if they had been set in place but weeks before.

"Maelen!" I lay there, my hands resting against the wall. "Maelen, where are you?"

"Krip—aid—aid—"

Faint, far away, a cry fast fading into nothingness. And the fear which had been riding me since first I picked up her send now struck deep into me. I was certain that if I could not find a way to her soon there would be no reason to go at all. Maelen would be gone for all time.

I had but one key left to use. And by using it I might throw away a means for my own defense. But again I had no choice. I edged back, out of the mouth of that cleft.

I lay flat outside, sighting inward with the blaster. Then I dropped my head to my bent arm, veiling my eyes against the brilliance of the blast I loosed as I fired.

Scorching heat beat back against me, though the worst was absorbed by my thermo clothing. I smelled the crisping of my mittens, felt a searing lick across the edge of my cheek. Still I held fast, giving that inner wall top power. What effect it would have on the blocks I could not tell; I could only hope.

When I had used all that charge I had yet to wait, not daring at once to crawl back within that cramped space until it had a little time to lose some of the heat. But neither could I wait too long.

At last impatience won, and I was startled at what I found. Those blocks, which to the touch had had a likeness to the native rock of the cliff wall, were gone—as cleanly as if they had only been counterfeits of stone. Thus I was able to enter the passage beyond.

Not that that was much larger. The cleft, or tunnel, or whatever it was, ran straight as a bore, with just enough room to wriggle. As I advanced I liked the situation less and less. Had I even been able to rise to my hands and knees, it would have given me a measure of relief. As it was, I had to edge on with a maximum of effort in a minimum of space.

Also, the farther I went, the less I liked the idea of perhaps coming up against a dead end and having to work my way out backward. In fact, so disturbing did I find that thought that I had to banish it as quickly as I could by holding to my mental picture of Maelen.

That journey seemed endless, but it was not. I used the blaster, now empty of charge, as a sounding rod, pushing it ahead of me through the dark, so feeling for any obstruction or fault which might cause trouble. And that did at last strike a solid surface.

I probed with the blaster in exploration, and it seemed that the passage was firmly plugged ahead. But I must make sure, so I squirmed on until my hand came against that surface. It did fill the space, and yet into my face blew a puff of air. Though hitherto I had not even wondered why I had been able to breathe in this tightly confined space.

As I slipped my hands back and forth, my fingers discovered a hole, through which flowed a distinct current of air. Hooking one hand to that, I strove to dislodge the whole plug. My effort moved it, though I found I must push instead of pull. It swung away from me and I shouldered through.

So I came not only to a much larger space, but to one with dim lighting. Or perhaps it was dim only in comparison with the outer world. To my eyes, used now to total dark, it seemed bright.

The hole of my entrance was some distance above the floor of this other space. I entered in an awkward scramble, half falling to the lower level. It was so good to stand erect again.

This chamber was square. And the light came through a series of long, narrow cuts set vertically in the wall to my left. Save for those, there appeared to be no other opening, certainly no door.

When I advanced to the light, I discovered a grating in the floor against the wall, wide enough for an exit if there were some manner of raising the grating itself. Just now I was more intent on looking through one of the slits.

It was necessary to squeeze very close to that narrow opening. Even then the area of vision was much curtailed. But I was looking down into a room or hall which was of such large proportions I could view only a fraction of it. The light came from the tops of a series of standing pillars or cases. And a moment's inspection of the nearest, though I must do that from some distance above, suggested something familiar. By almost grinding my face against the frame of the slit, I made a guess. These had a close resemblance to the box which had held that dead man above the valley. I was looking into a place for beings in stass-freeze!

"Maelen?"

Nothing moved below among the pillar-boxes. And—I had no answer to my call. I went on my knees, shed my charred mittens so I could lock fingers in the grating. And I had to exert all the strength I could summon before that gave, grudgingly. However, I was able to raise it. How I longed for what I did not have—a torch, for there was only dark below once more.

Lying flat, I tried to gauge what did lie below by letting the blaster dangle from its carrying strap. Thus I discovered what appeared to be a narrow shaft, its floor not too far below. And I dared to drop to that. Once down, I explored the wall which faced the sleepers' hall and was able to trace a line. Pushing outward brought no results. It was when my hands slipped across the surface of that stubborn barrier that it moved to one side and I was able to force it open a crack. Then the barrel of the blaster inserted there gave me leverage enough to force it the rest of the way.

How large that hall was I could not guess. It appeared to stretch endlessly both right and left. And there was such a sameness to those lines of boxes one could not find any guide.

"Maelen?"

I fell back against the very door I had just forced open. As it had happened before, my mind-seek brought such an answer as nearly struck me down. This response was no concentrated beam, but still it was a daunting blast, filling my mind painfully. So I crouched there, my hands raised to my ears in an involuntary response as if to shut out thundering shouts.

It was a torment, worse than any physical pain. A warning that here I dared not use the only way I had of tracing her whom I sought. I would have to blunder along, depending on the whim of fortune.

Shutting out mind-seek, I staggered forward in a wavering way between the boxes in the row directly before me. Now and then I paused to study the faces of those sleepers. There was a sameness about those. They might all have come from some uniform mold, as there appeared to be no distinguishing marks to make one case differ from the next. Then I became a little less dazed by that mental bolt which had struck me and noted that there was a change in the patterning of color sparks about the frame of each box.

I counted at first, but after I reached fifty, I decided there was no need for that. Beyond the rows where I walked now were more and more and more. It might be that the entire army of some forgotten conqueror was here laid up in stass-freeze. I laughed then, thinking what an excellent way to preserve troops between one war and the next, assuring a goodly supply of manpower with no interregnum living expenses.

Such a find as this had never been made before. In fact the treasure discoveries on Thoth had had no conjunction with the remains of bodies, a puzzle for the archaeologists, since it had previously been believed that such furnishings were placed with rulers as grave goods. So—was this the cemetery of those who had left their treasures on Thoth? But why, then, cross space to bury their dead on another world?

And if they were dead, why were their bodies in stass-freeze? It was a condition known to my own kind in the past, used for two purposes. In the very early days of space travel it had been the only way to transport travelers during long voyages which might last for centuries of planet time. Secondly, it was the one hope for the seriously ill, who could rest thus until some future medical discovery could cure them.

Nations, peoples, even species did entomb their dead, following beliefs that at the will of their gods, or at some signal, these would rise whole and alive again. Was this so profound a belief here that they had used stass-freeze to preserve their dead?

I could accept such preservation, but I could not accept the fact that, although dead, they apparently still used their esper powers. My mind shied away from the horror that a live mind could be imprisoned in a dead body.

There was an end at last to the hall. In the faint light of the boxes I could now see another wall, and in that an archway framing a wide door. A closed door. But I was so filled with a loathing of that place that I halted, fumbled for another charge for the blaster, determined to burn my way out if I found that portal barred to my exit.

However, at my urging it rolled aside into the wall. I looked into a passageway. It was lighted, though by what means I could not see, save that the walls themselves appeared to give off a gray luminosity. With the blaster ready I went along.

There were doors in this corridor, each tightly closed, each bearing on its surface a series of symbols which had no meaning for me. And where in all this maze could I find Maelen? Since my sharp lesson in the hall of the sleepers, I dared not risk another call. There was no help but to look within each of the rooms I passed.

The first door opened on a small chamber holding but two sleepers. But there were also chests ranged about its walls. However, I did not wait to explore those. Another room—three sleepers—more storage containers. Room three—two sleepers again—more chests.

I was at the end of the hall and here the way branched right and left. I chose the right. The hall was still lighted and it ran straight, without any break. How many miles did this burrowing run? I wondered. It might be that Sekhmet was half honeycombed with these tunnelings. What a find! And if those chests and boxes I had seen in the smaller rooms contained such treasures as had been found on Thoth—then indeed the jacks had uncovered a mine which the Guild would not disdain to work. But why had they jeopardized their operation by sabotaging the *Lydis*? They could have worked here for years and never been discovered, had we not been forced down and they overplayed their hand by the attack on us. Was it a matter of being over-greedy?

The corridor I now followed began to narrow; soon it was passage for one only. There—I paused, my head up as I sniffed. Some untrackable system of ventilation had supplied all these ways. But this was something different—it was an odor I recognized. Somewhere not too far away cyro leaves had been recently burned. There were other faint scents also—food—cooked food—but the cyro overlaid most of that so strongly I could identify little else.

Cyro is mildly intoxicating, but it is also used as a counter to both body fatigue and some nervous depressions. As a Free Trader I was and am conditioned against certain drugs. By the very nature of our lives we must keep ourselves alert and with top powers of reaction. Just as we are conditioned against a planet-side interest in intoxicants of any type, gambling, women not of our kind, so we know the drugs which can spell danger by a clouding of mind, a slowing of body. So well are we armored against such that the use of any can make us violently ill.

Now I felt myself swallowing, fighting the nausea that smell induced in me. But such an odor could mean nothing less than that somewhere ahead were, or had been, others than the sleepers. After such a warning my progress was doubly cautious.

The hall ended in a blank wall, but then I saw an opening to my right, framing a brighter glow some distance ahead. And so I came out on a low-walled balcony overhanging another large chamber. This in turn was partly open to the sky. And beyond, in that daylight, I caught a glimpse of a spacer's fins, as if one side of this cavern opened on a landing field.

There was no way down from the balcony. But from this perch I had a good view of all which lay below. And there was plenty to see. To one side was heaped a pile of such chests and boxes as had been in the rooms. Many of them had shattered lids as if they had been forced. And not too far away two servo robos were fastening up a shipping crate.

Off to the right was a plasta-bubble, the kind of living quarters used by explorers as a base camp. This was sealed. But two men sat on upturned boxes outside it. One was speaking into a wrist recorder. The other held a robo control board on his knee as he watched the two busy at the crate. There was no one else in sight.

I tried to gauge the ship's size from what I could see of its fins, and decided it must be at least equal to the *Lydis*, perhaps larger. But there was no doubting that I witnessed a well-established and full-sized operation, and that it had been going on for some time.

The last thing I wanted to do was attract their attention. But Maelen—had she wandered in here, to be caught in some trap? Indecision held me fast. Dare I mind-call? There were no sleepers visible. But that did not mean that the jacks might not be using one as a defense or a warning.

I was still hesitating when a man came in from outside. Griss Sharvan!

Griss—I still could not accept that he was a part of this, or that he had of his own free will gone over to the enemy. I had known him far too long, and he was a Free Trader. Yet he moved freely, gave no sign of being a prisoner.

He joined the two by the bubble. The one recording got to his feet hurriedly, as did his companion. They gave the response of underlings in the presence of a leader. What—what had happened to Griss?

Suddenly his attention turned from them. His head came up, he stared straight up—at me! I fell behind the low wall edging the balcony. His actions had been those of a man alerted to danger, one who knows just where to look.

I began to crawl back to the passage which had brought me here. Only I never reached it. For what struck me then was something I had never experienced before, in spite of my many encounters with different kinds of esper power.

The command of my own body was taken from me. It was as if my mind was imprisoned in a robo which was obeying commands broadcast by a board. I got to my feet, turned around, and marched back into the sight of the three below, all of whom now watched me.

Griss raised his hand, pointed a forefinger at me. To my complete amazement I was raised from the stone under my boots, lifted above the wall, carried out and down, all as if I had antigrav on me. Nor could I struggle against that compelling force which held me captive.

That energy deposited me, still on my feet, on the floor of the cavern. I stood there, a prisoner, as the two who had been checking cargo advanced on me. Griss remained where he was, that pointing finger aimed at my head, as if his flesh and bone had become a tangler.

The man who still held the robo control reached out his other hand and snatched the blaster from my hold. Even then my hands did not change position, but remained as if I still gripped barrel and butt with them. But the other jack brought out a real tangler, spinning its web of restraint around me. When he was done, Griss's hand dropped and that compulsion was gone, though now I had no chance at freedom. They had left my legs unbound, and the jack with the tangler caught my shoulder and gave me a vicious shove toward Griss.

Chapter 10

KRIP VORLUND

Only it was not Griss Sharvan who stood there. Though he—it—wore Griss's body as one might wear a thermo suit. The minute those eyes met mine, I knew. Nor did that knowledge come as too great a shock, since my own experiences had taught me such shifts were possible.

However, this was no shift for the sake of knowledge, nor for the preservation of life, such as the Thassa practiced. The personality which had taken over Griss was alien to our kind as the Thassa could never be. I had a swift mental picture of a terrifying creature—a thing with a reasonably humanoid body but a head evilly reptilian, a mixture which repelled.

Only for an instant did I hold that mental image; then it was gone. But with its disappearance there was also a flash of incredulous surprise, not on my part, but from the alien. As if he—it—was astounded that I had been able to pick up that image at all, as its true nature was so well concealed it never revealed itself.

"Greeting, Krip." Griss's voice. But I knew well that those slow, toneless words carried another's thoughts. I did not attempt any mental scanning, being warned by instinct that such would be the most dangerous thing I could do. "How many are with you?"

He held his head a little to one side, giving the impression of listening. A moment later he smiled.

"So you are alone, Krip? Now that was very foolish of you. Not that the whole crew could take us. But if they had been so obliging as to come it would have saved us much trouble. However, one more is a good beginning."

His eyes searched mine, but I had been warned enough to draw on the full resources of my talent, erect a mind-shield. Against that I could feel his probing, but surprisingly, he did not try to force it. I feared, guessed, that had he wanted to, he could easily have stripped me of any defenses, taken over my mind to learn all I had been trying to hide from him. This was a master esper, such as perhaps were the Old Ones among the Thassa, far beyond my own talent.

"A beginning," he repeated. Then he raised his hand in an arrogant gesture, crooking his finger to beckon me. "Come!"

I had not the slightest hope of disobeying that order. As before, I walked helplessly after him across the cavelike chamber. Never once did he turn his head to see whether or no I was behind, but wove a path in and out among the boxes.

So we came to another door and into a passage beyond. The light faded once again to that gray gloom which I had seen above, and the passage made several turns. Along its walls were open doors, but all the rooms were empty.

That this creature wearing Griss's body meant me no good was evident. I believed that my only defense against dire and instant peril was to dampen all esper talent, to depend only on the five senses of my body. But those I used as best I could to give me some idea of the territory through which we passed.

There were traces of odors from the cyro, but they were soon gone, leaving only an indefinable scent I could not name. Sight gave me the passage and the empty rooms along it. Sound—there was the faint rasp of two pairs of space boots against the stone floor, the fainter pulsing of my own breathing—nothing else.

And where was Maelen? A prisoner perhaps in the bubble? As quickly as I thought of her I thrust that thought again from my conscious mind. If she had not been discovered, I must not betray her.

My captor turned his head to glance back at me. And I shivered. He was laughing silently, his whole body quivering in a horrible travesty of the honest mirth my species knew. And his face was a mask of unholy and frightening joy—worse than any rictus born of torture or wrath.

Yet he made no effort to speak, either orally or by mind-touch. And I did not know whether that made his unseemly laughter, that silent gloating laughter, better or worse—probably the latter. Still laughing, he turned from the hallway into one of those rooms, and still helplessly in thrall, I followed.

The gray light of the corridor held here, but the room was empty. My captor stepped briskly to the left-hand wall. Once more he put out his hand, pointing a finger even as he had used it to make me prisoner. If he did not touch the surface of the stone, he came very close to it. So he began to trace a series of complicated lines. But as his finger moved there glowed on the wall a glistening thread, weaving in and out.

I knew that it was a symbol. We have devices such as persona locks which can be opened only by the body heat and thumb pattern of the one setting them. It could be that what I now saw was a very sophisticated development of such a safeguard, coming to life when will alone was focused on it.

He drew a design of sharp angles, of lines which to my eyes not only were distorted, but bothered me to look upon, as if they followed rules so alien that the human eye found them disturbing. Yet I could not look away.

Finally the alien seemed satisfied with the complicated pattern of line-cross-line, line-upon-line. Now his pointing finger indicated the very heart of the drawing. So he might have opened a well-concealed lock.

Sound answered, a grating—a protest, as if too long a time had passed since certain mechanisms had been activated. The wall split, a straight-edged crack down through the center of the design. One portion moved to each side to form a narrow doorway. Without hesitation he stepped within, and again I was drawn on.

There was no light here, and what sifted in from the chamber behind was sharply cut off as that crack closed. Where we stood now, in another chamber or a corridor, I had no idea. But that pressure kept me walking ahead. By the faint sounds, I deduced that he whom I trailed went as confidently as if he traveled a lighted and well-known road.

I fought an imagination which was only too ready to picture for me all which might lie underfoot, on either side, even overhead.

There was no way of escape. And I had best save my energy, hold my control, for a time when I might have some small chance against that which walked in Griss Sharvan's body.

To travel in utter darkness, and by another's will, distorts time. Minutes might have been stretching, or else they were less—I had no way of telling. It seemed to me that we went so for a long time, yet it may not have been that at all.

Then—light!

I closed my eyes against what seemed to be a wild burst of eye-hurting color. Blinked, closed, opened—

The chamber in which we stood was four-sided with walls which sloped inward, to meet at an apex well over our heads. And those walls were also transparent, so we might have been inside a pyramid-shaped room of crystal.

Through the transparent walls we looked into four rooms. And each had its occupant, an unmoving, unbreathing occupant, who yet seemed no statue but a living creature, or once-living creature, frozen into complete immobility.

I say "creature," for while these preserved beings beyond the walls were humanoid to at least the ninth degree outwardly, I had, as I looked upon them, the same sensation of an indweller wholly alien. For three I had that sensation. For the fourth—I gazed the longest at him—and knew, shocked into applying mind-probe to learn the truth.

Griss—that was Griss! As tightly bound within that body as I now was in the tangler's cords. He was only dimly conscious of what had happened to him, but enough so that he was living in an endless nightmare. And how long his reason could so endure—

I wrenched my eyes away, fearing to draw the crushing burden of his fear just when I needed a clear mind. Such would be no aid to him. Instead I made myself examine more closely the other three who waited there.

The rooms themselves were elaborately furnished, the furniture carven, inlaid with gems. Two had narrow beds, the supporting posts of which were the bodies of strange animals or birds; two, chairs which bore a small likeness to the Throne of Qur. Tables with small boxes; chests.

Then—the inhabitants. Whereas the bodies I had seen in the freeze boxes had been bare, these all wore helmets or crowns. They also possessed eyelashes and eyebrows. Each crown differed also, representing grotesque creatures. I shot another quick glance at that body now holding Griss's identity.

The crown it wore was a brown-yellow in the form of a wide-jawed saurian thing which was akin to the head I had seen in the mental image I had picked up earlier. It sat in a chair, but the one behind the next wall reclined on the narrow bed, head and shoulders supported by a rest of decorated material. The third was seated again. The crown of the second was a bird, and that of the third a sharp-muzzled, prick-eared animal.

But the fourth of that company was a woman! None of those behind the walls were clothed except for their crowns. And their bodies were flawless, akin to the ideal of beauty held by my species. The woman was such perfection as I had never dreamed could exist in the flesh. From beneath her diadem flowed hair to clothe her almost to her knees. That hair was of a red so deep and dark as to seem nearly black. Her crown was not as massive as those which seemed to weigh down her companions, but rather a band from which sprang a series of upstanding but uneven and unmatched filaments. Then I saw more clearly that each of these bore on its tip a small head like that mask of the cliff face. And each of those heads was equipped with gem eyes.

I gasped. When I had looked directly at the woman those cats' heads of her crown had begun to move, to turn, to rise, until they were all stiffly upstanding, pointing outward as if their jewel eyes were looking back at me in alert measurement.

But her own eyes stared beyond me as if I were so far outside her inner world that I had no existence for her.

A hand on my shoulder brought me around—to face the seated alien with the animal crown. And in my ears, Griss's voice:

"Attend, you! A great honor for this puny body of yours. It shall be worn by—" If he had meant to utter some name, he did not. And I think he cut short his words because of caution.

There is a belief, found mainly among primitive peoples, that to tell another one's true name puts one at his mercy. But that such a superstition would persist among aliens with manifestly so high a level of advancement I could not altogether believe.

However, that he intended now to force such an exchange as there had been for Griss, I had no doubts at all. And I was afraid as I never remembered being before in my entire life.

He caught my head from behind, held it in a vise grip, so that I had to look eye to eye with that one behind the wall. There was no fighting for freedom. Not physically. But still I could fight, I would! And I drew upon all the reserves of esper I had, all my sense of being who and what I was. I was only just quick enough to meet the attack.

It was not the harsh blanketing which had served as the knockout blow I had met in the ship valley, but rather a pointed thrust, delivered with arrogant self-confidence. And I was able to brace against it without bringing all my own power to bear.

Though I did not then catch any surprise, there was a sudden cut-off of pressure. As if he of the animal crown retreated, puzzled by resistance where he had thought to find none at all, retreated to consider what he might actually be facing. While I, given that very short respite, braced myself to await what I was sure would be a much stronger and tougher attack.

It came. I was no longer aware of anything outside, only of inner tumult, where some small core of my personality was beaten by smothering wave after wave of will; trying to breach my last defense and take that inner me captive. But—I held, and knew the crowned one's astonishment at such holding. Shock after shock against my will, still I was not engulfed, lost, borne away. Then I felt that other's growing rage, uncertainty. And I was sure that those waves of pressure were not so strong, that they were ebbing faster and farther as a tide might withdraw from a shore cliff which was mercilessly beaten by the sea but which still stood.

Awareness of the room returned. My head, still in that hold, was up, eye to eye with him beyond the wall. His face was as expressionless as it had ever been. Yet those features seemed contorted, hideous with a rage born of frustration.

"He will not do!" It was almost a scream within my head, bringing pain with the raw emotion with which it struck. "Take him hence! He is a danger!"

My captor jerked me around. Griss's face before me, but the expression was not his, an ugly, raw menace the real Griss had never known. I thought that he might well burn me down. Yet it seemed he might have some other use for me, for he did not reach for the blaster at his belt but rather sent me sprawling forward, so that I skidded up against the crystal surface of the wall behind which lay the woman, if woman she had ever been.

The cat-headed filaments of her crown quivered, dipped, their eyes glinting avidly as they watched me. I slid to my knees as if I were offering some homage to an unresponsive queen. But she stared unseeingly above my head.

The alien pulled me up, sent me on, with another push, toward the narrow slit of a doorway near one corner of the room. Then I was for the second time in the full darkness of that passage, this time ahead of my captor.

Nor was I to make the full return journey; for we were not far along that tunnel, in a dark so thick one could almost feel it, before I was again propelled to the right. I did not strike against any wall there, but kept on, brushing one of my shoulders against a smooth surface.

"I do not know what you are, Krip Vorlund," Griss's voice rang out of the dark. "'Thassa,' says that poor fool whose seeming I wear. It would appear that you are a different breed, with some armor against our will. But this is no time for the solving of riddles. If you survive you may give us an entertaining puzzle at a later hour. *If you survive!*"

Painfully alert to whatever guides I could use in this dark, I thought his voice sounded fainter, as if he no longer stood close by. Then there was only the dark and the silence, which in its way was as overpowering as the blackness blinding me. No compulsion to follow; I was as free as if a cord had been cut. But my arms were still tightly bound to my sides by the constriction of tangle cords.

I listened, trying even to breathe as lightly as I could so that would not hide any possible sound. Nothing—nothing but the horrible weight of the smothering dark. Slowly I took one step and then another from the wall, which was my only point of reference. Two more—three steps—and I came up against another wall. If I had only had the use of my hands, it would have been a small relief, but that was denied me.

Exploration, so hindered, told me at last that the narrow space in which I stood must be the end of another corridor. I found I could not return the way we had come—if my sense of direction had not altogether failed me—for that had been cut off, though I had not heard the closing of any door. There were left only the three walls, with the fourth side open. Leading perhaps to a multitude of possible disasters. But these I must chance blindly.

It was slow progress, that blind creeping, my right shoulder brushing ever against the wall, since I had to have some reference. I found no door, no other opening, always the same smooth surface against which my thermo jacket brushed with a soft rustling. And it went on and on—

I was tired—more, I was hungry, and thirst made my mouth and throat as dry as the ashy sand of the valley. To know that I carried at my own belt the means of alleviating all my miseries made it doubly hard. There was no fighting the grip of the tangle bond. To do so would lead to greater and more dangerous constriction. Twice I slipped to the floor of the passage. It was so narrow I had to hunch up with bent knees to rest, for the toes of my boots grated against the other wall. But then to get up again required such effort that the last time I did so, I thought I must keep on my feet and going, with a thin hope of survival. For if I went down again it could well be I would never have the strength to rise.

On and on—this was like one of those nightmares in which one is forced to wade through some muck which hinders each step, and yet behind comes a hunter relentlessly in chase. I knew my hunter—my own weakness.

Action held much of a dreamlike quality for me now. The four crowned ones—Griss Sharvan who was not Griss. Maelen—

Maelen! She had receded from my mind during that ordeal in the crystal room. Maelen! When I tried to see my mind-picture of her she flowed into someone else. Maelen—her long red hair, her—*Red* hair! No, Maelen had the silver hair of the Thassa, like that now close-cropped on my own skull. RED HAIR—the woman of the cat crown! I flinched. Could it be that some of that compulsion which had been loosed against me back there was still working on me?

Maelen. Laboriously I built my mental picture of her in the Thassa body. And despairingly, not believing I would ever again have any reply from her, I sent out a mind-call.

"Krip! Oh, Krip!"

Sharp, clear, as if shouted aloud in joy because, after long searching, we had come face to face, I could not believe it even though I heard.

"Maelen?" If thought-send could whisper, then mine did.

"Krip, where are you? Come—oh, come—"

Clear; I had not been mistaken, misled. She was here, and close, or that call would not be so loud. I pulled myself together, made answer quickly as I could:

"I do not know where I am, except in a very dark and narrow passage."

"Wait—say my name, Krip. Give me a direction!"

I obeyed, making of her name a kind of mind-chant, knowing that here perhaps there was power in a name. For upon such a point of identity could a mind-send firmly anchor.

"I think that I have it. Come on—straight ahead, Krip."

I needed no more urging; my shuffle quickened. Though I still had to go with my shoulder along the wall, since I could not bear to lose that guide in the dark. It was good that I kept it so, for there was another sudden transition from the dark to light, enough to blind me temporarily, so I leaned against the wall with my eyes closed.

"Krip!"

So loud she could be there before me!

I opened my eyes. She was. Her black fur was grayed, matted with dust. She wavered from side to side as if she could hardly keep her feet. There was a blotch of dried blood along one side of her head. But she was alive.

I slipped down by the wall, edging out on my knees to bring me closer to her. But she had dropped to the floor as if no reserve of strength remained in her. Forgetting, I fought my bonds, then gasped as the resulting constriction punished me.

"Maelen!"

She lay, her head on her paws, flattened to the stone, much as she had laid on her bunk in the *Lydis*. But now her eyes were fast closed. It was as if the effort of guiding me to her had drained her last strength.

Food, water—by the look of her, her need for those was greater than my own. Yet I could not help her, not unless she first freed me. And I did not know if she could.

"Maelen, at my belt—the cutter—"

One of those tools which were the ever-present equipment of an adventurer on an unknown world.

Her eyes opened, looked to me. Slowly she raised her head, as if to do so was painful, or so fatiguing she could hardly manage it. She could not regain her feet, and she whimpered as she wriggled on her belly to my side.

Bracing herself against my body, she brought her head higher; her dust-caked muzzle rubbed my side as she nosed against my belt. While she had once been so graceful of body, she was now clumsy and awkward, taking a long time to free the cutter from its loop, though I turned and twisted to give her all the aid I could.

The tool lay in the dust for a long time (or so it seemed to me) before she bent her head to mouth its butt, bring it up to rest against the lowest loop of the tangle bond. Twice the cutter slid away to thud to the stone before she could bite down on the spring releasing its energy. My frustration at having to watch her efforts and not be able to help made me ill.

But she kept to it stubbornly and finally she made it. The energy blade snipped into the thick round of the tangle well enough so that my own struggles parted it. Once broken, after the way of such, it shriveled away and I was free, though my arms were numb and I found it difficult to lift them. A return of circulation was painful, but I could grope for the rations in my supply bag. And I had those at hand as I pulled Maelen's body closer, supported her head against me, trickling water into her parched, dust-rimmed mouth.

She swallowed once, again. I put aside the water container, licking my own lips, to unscrew an E-ration tube, squirt the semiliquid contents into her mouth. So I fed her half of that restorative nutriment before I slaked my own thirst, fed my hunger-racked body.

For the first time, sitting there, holding the tube to my mouth, Maelen resting against my knee, I really looked about me. This was another of those pyramid-shaped chambers, though it did not rise to a point but was sliced off midway up with a square ceiling much smaller than the floor area.

Nor were these walls crystal, but rock. The ledge where we sat was about halfway between roof and floor. I turned my head to see the doorway through which I had come. But there was nothing—nothing at all! I remembered that quick transition from dark to light, as if I had pushed through a curtain.

There was a very steep stair midway along the ledge, descending to the floor. And that floor supported a series of blocks, some tall, others shorter, in uneven heights. Cresting each of these was a ball of some opaque substance which was not stone. And in the inner heart of each ball was a faint glimmer of light.

The balls were colored—red, blue, green, yellow, then violet, orange, paler shades, those closest to the walls the palest hues of all, deepening as one approached the core. The center one there was very dark indeed, almost black.

On the surfaces of the brighter and lighter-colored ones were etched patterns. And as I studied them I recognized some—there was a reptilian head resembling the crown of the body that now imprisoned Griss; I saw the animal one, the bird one, and, farthest away, a cat mask. But the meaning of this display or its use I could not guess. I leaned back against the wall; Maelen lay unmoving. I thought that she slept now and I had no desire to trouble her rest.

Rest—I needed that also. I shut my eyes to the dull light. Undoubtedly I should keep watch, for we must be in the very heart of enemy territory. But this time I could not fight the demands of my body. My eyelids closed against my will—I fell asleep.

Chapter 11

KRIP VORLUND

Now Maelen stood before me, not in animal shape, but as I had known her first on Yiktor. In her hand was that white wand which had been her weapon in those days, and which the Old Ones had taken from her. She was looking not at me, but rather at an inclining stone wall, and I knew that we were still in the burrows beneath the crust of Sekhmet. And she was using that wand as those with certain esper talents might to search out the presence of water, or any object worked by men, underground.

Save that her wand did not point down but stretched in a straight line before her. Holding it so, almost as if it were imbued with energy of its own to draw her after it, she walked forward. Afraid to lose her once again, even in this dream, I followed.

The wand touched the wall, and that barrier was gone. Now we passed into a space which had no boundaries, in which there was no substance. Until once more we stood in a chamber. Looking around, I knew where we were, though this time I was on the opposite side of the crystal wall.

There was that narrow bed, upheld by four cat creatures, on which lay the woman. And the gem-eyed heads of her diadem arose straight on their fine filaments. They did not all face Maelen; rather they twisted and made quick darts here and there until brought up short by the threads which attached them to the circlet about that red hair. It was as if they were alarmed.

Maelen paid no attention to the darting, almost frenzied activity of the crown. Rather she advanced to the end of the couch, her wand pointed at the other's body, her own gaze intent, measuring—

She glanced once to me, showing that she knew I had followed.

"Remember this one in time of need—" Her thought was faint, as if we were far separated, yet I could have put out my hand and laid it on her arm. Although I knew that I must not.

"Why?" Her words were too ambiguous. That they were of import I did not doubt, but for me they had no meaning.

She did not answer, only gave me a long, level look. Then she turned once more to the woman with her now wildly writhing crown, as if she must imprint that image so firmly in her mind that a hundred years hence she would still see it in detail.

The wand trembled, wavered from side to side. I could see that with both her hands Maelen fought to hold it steady. To no avail, for it leaped from her grasp.

I opened my eyes. My neck and shoulders were stiff where they rested against the stone of the wall. I felt an inner chill which my thermo clothing was no proof against. My hands moved over fur engrimed with dust and grit. I looked down. The glassia head rose from its pillow on my arm.

"Maelen?" So vivid had that dream been that I half expected to find her still as she had been moments ago.

"Look yonder!"

She used her nose as a pointer to indicate the globes. Some of those were glowing brighter, giving more light to the chamber. It took me only a moment or two to be sure that not all of them had so awakened—just those with the reptilian design.

"Griss!" I put the only name I knew to that menace.

"Griss Sharvan?" Her thought was surprised. "What has this to do with him?"

"Much, perhaps." Swiftly I told her of what had happened to me since I had been taken captive by that thing wearing Griss's body, and of the visit to the crystal-walled chamber where he had endeavored to give my body to his fellow being.

"She is also there, is she not?" Maelen asked.

I did not mistake her. There was only one "she"—the woman of the cat crown.

"Yes! And, Maelen, just now I dreamed—"

"I know what manner of dream that was, since it also spun me into its web," she interrupted again. "I had thought that no one could surpass the Thassa in inner powers. But it would seem that in some things we are as children playing with bright pebbles, making patterns on the earth! I think that these have slept here to preserve their race against some great peril in the past. But only those four you have seen survived, able to rise to full life again."

"But if they can be revived, why do they want our bodies?"

"It can be that the means of revival on their own cannot now be used. Or it may be that they wish to pass among us as beings of our own kind."

"To take over." That I could believe. Had the seeming Griss Sharvan concealed his alienness, posed perhaps as a captive among the jacks, we would have been deceived and so in saving him could have brought disaster among ourselves. I thought of the men I had left behind on the cliff. They were facing worse than jack blasters—and now I was impatient to be away, to warn them.

I had found Maelen. Now we must find our way out, return to the *Lydis*, or to the force of our men. What was happening here was vastly larger and worse than any jack looting!

"You are right." Maelen had followed my thoughts. "But as to discovering the path out—that I do not know. Can you even now find the door which you entered?"

"Of course!" Though I could not see any opening, I was sure I knew just where I had come through to this ledge. Gently I lifted her aside and arose. To make certain I would not miss what I sought if the opening were disguised in some manner, I put my fingers to the surface of the wall and edged along back toward that place where I thought I had entered.

I reached the far end of the ledge. There was no opening. Sure that I had made some mistake, yet somehow equally certain I could not have, I made a slow passage back, this time reaching both above and below my former tracing of the surface. I returned to Maelen. There had been no break in that solid wall.

"But I *did* come through!" I burst out, and my protest echoed hollowly through that space.

"True. But where?" Her question seemed a mockery of my vehemence.

Then she continued. "Such an experience is not unknown here. This has happened to me twice. Which is why I have been so completely lost."

"Tell me!" I demanded now.

So I learned how she had made her way from the ship valley, found the sleeper with the amplifier, how she had come to witness the looting of the cache, even as I guessed it might all have happened. But for the rest it was a tale of a strange journey, of her will battling that of another reaching out for her. Not, she felt, for her personally, but as one might fling a net in hope of catching something within it. But that compulsion was not continuous in its powers and she was able to fight it at intervals. It had brought her to where the ship of the jacks was finned down, and through the cavern there into the passages beyond. But there, bemused by the ebb and flow of the current which held her, she had been lost. Then she had contacted me, had been drawn toward my call in turn.

"I had believed that Thassa could not be so influenced," she admitted frankly. "Always I have been warned that I was too proud of my powers. If that was ever so, it is no longer. For here I have been as one played with by something infinitely greater, allowed to run a little, then put under restraint again. Yet this is the strangest of all, Krip—I will swear by the Word of Molaster that this power, this energy, whatever it may be, was not as conscious of me as I am of it. It was rather as if it flexed muscles in exercise so that it might be ready to use all its strength at a future call."

"The four of that inner place?" I suggested.

"Perhaps. Or they may be only extensions of something else, infinitely greater still. They are adepts, without question—very powerful ones. But even an adept recognizes something above and beyond himself. We name Molaster in our petitions. But that is only our name for what we cannot describe, but which is the core of our belief. These others are—"

What she might have added to her speculations was left unsaid. Those yellow globes with the reptilian masks, which had been glowing so much brighter, now gave off a low, humming note. And that sound, subdued as it was, startled us into immobility. We crouched, breathing only shallowly, our heads going right to left, left to right, as we went on guard against what this change might herald.

"Where is the door out?" I demanded.

"Perhaps you can guess better than I have been able to. Even as you, I went from dark to light, found this ledge, but no return. When your mind-send came I hoped it would direct me to an exit. But that was not to be. You came to me instead."

"Where did you come in?"

Her nose pointed to the other end of the ledge, well away from the spot where I was still sure my door existed. I went there, again running palms and fingers along the surface, hunting the smallest hint of an opening. I still had the cutter which Maelen had used on the tangler cords. Perhaps with that, or one of the other tools from my belt, I could force a lock, were I able to find it. A forlorn hope, but one clings to such.

The humming from the globes was continuous now. And it did something to my hearing. Or was there a more subtle outflow rising beyond the range of audibility to affect my thinking? Twice I found I had halted my search, was standing, gazing down at the globes, my mind seemingly blanked out. It could only have lasted a second or two, but it was frightening.

Now I believed that the globes were generating a haze. The forbidding representation of the designs on them was fading. However, that concealment acted in a strange way, just the opposite of what one might expect. One could no longer see those monsters, their elongated jaws a fraction open, their formidable fangs revealed, yet there was the feeling that so hidden, they were more alive!

"Krip!" Maelen's thought-cry dispelled what was building in my mind. I was able to look away, turn my head back to the wall. But now I feared that a danger worse than imagination presented was threatening us.

Solid wall. I thumped it now with my fist as I went, my blows faster, more savage. All they brought me was bruises and pain. Until—I had carried in mind so sharply the thought of a door, the need for a door—my fist went through!

To my eyes the stone was solid, as solid as it had ever been. But my hand had sunk in up to the wrist.

"Maelen!"

She needed no call. She was already padding towards me. Door— where had the invisible door come from?

"Think *door*—think it! See a door in your mind!"

I obeyed her. Door—there was a door there—of course there was. My hand had gone through the opening. There might be an illusion to deceive the eye, but there was nothing now to baffle touch. I rested my other hand on Maelen's head and we moved resolutely forward together into what appeared solid, unbroken stone.

Again we passed abruptly from light to dark. But also, as if a portal had slammed shut behind us, the humming was instantly silenced. I gave a sigh of relief.

"Is this your way?" I asked. Though how she could be certain of that in the dark, I did not know.

"I cannot be sure. But it is *a* way. We must keep together."

I left my hand on her head as she crowded against me. So linked, we went on, very slowly and cautiously, my other hand outstretched before me to warn of anything which might rise in our path.

Shortly thereafter I found a wall, traced along it until there was another way open to the left. Long ago I had lost all sense of direction, and Maelen confessed to a similar disability. We could do little until we found some lighted way. That we might not do so was a horror we refused to give mind-room to.

Whether the Thassa shared the ancient fear of the dark with my own race, I did not know. But the sense of compression, of stifling pressure, returned. Save that this time I did not walk with my arms bound to my sides.

"Left now—"

"Why? How do you know?"

"Life force in that direction."

I tried mind-probe for myself. She was right—a flicker of energy. It was not the high flow I associated with the aliens, but more like such as I could pick up when not too far from a crew member. And there was an opening to the left.

How far we were from the chamber of the globes now I could not guess. But a lighting of the way cheered us—and that grew ever brighter.

Only now there was sound also. Not a mutter of voices, but rather the clank of metal. Maelen pushed against me.

"He, the one who wears Griss's body—ahead!"

I tried no probe. I wished I could do just the opposite, reduce all mental activity so far down the scale he could not pick up any hint of us in return. I had not forgotten how easily he had found me out when I had spied on the jacks.

"He is one-minded now," Maelen told me, "using all his power for something which is of very great importance to him. We need not fear him, for he puts all to one purpose."

"And that?"

She did not reply at once. Then—

"Lend me of your sending—"

It was my turn to hesitate. To strengthen any mind-seek she might send out could make us more accessible to discovery. Yet I trusted her enough to realize that she would not suggest such a move unless she thought we had a fair chance. So I yielded.

Her probe sped out, and I fed my own energy to it. This we had not often done, so it was a relatively new experience for me, bringing with it an odd sensation of being pulled along in a current I could not fight. Then a blurred mind-picture came.

We seemed to be hanging in the air over a pit, or rather we were in the apex of one of those pyramid chambers. Below a robo was blasting away at the foot of one wall. There was already a dark cavity there; now the machine was enlarging that.

Behind the worker stood Griss. He did not hold any control board. It would appear that he was able to keep the robo at work without that. And his attention was completely absorbed by what he was doing. But that feverish desire which drove him was like a broadcast. He did not hold his defenses now, but fastened avidly on what he sought—an ancient storehouse of his kind, perhaps containing machines or weapons. His need was like a whiff of ozone. A whiff, I say, because I caught only the edge of it. Around the chamber, well above the level at which the robo worked, was another of the ledge ways. This ran across one wall, leading from one door to another. And without needing to be told, I recognized that this was the path we must follow.

Whether we could do it without attracting attention from below was another matter. But now that hole the robo battered was larger. The machine wheeled back, became inert. And the alien hurried to the break, disappeared through it.

"Now!"

We sped along the lighted corridor, and it was only a short distance until we ventured out on that ledge. It was so close to the apex of the pyramid that the opposite wall leaned very close. Maelen found it easier to take that route than I, for I could not stand erect but had to go on hands and knees.

Nor did I waste any time looking back at the hole the robo had opened. To reach the door on the other side, scramble within, was all I wanted.

"We made it!"

"For now, yes," she answered me. "But—"

She swung around, her head down. Her dusty body quivered.

"Krip! Krip, hold me!" It was a cry for help, coming so suddenly, without warning, that I was startled. Then I half threw myself over her, grasping her tightly around the body, holding on in spite of her struggles for freedom.

It was no longer Maelen whom I held so, but an animal that growled and snapped, struck out with unsheathed claws. Only by pure chance did I escape harm. Then she collapsed against me, her breath coming in deep gasps. There were flecks of white foam at the corners of her jaws.

"Maelen, what is it?"

"The calling—it was stronger this time, much stronger. Like—like to like!"

"What do you mean?" I still held her but she was far from fighting now. As if her struggle had exhausted her, she was in nearly the same condition in which I had earlier found her.

"The dream—she of the cat crown." Maelen's thoughts did not make a completely coherent pattern. "She is—akin to Thassa—"

But I refused to believe that. I could see no resemblance between her and the Maelen I had known.

"Maybe not to the sight," Maelen agreed. "Krip—is there more water?" She was still panting, the sound of it close to human sobbing. I found the flask, poured a little in her mouth. But some I must save, for we did not know when we could replenish that small supply.

She swallowed greedily, but she did not press me for more.

"The mind-call—the dream—I knew their like. Such are of Thassa kind."

I had a flash of inspiration. "Could it be adjusted? That is—having discovered you, could the pattern be altered to a familiar one, thus with a better chance of entrapping you?"

"That may well be so," she admitted. "But between me and that other there is something— Only when I face her, it will be on my terms and not hers, if you will give me of your strength as you did this time when she called."

"You are sure it was she? Not the one we just saw?"

"Yes. But when I go it will be at a time of *my* choosing. Which is not yet."

Having taken a mouthful of water myself, I brought out an E-ration tube, which we shared half and half. Made for nourishment during times of strain, it was high in sustenance and would keep us going for hours to come.

There was no sound from the chamber where the robo must still be on guard beside that hole. I wondered very much what the alien sought beyond the battered wall. But Maelen did not mention that as we went. On the contrary, she asked a question so much apart from the matters at hand I was startled.

"Do you think her fair?"

Her? Oh, I realized, she must mean the alien woman.

"She is very beautiful," I answered frankly.

"A body without blemish—though strange in its coloring. A perfect body—"

"But its mind reaches for another covering. That which walks in Griss was also perfect outwardly, yet its rightful owner saw fit to exchange with Griss. And I was taken there to exchange with another one. Are they in stass-freeze, I wonder?"

"Yes." She was definite. "That other one, he whom they used on the cliff top—"

"Lukas said he was dead—long dead. But those four, I am sure they are alive. The one in Griss *must* be!"

"Perhaps it may be that their bodies, once released from stass-freeze, will truly die. But I do not think so. I believe that they wish to preserve those for some other reason. And they seek *our* bodies as we would put on meaner clothes which may be soiled and thrown away once some dirty job is finished. But—she is very beautiful!"

There was a wistfulness in that, one of those infrequent displays of what appeared to be human emotion on Maelen's part. And such always moved me the more because they came so seldom. So I believed her a little subject to the same desires as my own species.

"Goddess, queen—what was she, or who?" I wondered. "We cannot guess her real name."

"Yes, her name." Maelen repeated my thought in part. "That she would not want us to know."

"Why? Because"—and I thought then of the old superstition— "that would give us power over her? But that is the belief of a primitive people! And I would say she is far from primitive."

"I have told you, Krip"—Maelen was impatient—"belief is important. Belief can move the immovable if it is rightly applied. Should a people believe that one's name is so personal a possession that to know it gives another power over one, then for them that is true. And from world to world degrees of civilization differ as much as customs and names for gods."

My head was up now, and I sniffed, alerted once again by a scent rather than a sound. Maelen must have been quick to catch the same trace of odor.

"Ahead—others. Perhaps their camp."

Where there was a camp there must also be some communication with the outer world. And I wanted nothing so much as to be free of these burrows, to return to the *Lydis*. At least my sojourn here had given me knowledge enough to warn and arouse my fellows to such danger as we had not known existed. So—if we did want to escape the heart of the enemy's territory, we must still push on into what might be open danger.

But I had not realized that my own wanderings must have been in a circle. For when we came to a doorway we were looking out into the cavern of the jack camp. The looted chests were piled about, and we could see, in the outer air before the entrance, a portion of the ship's fins.

There was a line of robos, all idle now, to the right. No sign of any men about. If we could keep to cover behind the boxes we might reach the outer opening—

But one step, or at the most two, at a time. Maelen was slinking, with her belly fur brushing the floor, along behind that line of empty chests. And I crouched as low as I could to join her. There was no sound; we could be totally alone. But we dared not depend on such good fortune. And it was well that we did not, for the side of the plasta-bubble tent parted as its entrance was unsealed and a man came out.

When I saw him I froze. Harkon—and not a prisoner. He carried a blaster openly, had turned to look back over his shoulder, as if waiting for someone else. Had the party from the *Lydis* taken, by some miracle of fortune, the headquarters of the jacks? If so, they must be speedily warned of what wore Griss's body. I had no illusions as to what would happen if that confronted them. The odds might be ten to one against that alien and yet he would come out the winner.

Chapter 12

MAELEN

We are told that all the universe lies on the balance of Molaster's unseen scales—good weighs against bad, ill against well. And when it seems to us most likely that fortune has turned, that is the time to be most wary. I had met much which was new to me since I had put on Vors's body and come to be one of this band of off-worlders. Yet I had always supposed that the core of the balance remained the same and that only the outer forms differed.

However, in these underground ways I had avoided challenges and learned things which were so outside the reference of all I had known before that many times I could only make blind choices. And to a Moon Singer of the Thassa a blind choice is an affront and a defeat.

Twice I had dreamed true—I could not be deceived in that—of her whom Krip had actually looked upon. Why was she so familiar to me when I had never seen her like before? There were no women on the *Lydis*, and those I had met on the three planets we had visited since first I raised from Yiktor were no different from the females of the plains people—never more than pale copies of what their men desired, creatures without rights or many thoughts.

But she—there was in me such a longing, a drive, to go and look upon her in body even as I had in dream, that I ever struggled against that compulsion, nor did I reveal it wholly to Krip. But that he had shared my second dream was to me proof that danger lay in actually facing her and I must not risk a confrontation yet. For what he had to tell me of the fate they had intended for him was a warning. I believe that it was perhaps that small bit of Thassa lurking in him which had defeated the takeover they had planned.

During the months we had voyaged together I had realized that Krip was a greater esper than he had been at our first meeting. It was my thought that this slow awakening of power, this development of his talent, was influenced by Maquad's body. Though I did not know how or why. Which again gave me to think about what a long indwelling in my present form might do to *me*!

I knew that the aliens had not been able to dispossess him, that the encased creature had ordered him taken away as a possible danger. And that small fact was the only favorable thing I had to hold to—save that we were together again and had found the door to the outer world.

It was pleasing that Krip did not move at once into the open when we saw the Patrolman. His care to remain in hiding, willing to accept nothing and no one unproved, reassured me. So we lay behind the boxes watching. Nor did either of us use mind-send. For if this Patrolman was not what he seemed, we would be thus betrayed to greater peril than we had lately been in.

Harkon moved away from the bubble and another came out—Juhel Lidj of the *Lydis*. He, too, carried his weapon; still, about both of them there was no sign that they feared any enemy. They were too much at their ease. And yet they were both men who had faced danger many times over, not foolhardy adventurers.

Together they passed us, moving toward the back of the cave and the mouth of one of the dark ways there. Still Krip did not stir nor try to hail them, and I waited his lead. But he edged around to watch them go. When he could be sure they were out of sight his hand touched my head for a close communication which could not be heard.

"They—I have a feeling all is wrong—not right."

"So do I," I was quick to answer.

"Could they have been taken over also? It is best we try to reach the *Lydis*. But if I have guessed wrong, and they are walking straight into what lies there—" I felt him shiver, his fingers on my head tremble slightly.

"If they are as you fear now, then they are masters here, and should they discover us— But if the others are still free from such contamination they must be warned. For the present we can hope such domination is confined to Sekhmet. Have you thought what might happen if their ship out there lifts off, carrying those who can change bodies as easily as you change the clothing on your back— spreading the contagion of their presence to other worlds?"

"Such evil as has never been known before. And there could be no finding them once they were off this planet!"

"Therefore—carry your message while still you may." In this I was urging what I had decided was the greater good. There was nothing one man and one glassia could do in these burrows to overset such enemies, but there was much which we could accomplish elsewhere.

"They could already have started it," he said then. "How do we know how many there are of them—how many voyages that ship out there has made?"

"The more reason why a warning must be given."

We were on the move again, using the looted chests as a shield as long as we could. Then we came into the pallid daylight at the cavern's entrance.

The cargo hatches of the ship were sealed, but her passenger ramp was still out. Krip looked up at her. He was far more knowledgeable of such than I. To me she merely seemed larger than the *Lydis*, and so I said.

"She is. We are D class; this is a C class ship, also a freighter, a converted Company freighter. She is slow, but can lift far more than the *Lydis*. And she has no insignia, which means she is a jack ship."

There were no guards to be seen, but we still kept to cover. And the broken nature of the country seemed designed to aid such skulking. That and the fact that the clouds were very dense overhead and a cold, ice-toothed rain began to fall. Shivering under the lash of that, we found a place where we could climb the cliff. We thought prudence dictated such an exit rather than use of the rough road beaten by many robo tracks.

Aloft, I could trust for our guide to the sense which was a part of Vors's natural equipment, and we headed in the direction where I was sure we would find the *Lydis*. But it was a nightmare of a journey, with the sleet sluicing around us and the dark growing thicker. We crawled where we longed to run, afraid of missteps which would plunge us over some rock edge.

There was a wind rising. I unsheathed claws to anchor me and crept close to the ground under the beating of its force and that of the sleet.

"Krip?" Here four clawed feet might manage, but I was not sure that two booted ones might do as well. And the fury of this storm was like nothing I had felt before. It was almost as if the natural forces of this forsaken world were ranged on the side of those who looted.

"Keep on!" There was no weakness in his reply.

I had come to a down slope where the water poured in streams about me as I twisted and turned, using every possible hint of protection against the worst blasts. As I went I began to doubt very gravely if we could press on to the *Lydis*, wonder whether it would not be much more prudent to seek shelter and wait out the worst of this storm. And I was about to look for a place where we could do so, when the stones my claws rasped were no longer firm, but slid, carrying me with them.

Over—out—into nothingness! An instant of knowing that I was falling—then a blast of pain and darkness.

Yet that dark was not complete, and I carried with me an instant of raw, terrifying knowledge—that it had been no normal misstep, no chance which had brought me down. I had been caught in a trap I had not suspected.

And, recognizing that, I knew also why it had been done and the full danger of what might follow.

But with Sharvan, again with Krip on Yiktor, there had been an exchange of bodies. Why need my present one be destroyed—why?

How better to enforce slavery upon an identity than by destroying the body which it inhabited?

Pain! Such pain as I had not believed could exist in a sane world. And in no way would my body obey me.

"Cannot—can never now—"

The message reaching me was erratic, such as a faulty line of communication would make.

"Leave—come—come—come!"

"Where? For what purpose?"

"Life force—life force! Live again—come!"

I made the great effort of my life, trying to cut off the pain of my body, to center all my energy and will on that which was the core of my identity.

"Come—your body dies—come!"

Thereby that which called made its grave error. All living things have a fear of being blotted out, of nonexistence. It is part of our armor, to keep us ever alert against evil, knowing that we have a certain way to walk and that how we walk it judges us on Molaster's scales. We do not give up easily. But also the White Road has no terrors for the Thassa, if the time has come for us to step onto its way. This which had entrapped me played upon the fear of non-existence, as if those with whom it had had earlier dealings could visualize no other life beyond what men call death. Thus it would readily gain what it wanted by offering life continuation quickly at the moment when that death approached.

"Come!" Urgency in that. "Would you be nothing?"

So I read its great need. My identity was not what it wished to take to itself, nor did it seek another's body. For to it its own covering was a treasure it clung to. No, it wanted my life force as a kind of fuel that, drawing upon this force, it might live again on its own terms.

"Maelen! Maelen, where are you?"

"Come!"

"Maelen!"

Two voices in my head, and the pain rising again! Molaster! I gave my own cry for help, trying not to hear either of those other calls. And there came an answer—not the White Road, no. That I could have if I willed it. But such a choice would endanger another plan. That was made clear to me as if I had been lifted once more to the cliff crest and a vast scene of action spread before me. What I saw then I could not remember, even as I looked upon it. But that it was needful, I knew. And also I understood that I must struggle to fulfill my part in that purpose.

"Come!" No coaxing, no promises now—just an order delivered as if it could not possibly be disobeyed. "Come now!"

But I answered that other call of my name, sent my own plea.

"Here—hurry!" How I might carry out the needful task I did not know. Much would depend now upon the skill and resources of another.

I could not make the glassia body obey me or even give me sight. To keep my mind clear, I had to block off all five senses lest pain drive me completely forth. But my mind—that much I had—for a space.

"Krip!" Whether he was still on the cliff top or beside me, I had no means of knowing. Only I must reach him and give him this last message or all would fail. "Krip—this body—I think it is too badly broken—it is dying. But it must not die yet. If you can get it into stass-freeze—You must! That box with the sleeper—get me to that—"

I could not even wait for any answer to my message. I must just hold grimly, as long as I could. And how long that might be—only Molaster could set limit to.

It was a strange hidden place where that which was the real "I"—Maelen of the Thassa, Moon Singer once, glassia once—held and drew upon all inner resources. Did that other still batter at my defenses, crying "Come, come—live"? I did not know. I dared not think of anything save holding fast to this small stronghold which was under attack. Weaker grew my hold so that at times the pain struck in great punishing blows. Then I tried only to form the words of singing, which I had not done since they took away my wand. And the words were like dim, glowing coals where once they had been leaping flames of light. Yet still there was a feeble life in them and they sustained me, damping out the pain.

There was no time in this place—or else far too much of it. I assured myself, "I can hold one more instant, and one more, and one more"—and so it continued. Whether Krip could accomplish that which would save me, or *if* it would save me— But I must think of nothing save the need to hold on, to keep my identity in this hidden place. I must hold and hold and hold!

But I could no longer—Molaster! Great were the powers once given me, much did I increase them by training. But there comes an end to all—and that faces me now. I have lost, I cannot remember that pattern of life which I was shown. Though I know its importance and know that not by the will of the Great Design was it interrupted for me. Yet it would seem that I have not the strength to finish out my part of it. I—cannot—hold—

Pain rushed in as a great scarlet wave to drown me.

"Maelen!"

One voice only now. Had that other given up? But I thought that even yet, were I to yield, it would sweep me into its web.

"Maelen!"

"Freeze—" I could shape only that one last plea. And so futile, so hopeless a one it was. There came no answer.

None—save that the pain grew less, now almost bearable. And I had not been cut free from the body. What—

"Maelen!"

I was in the body still. Though I did not command it, yet it served as an anchor. And there was a freedom from that pressure which had been upon me. As if the process of my "death" had been arrested, and I was to be given a short breathing space.

"Maelen!" Imperative, imploring—that call.

I summoned up the dregs of my energy.

"Krip—freeze—"

"Yes, Maelen. You are in the case—the case of the alien. Maelen—what—"

So he had done it. He had taken that last small chance and it was the right one. But I had no time for rejoicing, not now. I must let him know the final answer.

"Keep freeze—Old Ones—Yiktor—"

My hold on consciousness, if one could term that state of rigid defense "consciousness," broke. Did I walk the White Road now? Or was there still a place for me in the great pattern?

Chapter 13

KRIP VORLUND

The wind could not reach fully here, still my hands were numb. I watched the box. How I had ever mastered its catches, opened it long enough to pull out the body it had contained and put the broken, limp, bloodied bundle of fur in its place, I did not know. I shook with shock more than with chill, weak with the effort of transporting what had been Maelen across the rocky way, sure that she—that no living thing could survive such handling in the state I found her after that terrible fall. Yet she had lived, she was in freeze now. And I swore she would get to Yiktor—to the Old Ones—that she was not going to die! Though how I might do this I did not know.

I edged around. There stood the *Lydis* far below, the two flitters. No sign of life about them. Something else lay here among the rocks. I stared, and my shudders grew worse. The alien I had pulled so hastily from the freeze box—

But no body lay there—only a crumbling mass. I covered my eyes. Lukas had said it was dead, and his words were being proved now. Not that it mattered—nothing did, save Maelen. And the warning which must be delivered. Harkon, Lidj—were they still men or—

And who else? All those who had gone out against an enemy infinitely stronger than we had suspected?

I put out my hand to the freeze box as gently as I might have laid it on a furred head.

"I cannot take you with me now," I thought. Perhaps I could still reach her, perhaps not. But I had to try to make her understand that I was not deserting her. "I shall be back—and you shall see Yiktor, the Old Ones—live again. I swear it!"

Then I set about wedging that box even more tightly among the rocks, making very sure that it could not be shifted by any freak of wind or storm. If she was safe now, that covering must endure until I could fulfill my promise.

Having done what I could to ensure her protection, I descended through the lashing of wind and sleet to the floor of the valley. Reaching there, I used my wrist com, clicking out the code which ought to open the *Lydis* to me, waiting tensely for some sign that the call had been heard within the ship.

My answer came, not from the ship, but out of the night. A flash beam cut the black, pinned me against the rock wall of the cliff. Jacks—they had beaten me here!

I was so dazzled by that ray that I could not see who was behind it, though I believed they were moving in for the kill. I had no weapon now. Then someone stepped out into the light beam and I saw the uniform. Patrol! Only now that could be no reassurance either. Not since I had seen Harkon and Lidj in the cavern and knew what walked in Griss's body.

I tried to read in his face whether he was what he seemed or one of the enemy, but there was no clue in either eyes or expression. He motioned with his hand. The howling of the wind was far too loud to allow speech, but his gesture was toward the *Lydis*. Then the beam flashed downward, pointing a path to the ship, the upper edge of it catching the slow descent of the ramp. I went.

The *Lydis* had been my home for years, and I had felt privileged that that was so. But now, as I climbed her ramp, using handholds to drag myself up against the sweep of the wind, it was as if I approached something alien, with a whiff of trap about it. It could be just that, if the contagion of the aliens had spread this far.

I found myself sniffing as I came through the lock, the Patrolman behind me, as if I could actually scent that alien evil I feared to find here. But there was only the usual smell of a star ship. I began to climb the ladder to the control cabin. What would I find there?

"Vorlund!"

Captain Foss. And beyond him a Patrol officer with the stellar sword badge of a commander. Others— Though it was on Foss I centered my attention. If it *was* Foss. How could I be sure? What might have happened during that endless time I wandered underground? I did not answer but only stared at him, searching his face for any hint that he was not the man I knew.

Then one of the Patrolmen who had followed me up the ladder took me by the arm, turned me a little as if I were totally helpless, and pushed me down into the astrogator's chair, which swung as my weight settled in it. I dared to try mind-probe—for I had to know if there was yet time.

"You *are* Foss!" My voice sounded thin, hardly above a whisper.

Then I saw his expression change, recognized that slight lift of one brow—something I had seen many times in the past.

"You were expecting someone else?" he asked.

"One of them." I was near to babbling, suddenly so tired, so drained of energy. "Like Griss—one of them—inside your body."

No one spoke. Had I said that at all, or only thought it?

Then the captain turned to the emergency dispenser on the wall, twirled its dial, brought out a sustain tube. He came over to me. I tried to raise my hand to take that restorative. My body would not obey. He held it to my mouth and I drank. The stuff was hot, fighting the chill and shaking weariness in me.

"One of them—inside my body?" he said as if that were the most natural condition. "Perhaps you had better explain."

"Back there." I gestured to the wall of the *Lydis*, hoping I was indicating the direction of the burrows. "Aliens. They can take over our bodies. They did with Griss. He's—he's in the alien body now— behind a wall. He—" I shut out that memory of Griss imprisoned in the motionless body wearing the reptilian crown. "I think maybe Lidj, Harkon, too. They were too much at ease there in the cavern, as if they had nothing to fear. Maybe others— They tried to do it with me—didn't work. The alien was angry, said I was dangerous—to put me in the dark— Then I found Maelen."

Maelen! In that freeze box—on the cliff. Maelen!

"What about Maelen?" Foss had taken the pilot's seat so that his eyes were now on a level with mine. He sat forward, and his hands took mine from where they lay limp, holding them in a firm, warm grip. "What happened to Maelen?"

I sensed a stir, as if the Patrol officer moved closer. Foss frowned, not at me.

"What about Maelen, Krip?"

"She fell—onto the rocks—all broken. Dying—she was dying! Told me—must freeze—freeze until I could get her home, back to Yiktor. I took her—all broken, broken—" I tried to sever the compelling stare with which he held me, to forget that nightmare of a journey, but he would not let me. "Took her to the alien—opened the box—took the alien's body out—put her in. She was still alive—then."

"These aliens." Foss's voice was level, clear. He held me by it as well as by the grip on my hands and wrists. "Do you know who they are?"

"Lukas said dead—a long time. But they are esper. And the crowned ones are not dead. Bodies—they want bodies! Griss, for sure, maybe the others. There are four of them—I saw—counting the woman."

"He doesn't make sense!" cut in an impatient voice.

Again Foss frowned in warning. "Where are these bodies?"

"Underground—passages—rooms. The jacks have a camp—in a cavern—ship outside. They were looting—rooms with chests." Memories made dizzy, whirling pictures in my head. I had a bitter taste in my mouth as if the restorative was rising now to choke me.

"Where?"

"Beyond the cache. I got in through the cat's mouth." I tried to control that nausea, to remain coherent. "Passage there. But they—Griss—can hold men with thought alone. If the rest are like him, you have no chance. Never met an esper like him before, not even Thassa. Maelen thought they could not take me over because I am part Thassa now. But they did take me prisoner—Griss did—just by willing it. They used a tangler on me after."

"Korde." Foss gave a swift order. "Scrambler on—highest frequency!"

"Yes, sir!"

Scrambler, I thought vaguely—scrambler? Oh, yes, defense against probes. But would it work against the thing in Griss's body?

"About the others." The Patrol commander had moved around behind Foss. "Where are the others—my men—yours?"

"I don't know. Only saw Griss, Harkon, Lidj—"

"And you think that Harkon and Lidj may also be taken over?"

"Saw them walking around in jack camp, not taking any precautions. Had the feeling they had no reason to fear discovery."

"Did you probe them?"

"Didn't dare. Probe, and if they were taken over, they would have taken us, Maelen and me. Griss—he knew I was there even before he saw me. He made me walk out into their hands. But—they acted as if they belonged in that camp. And there was no sign of the others with them."

I saw Foss nod. "Perhaps the right guess. You can sense danger."

"Take you over," I repeated. The restorative was no longer working. I was slipping away, unable to keep my eyes open. "Maelen—" They must help Maelen!

Chapter 14

KRIP VORLUND

There was no night or day in the interior of the *Lydis*, but I had that dazed feeling that one has when one has slept very heavily. I put up one hand to deliver the usual greeting rap on the side of the upper bunk. If Maelen had slept too—

Maelen! Her name unlocked memory and I sat up without caution, knocking my head painfully against the low-slung upper bunk. Maelen was still out there—in the freeze box! She must be brought in, put under such safeguards as the ship could give. How had I come to forget about her?

I was already on my feet, reaching for the begrimed thermo clothing dropped in a heap on the floor, when the door panel opened. I looked around to see the captain.

Foss was never one to reveal his thoughts on his face. A top Trader learns early to dissemble or to wear a mask. But there are small signs, familiar to those who live in close company, which betray strong emotions. What I saw now in Foss was a controlled anger which I had known only once or twice during the time I had shipped on board the *Lydis*.

Deliberately he entered my cabin without invitation. That act in itself showed the gravity of the situation. For privacy is so curtailed on board a spacer that each member of the crew is overly punctilious about any invasion of another's. He pulled down one of the wall seats and sat in it, still saying nothing.

But I was in no mood to sit and talk, if that was his intention. I wanted Maelen as safe as I could make her. I had no idea how long I had slept, leaving her exposed to danger.

Since the captain seemed in no hurry to announce his business with me, I broke silence first.

"I must get Maelen. She is in an alien freeze box—up on the cliffs. I must get her into our freeze compartment—" As I spoke I sealed my thermo jacket. But Foss made no move to let me by, unless I physically pushed him aside.

"Maelen—" Foss repeated her name, but there was something so odd about the tone of his voice that he caught my attention in spite of my impatience to be gone.

"Vorlund, how did it come about that you weren't with the rest— that you found your own way into that chain of burrows? You left here in company." His eyes held mine in intent measuring. Perhaps, had my mind not been largely on the need for reaching Maelen, I might have been uneasy, or taken partial warning from both his question and his attitude.

"I left them on the cliff top. Maelen called—she was in trouble."

"I see." He was still watching me with a measuring look, as if I were a piece of merchandise he had begun to suspect was not up to standard. "Vorlund—" Suddenly he reached up and pressed a stud. The small locking cupboard sprang open. As the inner side of the door was a mirror, I found myself staring at my own face.

It always gave me a feeling almost of shock to see my reflection thus. After so many years of facing one image, it takes time to get used to another. My skin was somewhat browner than it had been on Yiktor. Yet it in no way matched the dark space tan which all the other crew members had and which I had once accepted as proper. Against even the slightest coloring my silver brows, slanting up to join the hairline on my temples, and the very white locks there, close-cropped as they were, had no resemblance to my former appearance. I now had the delicately boned Thassa face, the pointed chin.

"Thassa." Foss's word underlined what I saw reflected. "You told us on Yiktor that bodies did not matter, that you were still Krip Vorlund."

"Yes," I said when he paused, as if his words had a deep meaning to be seriously considered. "I am Krip Vorlund. Did I not prove it?"

Could he possibly think now that I was really Thassa? That I had managed to masquerade successfully all these months among men who knew me intimately?

"Are you? The Krip Vorlund, Free Trader, that we know would not put an alien above his ship—or his duty!"

I was shaken. Not only because he would say and think such a thing of me, but because there was truth in it! Krip Vorlund would not have left that squad on the cliff top—gone to answer Maelen. Or would he? But I *was* Krip. Or was it true, that shadowy fear of mine, that something of Maquad governed me?

"You see," Foss continued, "you begin to understand. You are not, as you swore to us, Krip Vorlund. You are something else. And this being so—"

I turned from the mirror to face him squarely. "You think I let the men down in some way? But I tell you, *I* would not have dared use esper—not around what controls Griss Sharvan now. Only such as Maelen might dare that. And *his* change was certainly none of my doing. If I had not acted as I did, would you have your warning now?"

"Only you did not go off on your own for us, to do our scouting."

I was silent, because again he was speaking the truth. Then he continued:

"If enough of Krip is left in you to remember our ways, you know that what you did was not Trader custom. What you appear to be is a part of you now."

That thought was as chilling as the fear I had faced in the burrows. If Foss saw me as an alien, what did I have left? Yet I could not allow that to influence me. So I turned on him with the best argument I could muster.

"Maelen is part of our safeguard. Such esper powers as hers are seldom at the service of any ship. Remember, it was she who smashed that amplifier up on the cliff, the one which held us all prisoner while you were gone. If we have to face these aliens it may be Maelen who will decide the outcome for us. She is crew! And she was in danger and called. Because I can communicate with her best, I heard her and I went."

"Logical argument." Foss nodded. "What I would expect, Vorlund. But you and I both know that there is more standing behind such words than you have mentioned."

"We can argue that out later, once we are free from Sekhmet." Trader code or not, I was ridden by the need to get Maelen into what small safety the *Lydis* promised. "But Maelen has to be brought to our freeze unit—now!"

"I'll grant you that." To my vast relief the captain arose. Whether he accepted my plea that Maelen was crew, that her gifts were for our benefit, I could not tell. It was enough for the present that he would go to her aid.

I do not know what arguments he used with the Patrol to get them to help us, because I left him behind as I climbed to the cliff crest. There was no alien face behind the frostless top plate now. Maelen's small body took so little room in the box it was out of sight. My quick inspection of the fastenings proved that the container had not been disturbed since I had left it. And where I had put the alien body, there was nothing at all. The winds must have scoured away the last ashy remains hours ago.

Getting the box down the cliff face was an awkward job, one which we had to do slowly. But at length we brought it up the ramp of the *Lydis* by hand, not entrusting it to the robos. And the Patrol ship's medic waited to make the transfer to the ship's freeze unit.

Every stellar voyaging ship has such a unit to take care of any badly injured until they can be treated at some healing center. But I had not realized, even when I labored to take care of Maelen, how badly broken her glassia body was. And I think that the medic gave up when he saw that bloody bundle of matted fur. But he got a live reading, and that was enough to make him hurry to complete the transfer.

As the hasps locked on the freeze unit, I ran my hand along the top. There was the spark of life still in her; so far had her will triumphed over her body. I did not know how long she might continue to exist so, and the future looked very dark. Could I now possibly get her back to Yiktor? And even if I tracked down the Old Ones of the wandering Thassa and demanded a new body for her, would they give it to me? Where would such a body come from? Another animal form, to fulfill the fate they had set on her? Or perhaps one which was the result of some such case as gave me Maquad's—a body from the care of Umphra's priests, where those injured mentally beyond recovery were tended until Molaster saw fit to set their feet upon the White Road leading them out of the weary torment of their lives?

One step at a time. I must not allow myself to see all the shadows lying ahead. I had Maelen in the best safekeeping possible. In the freeze unit that spark of life within her would be tended with all the care my people knew. A little of the burden had been lifted from me, but much still remained. Now I knew that I owed another debt—as Foss had reminded me. I was ready to pay it as best I could. And I went to the control cabin to offer to do so.

I found Foss, the Patrol commander Borton, and the medic Thanel gathered around a box from which the medic was lifting a loop of wire. From the loop a very delicate collection of metal threads arched back and forth, weaving a cap. He handled this with care, turning it around so that the light glinted on the threads. Captain Foss looked around as I came up the ladder.

"We can prove it now. Vorlund is our top esper."

"Good enough. I am a fourth power myself." Thanel fitted the cap to his own head, the loop resting on his temples, the fine threads disappearing in his fair hair.

"Mind-send," he ordered me, "highest power."

I tried. But this was like beating against a wall. It was not the painful, shocking task it had been when I had brushed against the broadcast of the alien or faced the crowned one; rather it was like testing a complete shield. I said as much.

Borton had been holding a small object in his hand. Now he eyed me narrowly. But when he spoke he addressed Foss.

"Did you know he is a seven?"

"We knew he was high, but three trips ago he tested only a little more than five."

Five to seven! I had not known that. Was that change because of my Thassa body? Or had constant exchange with Maelen sharpened and raised my powers?

"You try this." Thanel held out the wire cap and I adjusted it on my head.

All three watched me closely and I could guess that Thanel was trying mind-send. But I picked up nothing. It was an odd sensation, as though I had plugged my ears and was deaf to all around me.

"So it works with a seventh power. But another broadcasting body with an amplifier, and this alien able to exchange identities, may be even stronger." Borton looked thoughtful.

"Our best chance." Thanel did not reach for the cap I still wore. Instead he took out four more. "These are experimental as yet. They held up under lab testing; that's why they have been issued for trial in the field. Sheer luck that we have them at all."

"As far as I can see," Borton observed, "we have little choice. The only alternative is to call in strong arms and blast that installation off Sekhmet. And if we do that we may be losing something worth more than the treasure the jacks have been looting—knowledge. We can't wait for reinforcements, either. Any move to penetrate their stronghold has to come fast, before these body snatchers can rise off-world to play their tricks elsewhere."

"We can get in through the cat's mouth. They may not yet know about that." I offered what I had to give. "I know that way."

In the end it was decided that the cat's mouth did give us the best chance of entering the enemies' territory. And we prepared to risk it. Five men only, as there were only five of the protect caps. Captain Foss represented the sadly dwindled force of the Traders, I was the guide, and the medic Thanel, Commander Borton, and a third from the Patrol force, an expert on X-Tee contacts, comprised our company.

The Patrol produced weapons more sophisticated than any I had ever seen before—an all-purpose laser type which could serve either as a weapon or as a tool. And these were subjected to a very fine adjustment by the electronics officer of the Patrol Scout, so that each would answer only to the finger pressure of the man authorized to carry it. Were it to fall into strange hands it would blow itself apart at the first firing.

Wearing the caps, so armed, and with fresh supplies, we climbed back over the cliffs. Though I could not be aware of any sentries while encapped, we moved with caution, once more a patrol in enemy country. And we spent a long number of moments watching for any sign that the wedge opening of the cat's mouth had been discovered. But the Patrol's persona reader raised no hint that any ambush awaited us there.

I led the way to the opening, once more squirming on my belly into that narrow passage. And as I wriggled forward I listened and watched for any alarm.

Though the first time I had made this journey I had had no way of measuring its length, I began now to wonder about that. Surely we must soon come to the barrier I had opened to allow me into the chamber above the place of the bodies. However, as I crawled on and on, I did not see it—though I carried a torch this time. Doubts of my own memory grew in my mind. Had I not been wearing that cap I would have suspected that I was now under some insidious mental influence.

On and on—yet I did not come to the door, the room beyond. The walls appeared to narrow, though I did not have to push against them any more than I had the first time. Yet the feeling of being caught in a trap increased with every body length that I advanced.

Then the torchlight picked out, not the door I had found before, but a series of notches in the walls, as the surface on which I crept slanted upward. This *was* new, but I had seen no breaks in the original tunnel wall. I was completely lost, but there was nothing to do but keep on. We could not retreat without great difficulty, strung out as we were without room to turn.

Those handholds in the wall allowed me to pull myself along as the incline became much steeper. I still could not understand what had happened. Only one possible explanation presented itself—that I had been under mental compulsion the *first* time I invaded this space. But the reason for such confusion? Unless the aliens had devised such a defense to discourage looters. There were warping devices. Such were known; they had been found on Atlas—small there, to be sure, but still working—a device to conceal a passage from the eye or other senses. There had been tombs on other worlds which had been protected by all manner of ingenious devices to kill, maim, or seal up forever those who dared to explore them without knowledge of their secret safeguards.

And if this was so—what did lie before us now? I could be leading our small party directly into danger. Yet I was not sure enough of my deductions to say so. There was a jerk on one of my boots, nearly strong enough to drag me backward.

"Where," came a sharp whisper out of the dark, "is this hall of the sleeping aliens you spoke of?"

A good question, and one for which I had no answer. I might only evade until I knew more.

"Distances are confusing—it must still lie ahead." I tried to remember if I had described my other journey in detail. If so, they must already know this was different. Now I attempted to speed up my wormlike progress.

The torch showed me an abrupt left turn in the passage and I negotiated that with difficulty, only to face just such a barrier as I had found before. With a sigh of relief, I set my fingers in that hole, tugged the small door open. However, as I crawled through, my hopes were dashed. This was not the chamber overlooking the hall of the freeze boxes. Rather I came out in a much wider corridor where a man might walk upright, but without any other doors along it. I swung out and tried once again to relate my present surroundings to what I had seen before.

Certainly if I had been under the spell of some hallucinatory trick the first time, I would not have been led straight to one of their places for freezing their army. That should have been the last place to which they would have wanted to guide any intruder. Perhaps the Patrol caps, instead of protecting, had failed completely—so that *this* was the hallucination?

I had moved away from the entrance. Now, one by one, the others came through to join me. It was Captain Foss and Borton who turned upon me.

"Where are we, Vorlund?" Foss asked.

There was nothing left but the truth. "I don't know—"

"This hall of boxed aliens, where is it?"

"I don't know." I had my hand to that tight cap. If I took it off—what would I see? Was touch as much affected as sight? Some hallucinations could be so strong that they enmeshed all the senses. But almost desperately now, I turned to the rock wall, running my finger tips along its surface, hoping touch would tell me that this was only an illusion which I could thereby break.

I was allowed very little time for that inspection. The tight and punishing grip of Foss's hand brought me around to face the four I had led here.

"What are you doing?"

Could I ever make them believe that I was as much a victim now as they? That I honestly had no idea of what had happened or why?

"This is not the way I came before. It may be an illusion—"

I heard a harsh exclamation from Thanel. "Impossible! The cap would prevent that!"

Borton cut in on the medic. "There is a very simple explanation, captain. It would seem that we have been tricked by your man here."

He did not look at me at all now, but rather at Foss, as if he held the captain to account for my actions.

But it was Foss's hand which went swiftly to my belt, disarmed me. And I knew in that moment that all the years of our past comradeship no longer stood witness for me.

"I don't know *who* you are now," Foss said, eyeing me as if he expected to face one of the aliens. "But when your trap springs shut, I promise you, we shall be ready to attend to you also!"

"Do we go back?" The other Patrolman stood by the tunnel door.

"I think not," Borton said. "I have no liking to be bottled up in there if we have to face trouble."

Foss had put my weapon inside his jacket. Now he made a sudden move behind me, caught my wrists before I was aware of what he planned to do. A moment later I found my hands secured behind my back. Even yet I could not believe that I had been so repudiated by my captain, that a Free Trader could turn on a crew member without allowing him a chance to defend himself.

"Which way?" he said in my ear as he tested my bonds. "Where are your friends waiting for us, Vorlund? But remember this—we have your Maelen. Serve us ill and you will never see her again. Or was your great concern for her only lip-deep and used as an excuse?"

"I know no more of what has happened than I have told you," I said, though I had no hope at all that he would believe me now. "The difference in the passages is as big a surprise to me as it is to you. There are old tales of tombs and treasures guarded by clever devices. Such a one could have been set here—perhaps this time defeated by our caps—"

"You expect us to believe that? When you told us that your very first explorations here brought you to a tomb, if tomb that hall was?" Foss's incredulity was plain.

"Why would I lead you into a trap, when I would also be caught in it?" I made a last try.

"Perhaps we have missed connections somewhere with the welcoming party," was Foss's answer. "Now—I asked you, Vorlund—which way?"

"I don't know."

The medic Thanel spoke up then. "That may be true. He could have been taken over, just as he said those others are. The cap might have broken that." He shrugged. "Take your choice of explanations."

"And choice of paths as well," Borton said. "Suppose we head right."

Borton and the Patrolman took the lead, Foss walked beside me, Thanel brought up the rear. The corridor was just wide enough for two of us to walk abreast. As was true elsewhere, there was breathable air introduced here by some ingenious method of the constructors, though I never sighted any duct by which it could enter. Underfoot there was a thick carpet of dust which showed no disturbed marking—proof, I thought, that this was no traveled way.

The passage ended abruptly in a crossway in which were set two doors, both closed. Our torches, shone directly on them, displayed painted patterns there. Each I had seen before, and perhaps I made some sound as I recognized them. Foss spoke to me. "This—you know it!" He made it an accusation rather than a question.

What was clearly there in bold lines inlaid with strips of metal (not painted as I had first thought) was the narrow cat mask of the cliff. The slanted eyes of the creature were gems which caught fire from our torches. The other door bore the likeness of the crown of another alien—that which resembled a prick-eared, long-muzzled animal.

"They are the signs of the alien crowns!"

Thanel had gone to the cat door, was running his hand along the portal's outline.

"Locked, I would say. So do we use the laser on it?"

Borton made his own careful inspection. "Don't want to set off any alarms. What about it, Vorlund? You're the only one who knows this place. How do we open this?" He looked to me as if this was some test of his own devising.

I was about to answer that I knew no more than he, when Foss gave an exclamation. His hands went to the cap on his head. He was not the only one to receive that jolt of force. Thanel's lips twisted. He spoke slowly, one word at a time, as if he were repeating some message to be relayed to the rest of us.

"The—eyes—"

It was Borton, now standing closest to the panel, who cupped one palm over each of those glittering gems. I wanted to warn him off; my effort to cry out was a pain in my throat. But my only sound was a harsh croak.

I threw myself forward, struck the weight of my shoulder against his arm, striving to dislodge his hands. Then Foss's grip dragged me back in spite of my struggles.

There was a grating sound. Borton dropped his hands. The door was moving, lifting straight up. Then it stopped, leaving a space through which a man, stooping, might pass.

"Don't go in there!" Somehow I managed to utter that warning. It was so plain to me, the aura of danger which spread from that hole like an invisible net to enfold us, that I could not understand why they did not also feel it. Too late; Borton had squeezed under the door, never glancing at me, his eyes so fixed on what lay ahead that he might be walking in a spell. After him went Thanel and the other Patrolman. Foss pushed me forward with a shove which was emphatic. I could not fight him.

So I passed under the barrier with every nerve alert to danger, knowing that I was a helpless prisoner facing a great peril I could not understand.

Chapter 15

KRIP VORLUND

I did not know what to expect, except that this place was so filled with a feeling of danger it might have been a monster's den. But what I saw looked far from dangerous, on the surface at least. I believe we were all a little dazed at the wonder of our find. The Throne of Qur, yes, that had been enough to incite cupidity as well as enchant the beholder. But that artifact was akin to a common bench in an inn compared to what was now gathered before us. Though I had not seen the temple treasures unpacked, still at that moment I was sure that all here outshone those.

There was a light which did not issue from our torches. And the contents of the chamber were not hidden from view in boxes and bundles, though there were two chests against the wall. The wall itself was inlaid with metal and stones. One section was formed of small, boxed scenes which gave one the illusion of gazing out through windows upon landscapes in miniature. I heard a sharp catch of breath from someone in our party. Then Borton advanced to the central picture.

That displayed a stretch of desert country. In the middle of the waste of sand arose a pyramid, shaped like those two rooms I had seen here. Save that this was out in the open, an erection of smoothed stone.

"That—that can't be!" The Patrol commander studied the scene as if he wanted someone to assure him that he did not view what his eyes reported. "It is impossible!"

I believed that he knew that building in the sand, that he had either seen it himself or viewed it on some tri-dee tape.

"It's—it's incredible!" Foss was not looking at the picture which had captured the commander's attention. Instead he gazed from one treasure to another as if he could not believe he was not dreaming.

As I have said, the contents of the room were all placed as if this chamber was in use as living quarters. The painted and inlaid chests stood against a wall on which those very realistic pictures were separated by hangings of colored stuffs, glowingly alive. Those possessed a surface shimmer so that one could not be sure, even when one stared at them, whether the odd rippling shadows which continually flickered and faded were indeed half-seen figures in action. Yet the strips hung motionless.

There were two high-backed chairs, one flanked by a small table which rested on a tripod of slender legs. Carved on the back of one chair was the cat mask, this time outlined in silver on a dead-black surface. The second chair was of a misty blue, bearing on its back a complicated design in pure white.

On the floor under our dusty boots lay a pattern of blocks, black as one chair, blue as the other, and inlaid with more symbols in silver. On the tripod table were small plates of crystal and a footed goblet.

Thanel crossed to the nearest chest. Catching his fingers under its projecting edge, he lifted, and the lid came up easily. We saw that the box was filled to the brim with lengths of color, green which was also blue, a warm yellow—perhaps garments. He did not take out any of them.

Chests, the two chairs, the table, and, directly facing the door, not another wall but a curtain of the same material as the wall panels. Foss started toward that and I followed close behind— *It* was beyond— He must not!

I was too late. He had already found the concealed slit which allowed one to pass through. I went closely on his heels, though I had already guessed what lay beyond. Guessed? No, *knew*!

And knowing, I expected to be met by a blast of the freezing air of stass-freeze— Come to think of it, why had we not already felt that in the outer chamber?

She lay with her head and shoulders supported by a thick cushion, gazing away from us, out through the crystal wall. But the tendrils of her crown swayed and entwined, moved, their cat-headed tips turning instantly, not only facing us, but making sharp jerking darts back and forth. It was as if those heads fought to detach the ties which held them to the circlet about the red hair, that they might come flying at us.

If she was not in freeze, then how had she been preserved? She could not be asleep, for her eyes were open. Nor could one detect even the slightest rise and fall of normal breathing.

"Thanel!" Foss went no further in. At the sound of his summons the cat heads spun and jerked, went into a wild frenzy of action.

I was shoved aside as the medic joined us.

"Is—is she alive?" Foss demanded.

Thanel produced his life-force detect. Making some adjustments, he advanced. And it seemed to me he went reluctantly, glancing now and then at the whirling crown. He held the instrument up before the reclining woman, studied its dial with a gathering frown, triggered some button, and once more took a reading.

"Well, is she?" Foss persisted.

"Not alive. But not dead either."

"And what does that mean?"

"Just what I said." Thanel pushed the button again with the forefinger of his other hand. "It doesn't register either way. And I don't know of any life force so alien that this can't give an instant decision on the point. She isn't in freeze, not in this atmosphere. But if she is dead I have never seen such preservation before."

"Who is dead?" Borton came through the curtain now with the other Patrolman, stopped short when he saw her.

I could no longer watch the woman. There was something in the constant motion of her cat-headed coronet which disturbed me, as if those whirling thumb-sized bits of metal wove a hypnotic spell. I made my last effort to warn them.

"Dead or alive"—my voice was harsh, too loud in the confinement of that room—"she reaches for you now. I tell you—she is dangerous!"

Thanel looked at me. The others stood, their attention all for her as if they had heard nothing. Then the medic caught at the commander's arm, gave a sudden swift pull which brought Borton around so he no longer eyed her squarely. He blinked, swallowed as if he had gulped a mouthful of some potent brew.

"Move!" The medic gave him a second push.

Borton, still blinking, stumbled back toward the curtain, knocking against Foss. I was already on the other side of the captain, had set my shoulder against his, using the same tactics Thanel had, if in a more clumsy fashion. And once shoved out of direct line with the woman, he, too, seemed to wake.

In the end we all got back on the other side of the curtain and stood there, breathing a little heavily, almost as if we had been racing. I was aware that the cap on my head was warm, that the line of wire touching my temples was near burning me. I saw Thanel touch his own band, snatch his fingers away. But Foss was at my side.

"Turn around."

I obeyed his order, felt him busy at my wrists. A moment later my hands were free.

"I can believe," he said, "in anything happening here, Vorlund. After seeing that, I can believe! She is just as you described her. And I believe she is deadly!"

"What about the others?" Thanel asked.

"There is one there." I rubbed my left wrist with my right hand, nodding in the direction where the next compartment must lie. "Two more on the other two sides. One held Griss when I was here before."

Borton went again to that picture of the pyramid. "Do you know what this is?"

"No. But it is plain to guess you have seen its like before, and not on Sekhmet," Foss returned. "Does it have any importance for us now?"

"Perhaps. That—that was built on Terra in a past so distant we can no longer reckon it accurately. By accounts the archaeologists have never agreed on its age. It is supposed to have been erected by slave labor at a time when man had not yet tamed a beast of burden, had not discovered the wheel. And yet it was a great feat of highly sophisticated engineering. There were countless theories about it, one being that its measurements, because of their unusual accuracy, held a message. It was not the only such either, but one of several. Though this particular one was supposed to be the first and greatest. For a long time the pile was said to be the tomb of a ruler. But that theory was never entirely proved—for the tomb itself might have been a later addition. At any rate, it was built millennia before our breed took to space!"

"But Forerunner remains," Thanel objected. "Those were never found on Terra. None of the history tapes records such discoveries."

"Perhaps no remains recognized as such by us. But—" Borton shook his head. "What do we even know of Terra now except from tapes copied and re-copied, some of them near-legendary? Yet—and this is also very odd indeed—in the land where that stood"—he pointed to the picture—"they once worshiped gods portrayed with human bodies and beast or bird heads. In fact—there was a cat-headed goddess Sekhmet, a bird-headed Thoth, a saurian Set—"

"But these planets, this system, were named by the First-in Scout who mapped them, after the old custom of naming systems for ancient gods!" Foss interrupted.

"That is true. The Scouts gave such names as suited their fancies—culled from the tapes they carried with them to relieve the boredom of spacing. And the man who named this system must have had a liking for Terran history. Yet—he could also have been influenced in some way." Borton again shook his head. "We may never know the truth of the past, save this is such a find as may touch on very ancient mysteries, even those of our own beginnings!"

"And we may not have a chance to learn anything, unless we get to the bottom of a few modern mysteries now!" Foss retorted.

I noted that he kept his head turned away from the curtain, almost as if she who waited beyond it might have the power to pull him back into her presence. The wires of my cap no longer were heated; but I was unhappy in this place, I wanted out.

"That crown she wears—" Thanel shifted from one foot to another as if he wanted to look at the woman again. I saw Borton shake his head. "I would say it is a highly sensitive communication device of some sort. What about it, Laird?"

"Undoubtedly—" began the other Patrolman. "Didn't you feel the response of your protect? The caps were close to shorting, holding against that energy. What about the crowns the others wear?" He turned to me. "Are they alive—moving—also?"

"Not that I saw. They aren't shaped the same."

"I want to see the alien body holding Griss," Foss broke in. "Is that in the next chamber?"

I shook my head. And I had no idea of how one reached either the interior of the crystal-lined pyramid room or the other chambers which formed its walls. There had been another door beside the cat one. But side by side—when the rooms were at right angles—how—

Foss did not wait for my guidance. He slipped under the outer door and we were quick to follow. Thanel brought down the cat door, it moving much more easily to close than it had to open. Foss was already at work on the other door. It yielded as reluctantly as the first had done, but it did go up. However, we did not look now on a room filled with treasures, but on a very narrow passage, so confined one had to turn sideways to slip along it. This made a right-angled turn and then there was a second curtained doorway ahead.

"This one?" Foss demanded.

"No." I tried to remember. "Next, I think."

We slipped along that slit between walls to a second sharp turn, which brought us so that we must now be facing directly across from the chamber of the cat woman, if we could have seen through solid walls. Once more there was a door, this one patterned with the bird head. A third turn and we found what I had been searching for—the saurian.

"This is it!"

The door panel was doubly hard to dislodge because there was so little room in which to move. However, it gave at last, Foss and I working at it as best we could.

Once more we were in a furnished room. But we spent no time in surveying the treasures there, hurrying on instead through the curtain to the fore part. I could see now the crowned head, the bare shoulders of him who sat there, staring stonily out into the space beyond the crystal.

Foss circled to be able to see the face of the seated one. There was no moving part of this crown, no stirring to suggest that we had found more than a perfectly preserved alien body. But I saw the captain's expression change, knew that he could read the eyes in that set face and felt the same horror I had felt,

"Griss!" His whisper was a hiss.

I did not want to view what Foss now faced with grim determination, yet I knew that I must. So I edged forward on the other side of the chair, looked into the tortured eyes. Griss—yes—and still conscious, still aware of what had happened to him! Though I had passed through body change twice, both times it had been with my own consent and for a good purpose. However, had such a change been wrought against my will—could I have kept such knowledge and remained sane? I did not know.

"We have to do something!" The words exploded from Foss with the force of a blaster shot. I knew that he backed them with that determination which he had ever shown in the face of any peril that threatened the *Lydis* and those who called her their home. "You"— he spoke directly to me—"have tried this body exchange. What can you do for him?"

Always in such matters I had been the passive one, the one who was worked upon, not the mover in the act. Maelen had sung me into the barsk body when the Three Rings of Sotrath wreathed that moon over our heads, when the occult powers of the Thassa were at their greatest height. And I had passed into the shell of Maquad in the shelter of Umphra, where the priests of that gentle and protective order had been able to lend to Maelen all the aid she needed.

Once only had I seen the transfer for another—that in a time of fear and sorrow when Maelen had lain dying and one of her little people, Vors, had crept to her side and offered her furred body as a refuge for the Thassa spirit. I had seen them sing the exchange then, two of the Thassa, Maelen's sister and her kinsman. And I had found myself also singing words I did not know. But that I alone could make such an exchange—no.

"I can do—" I was about to add "nothing" when a thought came from my own past. I had run as Jorth the barsk; I now walked as Maquad. Could it just be— If Griss tried, overcame his horror and fear of what had happened to him, could he command his new body, rule it until he could recapture his own? But I must get through to him first. And that would mean setting aside the protect cap.

I explained, not quite sure whether this could be done, even if I dared so break our own defenses and put us all in danger. But when I had made this clear Foss touched the butt of the laser.

"We have our defenses. You know what I mean—will you risk that also?"

Be burned down if I were taken over—no, I did not want to risk that, but want and a man's duty are two different things many times during one's life. I had turned aside from what the Traders considered my duty once already, here on Sekhmet. It seemed that now I had a second chance to repay old debts. And I remembered how Maelen had faced exile in an alien body because she had taken up a debt.

"It may be his only chance."

Quickly, before I could falter, I reached for the cap on my head. I saw them move to encircle me, weapons ready. They all eyed me warily as if I were now the enemy. I took off the cap.

My head felt light, free, as if I had removed some burden which had weighed heavily without my even being aware of it. I had a moment of hesitation, as one might feel stepping out into an arena such as those on Sparta where men face beasts in combat. From which direction could an attack come? And I believe those around me waited tensely for some hideous change in me.

"Griss?" The impression that time was limited set me directly to work. "Griss!" I was not a close comrade of this poor prisoner. But we were shipmates; we had drawn matching watch buttons many times, shared planet leaves. It had been through him I had first learned who and what Maelen was. And now I consciously drew upon that friendship of the past to buttress my sending.

"Griss!" And this time—

"Krip—can you—can you hear me?" Incredulous thankfulness.

"Yes," I came directly to the importance of what must be done. "Griss, can you rule this body? Make it obey you?" The question was the best way I knew of trying to make him break down a barrier which might have been built by his own fears. Now he must try to direct the alien husk, even as a control board directs a labor robo.

I had had a hard time adjusting to an animal form; at least he did not have to face that. For the alien, to our eyes, was humanoid.

"Can you rule the body, Griss?"

His surprise was easy to read. I knew that he had not considered that at all, that the initial horror of what had happened to him had made him believe himself helpless from the first. Whereas I had been helped through my transitions by foreknowledge, and also by the aid of Maelen, who was well versed in such changes, he had been brutally taken prisoner in such a way as to paralyze even his thought processes for a time. It is always the unknown which carries with it, especially for my species, the greatest fear.

"Can I?" he asked as might a child.

"Try—concentrate!" I ordered him with authority. "Your hand—your right hand, Griss. Raise it—order it to move!"

His hands rested on the arms of the chair in which lie sat. His head did not move a fraction, but his eyes shifted away from mine, in a visible effort to see his hands.

"Move it!"

The effort he unleashed was great. I hastened to feed that. Fingers twitched—

"Move!"

The hand rose, shaking as if it had been so long inert that muscles, bone, flesh could hardly obey the will of the brain. But it rose, moved a little away from the support of the chair arm, then wavered, fell limply upon the knee. But he had moved it!

"I—I did it! But—weak—very—weak—"

I looked to Thanel. "The body may be in need of restoratives— perhaps as when coming out of freeze."

He frowned. "No equipment for that type of restoration."

"But you must have something in your field kit—some kind of basic energy shot."

"Alien metabolism," he murmured, but he brought out his field kit, unsealed it. "We can't tell how the body will react."

"Tell him—" Griss's thought was frantic. "Try anything! Better be dead than like this!"

"You are far from dead," I countered.

Thanel held an injection cube, still in its sterile envelope. He bent over the seated body to affix the cube on the bare chest over the spot where a human heart would have been. At least it did adhere, was not rejected at once.

That body gave a jerk as visible shudders ran along the limbs.

"Griss?"

"Ahhh—" No message, just a transferred sensation of pain, of fear. Had Thanel been right and the restorative designed for our species proved dangerous to another?

"Griss!" I caught at that hand he had moved with such effort, held it between both of mine. Only my tight grasp kept it from flailing out in sharp spasms. The other had snapped up from the chair arm, waved in the air. The legs kicked out; the body itself writhed, as if trying to rise and yet unable to complete such movement.

Now that frozen, expressionless face came alive. The mouth opened and shut as if he screamed, though no sound came from his lips. Those lips themselves drew back, flattened in the snarl of a cornered beast.

"It's killing him!" Foss put out a hand as if to knock that cube away, but the medic caught his wrist.

"Let it alone! To interrupt now *will* kill."

I had captured the other hand, held them both as I struggled to reach the mind behind that tortured face.

"Griss!"

He did not answer. However, his spasms were growing less; his face was no longer so contorted. I did not know if that was a good or a bad sign.

"Griss?"

"I—am—here—" The thought-answer was so slow it came like badly slurred speech. "I—am—still—here—"

I detected a dull wonder in his answer, as if he were surprised to find it so.

"Griss, can you use your hands?" I released the grip with which I had held them, laid them back on his knees.

They no longer shook nor waved about. Slowly they rose until they were chest-high before him. The fingers balled into fists, straightened out again, wriggled one after another as if they were being tested.

"I can!" The lethargy of his answer of only moments earlier was gone. "Let me—let me up!"

Those hands went to the arms of the chair. I could see the effort which he expended to use them to support him to his feet. Then he made it, stood erect, though he wavered, kept hold of the chair. Thanel was quickly at one side, I at the other, supporting him. He took several uncertain steps, but those grew firmer.

The restorative cube, having expended its charge, loosened and fell from his chest, which arched and fell now as he drew deep breaths into his lungs. Again I had reason to admire the fine development of this body. It was truly as if some idealized sculpture of the human form had come to life. He was a good double palms' space taller than either of us who walked with him, and muscles moved more and more easily under his pale skin.

"Let me try it alone." He did not mind-speak now, but aloud. There was a curious flatness to his tone, a slight hesitation, but we had no difficulty in understanding him. And we released our hold, though we stood ready if there was need.

He went back and forth, his strides sure and balanced now. And then he paused by the chair, put both his hands to his head, and took off the grotesque crown, dropping it to clang on the seat as he threw it away.

His bared skull was hairless, like that of the body in the freeze box. But he ran his hands back and forth across the skin there as if he wanted to reassure himself that the crown was gone.

"I did it!" There was triumph in that. "Just as you thought I could, Krip. And if I can—they can too!"

Chapter 16

KRIP VORLUND

"Who are *they*?" Foss asked.

"Lidj—the Patrol officer—there and there!" He faced the outer transparent wall of the room, pointed right and left to those other two aliens on display. "I saw them—saw them being brought in, forced to exchange. Just as was done with me!"

"I wonder why such exchanges are necessary," Thanel said. "If we could restore this body, why didn't they just restore their own? Why go through the business of taking over others?"

Griss was rubbing his forehead with one hand. "Sometimes— sometimes I know things—things they knew. I think they value their bodies too highly to risk them."

"Part of their treasures!" Foss laughed harshly. "Use someone else to do their work for them, making sure they have a body to return to if that substitute suffers any harm. They're as cold-blooded as harpy night demons! Well, let's see if we can get Lidj and that man of yours out of pawn now."

Borton leaned over the edge of the chair, reaching for the crown Griss had thrown there.

"No!" In a stride Griss closed the distance between them, sent the crown spinning across the floor. "In some way that is a com, giving them knowledge of what happens, to the body—"

"Then, with your breaking that tie," I pointed out, "they—or he—will be suspicious and come looking—"

"Better that than have him force me under control again without my knowing when that might happen!" Griss retorted.

If the danger he seemed to believe in did exist, he was right. And we might have very little time.

Borton spoke first. "All the more reason to try to get the others free."

"Which one is Lidj?" Foss was already going.

"To the left."

That meant the bird-headed crown. We returned to the anteroom. Griss threw open one of the chests as if he knew exactly what he was looking for. He dragged out a folded bundle and shook it out, to pull on over his bare body a tightly fitting suit of dull black. It was all of a piece including footgear, even gloves, rolled back now about the wrists, and a hood which hung loose between the shoulders. A press of finger tip sealed openings, leaving no sign they had ever existed.

There was something odd about that garment. The dull black seemed to produce a visual fuzziness, so that only his head and bared hands were well-defined. It must have been an optical illusion, but I believed that with the gloves and hood on he might be difficult to see.

"How did you know where to find that?" Borton was watching him closely.

Griss, who had been sealing the last opening of his clothing, stopped, his finger tip still resting on the seam. There was a shadow of surprise on his handsome face.

"I don't know—I just knew that it was there and I must wear it."

Among them all, I understood. This was the old phenomenon of shape-changing—the residue (hopefully the very *small* residue) of the earlier personality taking over for some actions. But there was danger in that residue. I wondered if Griss knew that, or if we would have to watch him ourselves lest he revert to the alien in some more meaningful way.

Thanel must have been thinking along the same lines, for now he demanded: "How much do you remember of alien ways?"

Griss's surprise was tinged with uneasiness.

"Nothing! I was not even thinking—just that I needed clothing. Then I knew where to find it. It—I just knew—that's all!"

"How much else would he 'just know,' I wonder?" Borton looked to Thanel rather than to Griss, as if he expected a better explanation from the medic.

"Wasting time!" Foss stood by the door. "We have to get Lidj and Harkon! And get out before anyone comes to see what happened to Griss."

"What about my cap?" I asked.

Thanel had passed that to the other Patrolman. And in this place I wanted all the protection I could get. The other held it out to me and I settled it on my head with a sigh of relief, though with it came the sensation of an oppressive burden.

We threaded along that very narrow passage to the next chamber, where the alien with the avian crown half-reclined on the couch. Having freed one "exchange" prisoner, I now moved with confidence. And it was not so difficult, as Juhel Lidj had greater esper power.

Then we retraced our way and released Harkon also. But I do not believe that Borton was entirely happy over such additions to our small force. They had put aside their crowns, and they were manifestly eager to move against those who had taken their bodies. But whether they would stand firm during a confrontation, we could not know.

We returned to the cat door. There I lingered a moment, studying the mask symbol. Three men, one woman—who had they been? Rulers; priests and a priestess; scientists of another time and place? Why had they been left here? Was this a depository like our medical freezers, or a politically motivated safe-keep where rulers had chosen to wait out some revolution they had good reason to fear? Or—

It seemed to me that the gem eyes of the cat held a malicious glitter, mirroring superior amusement. As if someone knew exactly the extent of my ignorance and dismissed me from serious consideration because of it. A spark of anger flared deep inside me. Yet I did not underrate what lay beyond that door and could be only waiting for a chance to assume power.

"Now where?" Borton glanced about as if he expected some guide sign to flare into life.

"Our other men," Lidj answered that crisply. "They have them imprisoned somewhere—"

I thought that "somewhere" within these burrows was no guide at all. And it would seem Foss's thoughts marched with mine, for he asked:

"You have no idea where?"

It was Harkon who answered. "Not where they are. Where *our* bodies are now, that is something else."

"You mean you can trace those?" Thanel demanded.

"Yes. Though whether mere confrontation will bring about another exchange—"

"How do you know?" The medic pursued the first part of his answer.

"I can't tell you. Frankly, I don't know. But I do know that whoever is walking about as Harkon right now is in that direction." There was no hesitation as he pointed to the right wall of the passage.

Only, not being able to ooze through solid rock, I did not see how that knowledge was going to benefit us. We had found no other passage during our way in (I was still deeply puzzled about the difference between my first venture into the maze and this one).

Harkon still faced that blank wall, a frown on his face. He stared so intently at the smoothed stone that one might well think he saw a pattern there—one invisible to us.

After a moment he shook his head. "Not quite here—farther on," he muttered. Nor did he enlarge on that, but started along close to the wall, now and then sweeping his finger tips across it, as if by touch he might locate what he could not find by sight. He was so intent upon that search that his concentration drew us along, though I did not expect any results from his quest. Then he halted, brought the palm of his hand against the stone in a hard slap.

"Right behind here—if we can break through."

"Stand aside." Whether Borton accepted him as a guide or not, the commander seemed willing to put it to the test. He aimed his weapon at the wall where Harkon had indicated, and fired.

The force of that weapon was awesome, more so perhaps because we were in such a confined space. One moment there had been the solid rock of this planet's bone; the next—a dark hole. Before we could stop him, Harkon was into that.

We had indeed broken through into another corridor. This one was washed in gray light. Harkon did not hesitate, but moved along with such swift strides that we had to hurry to catch up.

That passage was short, for we soon came out on a gallery running along near the top of another pyramid-shaped chamber. This one was triple the size of the others I had seen. From our perch we looked down into a scene of clanking activity. There was a mass of machinery, installations of some sort, being uncrated, unboxed by robos. Pieces were lifted by raise cranes, transferred to transports. But those carriers ran neither on wheels nor—

"Antigrav!" Borton leaned nearer to the edge. "They have antigrav in small mobile units."

Antigrav we knew. But the principle could not be used in mobile units, only installed in buildings as a method of transport from floor to floor. Here these carriers, loaded with heavy burdens, swung along in ordered lines through a dark archway in the opposite wall.

"Where's the controller?" The other Patrolman peered over.

"Remote control, I would say." Foss stood up.

We had all fallen flat at the sign of the activity. But now Foss apparently thought we had nothing to fear. And a moment later he added:

"Those are programmed robos."

Programmed robos! The complexity of the operation here on Sekhmet increased with every discovery we made. Programmed robos were not ordinarily ship workers, like the controlled ones we had earlier seen and used ourselves. They were far more intricate, requiring careful servicing, which made them impractical for use on primitive worlds. One did not find them on the frontier. Yet here they were at work light-years away from the civilizations producing them. Shipping these here, preparing them for work, would have been a major task in itself.

"In a jack hideout?" Foss protested.

"Look closer!" Borton was still watching below. "This is a storehouse which is being systematically looted. And who would have situated it here in the first place—"

"Forerunners," Lidj answered him. "But machines—this is not a tomb, nor—"

"Nor a lot of things!" Borton interrupted. "There were Forerunner installations found on Limbo. The only difference is that those were abandoned, not stored away. Here—perhaps a whole civilization was kept—both men and machines! And the Forerunners were not a single civilization, either—even a single species. Ask the Zacathans—they can count you off evidence of perhaps ten which have been tentatively identified, plus fragments of other, earlier ones which have not! The universe is a graveyard of vanished races, some of whom rose to heights we cannot assess today. These machines, if they can be made to work again, their purposes learned—"

I think that the possibilities of what he said awed us. Of course, we all knew of such treasure hunting as had been indulged in on Thoth—that was common. Lucky finds had been made all around the galaxy from time to time. The Zacathans, that immensely old, immensely learned reptilian race whose passion was the accumulation of knowledge, had their libraries filled with the lore of vanished—long-vanished—stellar civilizations. They led their archaeological expeditions from world to world seeking a treasure they reckoned not in the furnishings of tombs, in the hidden hoards discovered in long-deserted ruins, but in the learning of those who had left such links with the far past.

And parties of men had made such finds also. They had spoken of Limbo—that had been the startling discovery of a Free Trader in the earlier days.

Yet the plunder from here had not yet turned up on any inner-planet market, where it would logically be sold. Its uniqueness would have been recognized instantly, for rumor of such finds spreads quickly and far.

"Suppose"—Foss, plainly fascinated, still watched the antigravs floating in parade order out of the storeroom—"the jacks, even the Guild, began this. But now it has been taken over by those others."

"Yes," came the dry, clipped answer from Lidj. "It could be that the original owners are now running the game." He raised both hands to his bald skull, rubbed his fingers across it. There was still a mark on his forehead from the weight of the crown.

"You mean—" Borton began.

Lidj turned on him. "Is that so strange? We put men in stass-freeze for years. In fact I do not know what has been the longest freeze time ending in a successful resuscitation. These might be awakened to begin life at the point where they left off, ready for their own plan of action. Do you deny that they have already proved they have secrets which we have not? Ask your own man, Harkon—how can he explain what has happened to the three of us?"

"But the others stored here—at least that one in the box above the valley—was dead." My protest was weak, because too much evidence was on Lidj's side.

"Perhaps most of them did die, perhaps that is why they want our bodies. Who knows? But I will wager that they—those three who took ours—are now in command of this operation!"

Harkon had drawn a little apart, perilously close to the edge of the balcony. Now he spoke in the same husky tone our cargomaster used.

"Can you set an interrupt beam on these lasers you have?" I did not understand what he meant, but apparently his question made sense to Borton, who joined him.

"Tricky—from here," the commander observed.

"Tricky or not, we can try it. Let me see yours—"

Did Borton hesitate for a moment before he passed over that weapon? If so, I could understand, since lurking at the back of my mind was a shadowy suspicion of these three. It is never easy to accept body exchange, even for one knowing the Thassa.

But Borton appeared willing to trust the pilot and passed over the laser. Harkon squatted against the sharply sloping wall, which made him hunch over the weapon. He snapped open the charge chamber, inspected the cartridge there, closed it once more, and reset the firing dial.

With it in his hand he went to peer down, selecting a victim. There was a robo to his left, now engaged in shifting a metal container onto one of the waiting transports. Harkon took aim and pressed the firing button.

A crackle of lightning sped like a whiplash, not to touch the robo itself, but to encircle its knoblike head. The robo had a flexible tentacle coiled about the container, ready to swing it across to the platform. But that move was never completed. The robo froze with the container still in the air.

"By the Teeth of Stanton Gore, you did it!" Borton's voice was almost shrill.

The pilot wasted no time in waiting for congratulations on his skill. He had already aimed at the next robo and stopped that one dead also.

"So you can knock them out," Lidj observed. "What do we do now—" Then he paused and caught at Borton's arm. "Is there a chance of resetting them?"

"We can hope so."

The robos I knew and had always used were control ones. Free Traders visited only the more backward worlds where machines were simple if used at all. I had no idea how one went about reprogramming complex robos. But the knowledge of a Free Trader was not that of a Patrolman. Plainly Borton and Harkon hoped the machines could be made to work in some manner for us.

Which is what they proceeded to find out. When the six robos were halted we came down from the balcony. The antigrav transports still moved at a slow and even pace, though those now edging away were only partly loaded. Foss and the other Patrolman went into action, turning their lasers with less precision but as great effect on the motive section of those. The carriers crashed to the floor with heavy jars which shook even this rock-walled chamber.

The Patrolmen gathered about the nearest robo. Harkon was already at work on the protective casing over its "brain." But I was more interested in the transports. Basically these were nothing more than ovals of metal, with low side walls to hold their loads in place. The motive force of each lay in a box at the rear. The principle of their construction was unlike anything I had ever seen before.

"Something coming!" At that warning from Griss we all went to ground. But what loomed into view out of the opening was an empty transport back for another load. Foss had raised his laser to short it when Lidj jerked at his arm to spoil his aim.

"We can use that!" He made a running jump, caught the edge of the carrier's wall, and swung up on it. It did not halt its forward movement, proceeding steadily down a row of boxes until it came to a stop beside a motionless robo, still holding a crate aloft between clawed appendages.

Lidj was squatting before the controls, trying to make sense of them, when we clambered on board to join him. Unloaded as it was, the carrier bucked a little under our movements and shifting weight, so we had to take care.

"Could be set either of two ways," he said, "ready to go either when there is a certain amount of weight on board—or after a predetermined time. If it is the latter it's more risky. We'll have to either knock it out or let it go. But if it is a matter of weight—"

Foss nodded. "Then we can use it."

I could guess what they planned. Build a row of boxes around the edge of the carrier, then take our places inside that and have transportation out without fear of getting lost. We would, of course, be heading toward the enemy. But we would have the element of surprise on our side.

"Time it," Foss continued.

I looked around. A second empty carrier was now coming in, heading, not to where we waited, but to the loading site, where the Patrolmen now had the upper casing of the robo free.

"Look out!"

Those workmen scattered as the carrier swung in, just missing the upraised load arm of the robo. Then the platform halted, waiting to be loaded. The men arose to tug at the squat robo, pulling it out of the way to where they could get at it without any danger of being knocked out by a transport.

Lidj still knelt by the motive box. He had stopped trying to find any lever or control button. Foss had said to time it, and we were all counting furiously during long minutes as we stood tensely alert for the first sign that the carrier was preparing to move. But it hung there, still waiting. I heard the captain's sigh of relief.

"One hundred," he repeated aloud. "If it doesn't start up by five, now—"

His lips shaped the numbers visibly. The carrier did not stir.

"So far, so good. Weight must be what triggers it."

While we had conducted our crude test a third carrier had come nosing back. Counting the three which had been immobilized, there were now six. How many could there be in all? And how soon would someone come looking if they did not return?

Foss and Lidj went to one of the loaded ones which had been halted. Part of a cargomaster's duty is the judging of cargo loads, an ability to estimate, by eye, bulk and weight for stowage. Lidj was an expert. I was not so experienced, but I had had enough general training under his stiff tutelage to be able to come close to guessing the weight load on the downed platform.

Once we knew that, we moved along the still-racked boxes to pick out those which would give us protective bulk without too much weight—weight which our bodies must partly supply.

Having made our choices, we began to load by hand, a wearying process which was foreign to usual ship work. But in times of stress one can do many things he might earlier have thought impossible. We stacked our chosen boxes and containers as a bulwark running along the edges of the platform, leaving an open space between. Borton came to inspect our labors and nodded approval.

"Just let us get one of those boys going"—he nodded to the robos—"and we'll move out."

What he intended the reprogrammed cargo handler to do, I could not guess. Nor did we take time from our own labor to watch their struggles. There came a whir of sound. The robo brought down its upright arm, dropped the box it held. It turned on its treads to face the wide doorway.

"Now—" Harkon was moving to a second robo as if he planned to use that also. Then his hands went to his head.

"Time's just run out." His voice lacked the jubilation of seconds earlier. "If we make a move—it must be now!"

Chapter 17

KRIP VORLUND

No other carrier had returned for some time now. But Griss, Lidj, and Harkon all faced the doorway as if they heard some call.

"They are uneasy, those who wear our bodies," Harkon said to Borton. "We shall have to move fast if we would keep any advantage."

Borton triggered the robo and it moved out, heading for the door. With it as a fore guard, the rest of us took to the carriers. And as those edged away from the loading sites, picking up speed as they went, I could have shouted aloud in my relief. Our calculations had been proved right so far. Weight sent the carriers on their way.

Once airborne, I longed for the speed of a flitter. But there was no hurrying the deliberate pace, any more than we could urge on the robo rumbling ahead. Perhaps it was just as well we did not approach too near that. For as it went it came alive. It had been using two long, jointed arms, ending in clawed attachments. And it was also equipped with flexible tentacles, two above and two below those arms. Now all six of the appendages flailed the air vigorously, whipping out and around.

Though men have depended upon the services of machines for such countless ages that perhaps only the Zacathans can now reckon the number of those dusty years, yet I think deep inside us all there lingers a small spark of fear that some day, under some circumstances, those machines will turn on us, to wreak a mindless vengeance of their own. Long ago it was discovered that robos given too human a look were not salable. Even faint resemblances triggered such age-old distaste.

Now as I lay beside Foss and Lidj on the carrier and watched the wildly working arms of the robo, which seemed to have gone mad, I was glad that ours was not the first transport riding directly in its wake, but the second. Let the Patrol enjoy—if one might term it that—the honor of the lead. The farther I was from that metal monster seemingly intent on smashing the world, the better.

"They are not too far ahead now." Lidj's words reached me through the *clank-clank* of the robo.

"How many?" Foss wanted to know.

"My powers are not that selective; sorry." There was the ghost of Lidj's old dry humor in that answer. "I just know that my body is somewhere ahead. My body! Tell me, Krip"—he looked to me then—"did you ever stand off and watch yourself, back there on Yiktor?"

I remembered—though then the transition had been so great, my own adaptation to an animal's body had put such a strain on me, that I had been far more concerned with my own feelings at the moment than with what was happening to the body I had discarded.

"Yes, but not for long. Those men of Osokun's took me—it—away. And at the time I was, well, I was learning what it meant to be a barsk."

"At least we did not have that factor. It is hard enough to adapt to this covering," Lidj commented. "In fact, I must admit it has a few advantages over my own. Several aches and pains have been eliminated. Not that I care to remain in my present tenancy any longer than I have to. I fear I am conservative in such matters."

I marveled at what seemed my superior's almost complacent acceptance of a situation which might have unseated the reason of a less self-controlled man.

"I hope," he continued, "that the one wearing *me* has no heroic tendencies. Getting my body smashed up before I can retrieve it would be a disappointment—to say the least!"

With that he resurrected my own worries. Maelen—her present body could not continue to live, not long, if we roused her from freeze. And could it last, even in that state, long enough to get her back to Yiktor? How—I tried to think of ways that journey could be accomplished safely, only to reject each idea, knowing all were such wild plans as could be dreamed by graz chewers, and as likely to be realized.

The light ahead was brighter. Now the robo clanked on into the source of that, the first of our carriers closely behind him, ours drawn after without our guidance. We had our weapons and the protection of the bulwarks we had built about the edges of the platforms. Though those now seemed very thin shells indeed.

Here were piles of goods out of the storage place. And moving among them were the common controlled robos, sorting and transporting to a cargo hoist which dangled from the hatch of a ship. A single glance told me that we were in that landing valley and that this was the same ship Maelen and I had seen when we fled the burrows. How long ago had that been? We had eaten E rations, gulped down sustain pills until I was no longer sure of time. A man can exist long on such boosters without even being aware that he must rest.

Our carriers kept on at the same even pace, but the robo was not so orderly. Its path was straight ahead, and it did not try to avoid anything in its path. The whiplash of its tentacles, the battery of its arms crashed into the cargo awaiting stowage, sweeping away battered and broken boxes, some to be crushed beneath its own massive treads.

The surprise was complete. I heard shouting—saw the lightning fire of lasers, bringing down more of the cargo, melting some of it. And the shock of those energy waves did their work. Men toppled, to lie clawing feebly at the ground, their minds knocked out for a space by the back fire of such force. We tumbled from our transports, took to cover among the cargo.

Producing tanglers, the Patrolmen moved in toward those feebly moving jacks while we slipped ahead, searching for more humans among the working robos. The reprogrammed one smashed on and on until it came up with a crash against one of the ship's fins. There it continued to whir sullenly, not backing away, unable to move on. An arm caught in the dangling chains of the hoist. Having so connected, it tightened hold with a vicious snap. Before whoever was running the crane could shut it off, the robo had been lifted a little. Then the strain of its weight told, broke the hoist chain. That small

shift of position had been enough to pull the robo away from the fin.
Dropped to the ground again, it still moved—though its assault on
the fin had damaged it, and it proceeded with an ear-punishing
grating noise. One of its arms hung limply down, jangling back and
forth against its outer casing; the other clutched and tore with as
much vigor as ever as it rumbled on the new course.

I saw Lidj as I rounded a stack of boxes. He was heading, not
toward the scene of action, but away from it, crouching low as if he
expected blaster fire. And there was that in his attitude which drew
me after him. A moment later Harkon closed in from the left, his
black suit conspicuous here in the open. Then came another dark
figure—Griss. They were running, dodging, their empty hands held
a little before them in an odd fashion, with the fingers arched,
resembling the claws of the robo still engaged in senseless
destruction near the ship. And they did not look right or left, but
directly before them, as if their goal was in plain sight.

Watching them, I knew a rise of old fear. It could be that they
were again under the command of those aliens who had taken over
their bodies. And it might be better now for all of us were I to use
the side wash of my laser to knock them out.

I was beginning to aim when Griss shot forward in a spring,
launching himself into the mouth of the cavern where the jack camp
was. By that leap he barely avoided a burst of greenish light. Another
of those bursts flowered where Harkon had half-crouched as he
ran—but the pilot was no longer there. His reactions were quicker
than human. It was almost as if he sensed danger and his fear
brought about instant teleportation. Yet I saw him only a little
beyond where that green bubble had burst.

That the aliens must be in there was plain. I did not have the same
agility which the three ahead of me possessed; yet I followed. What a
meeting between the three and their alien enemies would bring
about, no one could tell. It might well be that confronting them
would reduce our men to puppets. If that were so—well, I held a
laser and knew what to do.

But, try my best, I could not keep up with the three. I did see
them by the plasta-bubble. The piles of loot had been much reduced
since I had last seen them—there was not enough left to provide
much cover. But the three were not trying for any concealment now.
Instead they had drawn together, Harkon in the center, my two
shipmates flanking him. Were they under control? I could not tell

and, until I was certain, I must not venture too close. I lurked in the shadows by the entrance, berating myself for my own indecision.

Those whom the three sought were there, back in the greater gloom under the overhang of the balcony where I had once been trapped by him who wore Griss's body. Lidj, Harkon, Griss—yet they were not the men I knew. *Those* were the three apparent aliens advancing toward them. There were others there also, those with whom I had begun that scouting patrol, the men from the *Lydis* and the Patrol.

They were ranged against the wall, standing very still, staring straight ahead, no sign of emotion on their set faces. There was a robo-like quality to their waiting. Nor were they alone. Other men, jacks probably, were drawn up flanking them. All were armed, blasters ready in their hands, as if their alien leaders had nothing to fear from any revolt on their part.

Yet they did not aim at the three advancing. Slowly that advance faltered. The black-clad alien bodies came to a stop. Wearing the protect cap, I received only a faint backwash of the struggle in progress. But that the aliens were striving for control over their bodies was plain.

Of the three, Griss was the first to turn about and face outward, his expression now as blank as those of the men under alien domination. Then Harkon—and Lidj. With the same uniformity with which they had entered the cavern, they began to march out, and behind them the rest of the controlled company followed.

Perhaps the aliens thought to use them as a screen, a way of reaching us. But if they did so, they were not of the type who lead their own armies, for they themselves did not stir away from the wall.

Had I waited too long? Could I use the laser with the necessary accuracy the Patrolmen had shown? In any case even death, I believed, would be more welcome to those I saw under control than the life to which these others had condemned them.

I sighted over the heads of the three at the fore and fired.

The crackle of the released energy was twice as spectacular here. Or else I had not judged well and set the discharge too high. But those over whose heads it passed cried out, loosed their weapons, staggered, and went down. The three at the van marched on a step or two, and I thought I must have failed to knock them out, save that their strength did not hold for long and they wilted, going to their knees, then lying prone. Yet their outstretched hands scrabbled on the floor as if they still sought to drag their bodies on.

At the same time that backwash of compulsion I had felt, even when wearing the cap, strengthened. The enemy did not have to seek me out! They knew where I was as well as if I stood in the open shouting for their attention. But it was by my will alone that I came out of cover, walking through the prone ranks of their stricken attack force to face them.

Their arrogance, their supreme confidence in themselves and their powers, was not betrayed in any expression on the three faces which I knew well but which now wore a veil of strangeness, as if the Terran features formed a mask for the unknown. No, their belief in themselves and their powers was an almost tangible aura about them.

Still I did not surrender as they willed me to. Or perhaps they were striving to launch me, as they had those others, as a weapon for the undoing of my own kind. Instead I walked steadily ahead.

They had depended so much on nonphysical power that they were late in raising material weapons. I fired first, another blast of that shocking energy, aiming above their heads, though I longed to center it on them. But I thought that must only be done as a last resort; those bodies must not be destroyed.

The energy crackled, died. I realized uneasily that I had now exhausted the laser charge. There was another cartridge in my supply belt, but whether I would have time to recharge—

I had never believed my reaction or my senses more acute than those of most other men. But, almost without thinking, I made a swift leap to the left. Yet I did not wholly escape the menace which had crept on me from behind. An arm flung out half-tripped me. I staggered, keeping my balance only by happy chance. And I saw that Griss had crawled on hands and knees to attack. But whatever small spark of strength had supported him now failed. He collapsed again, face down—though the length of his alien body twitched and shuddered, as if muscles fought will, will flesh and bone in return.

So I edged backward at an angle to give me vision of both the three by the wall and those they possessed. There was a writhing among the latter, as if they fought to get to their feet yet could not summon strength enough. As far as I could see, those who believed themselves masters had not changed position, save that they no longer raised their hands with the round objects I suspected were weapons. Instead those arms hung limply by their sides.

Then he who wore Lidj's body toppled forward, crashing to the hard stone of the floor, making not the least attempt to save himself. And the other two followed. As they did so, that tortured movement among their slaves was stilled. I could have been standing among dead.

"Vorlund!" Foss and Borton both shouted my name so that it sounded as a single word.

I looked around to see them at the cavern entrance. And I believe they, too, thought I had fought a fatal battle. For Borton hurried forward, went down on one knee beside the inert form of Harkon, then, having laid hand on the shoulder beneath that black covering, looked to the three by the far wall.

"What did you do?"

"Used laser shock." I holstered the weapon I still held.

Foss was beside Lidj. "Dead?" he asked, but he did not look at me.

"No."

They went on to the three by the wall, stopped to turn those over so they lay on their backs. Their eyes were open, but there was no hint of consciousness. It was as if the essence of the alien personalities had withdrawn—or else—

I had gone to look at them, too. Now I wondered. Could that shock have brought about a switchover? If so—or in any case—we should have both sets of men under guard before they returned to consciousness. I said so.

"He's right." Borton, rather than Foss, backed my suggestion. He produced a tangler, used it with efficiency. First he bound the three by the wall, then he attended to those in the alien bodies, putting all the others of that band under restraint as well for good measure. In addition the three aliens were given stiff injections to keep them unconscious—or so we hoped.

We were masters now of the jack headquarters, though we put out sentries and did not accept our victory as total. There was too good a chance of others' still occupying the ship or the burrows. And the whole nature of this site was such as to make a man very wary of his surroundings, only too ready to hear strange noises, start at shadows, and the like.

We made use of the bubble in the cavern as a prison, stowing there our blacked-out prisoners. Borton used the jacks' com to summon the rest of his men from the outer valley. The energy which sustain pills and E rations had given us was ebbing. This time we did not try to bolster it. Rather we took turns sleeping, eating rations we found in the camp.

There was evidence that the jacks had been here for some time. Signs, too, by deep flare burns left on the valley floor, that there had been more than one ship landing and take-off over a period of perhaps a year, or longer, planet time. But after sleep-gas globes had made the ship ours, we discovered very little more of the setup which had been made to market the loot or otherwise do business off-world—there were only faint clues for the Patrol to follow up.

Our prisoners did not revive quickly and Thanel was loath to use medical means to induce consciousness. Too little was known of the stresses to which they had recently been subjected. In all there were some twenty jacks, and the men of our own party which had been taken—including Hunold. And our only safe control on the alien three was to make sure they could not use their esper powers.

Thanel ordered these three, plus their alien bodies, to be put in a separate division of the tent. There he spent most of his waking time keeping them under observation. They still breathed, all six of them. And the detect showed a life signal whenever he used it on them. Yet the vital processes were very slow, akin to the state of one in stass-freeze. And how this state could be broken, he admitted he did not know. After a certain time had passed he even experimented by taking off his protect cap (having first stationed a guard to watch him and move in at the first hint he might be taken over) and trying to reach them via esper means—with no result.

I had fallen asleep. And I did not know how long it was before I was shaken awake again. Foss was the one who had so abruptly roused me.

"Thanel wants you," he said tersely.

I crawled out of the pheno-bag I had found in the camp. Foss was already heading into the open where the darkness of night had largely concealed the standing ship.

But it was not the chill of the night wind probing now and then into the cavern which set me shivering as I watched him go. I have known loneliness in my life. Perhaps the worst was when I realized on Yiktor that I might never return to my human body, that it was possible I might be entrapped for years in animal form. Then I had literally gone mad, striking out into the wilderness, allowing the remnant of beast in me to take over from the human which had been transplanted. I had run, I had killed, I had skulked, I had—Today I cannot remember all that happened to me, nor do I wish to. That was loneliness.

And this—this was loneliness of another type. For in that moment when Captain Foss walked away I saw the wall which was between us. Had the building of that wall been of my doing? Perhaps, though looking back, I could not deny that given the same choices I would have done no differently. Yes, I was no longer of the *Lydis*. I could ship out on her, do my duty well, maybe better than I had a year ago. But for me she was no longer the sole home a Free Trader must have.

What had happened? I was as lost as I had been when running four-footed across the fields of Yiktor. If I was not Krip Vorlund, Free Trader born, who wanted nothing more than a berth on the *Lydis*, then who *was* I? Not Maquad—I felt no closer kinship with the Thassa than I did with the crew; even less.

I was alone! And I shuddered away from that realization, getting to my feet, hurrying to obey Thanel's summons, hoping to find forgetfulness in this task, if only for a short time.

The medic was waiting for me as I came into that inner section where the six bodies still lay on the floor, looking just as they had when I had helped to bring them in. But Thanel had the appearance of a man who had not had any rest. And to my surprise he was not alone.

Lukas, whom I had last seen lying in tangle cords, stood beside him. It was he who spoke first.

"Krip, you are the only one of us who has been through body switch. The Thassa do it regularly, do they not?"

"I don't know about doing it regularly. Anyone who wishes to train as a Moon Singer does it. But there are only a limited number of Moon Singers. And so it may not be well known to the others. They have their failures, too." My own present body was witness to that, if one was needed.

"The question is, how do they do it?" Thanel came directly to the point. "You have been through it and witnessed it done for that Maelen of yours. Do they use some machine, drug, type of hypnotism—what?"

"They sing." I told him the truth.

"*Sing!*"

"That's what they call it. And they do it best when the moon there is three-ringed, a phenomenon which only occurs at long intervals. It can be done at other times, but then it needs the combined power of quite a few Singers. And the expenditure of their energy is such that it is only tried when there is great need. The rings were fading when Maelen was transferred to Vors's body—so there had to be more Singers—"

"Maelen was a Moon Singer, is one," Lukas said thoughtfully.

"Her powers were curtailed by the Old Ones when she was sent into exile," I reminded him.

"All of them? The fact remains that we have body transfer here and the only other cases known are on Yiktor. It might be possible to load these"—he indicated the sleepers—"into a ship and take them there. But there is no guarantee that your Thassa would or could make the exchange. But Maelen is here—and if she knows what can be done—"

He must have seen my face then, understood to the full my reaction to what he was proposing.

"She is not an animal!" I seized upon the first argument he might be tempted to use. But how could I make him understand, he who had never seen Maelen the Moon Singer in her proper form, only as the small, furred creature who shared my cabin, whom he rated as lower than any wearing human guise—a *thing* expendable for the crew's good.

"Who said she was?" Thanel might be trying to soothe me, but I was wary. "We are merely pointing out that we do have on this planet, here and now, a being—a person who is familiar with our problem, who should be approached in the hope that we have a solution to it here, not half the galaxy away."

But the very reasonableness of his argument made it worse. I flung the truth at them.

"You take her out of stass-freeze and she dies! You"—I centered on Thanel—"saw her condition, worked to get her into stass. How long do you think she might have if you revived her?"

"There are new techniques." His low voice contrasted with the rising fury of my demands. "I can, I think, promise that I can retard any physical changes, even if her mind is freed."

"You 'think.'" I seized directly on that qualifying phrase. "But you cannot be sure, can you?" I pressed and he was frank enough to admit the truth with a shake of his head.

"Then I say 'no!' She must have her chance."

"And how are you going to give it to her? On Yiktor? What will they do for her there, even if you can get her so far? Do they have a reserve of bodies?"

Chapter 18

MAELEN

It is true that sometimes we can remember (though that memory is as thin as the early-morning mist) a way of life which is larger than ours, into which dreams or the desire to escape may lead us. Where did I roam during that time I was apart from my broken body? For it was not the nothingness of deep sleep which had held me. No, I had done things and looked upon strange sights, and I came back to the pain which was life, carrying with me an urgency that would spur me to some action I did not yet understand.

Returning, I did not see with the eyes of the body which held me now so poorly. Perhaps those eyes no longer had the power of sight. Rather did Krip's thought reach mine, and I knew he had brought about my awakening, and only in dire need.

That need worked upon me as a debt-sending, so that I knew it was one which I must answer. Tied are we always to right our debts so the Scales of Molaster stand even!

Only with that summons came such pain of body as blotted out for a breath, or four, or six, my ability to answer. I broke contact that I might use my strength to cut off the communication ways between my body and my mind. I did this quickly, so that pain was lulled to a point where it could be endured, remaining as only a far-off wretched wailing of a wind which had naught to do with me.

Andre Norton

So armored, I sought Krip once more.

"What would you?"

"—body—change—"

I could not understand clearly. Body change? In me memory stirred. Body change! I was in a damaged body, one for which there was no future. A new body? How long had I existed in that other place? Time was always relative. Was I now back on Yiktor, with a new body awaiting me? Had as much time as that passed in the real world? For now it appeared that I was no longer closely tied to Krip's world, though that had once been the one I also knew best.

"Body change for whom?"

"Maelen!" Even stronger his thought-send. As if he were trying to awaken some sleeper with a shout of alarm, as does the horn man on the walls of fort keeps, where death by sword can creep out of the night unless a keen-eyed sentry sees it to give warning.

"I am here—" It would seem he had not heard my earlier answer. "What would you have of me?"

"This—" His thought became clear and he told me how it was with those of the *Lydis* and their allies.

Part of that tale was new. And, as his mental pictures built in my mind, my own remembrance sharpened. So I was drawn yet farther from the clouding mists where lately I had had my being.

Body exchange—three humans for three aliens. But—there had been a fourth alien. A fourth! Sharply clear in my mind she suddenly stood, her hair falling about her shoulders as a dark fire cloak, and on her head— NO!

My mind-touch broke instinctively. In her crown lay the danger, an ever-present danger. But she was there—waiting—ever waiting. She could not take over any of the others, even suck their life force, since they were male—she must have one of her own sex in order to exchange. That was it! She had called me (clear was my memory now). Yet while I kept apart she could not control me, force the exchange as her kin had—force the exchange? No, that had not been her desire as I had read it last—she had wanted my life force—not my body.

"Maelen?" Krip was sensitive to my preoccupation with the woman, though he may not have known my reason. "Maelen, are you with me? Maelen!" His call was stark now with fear.

"I am here. What do you want?"

"You changed me. Can you tell us how to exchange these?"

"Am I still a Moon Singer?" I demanded bitterly. This was no proper debt, for I could not supply payment. "Is Sotrath above our heads wearing Three Rings? Where is my wand? And can animal lips, throat, bring forth the Great Songs? I am of no use to you, Krip Vorlund. Those upon whom you must call stand tall on Yiktor."

"Which means well beyond our reach. But listen, Maelen—" He began with the haste of one who has a message of importance, and then his thought wavered. But I caught what he would say. Perhaps I had known my fate from the beginning, in spite of all his efforts to save me from it.

"If you would say that this body I now wear so badly will not continue long to hold me—that I have already guessed. Have you any answer for me, since I have given one which is no help to you?"

"She—the woman of the cat crown—she is a body!"

Once more I drew upon my power, probed behind his words seeking her insidious prompting, the setting of that thought in his mind. So that was to be the method of her attack? She would use Krip to reach me with temptation. For it is very true that living creatures, offered a choice of life or the unknown ways of death, will turn to life. And in the past I think that those with whom she had had dealings were much lesser in power, so that she had grown very confident, arrogant, in her reckoning.

But I could not discover any such prompting in his mind. And I was sure he could not have concealed that from me; I knew him too well and too deeply. There was nothing there but concern and sorrow lacing around his mental image of Maelen as he had seen me on Yiktor when I had been so sure of *myself* and the powers *I* held.

Knowing that this was not an implanted idea, I began to consider it. I could surrender to the mist and darkness, release the anchorage which held me in this body which could not be repaired in spite of all their science. We of Molaster's people do not fear to take the White Road, knowing that this life is only the first stumbling step on a long way leading to wonders we cannot know here and now.

Yet it is also true that we *know* when the time comes for such release, and I had not received such a message. Instead there was that pattern of which I was a part and which was unfinished—of which I had been shown a glimpse. If I chose to go now out of pain, or timidity, it was not right. And so my time was not yet. But I could not remain in this body, and there was only one other—that of her who waited. For it I would have to fight, and it would be fair battle, my strength against hers; a fairer war, I believed, than she had ever fought before.

If I had had but one of the Old Ones by my side my fear would not have been so great. But this was my battle only. Had the whole rank of them stood behind me at this time I could have asked no aid from them. But where was my wand; who would sing? Suppose I entered into that waiting alien and found myself a helpless tenant—

"Maelen." Krip's call was tentative now, almost as if he only wanted to know if I could still be reached.

"Take me to the woman. Do not try to contact me again until we are there. I must conserve my strength."

Sing? I could not sing. We were not under a three-ringed moon whose glory could enhance my power. I had no one of the Thassa to stand with me. No one of the Thassa—Krip? But he was only outwardly Thassa. Yet—and now I began to consider the problem with objective concentration, as if this action did not affect me at all but dealt with others with whom I had no emotional involvement.

Exchange needed a linkage of power. Once I fronted the alien it would be my battle, but to bring her to bay I might lawfully call upon aid. There had been that dead man—or seemingly dead man— who had broadcast to keep the crew of the *Lydis* and the Patrolmen under control. He, or the will behind him, had made use not of the traditional tools of the Thassa, but of mechanical means. What one could do, could not another do also?

For long ages the Thassa have shunned the aid of machines, just as we long ago went forth from cities, put aside possessions. I knew not the way of machines. However, to say in any crisis "because I do not know this thing, it will not aid me" is to close the mind. And neither have the Thassa been given to such narrowness. Even though we withdrew from the stream of life wherein swim the plainsmen and these star travelers, we do not stagnate.

So—a machine to aid. And a machine of the *Lydis* or the Patrol that was on my side, not that of her who watched and waited. Also— she had not seen me in body. Let me be brought before her. Shock had value. And if my mind was seemingly lulled—could she so be pushed off balance, made more receptive to counterattack?

Having made my plans, I spoke to Krip again, letting him know my decision, what I would need, then as swiftly retreating once more into my safe-keeping silence, while I waited, storing up what energy I could summon. Also I must prepare for this new technique—no wand, no songs. I would instead have to funnel what power I had through a machine. But behind me would be Krip and upon him I could depend, that I knew.

Though I had shut off contact with Krip, I became aware now of mind-send. That did not come boldly and openly, but was rather like the barsk, wily, untamed, prowling at the gate of a holding, scenting the uneasy herd within, working to find the best way of breaching the barrier between it and its victims.

I wanted to explore that skulking identity, but the need in my own plan for surprise kept me back. How great an adept did I now face? I am as a little child compared to some of our Old Ones. Would I now discover that the same held true here? I could only wait for the final confrontation, and hope the machine would aid.

Though I was not aware of any change in my own surroundings, I guessed, from the increased pressure from that would-be invading mind, that I must be approaching its lair. To hold barriers on two levels of consciousness is very difficult. As I allowed that invader to edge into my—as one might term it—outer mind, I had to stage that intrusion with more care than I had ever before taken in my life. For the enemy must believe that she was succeeding in her take-over— that there were no depths beneath which I marshaled forces, prepared a counterattack.

Perhaps I reached heights that day—or night—which I had not known were possible, even for a Moor Singer. But if I did, I was not aware of my feat. I was intent only on holding the delicate balance, lulling my enemy, being ready when the moment came.

There was a sudden cessation of that cautious invasion. Not a withdrawal, but further exploration had halted. Though I could see only with the mind's eye, I saw *her*! She was there in every detail, even as Krip had showed her to me, as she had been in my dream.

That had been blurred, filtered as it had been through his reaction to her. This was as sharp and clear as the Stones of Yolor Plain where they lie in the cruel moonlight of Yiktor's midwinter. Only she did not half recline on a couch as Krip had described. Rather in this place she sat enthroned, her cloak of hair flung back to bare her body, her head a little forward as if she wished to meet me eye to eye. And the writhing cats' heads of her diadem were not in play, but all erect on their thread-thin supports, their eyes turned also upon me—watching—waiting—

Diadem! I had had my wand, through which to center my power, when I had sung the small spells and the deep ones. Even the Old Ones possessed their staffs to focus and hold the forces they controlled. Her diadem served her so.

Perhaps I erred then in revealing my sudden enlightenment. I saw her eyes narrow. The hint of a cruel twist of smile about her lips vanished. And the cats' heads—a quiver ran along their filaments, a ripple such as a passing wind brings to a field of grain.

"Maelen—ready!"

Krip broke through the shield I did not try to hold against him. I saw the cats' heads twist, turn, whirl into a wild dance. But I turned from them to join Krip's guiding thought.

By some miracle of Molaster's sending, I could follow that mind-directive. I "saw" the machine before me. Its shape, its nature were of no interest to me, only how it was to act as my *wand*, my own diadem. To it Krip must link me, since it was of his heritage and not of mine.

Link and hold—did he understand? He must, for the mental image of the machine was now clear and solid. I directed power to it.

Recoil—a frenzied recoil from that other—rooted in fear!

Even as she withdrew, so did my will and purpose flood behind her. Though I did not quite reach my goal. She steadied, stood firm. The diadem braced her—

Between me and my mental image of the box the cats' heads danced a wild measure. To look beyond those, focus on the box was almost too much for me. And pain—pain was beginning to gnaw once more. I could not hold the blocks I had set up in that broken body, evade the spell of the cats' heads, concentrate upon the amplifier—not all at once!

Strength feeding me—that was Krip. He could not sing where there was no true Thassa to guide him. He could only support my link with the box. And then—more—small, but holding steady. I did not know from whence that came (Molaster's gift?)—I was only glad I had it.

She had driven me back a little from the advance point I had reached. But I was still ahead of where I had begun. Look not on the cats. The amplifier—use that! Feed it with a flow of will—feed it!

A broken image—that was a flash of physical sight. Blot it out! See only what is within, not out—this battle lies within! I knew now that the ending must come quickly or else I was lost. Once more—the amplifier, call all my resources—Strike!

I broke through some intangible defense, but I allowed myself no feeling of triumph. Success in one engagement does not mean battle won. What did face me now? Almost I recoiled in turn. I had thought that what I fought was a personality, one as well-defined as I saw myself—me—Maelen of the Thassa. But this was only will; a vicious will, yes, and a dark need for domination, but still only a husk of evil left to go on running—a machine abandoned by its onetime owner, left to "live" through the mists of unnumbered years. There was no inner self wearing the diadem, just the dregs of the will and forgotten purpose. So when I broke through the shell maintained by those, I found an emptiness I did not expect. Into that space I flowed, making it my own, then barricading it against the remnant of that other.

That remnant, robo-like, was far from being vanquished. Perhaps the many years it had been in command had developed it as a form of quasi-life. And it turned on me with vicious force.

The cats! Suddenly I could see nothing but the cats, their narrow heads, their slitted eyes, crowding in upon me! They began a whirling dance around and around—the cats! They were the focus through which this thing could act!

Dimly, beyond their attempt to wall me away from the world, I could see. Not with the mental sight, no, but truly. Forms, though I found them hard to focus upon, were there. Then I knew that I was not looking through the eyes which Vors had long ago given me. I was in another body. And I realized what body that was!

The pressure on me, the waves of enmity which were as physical blows against cringing flesh—those came from the cats. I was in a body, a body which had arms—hands—I concentrated my will. And all the way that other half-presence fought me. I did not feel as if I were actually moving; I could only will it so.

Were those hands at my head now? Had the fingers tightened around the edge of the cat diadem? I set my mental control to lifting the crown, hurling it from me—

The cats' heads vanished. My vision, which had been blurred, was now vividly clear. I knew that I had a body, that I was living, breathing, with no more pain. Also—that other presence was gone as if it had been hurled away with the crown.

They stood before me, Krip, Captain Foss, strangers in Patrol uniforms. There were others on the floor, encased in tangler cords: Lidj, Griss, the Patrol pilot—and three alien bodies.

Krip came to me, caught my two hands, looked down into my new eyes. What he read there must have told him the truth, for there was such a lighting in his face as puzzled me. I had not seen that expression before.

"You did it! Maelen, Moon Singer—you have done it!"

"So much is true." I heard my new voice, husky, strange. And I looked down upon this new casing for my spirit. It was a good body, well made, though the flow of dark hair was not Thassa.

Krip still held my hands as if he dared not let them go lest I slip away. But now Captain Foss was beside him, staring at me with the same intensity Krip had shown.

"Maelen?" He made a question of my name as if he could not believe that this had happened.

"What proof do you wish, captain!" My spirit was soaring high. I had not felt this way since I had donned fur and claws back on Yiktor.

But one of the Patrolmen cut short our small reunion. "What about it? Can you do the same for them?" He gestured to the men in bonds.

"Not now!" Krip flung at him. "She has just won one battle. Give her time—"

"Wait—" I stilled his bristling defense of me. "Give me but a little time to learn the ways of this body."

I closed off my physical senses, even as I had learned to do as a Singer, sent my inner questing here and there. It was like exploring the empty rooms of a long-deserted citadel. That which had partially animated this fortress had occupied but little of it. My journey was a spreading out, a realization that I had new tools ready for my hands, some as yet unknown to me. But there would be time to explore fully later. Now I wished most to know how I who was Maelen could make best use of what I had.

"Maelen!" That call drew me back. I felt once more the warmth of Krip's grasp, the anxiety in his voice.

"I am here," I assured him. "Now—" I took full command of this new body. At first it moved stiffly, as if it had been for long without proper controls. But with Krip's aid I stood, I moved to those who lay in bonds, alien flanking Terran. And their flesh was like transparent envelopes to my sight. I knew each as he really was.

As it had been with the woman into which I had gone, those which now occupied the Terran bodies were not true personalities, but only motivating forces. It was strange—by the Word of Molaster, how strange it was! I could not have faced those who had originally dwelled therein. I doubt if even the Old Ones could have done so. Whatever, whoever those sleepers had been, that had once been great, infinitely more so than the men whom only the pale remnant of their forces had taken over.

Because I knew them for what they were I was able to break them, expel them from the bodies they had stolen. Krip, still hand-linked with me, backed me with his strength. And, once those aliens had been expelled, to return the rightful owners to their bodies was less difficult. The Terran bodies stirred, their eyes opened sane and knowing. I turned to Captain Foss.

"These wore crowns, and the crowns must be destroyed. They serve as conductors for the forces."

"So!" Krip dropped my hand and strode across the chamber. He stamped upon some object lying there, ground his magnetic-soled space boots back and forth as if he would reduce what he trampled to powder.

In my mind came a thin, far-off wailing, as if somewhere living things were being done to death. I shivered but I did not raise hand to stop him from that vengeful attack upon the link between the evil will and the body I had won.

It was a good body, as I had known when first I looked upon it. And I found in the outer part of the chamber the means to clothe it. The clothing was different from my Thassa wear, being a short tunic held in by a broad, gemmed belt, and foot coverings which molded themselves to the limbs they covered.

My hair was too heavy and long and I did not have the pins and catches to keep it in place Thassa-fashion. So I plaited it into braids.

I wondered who she had been once, that woman so carefully preserved outwardly. Her name, her age, even her race or species, I might never know. But she had beauty, and I know she had power— though it differed from that of the Thassa. Queen, priestess— whatever— She had gone away long since, leaving only that residue to maintain a semi-life. Perhaps it was the evil in her which had been left behind. I would like to believe so. I wanted to think she was not altogether what that shadow I had battled suggested.

But the exile of that part, and of that which had animated the three male aliens, opened a vast treasure house. Such discoveries as were disclosed will be the subject for inquiry, speculation, exploration for years to come. As the jack operation (so swiftly taken over by the aliens) had been illegal by space law, those of the *Lydis* were allowed to file First Claim on the burrows. Which meant that each and every member of the crew became master of his own fate, wealthy enough to direct his life as he wished.

"You spoke more than once of treasure." I had returned to the chamber of the one in whose body I now dwelt to gather together her possessions (the company having agreed that these were freely mine), and Krip had come with me. "Treasure which could be many things. And you said that to you it was a ship. Is this still so?"

He sat on one of the chests, watching me sort through the contents of another. I had found a length of rippling blue-green stuff unlike any fabric I had ever seen, cat masks patterned on it in gold. Now they had no unease for me.

"What is your treasure, Maelen?" He countered with a question of his own. "This?" He gestured at what lay within that chamber.

"Much is beautiful; it delights the eye, the touch." I smoothed the fabric and folded it again. "But it is not my treasure. Treasure is a dream which one reaches out to take, by the Will of Molaster. Yiktor is very far away. What one may wish for on Yiktor—" What had I wished for on Yiktor? I did not have to search far in memory for that. My little ones (though I could not call them "mine" now, for I had sent them to their own lives long since). But—with little ones of their kind—a ship— Yiktor did not call me strongly now; I had voyaged too far, not only in space but somehow in spirit. Someday I wanted to go there again. Yes. I wanted to see the Three Rings of Sotrath blaze in her night sky, walk among the Thassa, but not yet. There remained the little ones—

"Your dream is still a ship with animals—to voyage the stars with your little people, showing others how close the bond between man and animal may truly become," Krip said for me. "Once I told you that you could not find treasure enough to pay for such a dream. I was wrong. Here it is, many times over."

"Yet I cannot buy such a ship, go star voyaging alone." I turned to look full at him. "You said that *your* dream of treasure was also a ship. And that you can now have—"

He was Thassa and yet not Thassa. Even as I searched his face I could see behind Maquad's features that ghost with brown skin, dark hair, the ghost of the young man I had first met at the Great Fair of Yrjar.

"You do not want to return to Yiktor?" Again he did not answer me directly.

"Not at present. Yiktor is far away, born in space and time—very far."

I do not know, or did not know, what he read in my voice which led him to rise, come to me, his hands reaching out to draw me to him.

"Maelen, I am not as I once was. I find that I am now in exile among those of my own kind. That I would not believe until here on Sekhmet it was proved. Only one now can claim my full allegiance."

"Two exiles may find a common life, Krip. And there are stars—a ship can seek them out. I think that our dreams flow together."

His answer this time came in action, and I found it very good. So did we two who had walked strange ways choose to walk a new one side by side, and I thanked Molaster in my heart for His great goodness.

Chapter 19

KRIP VORLUND

When I looked upon her who had come to me, who trusted in me (even when I had called her back to what might have been painful death, because I believed that a small chance waited for her) then I knew that this was the way of life for us both.

"Not exile," I told her. "It is not exile when one comes home!"

Home is not a ship after all, nor a planet, nor a traveling wain crossing the plains of Yiktor. It is a feeling which, once learned, can never be forgotten. We two are apart, exiled perhaps, from those who once were our kind. But before us lie all the stars, and within us—home! And so it will be with us as long as life shall last.